THE LORDS OF
THE STONEY
MOUNTAINS

The Lords of the Stoney Mountains

Antony Swithin

Edited by Mark Sebanc

This edition first published in Great Britain in 2020 by Gollancz
an imprint of the Orion Publishing Group Ltd
Carmelite House, 50 Victoria Embankment
London EC4Y 0DZ

An Hachette UK Company

1 3 5 7 9 10 8 6 4 2

A CIP catalogue record for this book is
available from the British Library.

ISBN 978 1 473 23224 2

Typeset by Born Group

www.sfgateway.com
www.gollancz.co.uk

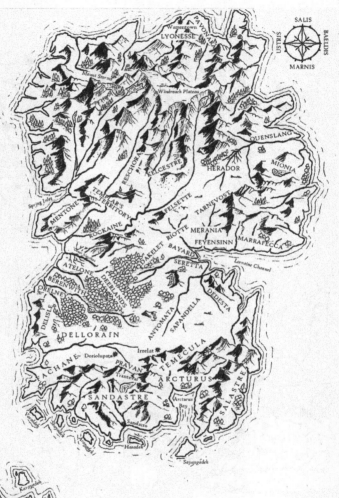

THE CONTINENT OF

ROCKALL

In the Year of Our Lord 1403

20 60 100   500
Km. |_____|
0 40 80   300

Green R.

Jarmswayle

Green Marshes

Quincemail

Thraincross

Etolen Dunes

R. Meriann R.

R. Mentone

R. Rondoleth

R. Aramasha

Valdevil

Wildfell

R. Aramasha

Tryad in Riotte

All Saints R.

Mentone Plateau

Takrallen

Falconward

Saint Lorraine

Wratney

Rewlenscrag

Merlinward

Great Marshes

Becketsward

Cat Crags

Amsetch

Blackhills

Owisgard

R. Atelone

R. Berenselth

Daincross

Dunfield

Chancelet

Skarngrove

R. Baldovney

R. Everdain

Everbrend

R. Worenthin

Irrelat

Doriolupata

Verumest

Trantevar

Brevolan

Argray

Andresellar

Peratenay

R. Sisheven

Sandarro

Southern and Central
Rockall

CHAPTER I

A Sojourn In Talestant

The approaching party had sighted me and was speeding up. I waved to them and gestured toward the fleeing grey riders, but it was not necessary. The Sandastrians had divided their ranks already. About two thirds of them set off at full tilt in pursuit, while the others continued at a more leisurely pace towards the ruined temple. Seizing the bow and quiver, I clambered down from the wall to join my friends.

During the fight, Rascal had wisely kept clear of me and hidden himself, but now he leapt onto my shoulder, crooning rapturously. Avran gave us a crooked smile.

'It was well that the mist lifted, Simon. My opponent was a better swordsman than me. Your friend Dermot Fitzstephen himself, I presume?'

I had known this from the moment Dermot shouted his order to the sevdru. 'Yes, it was, but Lednar, I'm grieved to tell you that he struck down your beast as he rode away. I hope she's not badly injured.'

'She's dead,' Lednar said quietly. 'She was a friend of many years and I shall miss her.'

As Lednar had not looked down into the quarry, I realized immediately that it was true that a rider did indeed know immediately when his sevdru was slain. He sighed, then continued: 'Yet we must give thanks to God that, against all odds in terms of both numbers and weapons, the three of us are not merely alive but unhurt. We owe much to Simon's markmanship, I suspect, since only two riders reached these walls. How many did you account for, friend?'

'Well, I brought down three,' I said, 'but one was not injured, for he was able to ride away.'

'And you finished another, Lednar, while the best I could manage was to kill that unfortunate animal.' Avran gestured at the dead sevdru. 'I hated having to do it, but Dermot would have ridden me down otherwise. Well, let's go out and meet our friends.'

The approaching riders, about ten or so of them, were understandably unsure of their reception, and each rode towards us sword in hand. However, as soon as they saw us, there was a chorus of joy and a swift sheathing of weapons. Their leader was burlier than Lednar, but otherwise so much like him that I recognized at once Esenar Estantesec. Seven of the others were Estantesecs as well, and there were two Derresdems in the party. I remember all their names, but there is no need to recount them.

Within minutes we were sitting on fallen blocks of stone, enjoying the sunshine and sharing a repast of dried meat, bread, and fruit. It was almost a full day since I had eaten. I was voraciously hungry, but even more welcome to me was the wine that was shared so generously all around. Nor were our sevdryen neglected. One of the Estantesecs went away to cut and bring fodder for Yerezinth and Zembelen, while another fetched them water from the spring.

Over the meal, Avran recounted our adventures, paying me tributes so excessively generous that more than once he caused my face to redden with embarrassment. There was much discussion about the identity of the grey riders, but no new suggestions were forthcoming. Afterward, we made a close examination of the bodies and accoutrements of the three who had been slain, in the hope that this might furnish useful information. It did not. The three men were personally unknown to the Sandastrians and not sufficiently distinctive in colouring or build to be of any obvious origin. They carried no papers and, apart from the rising-sun emblem stamped into their boot-tops and repeated on belt-buckles and cloak-clasps, they bore no identifying marks. Our examination of the two dead sevdreyen and their gear was no more informative, but it did furnish me with unexpected good fortune. The beast slain by my arrowshot from the wall chanced to be bearing the bundle containing my belt and weapons. Moreover, my bowstave had survived the sevdru's fall unbroken. It was with particular relief that I took up my belt, with its array of sheathed knives, for these were virtually irreplaceable. Though one knife, of course, was lost, I managed to have twelve again, including the little Italian knife my tutor had given me originally. It was a pleasure as well to have my own sword and quiver of arrows back. My pack, however, with the good brown pelican I had bought in Bristol, was never found.

While our investigations were in progress, the two Derresdems had ridden away, to follow and make contact with the party pursuing the grey riders. The rest of us decided to stay where we were for that night. In the bright sunshine, the old temple on its hilltop was a pleasant enough place. When evening came, there was cheerful talk and singing around a bright fire. If the temple held any ghosts, they did not trouble our sleep.

The next morning was one of sunshine and dew-sparkle, making the hills continue to seem a friendly place. It was only in mist that they took on an alien and hostile aspect. As we breakfasted, two messengers arrived from the pursuing party, bringing a captured sevdru and news.

The animal, it seemed, was one of the two whose riders I had killed, the other having been taken over by the grey rider whose sevdru had been slain. I had thought that the Estantesec party would have caught up speedily with the fleeing grey riders, but of course they also had been riding through the night. Pursuers and pursued were thus evenly matched, and the gap between them had not closed.

Just before nightfall yesterday, the grey riders had divided their ranks, two heading southeastward and two to the northeast. The Estantesec party had likewise divided, the two messengers being sent back at that point. The messengers had met the Derresdems and directed them onwards. Then they had rested for a few hours before coming to the ruins.

Their arrival, therefore, left us still uncertain as to the fate of the grey riders, but it did furnish us with a mount for Lednar. The captured sevdru was a male, as grey in hue as the riders' cloaks. Lednar tried him and pronounced him satisfactory, but he was clearly not much enthused by his new acquisition. However, he managed well enough when, in mid-morning, we rode away. The two messengers, with two other Estantesecs, were left resting by the ruins. Later they would ride east to rejoin their colleagues.

It was a relaxed and merry ride that day. After sixteen hours of recuperation, Yerezinth was full of energy again and touchingly affectionate. With Rascal crooning and content on the pack-saddle behind me and Avran chattering happily to his cousins close or distant, I felt wholly free of the tensions that had gripped me during three frightening days. Once again, I could notice the birds, the flowers, and the little lizards among the rocks, could enjoy the sunshine and feel the pleasure of travelling through new country. I had no particular desire to talk, but I found myself humming as cheerfully as Rascal.

There was no reason now to go to Trantevar and we did not even glimpse that town. Around midday, however, we turned north and began the leisurely descent into the valley of the Dalirond. I saw many trees below us, appearing so big that I presumed they must be already close. However, though they stood ever taller before us, we seemed to take a surprising time in reaching them . . . Then I realized that these must be the huge trees spoken of by Avran. I recalled that he had said they grew a hundred ells high – a full three hundred and seventy-five feet. Hard to believe.

Yet, as they towered ever higher before us and loomed above us, I admitted to myself that Avran had not exaggerated. Truly these trees were giants, their very trunks as large in circumference as a church tower – and so much taller. Their bark was thick and of a creamy-brown colour, full of little holes, like the crust that forms on solidifying honey. (Later I found that it was strangely soft and yet resilient. You could hit it hard without injury to your fist and without leaving any marks). The lowest branches were high overhead and, since the great trees did not crowd one another, there was not only space, but even sunlight between them. We rode through a dappled pattern of light and shade, with plants and smaller trees crowding the sunnier spaces.

In the glades, hasedain were grazing, under the watchful eyes of herdboys whose merry whistles and cheerful greetings enlivened our passage. Twice I saw fallen trunks that had been turned into hasedain-sheds, and several times we passed hasedu-drawn carts made from hollowed-out half-trunks. In the bigger glades there were padin much like those on the flanks of Sandarro hill. However, each was built wholly from wood, each decorated by careful carpentry into elaborate geometric or natural patterns, and each painted in cheerful colours, green, scarlet, yellow, brown, or azure blue. They were the brightest and most cheerful houses that I had ever seen.

'I like these padin,' I observed to Avran. 'Yours must be a happy people, to live in such habitations and to maintain them so well. Yet, if you were attacked, what would happen? Do you have any fortresses, any strong-points, in Estantegard?'

Avran laughed. 'Why, our strong-points are all around you.'

'The padin?'

'No, not them. I mean the trees. Those are our defensive towers, our refuges from aggressors. There are ladders up them, tunnels in them, platforms high in their branches, lookout points at their tops. And you need to understand as well that an invader could not even use fire against us. The bark, the very wood of these trees is proof against flames. Only the lesser vegetation would burn. Our trees, our residences even, would be safe enough. It's been many years since any enemy entered the forests of Estantevard and, believe me, they gained much in the way of pain but little profit.'

'Why don't you abandon your castles, then, and grow trees like this everywhere? If you did, presumably all of Sandastre would be impregnable.'

He laughed again. 'I very much doubt that. The ingenuity of evil and ambitious men is boundless. Yet it wouldn't work anyway. These trees, the great *pevenekar,* will grow only in the lands around Lake Vanadha. We've tried planting their seeds elsewhere. They sprout, but they never flourish. You'll discover that their seeds are tiny and even the cones are no bigger than the end of your thumb. Odd, to think something so mighty can grow from something so very small.'

I fell to remembering my early days in Sandarro. 'It was these forests, then, that your artists were remembering when they decorated the fifth level of your father's castle?'

'Yes, of course, and that's why we Estantesecs chose to have our own rooms there. When we're so far from our own lands, those corridors make us feel at home. Yet not all the peoples of my vard live in these forests. Some live in the hill country north of Lake Vanadha – and not even in Sandastre, but in Denniffey and Pravan. They're venturesome people – they need to be, in those troubled lands. And they, Simon, will be very useful to us when we venture on northward.'

For some time we had been riding along a road through the big trees – but it was not a straight, cobbled track like the old Roman roads that still traversed the moors near my home, nor yet one made of cut and fitted stones like those in Sandarro and its environs. Instead, this road was made of logs hewn from lesser trees, set at the level of the surrounding forest humus and laid transversely to the line of the road itself – if one might call it a 'line,' for the road meandered intricately around and between the massive boles of the peveneks. If the trees were to become strong-points, a road like this would bemuse and bring many hazards to any invader. Certainly it was not designed for folk in a hurry.

Eventually the road began to swing toward the north, not in a single turn, but in a series of curves. I noticed that it was beginning to rise above the surrounding land – or, rather, that the road was maintaining its level and the land falling away. We passed through a belt of lesser trees, then into open meadowlands with many grazing hasedain, the road rising ever higher above these fields. Soon we were ascending a steep ramp leading to a broad bridge. As we traversed it, the waters of the Dalirond sparkled beneath us in the sunshine. A little scarlet, spear-billed bird, much like a kingfisher, flew upstream with the speed of an arrow.

'Why is this bridge built so high?' I asked. 'Why, we must be five full ells above the water!'

It was Lednar who answered. 'On a sunny day like this, yes, it must seem strange indeed. But picture to yourself that you are here instead on a day of storms, with pevenekar being brought down into the Dalirond by lightning or by the undermining of river banks. Such great logs, floating downstream, would sweep away any bridge of lower span – as, indeed, our ancestors found, at much cost in effort.'

'And you must understand, Simon, that this bridge is made from the trunks of just two pevenekar,' contributed the rumbling voice of Esenar. 'My grandfather described to me how it was done. They built two sloping mounds of earth from either side of the Dalirond, when the river was at summer ebb. Then the trunks were tugged and heaved up till they met in mid-river and could be bound together. It took much effort, but the bridge has lasted eighty years and more already. See, we're approaching midpoint now. That's the line where the trunks are joined.'

Beyond the bridge and the meadowlands, the road forked into three. Accompanied by the two cousins, we took the west fork and were quickly back among the great trees again, but the other Estantesecs bade us farewell here, four going north and two east to seek homes nearby. Nor were we far from the ending of our own journey. Twenty minutes of steady jogging followed, with the big trees ever fewer and farther apart, until we found ourselves again among lesser trees. Mostly these were the slim-leaved estelens that the Estantesecs chose long ago as emblem for their vard, in modest preference to the giant peveneks. Already the estelens were in yellow bud, promising the golden glory of their spring flowering. Many sevdreyen browsed in content-ment among them. Ever ready to respond to the call of their masters or mistresses as they were, they required no herd-boys to keep them from straying.

We were riding slowly upward now. Ahead was a flat-topped hillock with a group of padin set upon it – five of them – arranged in stellate pattern around a central, large structure that seemed to be a sort of hall. The arrange-ment was reminiscent of the plan of Sandarro Castle, but here were no stone defence-works. Instead, these wooden houses were bright with paint, sky-blue, red and gold, as cheerful as booths at a fair and about as menacing.

Avran drew his sword, tossed it high in the air, caught it by the hilt and flourished it. 'Home at last – truly home, after so many years. Here my family lived for centuries before they became princes in Sandarro and here we'll return when we shed the burden of ruling. Welcome to Talestant, Simon!'

As we ascended the last rise, I saw beyond the padin a steep grassy descent, a curve of brown sand, and the blue waters of a great lake – Lake Vanadha.

It happened to be the case that, though Ilven had taken me on visits to shops and inns in Sandarro, I had neither stayed in nor even entered any typical padarn – that is, one used as residence by a family. I can't call it a house, for a padarn is more than that. Rather, it's like a group of small connected houses, set not in a row as are so many English cottages, but in a circle around a central open space. At opposite sides are two gateways, closed at need by massive doors. Normally the outer wall is high and windowless. At the top of that wall is a steep, outwardly-sloping rampart and within this is a circular walkway extending all the way round the padarn, on which defenders may patrol at times of need. Within the walkway, a roof slopes gently inward, with regularly spaced grooves that convey rainwater down into a gutter. The rainwater then drains down into two large, covered tanks, one for humans and one for beasts, furnishing an ample supply of drinking-water for times of siege. Altogether, the padarn has a defensive design. Even the garden at centre, stocked as it is with vegetable beds, fruit-trees, and fodder-bushes for sevdreyen, is a part of that design.

The padin of the region about Lake Vanadha accord in general with that pattern, but the differences are significant. The circular walkway is bounded upon its outer side only by a fence, not by a solid rampart. Moreover, it has seats at intervals, so that its inhabitants may be at ease while enjoying the view. There are windows in the outer wall, with many little panes of thin, polished horn to admit the light and yet keep out cold winter winds. The gardens contain more flowers than feed-plants, and the padin never have gates. Of course, they are inhabited only when the land is at peace. At times of war, as Avran had told me, the Estantesecs and their neighbours take refuge in the great

ANTONY SWITHIN

trees. All in all, while the padin of Sandarro are pleasant
enough, those of Estantegard have a joyful lightheartedness
of design that quite charmed me.

Whether in Sandarro or on the shores of Lake Vanadha,
each padarn is divided into a number of units, set about the
central garden like the spokes of a cartwheel. Each unit,
or *aspadarn,* is comparable with an English town-dweller's
house of two storeys. The ground floor has a kitchen and
retiring room at back beside the outer wall and a living
room on the garden side, while the second floor has three
or more bedrooms and is connected to the kitchen by a
steep staircase or ladder. However, in sunny weather, life is
largely lived in the garden, where there are tables and seats.

Most often a padarn belongs to a single large family,
grandparents living in two of the aspadin, their children
and grandchildren in the others. Sometimes one padarn
may be shared by two or more smaller families or by a
group of unmarried men or women.

In an English castle, only the nobility have private quarters and even they must spend much of their lives in the
hall. A padarn, in contrast, gives a choice of communal or
private activities to all that live in it.

The padarn belonging to Avran's own family was one of
the two on the lakeside. Since out of necessity the prince's
family had to reside in Sandarro, it was used only during
periodic summer visits and taken care of by the families
in the neighbouring padin. In midwinter, the time of our
visit, it had long been closed up; nor did we intend to stay
in Talestant long enough to justify its being opened for us.

Instead, we resided with Lednar and Esenar Estantesec
in a padarn on the forest side of Talestant. We were
welcomed by their grandparents (great-uncles and aunts

of Avran and Ilven), all four of them healthy and hearty, by Esenar's wife and six lively children, and by two other brothers and their families. Since Lednar the hunter was unmarried, it was in his aspadarn that we slept, though all our meals were taken in other aspadin.

These were cheerful, energetic, and industrious people, whom I came to like very much. Yet, in my English fashion, I considered it strange and wonderful that members of the ruling family of Sandastre should be content to live so far from that land's capital city and so simply. When Avran told me that both great-uncles had formerly held high positions in Sandarro and that Esenar had been a quincentenar in the Sandastrian army, my sense of wonder only increased.

I was delighted to find Rokh browsing cheerfully among the estelen trees close by. He had been brought back there by cart, I learned. His broken leg had been examined and redressed by Esenar's wife, a skilled animal doctor, and promised to heal wholly within a few weeks.

Yet, fond though I was of Rokh, I could not await the healing of his forelimb. My quest was too urgent for that. Moreover, I had Yerezinth now. Remembering my indebtedness to Lednar, I offered Rokh to the hunter. This was a transfer of ownership that delighted our friend, since the grey rider's sevdru had proved uncongenial to him – and it was accepted readily enough by Rokh.

We stayed in Talestant for six days – six relaxing days, spent talking or singing in the garden, sauntering among the great trees (though I was given no chance to explore their 'fortifications'), lazing on the quiet shore of Lake Vanadha, or swimming in its waters. I took the opportunity to write a long letter to Ilven, shaping my letters carefully in order to demonstrate to her how well I had profited from her tuition. Though I told her something of our doings, much of that letter inevitably became an expression of love and of longing. As it was, it made it all the more painful to think that our journey had yet barely begun. Much though I liked Talestant, I was eager to be leaving.

Avran, in contrast, was disposed to linger. He was happy to be back in the lands of his vard, of course, but, no less than myself, he was eager as well for news. We were both of us anxious to know if Dermot Fitzstephen and his three associates had been captured. If so, we were hoping Dermot could be persuaded to forsake his loyalties and name his employers. Already Avran had transmitted all the information he had gained about the grey riders to his father the Prince by way of the system of royal messengers whose swift passage binds together the bundle of vardlands that is Sandastre. It was possible that the riddle of the riders might be solved for us from Sandarro.

It was on the fourth day that we received an answer to the question of Dermot Fitzstephen's fate and on the sixth day that messages came from Sandarro. For both pursuing parties, the trail of the grey riders had proved a long one. While we were resting in the ruined temple, the Sandastrians had continued that pursuit until the fall of night prevented any further reading of tracks. The grey riders must have rested as well and, though they were up and away earlier, their tracks were soon rediscovered. And so the hunt had resumed. It was to continue throughout much of the day on which we rode to Talestant.

By the afternoon, the gap between the pursuers and the two grey riders who had headed south-eastward was closing fast. In a gully somewhere above the lands of Indravard, they turned at bay and spurned an invitation to surrender.

Instead, there had been an exchange of darts from sasayin during the course of which two of the Estantesecs were injured and one of the riders killed. Again there was a call to surrender, but the surviving grey rider ignored it. Desperately he charged his pursuers. When his sevdru was cut from under him, he fell on his own sword rather than be taken. Neither of the dead men was Dermot Fitzstephen.

It was Dermot and a companion, then, who had turned northeastward, riding so desperately fast that they were not even sighted by the other pursuing party till late afternoon on the second day. By then they were in a region of crags and broken rocks, where tracking was difficult and a passage not easy even for sevdreyen. The gap between pursuers and pursued had not closed before darkness again fell.

Next morning, the Sandastrians discovered the tracks of the grey riders' sevdreyen only after much trouble. They followed and eventually caught up with those animals, only to discover that both were now riderless. Somewhere among the rocks, Dermot and his companion had slipped away. Though the Sandastrians alerted the surrounding vardai – Derresdavard, Kevessvard, Indravard, even Predaravard on the shore of Arcturus Bay – no trace was found of those two.

Nor did the message from Sandarro furnish any new information. It turned out that Prince Vindicon and his councillors knew nothing either of the grey riders or of any new plot against the realm of Sandastre. They were quite as puzzled as we were and even more uneasy.

The messages to Avran, then, brought him no comfort. On the other hand, a message sent to me by Ilven was an occasion for me of great contentment. Though I remember exactly what she wrote, I will not divulge her words, for they were written for my eyes alone.

CHAPTER 2
The Forgotten City

So it was that, seven mornings after we had reached Talestant, Avran was persuaded to journey forth again with me. We had decided we would be wise to continue to wear soldiers' garb, inasmuch as wandering mercenaries are common enough in the lands to which we were going. Both Zembelen and Yerezinth were joyful at being on the road once more, but Rascal, squatting atop my new pack-saddle, was sulking. I was not sure if this was out of resentment at having to leave those luscious estelen groves or on account of a growing awareness on his part that, before long, he and I must go our separate ways. (For that matter, this realization did not provoke any joy in me either.) Soon the steady jogging sent him to sleep, and, when he awoke, he was cheerful enough.

After discussions with Avran's cousins, we had decided to ride northward into Denniffey rather than northeastward through Pravan and Volendar. Since the lands of the Estantesecs extend further into Denniffey than into Pravan, our decision was an obvious one. It made sense for us to want to remain as long as possible among people who were apt to be our friends. Elsewhere in those realms, there were indeed few places that inspired any trust.

However, there were other reasons as well. Pravan's ruler, styled an earl, had taken to himself the powers of a petty king of the worst sort. He lived in tarnished state among servile courtiers and plundered whenever and wherever he might. The Estantesecs, with their powerful southern connections, tended to be left alone, but beyond their lands there was no safety for travellers. Volendar was equally unsafe. It was a tiny realm beyond Pravan on the edge of the plains, with a Temeculan ruling family uneasily governing a handful of Montariotan subjects who, having given up nomadic life, were perpetually under threat from their wandering kinsmen. It was most definitely not the place from which to begin a crossing of the plains and, with Antomalata and Sapandella at war close by, we would have been quite unwise to choose the northeastern route.

Denniffey was a *naradat,* a republic somewhat on the ancient Athenian model about which my tutor had taught me. In theory at least, the *narat,* its ruler, was elected on the death or resignation of his predecessor by free vote of all adult citizens. The idea was attractive, and I was disappointed to learn that practice fell far short of precept.

For almost two centuries, each successive narat had been a member of the powerful Abaletsen family. Since no other candidates had dared to stand in opposition, naturally there had been no need for elections. Yet the long rule of the Abaletsens had not been benign. Long ago Denniffey had been a rich and densely populated land, powerful enough even to rival Sandastre. However, years of almost incessant warring with adjacent realms to east, west, and south and repeated attacks from the north by Montariotan marauders had pushed Denniffey into a long decline.

Presently, however, Denniffey was at peace. Although, with neighbouring Darrinnett in fiery revolt against the Fachnese, that peace looked fragile, we trusted we might traverse Denniffey without incident and find ourselves beyond its frontiers before any new conflict flared up.

The sunshine continued through the next three days. After a few hours of riding through pasturelands beside Lake Vanadha, with brown sands at our left, where shore-birds probed for food and peeped plaintively, we crossed another high-arched bridge to enter the realm of Denniffey. This frontier was not guarded, inasmuch as both banks lay within the lands of Estantegard. Onward we rode, north up the narrow valley of the swift-flowing Demdelet, under the intermittent shade of giant pevenekar. On that night and the one following, we slept in padin as colourful as those of Talestant. The evenings were passed in song and celebration. While Avran's rank was being discreetly ignored, he was after all an Estantesec and honoured at least as a visiting relative.

On the third morning, however, the character of the landscape began to change. The Demdelet, narrower and more turbulent now, was still at our right, but the huge pevenekar were succeeded by lesser trees, and even those became ever fewer and smaller. There were sevdreyen browsing among these trees, but always under the eye of a heavily armed guard, watchful, not for beasts of prey, but for marauding men. The padarn we slept in that night was built of stone and set high on a crag.

Our host was Senraidar Estantesec, a man of Temeculan descent in part, as his first name indicated. (Senraidar had been a name borne by many of the Earls of Stavrasard, one of whom became the first King of Temecula). He was tall, lean and wiry, with a nervous watchfulness evoked by years on the uneasy edge of the lands that fell under the sway of the Estantesecs. His wife was prematurely grey, and his children struck me as too steady and sedate for their years. However, his two sons played happily with Rascal, while his daughter seemed especially enthralled by the little vasian.

We watched the children's games and talked in an easy, relaxed spirit till they were taken away to bed. After that, we began questioning our host about his land, for there was much we needed urgently to know.

'Yes, indeed, there were once many people living hereabouts,' Senraidar said, in response to an enquiry from Avran. 'This would be a good land yet for men and beasts, if people could just remain in peace. But when it comes to the folk of Denniffey, it seems they can never rest easy. There's always soldiers being sent out from Doriolupata to enlist recruits or collect taxes for some new war – a campaign against Volendar or Siasaph, maybe, or what they style a retaliatory raid against those accursed nomads of the plains. Sometimes there is in fact a campaign, but more often than not the taxes disappear into the coffers of the narat, and the soldiers are employed merely to extort more money. So why should folk trouble overmuch to grow bigger crops or breed larger herds of beasts, when it'd simply mean paying higher taxes to those money-grabbing Abaletsens?'

'Well, you're Estantesecs. Doesn't that help?'

'Aye, of course it does – if you're down in the forests, with the pevenekar about you and Sandastre nearby. Up here, though, it's not so handy. It's just too easy for them soldiers to pick up a man and carry him off to Doriolupata, where he must explain to the narat and his fat cronies exactly why the taxes fell short, on pain of being clapped into prison if they don't like his answers. Or else there's what they call an unfortunate accident, and you're found with a hunting-spear embedded in your spine. And then, look at our neighbours, if one can honour them with that title. The Sambrelans down on the lakeshore, they're not bad folk, but those Vaghats over to our west are a perverse bunch. If they don't chance to be fighting the Baroddans, you may be sure they'll be quarrelling with someone else. And you'll know all about the Lenavvars, I'm sure. I could do without that thieving, traitorous crew nearby.'

Avran did indeed know of the Lenavvars, who had played a black part in the history of southern Rockall. 'I wonder that you stay on up here, when the problems are so great.'

Senraidar's lined face creased into a smile. 'Well now, it does make life interesting, you know. And' – his eyes twinkled – 'I won't say but that the Lenavvars and Vaghats don't lose the odd beast on occasion.'

Avran laughed heartily. 'Why, you old battler, you! Well now, can you tell us what's happening in Doriolupata these days? As I mentioned, we're bound northwards. Somehow, we need to find a way across the River Werenthin and the plains beyond.'

Our host grimaced. 'Crossing that river's difficult enough. It's wide, and there are neither bridges nor ferries, as well you must know. And traversing the plains – well, you *might* manage it, but I wouldn't give two asalbek berries for your chances. Best turn back while there's yet time. As for Doriolupata, it's the same old brew of politics and corruption that ever it was. Our beloved President Vizien Abaletsen' – he spat with disgust – 'is just the right spice for such a brew.'

Senraidar helped us to more wine, but he would not say more about his land and its ruler. Instead, he told us much about the Montariotans. He had fought against them during past years and he knew much more about them than had Enar Servessil and his colleagues.

On more immediate matters, he gave us specific advice in two regards. He recommended that I should send back Rascal to Sandarro at the first opportunity and that Avran and I should henceforward conceal our familiarity with the longbow. In the first place, concerning Rascal he pointed out that fodder trees for vasianar would become ever harder to find as we rode northward and, secondly, that a vasian would attract unwanted attention in lands where such beasts were scarcely known. Concerning our longbows, he commented that the word of my doings in Sandarro had spread widely already. To be seen carrying a strung longbow would not only identify us unmistakably, but might well cause us to be pressed into teaching the use of that weapon to the soldiers of Denniffey.

Senraidar was able to be helpful in both respects. He offered to furnish us each with one of the light game-hunting bows of southern Rockall, as explanation for the quivers of arrows we carried. The longbow staves, he suggested, might be passed off as sticks for quarterstaff combats, which are as common an amusement among the Temeculan tribes as they are in England.

As for Rascal, Senraidar had an excellent proposal to make. The children of Estantesec families resident outside Sandastre are quite regularly sent to Sandarro, there to gain education of a quality not available in these borderlands. Senraidar's daughter and elder son, along with children from several neighbouring padin, would be travelling south within two days under strong escort. He suggested that Rascal travel with them. The children would be thrilled to have him in their charge. They would take good care of him and deliver him safely to Ilven.

This idea I found both comforting and disquieting. I knew that a parting from my vasian could not be long delayed, but I had become so fond of him that the prospect caused me great dismay. However, the offer was too good to be refused. I summoned up a smile of thanks and accepted.

When I sought my bed that night, I found myself having to undertake the task of mentally explaining his future to Rascal. Somehow I managed it. Though I could feel his pain, I could also sense that my vasian had been anticipating the parting and was ready for it. Even more strangely, I became aware that, though Rascal would miss my company, he would not pine. Instead he would wait for me, secure in the certainty that I would be returning to him some day. The confidence and trust of that little animal were both astonishing and humbling. Though I found my eyes welling up with tears, I could not help but experience a lifting of my heart at the same time.

Nor, next morning, was the actual parting difficult. Certainly Rascal's ears were drooping a little and, when I gave him a farewell hug, he was reluctant to be loosed. However, when I handed him over to Senraidar's little daughter, he settled on her shoulder without any sign of sulking or sorrow. Though certainly saddened by that parting, I rode away in better spirits than I had expected.

It was well that my spirits were good, for the day was a bleak one. The sky was leaden-grey and the clouds lowering. A strong, cold wind from the northeast bowed the grassheads and stirred the dead leaves by the gate of the padarn into a dance. The path down the crag was both steep and exposed. Both we ourselves and our sevdreyen were glad to reach the shelter of the Demdelet valley again.

Not that this served us as protection for long. Soon the river was branching into smaller, swifter tributary streams, the deep slots of whose channels were too narrow to allow the passage of riders. We were forced instead to endure the wind, following an ill-maintained road across uplands where tumbled walls divided abandoned fields. Here and there, heaps of stones marked the former positions of buildings so completely collapsed that their purpose and character could no longer be determined. It was all too evident how the population of Denniffey had dwindled, when so much cultivable land had fallen into such complete neglect.

Yet, though it appeared so desolate, this landscape was not depressing, even on such a bitter day. Perhaps this was because grasses and weeds had grown up so luxuriantly around those tumbled stones, perhaps merely because the structures were so long fallen that they had lost the poignancy of recent ruins.

By then we had left the lands of the Estantesecs and were riding through the western fringes of those of the Lenavvars. Several times we saw, away to the east, herds of hasedain or sevdreyen grazing among the overgrown fields under the watchful eye of some cloak-huddled warrior. However, in these lands there were no songs, no merry calls to greet our passing, but only a silent, suspicious watchfulness. A few birds fought the wind in brief flights from covert to covert, but the cold had also subdued their songs. All other wild creatures were keeping safe within shelter.

Around midday we found ourselves approaching what once had been a padarn – a larger ruin, set on a mound built from the earth and stone rubble excavated from a surrounding ditch. The ditch was still water-filled, though green now with weed, and three walls of the padarn still stood, although blackened by the smoke of the consuming fire that had burned it long ago. Since they promised shelter from the relentless wind, it was within those walls that we decided to take our noon repast. The grasses stood high and green in the lee of the ruin.

As we rode up onto the mound, some small animal grunted in fright and hastened away unglimpsed, the grasses rippling at its passing like water flowing over a submerged swimmer.

Senraidar's wife had furnished us with a generous store of food: compact rations for the days to come and cheeses, salads, and fruits for this first day. Once out of the wind, we were warm enough to enjoy our repast in comfort. While we ate and talked, our two sevdreyen foraged contentedly among the tall weeds that grew round about. However, I found myself missing Rascal's happy crooning – and not for the last time.

Our afternoon road led us ever upward, onto the main mass of the looping Heights of Denniffey. The ruined field walls became fewer and more widely spaced, the vegetation less green and progressively sparser. Soon we were traversing moorland that was stonier and more barren than even the Trantevrin Hills. Our uphill ride was ever more of a fight against the bleak wind. I found this familiar and exhilarating, for it reminded me of days on the windy moors of the Pennines back in England. Avran, on the other hand, accustomed to the benign climate of Sandastre, was shivering, while the sevdreyen were cold and unhappy.

As we topped a minor ridge, I was reminded again of my homeland. Ahead was a sandstone cliff that seemed to have been shaped by wind and weather into masses and pillars, much like the gritstone crags of Wharncliffe close to my Hallamshire home. Below were ridges of rubble and scattered larger blocks of sandstone, some square, some rounded. For me, these too recalled Wharncliffe, where, for uncounted centuries, men had shaped the coarse gritstone into querns and millstones for grinding corn.

However, as we rode closer, I saw that these blocks and mounds were not the residue of a stone-trimming industry, but the tumbled ruins of a town. What I had thought to be crags were the crumbling towers and broken walls of the ridge-top castle that had once watched over that town. Below them, the whole broad face of the sandstone had, at some distant time, been elaborately graven and polished.

Though the stone had flaked or discoloured in places, and lichens and mosses had rooted wherever they might, the theme of these carvings remained evident. A triumphal procession was depicted, featuring warriors returning from victory. Their helmets were wreathed with blossoms, their spears bedecked with flowers, and the horns of their sevdreyen caparisoned with feathers. Behind the warriors, to our right as we looked at the cliff, were depicted hasedain laden with booty and led by servants or prisoners (it was not clear which), while captured sevdreyen, roped together in threes, followed. Shown at lesser scale below the victorious warriors was a line of onlookers, men, women and children, their gestures expressive of their joy.

Above the carvings, an inscription in archaic Sandastrian characters was yet decipherable, even though worn away in places. As we threaded our way through the ruins and drew closer to the rock face, Avran strove with furrowed brow to read the inscribed characters.

'I cannot clearly understand it,' he remarked at last. 'The words are like ours, yet unlike them too. However, I think this must, long ago, have been a fortress city of the Kingdom of Elvenost. Nowadays Elvenost is a very minor realm, just one of several small states huddled along the border of Temecula. There was a time, however, when Elvenost grew great and powerful, holding in thrall most of the lands around Sandastre.'

'I've barely even heard of it,' I confessed. 'How long ago was that?'

He laughed. 'Oh, quite a long time – twelve hundred years or so. We Rockalese have long memories, you know. But I remember Elvenost particularly because its most powerful king had the same name as my eldest brother – Helburnet. Helburnet the Triumphant, his people called him in the days of his greatness; and I presume that this carving must commemorate his conquest of Denniffey. If his luck had held, he might also have conquered Sandastre. Our eslef of that time, Falco Serrad I Vednetren, was a devious man but without the qualities of a warleader. However, Helburnet was assassinated – by one of his generals, I believe – and his whole empire collapsed almost overnight.'

Avran directed a more intent gaze at the carvings, then pointed. 'You see the figure over there – the rider on the unusually large sevdru? The rock has flaked badly, but he appears to be wearing a crown of Temeculan style. I presume that must be Helburnet. Odd, isn't it, that his figure should be the most severely damaged of all?' He paused, then added reflectively: 'Yet perhaps that's appropriate enough, since his own demise preceded the fading of his empire. And now, from all those conquests, nothing remains but a few ruins and these crumbling carvings.'

'What was this city called?' I wondered.

Avran shrugged. 'I've no idea. I doubt if even the Denniffeyens recall its name. What does it matter? Now, its only inhabitants are lizards and other small beasts, and they have no language.'

Since the fortifications occupied the whole ridge, we had to find a way through them. This proved easy enough. A steep earthen ramp led up to where an ancient gate once had stood, its arch now fallen in. Beyond was the courtyard of the old castle, grass-grown now and with a few bedraggled bushes rooting among its stone flags. Beyond again, there was a second gate, its arch substantially intact but its doors long vanished. There had been a moat on its outer, northern side. This was dry now and overgrown, but still bridged by an arch of carved stone. With some trepidation, we rode over this arch, but fortunately it remained solid.

However, now we were again riding into the teeth of the wind, which seemed yet more biting after the temporary shelter. A long slope of moorland lay before us, affording no prospect of further protection for many leagues. Beyond, indeed, there was only the grey sky.

After about quarter of an hour of dogged riding, Avran slowed his mount and addressed me. 'I've had quite enough of this. There's a refuge of a sort behind us, but none at all ahead. It would be stupid to go on. Let's turn back and spend our night in the old city.'

I hesitated. What Avran said made sense, yet his proposal made me uneasy. Or was it Yerezinth who was uneasy?

'Very well,' I said reluctantly, and we turned our mounts around.

Riding into the wind had been hard. Riding with the wind behind us was a delight. Avran turned a laughing face to me. 'This is wonderful! Come on, Simon, we'll race you back to the ruins.'

In a moment, Zembelen was galloping away at full tilt, with Avran shouting in joy and urging him to yet greater speed.

After my earlier misadventure, I did not really make an effort to match Avran's pace. But, since Yerezinth was a bigger animal than Rokh and his stride longer, we were soon catching up. Within minutes we were approaching the castle again. Yerezinth was only a few paces behind Zembelen when we crossed the stone bridge and even closer as we traversed the grass-grown courtyard. Through the broken gate we rode neck and neck, to cascade down the steep slope beyond, warm now, breathless and laughing.

Yet, for a second time, the reckless abandon of speed had carried us into trouble. When we had left the ruins of King Helburnet's city, it had indeed been populated only by lizards and other small beasts. In our myopic lack of wisdom, we had presumed all would remain unchanged. Now, however, it was aswarm with soldiers.

They seemed to rise from nowhere to surround us from all sides, burly men in jupons and hose as brown as the tumbled stone, with surcoats as green as the weeds and with drawn swords or axes in their hands.

Any resistance would clearly be vain. Avran raised his arms outward and forward, in the Rockalese gesture of surrender that shows no weapon is held.

As I followed suit, I noticed on each surcoat a heraldic device and read it automatically. 'Per bend argent and vert, a cockatrice sejant purpure,' I muttered to myself – an

obliquely divided shield, silver and green, bearing in purple
the device of a sitting creature that looked like the cockatrice
of legend. My studies in Sandastre had not been in vain.
Even before Avran could tell me so, I knew that we were
surrounded by soldiers of Denniffey.

CHAPTER 3

Captives In The Rain

They were soldiers, but their intentions towards us did not appear hostile. While their swords were drawn, they seemed more startled than threatening. An immense man, clad beneath his surcoat in rather rusty chain mail and with the cockatrice device repeated on his iron helmet, appeared to be their leader. It was he that addressed us.

'Why so hasty, brothers? Be ye in pursuit or in flight? Neither beast nor man has passed hereby. What is it that ye are about?'

His voice was a sort of dry roar, like waves breaking on a pebble-bank. Its inflexions were hard to read, yet I thought indeed it contained more in the way of puzzlement than of threat.

'Might I ask, sir, whom I am addressing?' Avran enquired, breathless but polite.

'I am Burak Ekonar, quincentenar of the army of Denniffey. I am warden of these lands under the authority of the narat and responsible for all deeds done here or left undone. Who be ye, that come as strangers?'

Avran laughed gaily and lowered his hands. 'Why then, it is you whom we were seeking! My companion and I are soldiers of fortune. We are come to find employment in this land, for we are told that you welcome good warriors and offer them high rewards.'

29

The soldier eyed him suspiciously from under brows as shaggy as old thatch. 'Indeed! So ye were seeking us, were ye? Yet ye seemed greatly surprised at finding us.'

'True enough,' Avran responded easily. 'We thought you were many leagues away to the west. That was the cause of our surprise, for we had not reckoned on encountering you so soon. And it was the cause of our haste also, for we were trusting to locate you before sunset. There is little shelter in this land. We hoped to find refuge in your camp, for the wind is cold.'

'It is that.' The massive head was nodding slowly. 'A bleak day it has been, one of the hardest I remember. Where be ye from, may I ask, and what be your name?'

Avran's smile vanished like a chalk-mark wiped from a slate. He spoke very coldly now. 'As to where I am from, let us just say, from the south. And it is enough to add that my forename is Avran. My surname I mislike, ever since they placed a prefix before it; so I will not quote it.'

At this the listening soldiers smiled or even chuckled, perceiving that Avran was referring to the 'biek' placed before the vard name of a convicted Sandastrian criminal. Their leader said drily: 'Ay, well, we'll not press you for it. And your friend?'

'His name is Simon and he's from the east.' (True enough, since England lies far to the east of Denniffey.) 'He has a surname so barbarously strange that I can't set my tongue to it. What is it, Simon? Bransait? Branthait?'

'Branthwaite,' I managed to respond gravely, though I was bubbling with amusement inside at Avran's adroit deceptions.

Their leader considered this, his brows knotting. 'A difficult name indeed, and not one that I have ever heard.

Certainly not Temeculan, nor Salastrian either. You must come from beyond the Arctorran lands, I guess?'

I assented solemnly, which was easy enough, since what he said was true. 'To my own people, such names are commonplace. However, you will surely find it easier to call me just Simon, as does Avran. Among comrades, there is no need for formality. If you accept our services, soon we shall be comrades indeed.'

Burak Ekonar had lowered his sword by now, as had the other soldiers. However, none of those swords had yet been sheathed, and the huge soldier still appeared dubious. His brows had relaxed, but his rather small pale brown eyes were busy assessing us.

'Well, as to that,' he rumbled, 'it is not for me to decide. Tonight you may remain with us, but you will be under guard. We return tomorrow to Doriolupata, where our commander can decide your fate. Maybe, when all is said and done, you'll be recruited to the service of the narat – who knows? Yield your swords to me, please, and dismount.'

Our swords were examined with interest, for they were better blades than are commonly carried by Rockalese soldiers. In consequence, they earned us further suspicious looks from the massive quincentenar. However, our bowstaves were not examined, nor were we searched.

Moreover, though certainly we were watched, we were treated well enough that evening. Indeed, these soldiers were travelling in comparative luxury. Both we ourselves and the soldiers fed well on broth that had been heated in a big iron pot, together with hunks of bread (rather dry, but tasty enough when dipped in the broth) and beakers of ale freshly tapped from a wooden cask. The soldiers' pack-hasedain carried not only bedding and provisions, but also fodder and water for their sevdreyen. Thus Yerezinth and Zembelen were treated as well as we were. However, they were likewise kept under guard, for Burak Ekonar understood fully the abilities of a sevdru and was taking no chances.

The soldiers themselves were a pretty rough bunch. A few were Denniffeyens of the lower sort, but the majority were mercenaries coming, it seemed, from most parts of southern Rockall – Arctorrans, Baroddans, Fachnese, and men from several Temeculan and Salastrian tribes. Avran told me later that the surname of their leader showed him to be from Skayarock, a realm north of Fachane and now reluctantly under the governance of that kingdom.

Only the strength and force of personality of Burak Ekonar maintained any coherence or discipline in this motley band. And indeed, on that first evening, the discipline seemed tight enough. Though Avran's ready tongue and easy humour elicited both attention and laughter from the soldiers sharing our shelter, their watchfulness never ceased. That night, we went to sleep wrapped warmly in blankets beneath a shelter of hides erected in the lee of one of the more substantial ruins. However, we slept under the steady eyes of guards and, when we woke next morning, new guards were watching us with equal vigilance.

That morning was a grey one. The wind had veered overnight and now was blowing from the southwest. It was a much warmer wind, but the massing, hastening clouds were an augury of rain soon to come. Under this threat, the soldiers and the two of us breakfasted with such speed that, within forty minutes of our rising, the shelters were down and the hasedain being loaded. Even so, as we were mounting our sevdreyen, the rain began.

Only at this time did Avran and I realize we were not the only prisoners. Two other men were enduring a much more rigorously enforced confinement. Each had been bound to the pack-saddle on which he was mounted, the ropes being further tied to the pack-saddles of soldiers on either side.

One of these men was dark-bearded, with eyes deeply shadowed by lowering brows. Almost as massive as Burak Ekonar, he was guarded by two of the strongest of the soldiers. However, he appeared so wrapped in gloom that he was unaware of them. The other prisoner, a lean man of middle height, whose bright red hair was somewhat muted in hue by the onset of greyness, was in contrast looking at the scene about him with sharp eyes. When he perceived Avran, I saw him start in surprise. However, he made no comment and instantly looked away.

There were around fifty soldiers in Burak Ekonar's band. They rode in the formation of an open wedge, with their leader, riding the biggest sevdru I had ever seen, in the vanguard – at the point, as it were. Avran and I, though still without our swords, were not under any restraint. We were, however, placed firmly at the centre of the wedge. The two captives and their guards were some way behind us. At the back of the wedge, which is to say its blunt end, the pack-hasedain patiently trotted along in line abreast.

In such open country, our placement among the soldiers left us no chance of escaping. Yet it had its advantage, for we were protected somewhat from the rain. This came in large drops, driven obliquely by gusty wind buffets that set the soldiers – especially those to our left, who bore the brunt of the weather – grumbling and cursing. Like them, Avran and I were wearing cloaks and had pulled the hoods forward over our heads. Our cloaks were good, yet the wind-driven rain found its way into and beneath our garb in warm runnels until our necks, arms, and legs were soaked. Not since those days of riding to Bristol had I been so thoroughly uncomfortable.

Moreover, this day's ride was infinitely more boring, for the press of surrounding soldiers prevented any extensive view of the moorland about us. The distant prospects were, in any case, veiled by cloud. Even so, I was aware that we were heading northwestward, obliquely down the long northern flank of the Heights of Denniffey.

During the first three hours of riding, the surface beneath us changed little; but, after that, the stones became ever fewer till they vanished amid a deeper, greener herbage. Once we picked our way across a marsh, the wedge of soldiers and beasts narrowing before and widening after it in hourglass fashion. And twice we splashed through the waters of shallow, swift streams. There were increasing numbers of bushes, and I began to glimpse, through the wet mist, dark shapes that must be small trees. The wind was blowing more steadily by then and the rain coming at us in ever more drenching bursts.

In such conditions, the vigilance of the soldiers had understandably waned. Avran was riding quite close by me, and we were able to talk in low tones. He was inclined to self-recrimination.

'Brrh! What weather!' he said, shaking his head so that the water spattered from his hood. 'And what a fool I am, plunging us into this mire of trouble! After that earlier episode, I ought to have known better than to race along so heedlessly. It serves *me* right for sure, but I grieve at having brought you into such a predicament.'

'Actually, I thought you did us pretty well, Avran,' I responded honestly. 'I'm sure the soldiers truly believe you to be a criminal on the run and me just some harmless wanderer with an appetite for adventure. If they realized who we were, matters might be much more serious. As things are, the worst that can happen is that we might be forced to serve awhile in the Denniffeyen army. And surely we'll be able to slip away soon and that without too much difficulty.'

Avran snorted and gave another angry toss of his head. 'As to that, it might not be so easy, from what I've heard of the walls of Doriolupata. However, there's worse yet. Do you know who those prisoners are?'

'No. I presumed they were just farmers who'd fallen foul of the narat and his cronies.'

'It's much more serious than that, I regret to say. The redheaded man is an Estantesec, a distant cousin of mine. Darolayn is his name, a member of our vard who lives in Denniffey just a few leagues east of Senraidar's home. Before you awoke two mornings back, I was talking with Senraidar and he told me that cousin Darolayn has been dabbling in politics. It seems that there are signs, at long last, of an uprising against the Abaletsens. Darolayn is in the very forefront of the discontented, so much so in fact that the narat has outlawed him and set a price upon his head. Senraidar was rather gleeful about that – he was sure they'd never catch Darolayn. He was wrong. They've caught him. The other man they've captured is less important, just a bodyguard, I would guess. However, without Darolayn, the uprising may collapse – and, Heaven knows, it's past time that the Abaletsens were overthrown.'

I gave out a low sigh. 'Well, that's sad news. How did they catch him?'

'I don't know yet. I'll try to find out. However, there's another problem. Darolayn knows me well. He's been to Talestant several times and also to Sandarro. He wouldn't denounce me willingly, but, if the narat's torturers should get at him, he might do so involuntarily. And I'm quite sure that Vizien Abaletsen would love to have me in his dungeons. He's well aware that my father dislikes his rule, even though Sandastre has never interfered in the affairs of Denniffey. Think how the narat might use me, either to secure a ransom or, more likely, to obtain political favours for his accursed family.' He groaned at the very thought.

I tried to respond with bracing optimism. 'Well, it hasn't happened yet, so keep your spirits up. Much may happen yet before we reach Doriolupata. How far is it, anyway?'

He considered the question briefly, then shouted to the nearest soldier: 'How much longer must we endure this rain, friend? Shall we reach Doriolupata tonight?'

'That we won't,' came a growled response. 'Given decent weather, we'd be there by noon tomorrow. In conditions like this, who can say? It's my belief we ought to be seeking shelter, not riding on and on across these accursed hills.'

Avran gave me a covert smile and muttered under his breath that he hoped the rain would continue. Aloud, he said: 'Quite right, friend. You're soldiers – fighting men, not *festikieren*' (The *festikier* is a common waterbird of southern Rockall). 'Why endure this weather, when there's no enemy to be attacked and no other reason for haste?'

'Ay, that's right enough!' the soldier said. At this, he rode over to one of his fellows to pass along this sentiment. In fact, the soldiers were becoming ever more restive.

The close formation in which we had ridden forth was becoming ever looser, as they straggled or clotted into grumbling groups. Burak Ekonar's tight discipline was dissolving progressively in the steady downpour.

After the soldier had gone, Avran addressed me again. 'Well enough as far as it goes, but all it may gain us is a wet night in some meagre shelter. I see small hope of our escaping and none at all of our freeing Darolayn.'

I tried a second time to cheer him. 'Don't be so glum, Avran, friend. We've been fortunate before. Maybe we'll be so again.'

Almost as I spoke, the whole column of riders came to a straggling halt, and a message was passed back that cheered the soldiers immensely. The one whom Avran had addressed hastened back toward us.

'Ah, now, here's good tidings!' he crowed. 'There's a stand of trees not far ahead where we can find shelter. We'll be camping there till tomorrow morning or whenever this infernal rain stops. Burak Ekonar's no sort of a fool, after all.'

Nor was he, for he had sensed the mood of his rabble of followers and, being well aware how slight was their loyalty in any adversity, had adjusted his plans accordingly, as a sea-captain trims his sails to the wind. Though the rain did not abate, it was with a new enthusiasm that the ride was resumed.

Within another hour we were descending a slippery, rock-strewn slope into a saucer-shaped depression. Once there might have been a lake here, but, if so, its waters had long since drained away. Now it was overgrown densely by trees of a sort I had not seen before, with dark-green foliage opening out above their trunks as abruptly – and in much the same fashion – as does an open fan above its handle. Avran called the trees *tavelnekar* and told me their bitter yellow berries were used in Sandastre to cure agues. Though, to be sure, the trees could not keep out all the rain, they formed a welcome protection from the wind and allowed the hide shelters to be erected without much effort in their lee.

Since dry wood had been brought along in the hasedain packs, fires were soon burning and the stewpots bubbling merrily. Around each of the fires, four shelters were set in an inwardly-facing ring so that the soldiers might each enjoy the warmth. As food and drink began to circulate, their spirits picked up, and the talk became loud and cheerful.

Accepted into the communality of one such circle, Avran and I, though in theory still prisoners under guard, were in practice being treated more and more as equals. Avran's good-humoured badinage made him ever more popular and brought with it a corresponding increase in tolerance for me.

The two other captives were very much less fortunate. Each had been roped to a tree and, though fed and given water, was left to find what shelter he might in the lee of its trunk. I could not see the dark-bearded man, but the red-haired captive, Avran's cousin, was not far distant from our tent. Technically, indeed, he was under the surveillance of the soldiers in our shelter-ring. It must have been a thoroughly miserable afternoon for both prisoners; and, though the rain continued steadily into the evening, they were afforded neither coverings nor any other protection from the weather. On the excuse of a call of nature, I left our shelter shortly after dinner. I did not dare to stray far, for I was still under observation. However, the two soldiers appointed to the task of watching me were not disposed to follow me out into the rain. Moreover, they were much more interested in a game of chance that was in progress by the fireside. It was being played with octahedral garnets on the faces of which numbers had been scratched.

The red-haired prisoner was reclining wearily in the encumbrance of his ropes, about twenty yards away. Though the sky was darkening now, he saw me against the fire-glow and looked toward me in appeal, half-rising. However, the guards were also looking toward me, and I did not dare approach him. Instead, I turned away. As I did so, I saw him slump back in despair.

The daylight was fading now, and the background of trees was dark. I was sure that the guards, though still able to see me, could not perceive all my movements. As I turned back toward the shelter, swiftly I snatched one of my throwing-knives from its shoulder-sheath and hurled it toward the prisoner.

I heard the slight thwack as the knife plunged into the soil somewhere by him in the gloom, but I could not determine how accurate that hasty throw had been. Nor did I dare attempt to check. Instead, with the haste appropriate to such wet weather, I returned to the shelter.

The game was at a tense stage. Caught up in it as they were, the two guards noted my return with relief and switched their entire attention to the rolling garnets. I sat down by Avran, my heart beating fast, wondering if I had thrown the knife far enough and if Darolayn Estantesec would be able to reach it. This set my mind racing with further questions. Did he have sufficient skill to free himself and escape the soldiers? Would he have sense enough to take the knife with him, so that his escape was not laid to my account?

As for Avran and me, no chance of escape was afforded us. Within minutes, the massive figure of Burak Ekonar followed me into the hide shelter. He had come to ensure that, in such cramped quarters, Avran and I were separated for the night and kept under close guard. Also, he arranged a rota of hourly inspection for the other two prisoners. When he left the shelter, he was accompanied by a disconsolate Avran and the two soldiers charged with guarding him.

That night, again I slept with two guards watching me. Nor, on this occasion, did I find sleep quickly. Our capture by the Denniffeyan mercenaries had delayed our quest already. And, if their guard over us continued to be so very close and careful, it might be long before we were able to evade them and resume our search for Lyonesse. Well, the good thing was that at present we were not in any real danger. 'Be content, Simon, be content,' I urged myself, even as I slipped away into a deep slumber.

CHAPTER 4

The Walls Of Doriolupata

A clamour of voices awakened me. Burak Ekonar was standing close by our shelter-ring, roaring with fury, and other soldiers were shouting feverish responses, transmitting his orders or giving their own.

It was natural enough that I should ask my guards what was the matter. Their answer startled me. Not one, but both of the other prisoners had escaped.

That much, at least, was clear. But otherwise no one seemed to clearly comprehend quite what had happened. One theory seemed to be that the big black-haired man had burst his bonds, released his comrade and, after felling several guards, fled with him. Another was that both men had been freed by a rescuing party after a bloody – but mysteriously silent – affray. And a third was that they had been treacherously released by one of their guards during the night.

Whatever the truth of the matter, the soldiers were as stirred up by the event as ants in an unroofed nest – and their activities were almost as frantic and purposeless.

Burak seemed to be dispatching parties of pursuers at random in all directions. So angry was he, in fact, that all logical thinking had deserted him. He had lost two prisoners whose capture would have brought him reward and high honour. In his rage, he was stamping, spluttering and hoarse, like a great brown bear at a baiting, throwing out profligate blame on his soldiers. He railed at them as stupid buffoons rather than soldiers and insisted that he was afflicted by as incompetent, unreliable, untrustworthy, and brainless a lot of subordinates as ever a man could be cursed with.

Soon Avran was permitted to join me. He was finding it hard to conceal his glee at the news of his cousin's escape. For the moment, he also was attributing this to the sheer strength of the black-haired man. The ropes by that man's tree had been so much stretched and chafed that his bursting of his bonds seemed quite feasible. Nor, in a disorganized and chaotic morning, did I have chance to tell Avran the truth. Instead I learned how Darolayn had been captured – by treachery and a trap.

'Do you recall seeing a rather sly-looking man yesterday, Simon? – the only one, other than the escaped prisoners and ourselves, who was not in soldiers' gear? He was riding over to our right, if you remember.'

I told Avran I did not remember him, and he continued.

'Well, that man is a leader of the Lenavvars. His name is Zeladh Lenavvar. Darolayn properly distrusted that family, but he was anxious all the same to secure their aid against the Abaletsens. In consequence, having quietly secured the promise of a substantial reward beforehand from the narat, Zeladh Lenavvar proceeded to play Judas. It's something his accursed family has done all too often.'

As Avran paused, I asked: 'Yet Darolayn must have been watchful. How did they entrap him?'

'Yes, he was watchful, but they were too cunning for him. Darolayn was invited to a very private dinner, to explain to the Lenavvars his plans for the uprising. He was careful to take along his bodyguard, but that did him no good. They were both given drugged wine, and it came in the second bottle, not in the first. No doubt Zeladh thought that was a very clever touch, a way to work around Darolayn's wariness. Now he's not so sure. When Darolayn recovered consciousness, he vowed swift vengeance. Well, at the time, that didn't concern our dear Zeladh Lenavvar, so long as Darolayn was safely in custody. When I saw Zeladh just now, though, his face had a distinctly greenish tinge. Despicable coward!' Avran hissed his contempt.

Breakfast was prepared and eaten at leisure amidst an uneasy hum of talk. The rain, which had slackened overnight, ceased altogether by mid-morning. The shelters were taken down and the hasedain loads prepared, but the fires were kept burning, and the talk continued around them while the return of the search-parties was awaited.

Though Burak Ekonar had fallen silent, he seemed about as tranquil as a hive of bees newly overturned. He had put eight of the guards under arrest for incompetence and possible culpability in the escape. These were chained in a disconsolate ring around the tree from which the massive, dark-bearded man (no-one seemed to know his name) had been freed. Moreover, though the sun was soon shining and the air becoming warmer, the spirits of the other soldiers remained low. Unless the prisoners were recaptured, there was trouble ahead for all upon return to Doriolupata.

For some hours I was on tenterhooks, fearing I would surely be searched and my other throwing-knives discovered. However, this did not happen. As I came slowly to realize, Avran and I were the only ones considered exempt from suspicion, for we had been under the continuous surveillance of guards. As the soldiers reasoned, if we had been associates of Darolayn, we would have fled with him. The result was that even Burak Ekonar's suspicions of us diminished from that time on.

By mid-afternoon the search-parties were back, all of them reporting failure. The grass was too wet and the wind had been too continuously strong overnight for tracks to persist. Moreover, the fugitives' lead was too long, and there were too many possible hiding-places. Such was the reasoning for their lack of success. With an air of weary resignation, not having expected anything better from his men, Burak responded to their excuses with nothing worse than disgusted words of dismissal.

At last the fires were put out and we were on our way again. Under the twin pressures of their leader's simmering anger and their own sense of failure, the soldiers rode faster and observed closer formation than they had done yesterday. Avran and I were kept too firmly apart to be able to talk.

However, on this part of the journey I did identify Zeladh Lenavvar, a thin man in a yellow cloak, the colour of which seemed to find a reflection in his facial features. He was so afraid of possible ambush that he stayed firmly in the centre of the wedge of soldiers and, even so, kept glancing around him uneasily.

The ride was not a long one. An hour before sunset, camp was made on the lee slope of a hill ridge, the fires lit, and a guard set. For the soldiers, it proved a depressing evening of uneasy conversation and recurrent, sulky silences. But Avran and I, no longer under serious suspicion, were allowed to walk around the camp and talk. When Avran learned that I was responsible for Darolayn's escape, his delight was unbounded and his praise unstinting. Together we wove the thread of the story of that escape. The following is what we surmised from what we knew and from the snippets of information we had gained.

My knife must have been quickly found and put immediately to use. After freeing himself, Darolayn must have lain quiet till a soldier came by. That man had been seized, choked into unconsciousness, and tied to the tree in Darolayn's stead. In the darkness and rain, this substitution had deceived the patrolling parties of guards until morning.

Meantime, Darolayn had found and freed his colleague, thoughtfully fraying the ropes so as to suggest a quite different means for their escape and thus diverting attention from Avran and me. The second patrol had blundered upon the escaping men and been quietly silenced, not killed, just rendered unconscious by blows from the dark-bearded man's massive fists. Thus, swiftly dealt with, those soldiers had not even glimpsed Darolayn. After that, the two escapees had located their own sevdreyen – no difficult task, given the mental guidance those animals could provide – and ridden away undetected into the night.

From what Avran had heard, the soldiers guarding the sevdreyen had been far from vigilant, not even noticing till daylight that two animals were missing. When he learned this, Burak Ekonar's comments took on an extra measure of vitriolic anger. Along with the guards charged with watching the prisoners, these men were under arrest. At the very least, all were likely to be dismissed from the Denniffeyen army.

Well, that was their problem. Ours was to escape northwards, and we were given no chance to do so either that night or during the rest of the journey to Doriolupata. The next day was cool, with flotillas of grey cloud passing overhead and rain seeming ever imminent. That last ride with Burak Ekonar's soldiers was much like that of the previous afternoon. Again, they rode without enthusiasm, like truant children returning home because they knew they had no other choice, even while remaining well aware that chastisement awaited them.

We followed a road between fields either cultivated or under grass, with barns at intervals. Occasionally we glimpsed a group of farmhouses, set on a mound surrounded by ditches. Always there was a round stone tower at centre, much like an English castle keep. The farmhouses were also of stone, elongated structures arranged around the tower in cruciform or star-shaped pattern. Though there were many trees amid the fields, none was permitted to grow where it might impede a view from the tower or mask the approach of an enemy.

They were strong structures, to be sure, and their defensive design as good as that of Sandastrian farms. All the same, they seemed relics of an earlier, more prosperous age. Grasses and weeds grew from crevices in their walls. Stones were missing. Doors were unpainted, ill-repaired, or lacking. Sometimes only one or two of the farms in a group were inhabited, the roofs and even the walls of the others having been allowed to fall in. While this had once been a prosperous countryside, it was no longer so. Moreover, the unpopularity of the soldiers was quickly apparent. Men working in the fields ignored our passing or turned away. Children ran from us. When we neared a farm, its women would retreat inside, locking the door and dropping the bar. We knew that, because we could hear those bars falling into place. A man leading a group of sevdreyen along the road turned abruptly onto a side-path and sent them scattering — fearful, presumably, that his beasts might be seized. Not beloved and welcome heroes, these soldiers of Denniffey, but hated despoilers of the land.

When first we glimpsed Doriolupata, it was from above and from the distance of a couple of leagues. Like a conical heap of grey stones it looked then, against a green background turned dark under the shadows of the clouds. However, as we rode steadily north and downhill, the city took on shape, seeming ever more massive and formidable.

Doriolupata must have been first settled long ago, because it was so excellent a site for a fortress — a hill of limestone, detached from the main mass of the Heights of Denniffey, with steep slopes on all sides and marshland to north and west. On such a strong site, even a conventional motte and bailey would have been adequate to deter aggressors; but the designers of this fortress city had been much more imaginative. With infinite labour over the centuries, they had quarried, delved, and built till they had produced a structure that was daunting and impregnable.

As Avran and I rode toward the city, we were struck more and more by the vastness and height of the walls that surrounded it. There seemed to be an impressive succession of curtain walls, enclosing a castle within on the hilltop. We were wrong in what we surmised on our approach. We learned after all that there was only one single, huge wall, eight poles high at least, climbing the hill in a great spiral from the city gate all the way to the castle at the top. If Sandarro had been designed on the plan of a flower, then it was surely the case that Doriolupata had been designed on the plan of a snail-shell.

A linear mound had been constructed to carry the road easily from the hill-skirts to the south over to the main gate of the city. There was marsh on both sides of this mound. Deeper marsh, with many pools a-clamour with waterfowl, lay to our left. (Indeed, these were called the Osumlet Marshes, which translates as the Wildfowl Marshes). To our right was a shallower marsh grading into meadowlands.

Two round towers guarded the outermost gates of the city, but their massive doors were standing open, and the soldiers on the towers regarded us without curiosity. Within was a bailey, overgrown with grass and weeds, and beyond were three great towers guarding twin gates: the Sovestegor, the 'gate of the strangers.' One of these, the one at the left, was closed. Weeds were growing high and untended against its great doors, and the huge, elaborate hinges were rusting. In contrast, the doors at right were in good order and, like the outer gates, stood open. Through these we passed.

It was a depressing entry to a city. This ward, the Sovensdort or 'stranger's ward,' was overshadowed not only by the great, spiralling curtain wall but also by a third, lower wall between its courses, separating the Sovensdort into an inner and an outer quarter. Built against, or out from, these three walls had been many fine houses of stone and wood, but these were now in sad decrepitude. All were neglected, many were ruinous, and some had collapsed entirely, their foundations tumbled and their stones overgrown by tall weeds and tangling creepers. The ragged men and women who watched us go by, and even the few half-naked children, were dully apathetic – a reaction worse, or so it seemed to me, than even the hostility of the country folk.

The median wall ended before we came to a third double gateway, the Koirustegor, which translates as 'gate of the merchants.' Once again, the gate at left was closed and neglected, that at right open and, this time, guarded. We were scrutinized carefully as we rode in. Intrigued by this disparity, I asked the soldier riding beside me to explain it.

'The left-hand gate is the ceremonial gate,' he explained gravely. 'It is to be opened only when our beloved narat rides forth. As it chances, that is seldom, for His Highness feels more at ease, shall we say, in the heart of his city. His delicate constitution is ill attuned to the rougher life outside.'

I glanced at him. His face was perfectly grave, but we both knew what he was implying – that the narat felt safe only in the heart of his fortified city. It was a sad commentary on the condition of this land of Denniffey.

Things were better in the second ward of the city than in the first, for here lived the protected merchant class and the servants of Denniffey's regrettable ruler. To our left, below the inner coil of the great wall, were warehouses and inns, which, if rather dirty and unpainted, were at least in vigorous use; to our right were lines of tall houses, with shops in their lowest storeys. There was a bustle of people in the street, most of them quite well-dressed. Though they made way for us quickly and paused to watch us ride by, they showed no particular apprehension of us. Indeed, from some doorways, painted ladies called out greetings or invitations as we passed.

All in all, it should have seemed much like an English town. Yet, here again, something felt wrong. An English crowd would have been noisier, more obviously cheerful. There would have been good-humoured gibes and catcalls as well as greetings, to which the soldiers would have responded in kind. These people were too quiet, in fact, too obsequious.

The next gate was the Bevnustegor, 'gate of the beasts,' beyond which we entered quietness and greenery. Here were trees and bushes, grass, flowers, and pools. Here sevdreyen and hasedain were grazing. True, there were stables and a few houses. True, there were soldiers patrolling the walls and towers on either side, but this was a pleasant place, a place of tranquillity. I could feel a new enthusiasm in Yerezinth, as he sniffed the clean freshness of this quarter. Meanwhile Zembelen was tossing his horns joyously.

A fifth double gate was passed, the Agirustegor, 'gate of the noblemen.' As usual, the gate at left was closed, but it was free of weeds and obviously in regular use – which meant the narat did at least ride out into the Bevnusdort. Within, there were again trees and bushes. Set among them, however, were handsome houses, the city residences of the great families of Denniffey. The houses of such families as had retained the favour of the Abaletsens during their long rule exuded opulence, with fresh gilt or silver on the heraldic devices over the doorways, rich furnishings and tapestries visible through the leaded panes of great windows, and a swarm of servants. Others, in contrast, seemed neglected, and several were shuttered or empty.

It chanced that, as we were passing one of these, Zeladh Lenavvar was riding just a little way in front of me. Since arriving in Doriolupata he had recovered his spirits. In a high voice, as unpleasant as the scratchings of an unrosined fiddle bow, he had been complaining of the soldiers' ineptitude in losing 'his' prisoners. Indeed, he was threatening that, if necessary, his reward money would be deducted from their pay.

Suddenly I heard an all-too-familiar whir above and behind me. I ducked, but was still looking forwards when the sasial dart struck the betrayer of guests full in the back. He gave a cry, crumpled sideways, and fell lifeless from his sevdru. Vengeance had indeed come swiftly.

CHAPTER 5

Within The Walls

In reflexive reaction, the soldiers broke and scattered, but there were no more darts. Already Burak Ekonar was howling with rage and pointing upwards. A lithe figure in brown tunic and hose was running swiftly along the roof of the house towards the wall. However, he was so high above us that neither hurled javelins nor even darts from the sasayins of the soldiers could hope to hit him. Some of the javelins that fell short clattered to the ground. There was a rope awaiting the fleeing figure and, above, a second man in the uniform of a soldier to haul him up.

As he reached the top of the wall, the first man turned and waved cheerily. To me, from my vantage point, it looked for all the world like Darolayn Estantesec. Then he and the supposed 'soldier' disappeared beyond the wall.

Predictably, there was utter confusion for a time. Burak's men had broken into the house and were soon up on its roof, while the guards from farther along the wall came running to investigate. Long before the two men could be intercepted, however, they had swarmed down another rope, to vanish among the hovels and ruins of the Sovensdort.

The ambush had been carefully prepared. The skull of a sevdru, with a sasayin ribbon between the horns, was found affixed to a beam on a swivel, in such a fashion that it might dispatch its dart downward at any required angle. I had not heard of such a device before, but it was used regularly in street fighting in southern Rockall, where the bows were found to be not as effective in man-killing. The soldier patrolling that section of the wall had been somehow silenced – later he was found, bound and gagged, in an upper room of the empty house – and another man had taken his uniform and place. The time of our arrival in the Agirusdort had been gauged very accurately, for a change of guards had happened only an hour earlier and the ambush set up in the ensuing short time.

If Burak Ekonar had been angry at the loss of the prisoners, he was even more furious now. Summoning most of his men, he rode away at frantic speed back down the spiral roads of Doriolupata, to begin an intensive search of the Filsovensdort, the inner and closer part of the Sovensdort, and then of its outer part, the Uldsovensdort. However, though much time was spent on this search and many citizens grievously mishandled, Darolayn Estantesec (if that in fact was who it was) was not found. A search of the Koirusdort over the next two days by a larger body of soldiers ended up arousing even more resentment, but produced no different a result.

Left behind with the remainder of Burak's troop, Avran and I were ordered to dismount. Their sevdreyen and ours were led away to be groomed and taken to pasture, not in the Bevnusdort – that apparently, was reserved for the beasts of the narat and his cronies – but in the meadowlands beyond the city. At the time, this seemed a considerable setback for Avran and me, since it meant we would have to either escape afoot from the city or await some future expedition before attempting an escape. In the end, however, it was to prove an advantage. For the moment, all we could do was to instruct our sevdreyen mentally to be ready for a call at any time.

The body of Zeladh Lenavvar had been wrapped in blankets and taken to the house of his family – not one of the most opulent – to await burial. For more than an hour, we and the remaining soldiers simply waited around. Having nothing to do, the soldiers discussed the Lenavvar's death in awestricken dismay.

Eventually one of Burak's centenars arrived bearing orders. Avran and I fell obediently into line with the soldiers. With packs on back, pack-saddles under our arms and bowstaves in hand, we marched with them onward up the road, past the last of the great houses, across a parade ground and through the innermost city gate, the Nostegor or 'heart gate' – this time just a single arch between two great towers – into the city's innermost ward, the Naradsdort or 'ward of the republic,' where the soldiers were quartered in great barracks below the castle.

There the adjutant dismissed the soldiers to their quarters. We were taken along to join them at dinner, in a small canteen just within the gate. Once again, that was an uneasy evening, as the soldiers could talk of nothing but the killing of the Lenavvar, the escape of the prisoners, and the likely consequences to themselves of both events. They considered us fortunate, since we could not be held responsible for either happening, and we were treated well enough. However, when we were taken to sleep, it was in a large and guarded dormitory, on pallet beds some way apart from one another and far from the doors. Escape from Doriolupata would not be simple.

Nor did it come to appear easier in the days that followed. The next morning, Avran and I were transferred away from Burak's troop into another barracks, where new recruits were accommodated. There were quite a lot of them, some being mercenaries like Burak's men, but most the scourings of the Denniffey countryside. Only a few of the latter had been willingly recruited to the Abaletsens' service. The majority had been entirely reluctant, yet forcibly impressed in view of the anticipated threat from rebellious Darrinett. Strangely enough, those who were the friendliest of all to us were the mercenaries. The willing Denniffeyen recruits were a pretty noxious gathering of thieves and rogues, while the unwilling classed us with all other foreigners and hated us accordingly.

Because so many of the recruits were as eager as we were to escape this service and were more obvious about what they wanted to do, we were all watched and guarded as if we had been prisoners. Though we were supposedly soldiers already, we were not trusted with weapons. Avran's sword and mine, my belt of knives and even our supposed 'quarter-staves' were taken away, with an assurance that all would be returned later. Instead, during the first week, we were permitted to drill and exercise only with sticks.

We were under the direct charge of a bitter-tongued serjeant and the indirect authority of a fat Denniffeyen centenar, who lolled on a stool and watched the proceedings with languid interest. All was done on foot, the sticks simulating swords, spears and javelins at different stages of the exercises. It was quite well managed – this was, after all, a highly professional army, whatever its moral quality – and, in a way, I enjoyed myself, hating only the recurrent bullying of the unwilling or incompetent. Though I saw

Avran every day, I had no chance to talk privately with him, for indeed there was no privacy between our morning rising and our being locked into the dormitory at night.

However, at the end of the week, the selection of the better soldiers began. In particular, we were given a test in swordsmanship. In this, of course, Avran excelled. Moreover, after the long hours of practice in Sandarro with Oled Orexin, my own performance – though not in the same class – was much better than that of most other recruits.

Twenty of us – almost all mercenaries – were selected for advanced training. We were given surcoats of green with the cockatrice emblem, swords were issued to us (or, as in the case of Avran and me, returned to us, along with our other possessions), and we were transferred to another barracks, joining one of the hundred companies into which the Denniffeyen army was divided. The centenar to whom we were assigned was a long-moustached Fachnese merce-nary, fierce and forceful enough during the day's training, but easy-going (and, by repute, hard drinking) out of hours.

While we had not yet been allowed outside to go beyond the Naradsdort, Avran and I were at least able to stroll around and talk together, watching the soldiers and courtiers come and go from the castle. On one occasion, we were ordered by a centenar to stand at attention while President Vizien Abaletsen himself, a surprisingly small man with a plump, pouchy face, rode by on a snow-white sevdru. As Avran commented sourly, the rider dishonoured the beast.

Though we discussed the question at length, we could see no immediate prospect of escape from Doriolupata. We were in the innermost coil of its high spiral of walls and we had not seen our sevdreyen since the day of our arrival, though assured we would do so 'when the proper time comes.' Not only that, but even if we escaped from the city and avoided the Osumlet Marshes, we had no idea how we might cross the River Werenthin – always a difficult task, as Senraidar had warned us.

These were serious problems, but we had certain advantages also. First of all, there were few Sandastrians in the barracks, and Avran had not been recognized. Secondly, though wearing the green surcoats, we were permitted our own clothes beneath. (Not until soldiers were finally admitted to the Denniffeyen army were they issued with full uniforms). My hidden knives remained undetected and the true purpose of our bowstaves passed unperceived.

As a precaution, Avran and I simulated quarterstaff fights on some evenings, receiving encouragement and advice from the other soldiers. When asked why our staffs were notched, Avran responded calmly that this was so they could be used to twitch the staff out of the hands of an opponent. In a grand display of misdirection, he bemoaned that he was not yet skilled enough to manage this.

All in all, that was not an unhappy time. Yet it was not possible for us to be at ease – in part, because our quest for Lyonesse (and, for me, my return to Ilven my beloved) was being so much set back, in part, because, for both of us, our future safety was a matter for question. While Avran had not yet been recognized, his eventual recognition seemed daily more likely and only a matter of time. That being the case, my fears for my friend were as great as his own fears for the effect it would have on his father's realm.

However, twelve more days passed by without untoward incident. On each Sunday, we were lined up with the other soldiers and recruits for a religious service of the most perfunctory kind, conducted by a stout cleric intoning scriptures in so formulaic a fashion that none of us even understood him. Later on that day and on all other days, we either paraded or exercised with simulated or real weapons. With my usual ability at throwing things, I found that I excelled at hurling the javelin, and there was none who could match Avran's swordmanship.

However, in our urgent desire to gain greater freedoms by doing well, we found a new problem suddenly pressing on us. Along with eight other recruits – the Denniffeyens seemed only to think in groups of ten, for some strange reason that bemused my English mind – we were brought before the centenar and informed of an imminent promotion. In three days' time, he told us with a beaming smile, the two of us and other recruits who had distinguished themselves would be admitted to the Denniffeyen army. Furthermore, he announced, we would have the honour of swearing fealty to the narat himself.

In the meantime, we were each presented with a bagful of kals, the etched quartz spheres that serve as low-value coins in southern Rockall (higher values are garnets or zircons, each facet bearing an inscription and the device of the realm). In addition, we were each given an engraved metal disc which, the centenar told us, would enable us to pass at will through the three inner city gates, though not through the two outer gates.

'Time to go and enjoy the Koirusdort!' he growled genially. 'Have a good time, but be back by sundown.' Waving dismissively at us, he turned to other concerns.

For almost three weeks we had all seen nothing but the grey buildings and high walls of the Naradsdort and the stones of the parade ground by the Nostegor. It was a pleasure for me even to walk among the tall houses and trees of the Agirusdort – I noticed again, with wry amusement, the roof from which the Lenavvar had been slain – and a positive delight to wander down through the trees and flowers of the Bevnusdort. The month of Devbalet (February) was well advanced now, and it was high spring in southern Rockall. More than ever, this was a beautiful place.

Seeing that Avran and I were disposed to linger there, the other eight recruits left us, hastening away to explore the delights of the Koirusdort, its inns, its shops, and its women.

When they were out of earshot, Avran, who had said little before then, burst out: 'Simon, we must leave this place – and quickly. Playing at soldiers is well enough, although a waste of time, but I refuse absolutely to take any oath of fealty to that greasy weasel, Vizien Abaletsen. Just like me, you've seen the evil that he's done to this land. Surely you can't take any oath to him? For my part, I'd rather die!'

Startled, I looked at him. 'You know, that question hadn't even occurred to my mind, I have to confess. I suppose I was getting too used to our life among the soldiers to be thinking clearly. You're right, of course, Avran. We can't swear any such oath. Yet, if we say we don't want to join the Denniffeyen army, they won't merely let us go. Most of the other recruits are just as unwilling. What can we do, though, to avoid taking that oath?'

Avran gave me a strained smile. 'Well, Simon, it was I who plunged us into this morass – as usual. Much use I've been to you on your journey so far! But I'm afraid it is you that needs to devise a means for our escape. You're the cunning one, not me.'

I looked at Avran bleakly, then at the high, guarded walls towering above us, and sighed. Today was Saturday. Sunday and Monday would follow, and then the oath-taking on Tuesday morning. Was it possible, in so short a time?

'Well,' I answered slowly, 'I'll try my best to think of something, but, at the moment, I'm quite without inspiration. We need to know more about this city. Let's go and look around the Koirusdort.'

When I had first glimpsed the merchants' quarter, its crowded, clamorous street and high, close-set buildings had reminded me of an English town. At second look, that impression persisted. Yet there were many differences – in the clothes of the people, of course, and their language, in the greater number of written signs, appropriate in a land where far more men and women were literate, but, most of all, in the behaviour of the people. I had felt this difference when we rode through. I felt it more strongly now – a submissiveness, an obsequiousness that surely sprang from unease, even from fear. It was apparent in the way that men looked at us in our soldier's garb, moved out of our path unnecessarily, smiled at us with nervous over-courtesy. It was apparent in the fashion that children's games were instantly stilled as we approached, only to be resumed when we had gone past. This might be a good city in which to have the privileges and money of a soldier, if one lacked sensitivity. It was not, however, a happy city. I hated it.

Yet there was a street life, and some of it was amusing. We stopped to listen to a trio of goliards, one strumming on an embelin, the second blowing powerfully on a horn-tipped pipe much like a hautboy, the third tapping away with his fingertips on a skin-covered double drum suspended from his belt. Wild, exhilarating music it was, as unfamiliar to Avran as to me, for these musicians were Montrions. Then there was a conjurer, producing amazing objects from the sleeves of passers-by or even from the air; and a juggler, manipulating ever-increasing numbers of coloured balls till the air seemed a-dazzle with them.

It was as we were watching this that Avran felt a touch on his sleeve. A slim, dark-haired young woman stood beside and slightly behind him. Her lips were tinted scarlet and her eyelids powdered a bluish colour, yet she seemed somehow different from the other painted beauties whose blandishments we had ignored.

'Come with me, young sir,' she whispered. 'Your cousin awaits you in the Inn of the Winged Fish. Follow me.' Instantly she turned away.

After a single, startled glance at me, Avran did indeed follow, and I came right after him. She led us along the main highway for some distance, weaving a graceful way through the jostling crowds, and then turned right down one of the short side-streets under the shadow of the inner city wall. It was a street mostly of warehouses, but at its end there was a tiny inn with the hanging sign of a fish improbably endowed with a bird's feathered wings. The woman beckoned, then ducked inside the rather low inn doorway.

Avran paused and glanced at me. Then, our hands on our sword hilts, we followed. It was gloomy inside, for, though there was no sunlight in the deep shade of the walls, no candles or dips had been lit. We hesitated under the lintel till our eyes adjusted to this dimness.

There were just four people in the little room – the girl who had led us there, still now and smiling at us; a diminutive man in an apron, surely the innkeeper; and, at a little table with goblets of wine before them, two other men. I recognized the massive figure of the first quicker than I did the leaner shape of the man behind him, even though I had seen the latter more recently, and I marvelled. All over Doriolupata, these two fugitives were being furiously sought, and high prices had been set on their heads. Yet here they were, sitting relaxed in the heart of the city of their greatest enemy.

CHAPTER 6

The Passage Of The Walls

The lean man rose to his feet and held out his clasped hands in greeting.

'Welcome indeed, Prince Avran,' said Darolyn Estantesec. 'We have been watching for you and hoping for your coming.' After his hands had been seized and shaken vigorously, he turned to me. 'And thrice welcome to you, Avran's friend. I do not know your name, but I know you to be my deliverer and shall be eternally in your debt.'

Blushing, I clasped his hands with pleasure. This was the first time I had seen Darolayn at close quarters. I liked what I saw. He was only a little taller than me, with a bush of hair and a trim Spaniard's beard, both of them having surely once been as flaringly red as Avran's but now fading into greyness. His face was creased and weathered, redeemed from grimness by the puckerings of good humour around his lips and eyes. Those eyes were of the same vivid blue as the wings of the little butterflies I had seen so often on the limestone uplands. They looked at you very directly and clearly missed little. I was pleased when I saw, by the broadening of his smile, that the liking was mutual.

Avran was also smiling. 'If you are in his debt, Darolayn, then so emphatically am I. Let me introduce you. This is

Simon, from Hallamshire in England. Since his true surname is almost unpronounceable, we call him Simon Vasianavar.'

Again, we solemnly exchanged clasped handshakes, then Darolayn turned to introduce us to the others in the room.

'These three are my good friends and trusted colleagues. First of all, my beloved cousin Dorren Estantesec, who risks more in my service than I dare to contemplate.' The dark-haired girl blushed and gave a little curtsey. 'And Radim Perilumin, who puts his house at our disposal to his peril.' The little innkeeper bobbed at us and grinned. 'And finally, this minute scrap over here' – he indicated his craggy, black-haired companion – 'is Vaien Vaghat, also very much in your debt.'

Vaien's huge hands engulfed my clasped ones, and his smile informed me that I had gained another formidable friend.

Three further stools were set around the table, and goblets of wine brought. Then the innkeeper went to keep watch in the doorway. However, no customers came, for the warehouses were quiet today and the inn too much off the main road to attract casual visitors. Soon, prompted by Avran's eager questioning, Darolayn was giving us an account of the situation in Denniffey.

As we were already aware, it was quite lamentable. The Abaletsens, it seemed, had been at the outset reasonable governors of the republic, but that was seventy years or more ago. The last three generations had treated it as a personal fiefdom, to be plundered at will and to the fullest possible extent. Under their misgovernment, Denniffey was tottering ever closer to complete ruin, Vizien Abaletsen proving even greedier and more corrupt than his father and grandfather had been. Moreover, after an assassination attempt had failed six years ago, Vizien had ceased ever to venture forth from the walls of Doriolupata, taking his unpleasant pleasures within the castle and never riding beyond the Bevnusdort. Thus, he saw nothing of the land that he ruled and cared nothing about it. The Ruling Council was a farce, being made up only of his close relatives and particular cronies, all of the Abaletsen or Elietin families. Complaints to the Council went unheard, injustice was rife and crimes left unpunished. Indeed, in their own view, the narat's party and the army that was their instrument were above the law and could do no wrong.

Though the whole land was seething with discontent under this misrule, Darolayn and his colleagues were, however, pessimistic about the prospects of its being ended.

'The army is our greatest problem,' Darolayn said sadly. 'With so many imported mercenaries, it is too strong and too skilled. If the power of the Abaletsens were broken, those men would gain nothing and lose much. My people hate the Abaletsens and would like to rise against them, but they are afraid.'

'Is there no hope, then?' Avran asked.

'Oh yes, there is hope; one can always hope. As you know, after their successful revolt against the Fachnese, the Darrinnettans are in high fettle. They claim some of our territories and might decide to invade Denniffey. If they do, who knows what might chance? And of course, were our Sandastrian cousins to choose to intercede . . .?' Darolayn gave Avran a questioning look.

'Small chance of that, I fear,' he responded. 'Our people have no desire for war, now or ever in the past, as you know well. Moreover, we've been coping with our own internal problems.'

Avran told the three something of recent happenings in Sandarro, making overmuch of my contributions, but saying nothing about the grey riders. He went on to recount how we had been captured and brought to Doriolupata and of our wish to escape from that city.

Darolayn smiled at this. 'If Vizien Abaletsen knew he had you under his hand, Avran my cousin, how he would crow! But he must never know. Even if I were not indebted to you, I would want to ensure that you escape from Doriolupata. As matters are, I am entirely at your service. But why did you venture into Denniffey and with what aims?'

Briefly I explained, to see Darolayn's brow wrinkle in puzzlement. 'I have never heard of Lyonesse. Have you, Vaien, or you, Dorren my dear?' Both shook their heads, and he went on: 'It may be in the great forests, as you say. We learn little from those lands. As for a crossing of the River Werenthin, that can be arranged, I am sure. But you will be fortunate indeed if you can traverse the yellow plains in safety. Yet, if the hand of God be upon you, perhaps you may. Others have done it, though not often.'

He pondered for a while, then said: 'Excuse us a moment.' At the jerk of his head, the big man and the girl followed him out to the doorway, where all three were soon in earnest conversation with the innkeeper.

Avran looked at me and smiled, the shadow of strain quite banished from his face. 'It seems we are to be fortunate again, Simon. If Darolayn was so readily able to ease himself into this city, surely he can ease us out of it.'

I nodded with relief. 'If so, that's as well, for I've not been visited by any inspirations. You put your trust in me in vain, I'm afraid.'

He laughed. 'Not at all. Was it not the knife you threw to Darolayn that made this encounter possible? Well, they're returning. Let's hear what they propose.'

However, only Darolayn and the mighty Vaien Vaghat were coming back. The innkeeper was resuming his watch, while Dorren, with a farewell wave, had slipped out of the inn door. The two men sat down again at our table.

'We can do nothing for you today,' Darolayn said flatly. 'Not only will the arrangements take time, but also you have been seen with Dorren and I cannot put her in danger. She will be returning shortly with a friend. The two girls will escort you during the rest of this day, when you must visit the inns and appear to be carousing. Your lengthy stay in this inn will be attributed to quite other pursuits, of course, which is all to the good. By sundown, you must be back in the Naradsdort, like good little soldiers should be. Tomorrow is Taltegis [Sunday], with its religious services and parades. You will not be allowed past the Nostegor before late afternoon. But, given even ordinary good fortune, you should be allowed free time then. It is usual. Now, pay close attention while I tell you what you must do.' He proceeded to give us detailed and careful instructions.

Twenty minutes later, we were walking and chattering among the stalls, Avran arm-in-arm with Dorren Estantesec and I with a curly-haired, brown-eyed girl whose name I do not recall and whom I never saw again. Even though our dalliance was entirely feigned, it provided a pleasant enough interlude. We dined and drank wine with the two girls in an inn so noisy with music and song that there was little need for conversation. We lingered with them to watch the street entertainers and then we bade them protracted and affectionate farewells under the indulgent eyes of the Bevnustegor guards, before hastening back to our barracks in the waning evening light.

The Sunday morning was one of gusty wind and shifting cloud. In alternating sunshine and shade, we endured, along with the other soldiers, the bumbling intonations of the stout cleric and performed elaborate military exercises under the bored and uninterested eyes of a group of councillors, who hastened away as soon as they could. Under a sky that was ever more heavily clouded, the afternoon brought further exercises, among them hand-to-hand combat, sword-fighting, and javelin throwing. I was nervous that some trivial accident might occur that would upset our plans. Nevertheless, I performed better than usual, gaining generous praise from the large-moustached centenar. Under the circumstances, this embarrassed rather than pleased me. He and some of the other mercenaries were worthy men, however unworthy the ruler they served, and it caused me no pleasure to know that I was deceiving them. It was late afternoon before we were dismissed. Hastily we returned to our quarters. Obviously, we dared not be seen leaving with our packs, nor with the quivers of arrows. These would have to be forfeited. However, we detached the arrowheads and secreted them in our money-purses. The bowstaves would be a more serious loss, and so it was worth taking a chance to preserve them.

Thus it was, with each of us holding a bowstaff in hand, that we walked boldly toward the Nostegor. My heart jumped with dismay when the guards stopped us.

'Hola, you recruits; your passes, please!' And, after we had showed them: 'Why those great sticks, pray?'

'Well, sir, we've been invited to take part in a quarterstaff contest in the Koirusdort. For the honour of the
army and – er – a small wager.' Avran coughed discreetly.

The guards laughed. 'Why then, we must not hold you
back. And make a wager for us as well, provided you're
quite confident of winning – but we want no losses, mind!'
With that, we were waved through the gate.

Swiftly we walked down through the Bevnusdort,
hastened on our way by a sprinkling of heavy rain. At
the Bevnustegor we were stopped again and Avran told
the same story. These guards were puzzled and suspicious.

'A quarterstaff contest? We've had no word of it. Where
is it to be held?'

'Oh, it's quite a small affair,' I interjected hastily. 'Just
for the wager. It'll be held in the yard of the Star and
Crescent Inn, if the rain keeps off. But I fear' – I glanced
at the sky with feigned disgust – 'that the contest may be
cancelled and the wager with it. Curses be on this weather!'

At this these guards laughed as well. 'I don't fancy your
chances,' said one. 'Well, get along with you!' And again we
were waved through. As we walked out from the shadow
of the gate, I found that my knees were trembling. The
streets of the Koirusdort had been almost as crowded as
yesterday, but the crowds were dispersing, for the rain was
coming on harder. The pedlars were putting their wares
back into their packs, and the goliards wiping and packing
away their instruments. This was fortunate, for, in such
general movement, our own proceedings were likely to
pass unperceived. Indeed, with the people about us hastily
seeking shelter, our own haste appeared entirely reasonable.

As we went along, we counted the streets to our left,
seeking the ninth as instructed. Before long, we were

running through a downpour that entirely emptied the streets and turned the colour of our surcoats to a darker green.

At last, we reached the ninth street. A rather ramshackle one for this quarter, with sheds built against the houses and piles of planks, stones, and sand, evidently intended for sale, in its middle. There were few signs of life, yet we were conscious of being watched as we walked along.

'The sixth house on the right-hand side,' Avran muttered. 'Four, five – this must be the one. My, but it looks a dingy place.'

So it did. The woodwork was chipped and discoloured, the windows closed with sacking instead of the usual fine cloth or horn, and the steps to the front door ill-set and cracked. The door stood open, but such was the gloom inside that it was not inviting. However, any shelter from such rain would be welcome, and so in we went.

I did not see the black-haired giant until he spoke. 'Greetings again!' said Vaien Vaghat. 'You are in good time – excellent! Follow me.'

The stairs were rickety and creaked under our weight as we ascended. Though the light was so poor, I could see how very filthy and ill-maintained this house was and I guessed correctly that no-one lived in it.

On the second flight, there came a surprise. Vaien turned abruptly and pressed a panel with his palm. Immediately a section of the wall swung inward, revealing a narrow passage.

'These places were not built for such as I,' he grumbled. 'More for small folk like you, Simon. Don't follow me too closely. I may become wedged.'

However, having turned right side foremost, he edged along the passage successfully enough. Since, at his behest,

Avran had swung the panel shut behind us, it was a traverse in darkness and seemed to take a long time. Eventually I heard Vaien's grunt of satisfaction and was dazzled as another panel swung open, to reveal a brightly lit room beyond. Stumbling after him, I tripped on a board and was prevented from falling only by his massive arm.

As I recovered my balance, I saw that we had come through into a very different house, if it could be judged by the room we entered. For here were tapestries on the walls, fresh rushes on the floor, a handsomely-wrought table laden with good food and drink, and two welcoming figures – Darolayn Estantesec and Dorren. Their lack of surprise indicated that they had been informed already of our arrival. Indeed, the eyes that we had been conscious of in the street had been those of Darolayn's watchers. Although, in both our encounters, he appeared to be unguarded, that was evidently not the case.

We were urged to remove our sodden surcoats and hose in exchange for fresh garments. Someone – Dorren, perhaps – had a good eye for estimating measurements, for they fitted perfectly. There were brown tunics of the length, though not of the cut, of a cotehardie and hose of a moss-green for each of us.

Avran, with his love of bright colours, winced a little at the prospect of having to wear garments of such subdued hues. Our new surcoats, however, pleased him better. Though moss-green on the outer side, they proved to be reversible; the inner side was of as vivid a yellow as a wagtail's breast in springtime. Dorren, after watching us change our clothes with a cool interest that I found embarrassing, told us that we must wear the surcoats green side outermost until we had crossed the Werenthin, but yellow side outermost to evade notice in the grasslands beyond. The prospect of yellow grasslands was a startling one.

As for our military surcoats, they were folded carefully and taken away, useful no doubt for their store of props in future schemes against the narat and his minions.

After that, the four of us had a meal which surpassed any since leaving Peratenay. It included roast waterfowl, an array of salads and fruits, tarts made from sweet yellow berries, and a golden wine that frothed from flasks into glasses and was strangely exhilarating stuff to quaff.

Over the meal, we talked about many matters. I learned that we were in the last house of the row, that closest to the wall. It was owned ostensibly by a wealthy trader in builder's materials, but actually by Darolayn. This was only one of several centres for the rebels in the Koirusdort and Sovensdort, the old houses of which had many concealed doors, secret passages, and hidden chambers.

Dorren railed against the lack of spirit displayed by the Denniffeyens, who, though so frustrated and unhappy under Abaletsen rule and quite willing to aid Darolayn and his associates covertly, were yet unwilling to take up arms and free themselves. Darolayn was more understanding.

'The problem is that, after more than a century under the Abaletsens, we Denniffeyans have become accustomed to misgovernment. We've been trampled down so often that we've forgotten what it is to stand upright and free.'

'Can you ever convince your people to rise?' I asked.

He looked at me rather sadly. 'I try, Simon, and I hope. Yet I do not know . . . I do not know.'

Darkness came early that wet night and, with dark-ness, action. Equipped with new packs containing spare clothing, food, and horn flasks of wine, Avran and I followed Darolayn, and were followed by Dorren and Vaien, down four flights of stairs into the cellars of the house. A barrel was rolled away to reveal an iron ring set flush with the floor. This was grasped and pulled upward without effort by the mighty Vaien. What appeared to be a stone flag, but was actually a wooden trapdoor, rose with it, revealing a vertical shaft into whose dark abyss there descended a narrow-runged ladder.

Darolayn descended first, Avran and I following, with Vaien, grumbling again at the narrowness of such places, last. After giving us a farewell smile and wave, Dorren stayed behind to shut the trapdoor and conceal it anew.

When the light above us was shut out, the descent became a matter of rhythm and endurance. Extend a left foot down; find the rung; put one's weight on it; reach down with the right foot. Again and again, endlessly, in pitch-black darkness, with the sounds of Avran and Darolayn moving below me and Vaien grunting with ill-temper above. The bowstaff in my hand was an ever-present nuisance and, at times, my sword-sheath caught tiresomely against ladder or walls, causing the hilt to press with bruising weight into my stomach. Down, down, down we went with no pause for breath, till my calves and knees were aching.

At last Darolayn called up: 'Easy now! Solid ground below.'

Twelve more downward steps and my foot found a stone flag instead of a ladder-rung. A hand – I supposed it was Darolayn's – steadied me and guided me aside to make way for Vaien. Then we were walking along a narrow tunnel that sloped gently downward, its walls so close upon us that we seemed to be ever brushing against one side or the other. The ground became slippery with water, then muddy. Another pause, then a door was swung inward. I saw before us the greyer darkness of a cloudy night and smelled the fresher moistness of recent rain.

'Wait a moment,' came Darolayn's whisper, and then he added: 'All is well, but quietly now!'

We emerged into a dimple of the northern slope of the hill of Doriolupata, or rather, at the point where the steep earthwork below the great walls arose from the gentler natural slope. The door to the passage was shut carefully behind us. Its handle was what appeared to be the stump of a dead bush in the shade of a cluster of living bushes. When closed, the door was quite indistinguishable from the wet earth of the hillside, so carefully had it been concealed.

'Now we must summon our beasts,' Darolayn said quietly.

'You as well?' Avran said.

'Vaien and I, we'll journey with you to the river. It's better that way, although we won't be returning to the city by this route. That ladder is too arduous a climb. Besides, we have business to attend to, up in the hills. Let's go on down.'

The grasses and weeds of the hillside were slippery with moisture. For the first time I was grateful for the bowstaff. I could use it to probe my path and as an anchor when my boots slipped. Darolayn moved quite swiftly, but Vaien followed slowly. He had broken off a leafy branch from a bush and was employing it to obliterate the signs of our passage. Some way to our left below, I could see a gleam of waters and knew we must be close to the edge of the Osumlet Marshes. Immediately below us was a coppice and, to our right, parklands with many shrubs and small trees.

It was in the coppice that we awaited the coming of the sevdreyen. We knew they were coming, of course. I could clearly sense the responsive gladness of Yerezinth. Yet they must have been many miles distant, for it was almost a half-hour before we saw their graceful shapes gliding through the trees toward us. By then, Darolayn and Vaien had long since greeted and fondled their own beasts.

It was a delight to be mounted again and in open country, after so many days afoot and pent up in a city. As if in response to the pleasure I was feeling, the moon sailed forth from the clouds, silvering the bushes and trees with its light. We rode contented through a long night into a bright dawn and continued riding, while trees and bushes became ever fewer and the green weeds and grasses of the parklands ever more densely flecked with the yellow of the coarser grasses of the Werenthin plains. Several times we passed barns or ruined padin, and many times we saw groups of grazing hasedain. However, in this land forever threatened by Montariotan raids, no men ventured far from their homes before full daylight.

Lulled by the steady pace and entire trustworthiness of my mount, I was beginning to doze when, abruptly, Darolayn checked his mount and pointed. Ahead was a green line of bushes, wrapped in a billowing sheath of ground-mist.

'The Werenthin,' he said simply.

We rode on for another hour or more, till the sun had climbed high in the sky and the mist dispersed. We came to that line of vegetation and then moved along its edge eastward, until we reached a place where a cluster of small trees furnished shelter and concealment. While the sevdreyen browsed discreetly and Vaien Vaghat, seemingly tireless, kept watch, Avran, Darolayn, and I wrapped ourselves in our cloaks and slept.

I awoke to find the afternoon well advanced and Darolayn deep in conversation with a little gnome-like man, who had a stiff fringe of a grey beard, a red, rather bad-tempered face and pale blue, rheumy eyes. He was clad in what looked like a collection of cloth rags stitched together arbitrarily by someone who knew the principles of sewing, but entirely lacked skill in that art. Avran was also awake, while Vaien Vaghat was deeply asleep and snoring like an old hound on a hearth.

'This is your boatman, Simon,' said Darolayn. 'He is a shy man, and with good reason, so he prefers that you should not learn his name. He will convey the two of you across the Werenthin, which is at present too deep in flood to be forded. As for me, I must watch while my friend slumbers. I shall say farewell and Godspeed here.'

Avran took his clasped hands. 'We are profoundly grateful to you already, cousin. If you send word to Sandarro that we have safely crossed the Werenthin, you will place us yet more deeply in your debt. Be sure I shall try, upon return, to repay it.'

'To speak thus of debts, Avran, is ridiculous. Have you and Simon not given me life itself?' He turned to me. 'Avran tells me that you have been accepted by his family as a new brother. That means you are an Estantesec in actual fact, if not in name, and thus my cousin. I take great pleasure in that knowledge.'

I clasped his hands in my turn. 'Thank you, Darolayn. I hope all goes well for you, that you succeed in all your aims. Maybe we'll meet again someday?'

A smile flickered across his face, a strange, almost mystic smile. 'Oh yes, we'll meet again. The fates of the three of us are interwoven closely, of that I'm sure. I shall look forward to that next encounter. Before parting this time, though' – he delved into an inner pocket of his cloak – 'I must return this knife to you. I shall hope not to need it again. Good travelling!'

Pleased, I returned the throwing-knife to its sheath, shouldered my pack, and picked up my bowstaff, while Avran did the same. Then, with a farewell wave, we followed the boatman out of the grove, to be followed in turn by our two sevdreyen. So dense was the foliage that, within seconds, the two Denniffeyens were lost to view.

There was no path from the grove to the riverside, but the boatman found his way through the bushes with the ease and speed of a weasel. Suddenly he stooped and pushed. The boat he had concealed slid easily before him, down a short slope and into the water with never a splash. He leapt in lightly, stooped again, and produced a length of rope, the middle portion of which he tied around the boat's sternpost.

'Step in, will ye? Gently, now. Ye're not hasedain seeking a mud-wallow.'

Avran managed it well enough. However, when with trepidation I followed, the boat rocked violently and sent me tumbling into the old man's lap, causing him to splutter indignantly. Remembering Bristol, I wondered whether it would always be my fate to be clumsy in boats.

I was sent to sit in the bow, while the old man remained amidships. Avran, under his instruction, tied one end of the rope about the horn-bases of Zembelen, the other about those of Yerezinth. Both sevdreyen were made unhappy and nervous by this, and, uncertain ourselves, we found it difficult to calm them.

The boatman mumbled to himself in disgust, then unshipped two oars and, with a single powerful stroke, sent his craft skimming out into the river. As the ropes tightened, the sevdreyen perforce splashed out into the water. Soon they were swimming behind the boat.

The Thames at London was the biggest river I had seen hitherto, for one could not count the Severn's salt estuary. After the winter rains, the Werenthin was at least three times as wide as the Thames and flowing much more swiftly. Moreover, we were crossing it obliquely with the current, making the traverse even longer. The river waters were so clear that we could see waterplants fluttering beneath us and strange fishes swimming among them.

I was so engrossed in watching these that I did not see the other bank approaching. We struck it with a thump, and, for a second time, I was sent tumbling against the boatman.

This time he was rendered positively inarticulate with rage, his eyes popping and his whiskers seeming to bristle like a cat's. It was some minutes before I could distinguish his words: 'Get out, damn you, get out of my boat! Call yourself a waterman? Why, I'd sooner have a galikhu in my boat. Get out, get out!'

Hastily I did so. Meantime, Avran was unfastening the sevdreyen's horns. They had swum well. All the same, but for the pull of the boat, they would surely have been carried away by the river's strong current. Then Avran leapt up onto the bank neatly. As he turned, the old boatman drove in his oars and shot away from the bank, too swiftly to be offered any reward. If he heard our cries of thanks, he did not respond to them.

As we watched him out of sight, I realized that Avran was quivering with laughter. 'Oh Simon, that was hilarious!

You should be a tumbler – or rather, that's what you truly are. Poor old man, he'll not forget you in a hurry.'

I smiled sheepishly. 'Well, anyway, Avran, we're across the Werenthin.'

He sobered instantly. 'Yes indeed, and from now on we must take even greater care. On this side of the river, there are no friends to be found.'

79

CHAPTER 7

The Yellow Grasslands

Back in Sandarro, Enar Servessil had told us a little about the Montariotans, and Senraidar Estantesec, who had fought against them, had told us more. Yet, in sum, Avran and I knew far less than we would have wished about these people of the plains.

There were seven principal tribes, each with its own ruler, customs, and territory. Though the boundaries of these seven territories shifted somewhat according the fortunes of war, we knew their position with fair accuracy. Matruvak was the westernmost tribe, its lands close to where the Werenthin debouched into the sea. Mestei came next, north of the former Baroddan realm of Aldagard. Sedlaviss occupied the grasslands north of Darrinnett. And the easternmost Montariotan realm was Brantava, at perpetual war with neighbouring Volendar.

Unless we missed our way on the plains, we should be in no danger of encountering any of those four tribes. Nor did we expect to be in danger from the riders of Ayanessei, whose lands lay north of Mestei. Instead, our path lay through the territory of the two remaining tribes. Our passage of the Werenthin had brought us into the plains where roamed the turbulent Amatomarr, the particular enemies of Denniffey. And, if we succeeded in safely crossing their territory, we would have to traverse that of the Eldernet as well.

While the Volendarans had ceased to roam and had accepted Christianity, the other Montariotans – some called them Montrions – remained wanderers and heathens, worshipping gods of the sky and wind. They wore grass-yellow robes, carried bright, strangely shaped banners and were armed with broad-bladed spears as long as lances. They lived in tent-cities, moving with the seasons or at the whim of their rulers. Mostly they rode the heavier, slower hasedu rather than the lighter, fleeter sevdru. Hasedain are close grazers and can find food enough to survive in the grasslands even in summer, when aridity kills off the taller plants and sevdreyen would die. However, so early in the spring, there should be fodder enough for our sevdreyen and, with luck, our swifter mounts would enable us to outride any pursuing Montariotans. That, at least, was our plan.

We spent the rest of that day in concealment among the bushes on the Werenthin's banks, but not in idleness. I was eager to restore our longbows to usefulness. Having found a straight-branched shrub much like a withy, though with broader leaves, I proceeded to cut for us some new steles, using the newly-returned throwing-knife as whittle. To these steles Avran affixed the arrowheads we had salvaged.

The fletching was more of a problem, for it had not been possible to detach and bring with us any of the stiff leaves with which the Sandastrian arrows had been fletched. However, after I had finished cutting the steles, I ventured prospecting along the bank and chanced on a dead waterfowl caught up in some grasses by the water's edge. Its pinions served, when trimmed, as perfectly adequate fletchings. Our arrows would not carry quite so far as usual, perhaps, but they would nevertheless serve to surprise any assailants.

The making of quivers proved easy. We found needles and coarse thread in our packs, placed there no doubt by the thoughtful Dorren. The inner bark of the withy-like bushes, which Avran could not find a name for, was flexible enough to be shaped and sewn into a satisfactory form. Since we had no saddles, the quivers that we fabricated were fixed to our belts, and they fulfilled their purpose admirably.

By the time all this had been done, the evening was already well advanced. We ate sparingly of the bread and dried meat stored in the packs and then, worming our way into deeper shelter, went quickly to sleep. We knew that our sevdreyen, who had rested since their swimming of the river, would guard us adequately and waken us at dawn.

I was roused by the gentle pressure of Yerezinth's soft muzzle. It was dark still under the bushes, but, when I stretched and rose, I could see the first pale light of a new day edging the Werenthin's waters upstream with brightness.

Zembelen was trying to awaken Avran, but having much less success. In the end, to my amusement, he prodded my friend's cheeks quite sharply with his two nasal horns. At this Avran awoke with a startled cry, rubbing his face indignantly. Zembelen stepped back quickly, tossing his head in fright. However, when I had told Avran what had transpired, he smiled ruefully and gave his sevdru the caress he deserved.

Hastily, we ate hunks of bread and meat and took swigs from our wine flasks. We turned our cloaks yellow side outermost and then, followed by our beasts, made our way cautiously up through the tangle of bushes, across a broad berm that paralleled the river's course and, through diminishing cover, out into the grasslands. In the pale morning light, the grasses seemed the colour of cream atop a butter churn. As there was no wind yet, their colour and their stillness gave our venturing forth a strangely dream-like quality.

The view was not far-reaching, for we were on a low step of land with two higher steps beyond. We mounted our sevdreyen quickly and, alert for danger, rode upward until we had ascended both those steps. As we did so, the light brightened, and a little breeze began to stir the grass-heads into a motion reminiscent of the surface ripple of a gently flowing stream. Neither on those three valley terraces nor in the much broader view now opening before us could we detect any sign of human life. Far away to the west, a few black dots were moving away from us, wild creatures of some kind, though we could not tell what. Some wading birds made their way toward the river in random flight, like shreds of cloth blown by a gusty wind. Otherwise, the landscape seemed quite empty.

So it continued to seem throughout a long day's riding. Never before had I traversed grasslands so vast and so open. The view changed so little that I felt almost that Yerezinth and I were not moving, but the ground was flowing slowly past us.

As the sun rose higher, the grasses changed in hue from cream through a pale yellow to the rich colour of wheat at harvest-time. Just as such wheat is flecked by the scarlet of poppies and the blue of cornflowers, so also these grass-lands were flecked by the blues, violets, and reds of spring flowers whose names we did not know. The buzzing of the insects that haunted them was lost in the continuous susurration of the wind-stirred grass. Only our own voices and, occasionally, the calls of birds overhead rose above that steady murmur.

By late afternoon, our sevdreyen were tiring, and we knew our ride must be brought to an end. Yet, in this monotonous landscape, shelter and concealment were scarcely to be found. Only our cloaks could furnish either. Arbitrarily we decided to stop for the night. While our two beasts cropped the coarse herbage with evident reluctance and distaste, we ate a sparing supper. Then Avran wrapped himself like a caterpillar into the cocoon of his cloak and went swiftly to sleep, while I kept watch.

The sun went down in a splendour of colour that would have delighted any herald. For a brief while, I could see an irregular purple line on the southern horizon that must be the Heights of Denniffey. The night sky was clear, and the waning moon washed the landscape with a pale light, making me feel as lonely and as conspicuous as a black-beetle on a flaxen sheet. I shivered and huddled deeper into my cloak.

The wind had dropped with the rising of the moon, and I was aware of much movement about me. Furry-winged moths blundered buzzing from flower to flower. A cricket-like creature made a high humming sound, like the whir of a metal ring rotated rapidly at the end of a string, while another shrilled like an indignant starling. There were nightjar-like birds pursuing insects overhead, diving again and again with a flurry of wings and a soft, moaning cry. And several times I glimpsed a night-hawk hastening above me on silent wings. Small animals rustled and chittered among the grass-roots and, quite close by, a subdued gnawing sound told me that one of them was feeding. Twice, I saw the black shapes of deer-like creatures running by, and, once, a badger-sized creature trundled past, grunting and heeding me not at all. Though the grasslands might seem empty under the bright sun, they teemed with nocturnal life.

As the hours crawled by toward the time at which I should rouse Avran, I found it harder and harder to avoid falling asleep. I stretched and shifted at intervals, but was reluctant to rise and move about, for fear of disturbing him prematurely. The sevdreyen had stayed close to us, but they were asleep as well, trusting in me as I had trusted in them.

Abruptly I became fully awake. There was a strange new sound, almost a rumbling, distant yet, but coming closer. Some large creatures, I surmised, and running quite fast. I could hear heavy hooves and a curiously unattractive bubbling grunt that made the hairs rise on my neck.

Yerezinth and Zembelen were also awake and on their feet, gazing tensely, alternately at me and toward that sound. Like me, they were unsure of its meaning, but sensed danger.

With sudden decision, I bent over my friend and shouted into his ear. 'Avran, rouse yourself! Something is coming towards us – some animals, I mean! They may not be dangerous, but I think we'd be wise to be ready.'

My friend shook himself into wakefulness, like a dog shaking off water after a swim, and sat up, listening. The pounding hooves approached closer and closer, the bubbling grunts sounding ever louder and more unpleasant. Suddenly I found I could see the creatures, a tumbling mass of them, approaching us at a rapid rate.

Avran stood up. 'I don't like this. I'm going to mount.' In a moment, he was a-straddle Zembelen.

That was not a wise move, for the creatures sighted him instantly. There was a burst of horrid cachinnating laughter, and they were racing toward us. For a moment I stood frozen, then I leapt onto Yerezinth's back. He needed no urging. In a moment, he and Zembelen were in full flight from the pursuing creatures.

It was a mad ride across grasslands that gleamed a pale gold in the moonlight, with Yerezinth and Zembelen galloping at the limit of their speed. Yet, fast though a sevdru can travel, the creatures were gaining on us steadily.

Huge they were, quite as long-legged and high-bodied as horses, but bigger than the largest horse I had seen and moving more as would running pigs. As they closed upon us, I glimpsed them in the moonlight and recognized them. The short, gleaming tushes, the squared-off snout, the distorted warty cheeks and swollen-tipped, hairy ears: these were the nightmare, hoglike creatures I had seen depicted on that wall-painting in Sandarro Castle and had believed could not be real. Nightmare had turned into reality with a vengeance.

One of the creatures had outdistanced the rest and was almost upon me, the sound of its drumming hooves and its obscene, gurgling cry loud in my ears. There was no hope of using my bow against it, and I did not think of my sword. Instead, I seized a throwing-knife from my belt and half-turned.

It was almost alongside me already, its yellow teeth champing, its nostrils flaring red and its eyes a baleful, blood-shot yellow. I could even smell the creature, a horrible whiff of ordure and decay. As it reached to seize me, I rammed the knife straight down into that gaping throat, snatching my hand away barely in time before its jaws closed.

The creature gave a choking, gurgling groan and lurched against Yerezinth's flank, causing him to gasp in frightened pain, stagger, and almost fall. My heart skipped wildly in fear, but then we were past and the beast fell away from us, becoming entangled with its pursuing fellows and bringing some of them down.

I heard an unpleasant tearing sound, as if they were savaging it, but some of them, at least, were surging past to continue pursuing us.

Our headlong flight went on for almost an hour longer. However, the creatures never again came so close, their stamina fortunately not matching their speed. There came a final, braying cacchination that had a note of frustration, then the pounding sound of their pursuit slackened and ceased altogether. Nevertheless, we rode on at undiminished speed for fifteen more minutes before we felt safe enough to slacken pace.

'That was an unpleasant awakening, to say the least!' Avran gasped. 'Vile beasts! Our legends tell of them, but no Sandastrian has seen one for centuries. *Ukhuren* they are called, ghost-hogs, as they hunt and scavenge only at night.' He sighed again. 'I'm glad we got clear of them – they'd have finished us pretty quickly.'

'I remember a picture of them, in the castle. Are all the creatures in those pictures real? I thought those, at least, must be legendary.'

'I'm not sure. Some of the pictures are of creatures long gone from our lands, like the *ukhur* and the *ramora* – the big, blue creature with the massive horns. Others have never lived in Sandastre, to my knowledge, though traveller's tales tell of them. The *xalihu*, which you'd call a unicorn, is one. Does it live in England? I never did see one there, though I heard strange stories of how it was hunted – if I recall aright, they said that it could be lured only by maidens.'

'There are no unicorns in England nowadays,' I answered pensively. 'Once, though, at a fair, I saw a twisted, ivory horn they said was a unicorn's horn. I believe it was ground up afterward to make love-potions. People say the unicorn lives far away in the east, in the lands of the infidels, where the Crusaders fought.'

'Well, after tonight, I'm prepared to believe that *all* those creatures exist somewhere, but I trust that none of them will disturb my slumbers in the nights that await us. You need to dismount and rest now, Simon. I'll watch for what remains of this night.'

Very glad was I to do so. Sleep came over me swiftly, and it was undisturbed by any further visitations of animals either real or unreal.

CHAPTER 8

The Montariotan Camp

Dawn was amply past when I awoke, and the shadows of the sevdreyen were long on the yellow grass. For a while, the events of the night seemed to me too dream-like to be real, but were confirmed when I groped for my belt and found that one throwing-knife was missing. Avran was still on guard. On glancing up at him, I was disturbed to see that he was looking more than a little worried.

'We came closer to disaster with those ukhuren last night than I realized,' he said. 'Did you know that Yerezinth has been injured?'

I sat up hastily, remembering my realization of my sevdru's pain and chiding myself for not examining him. 'No, I didn't. Is it serious?'

'I hope not. I did my best to treat it, but summon him and look.'

Yerezinth's movements, as he obeyed the summons, were decidedly stiff. He was limping a little on his left hind leg, and along his left flank was a gaping, zigzag gash cut by one of the sharp tusks of the falling ukhur. I examined this wound with concern. I was relieved to see that, though deep, it was clean and appeared already to be showing signs of healing.

'I noticed the cut at first light,' Avran said. 'There was quite a heavy dewfall. I used a damp cloth to wash the wound, then washed it again with a little of the wine. I think it will close up quickly, though it will leave a scar. The problem is that, to allow it to heal, we'll have to ride slowly today.'

Grieved at my own lack of attention to my sevdru, I was caressing his head and horns. 'Thank you anyway, Avran. Well, if we can only travel slowly, so be it.'

'However, we face another problem, Simon. I don't have a clue where we are. Do you? Those ukhuren chased us a fair distance. Was it to east, west, north or south? For obvious reasons, I wasn't thinking about all this while they were pursuing us, and now I'm not sure.'

'When I first heard them, they were over to the east of us. I'm not sure either, Avran, but I believe we must be a fair ways west of our original course.'

Avran sighed. 'Well, that accounts for it. We must be in the western reaches of Amatomarr, where its territories march with those of Eldernet and Mestei – disputed terrain, I gather. That might prove good for us, or it might prove ill. Such lands are likely to be empty of permanent settlement, but we'll be in considerable peril from raiding parties. *Not* the place to be slowed by an injury to one's mount, I'm afraid.'

I stroked Yerezinth's soft nose, and he snuffled with affection in response. 'Well, I'm only grateful that I killed the beast in time.'

Avran was clearly startled. 'It was that close? What happened?'

So I told him how the ukhur's attack had been foiled, ending lightly: 'I suppose we ought to ride back and look for my knife, but I'm inclined to let the creature lie.'

He gave a quirky smile in response. 'No, Simon. It would be easy enough, I'm sure, to backtrack our course, but we've been fortunate once, and I thank God for your quick thought and quick hand. To risk another encounter with the ukhuren, especially with a lame sevdru, would be sheer folly. No, whatever direction we ride today, it can't be eastward.'

We breakfasted quickly, then set off again northward across the grasslands. At first, I walked alongside Yerezinth, to give him chance to rest that injured leg. However, I could sense his feelings of inadequacy and the keenness of his wish that I were on his back again. As soon as I was confident that he was walking more easily, I mounted him. Nevertheless, we went along at a pace no faster than a horse's walk.

Avran preferred to prospect the way ahead for hidden dangers. He was riding about ten poles in front of us when, suddenly, he and his mount stopped. Waving me to be still, Avran climbed down from his sevdru and walked forward on foot. I looked past him. In my concern for Yerezinth and dazzled as I was by the bright colour of the grasses in the morning sunlight, I had not realized that the land, flat for so long, was beginning to dip downwards. Avran was on his knees now, gazing ahead intently.

'Simon!' He called, his voice low, but urgent. 'Dismount, then come and take a look – quietly, now!'

I obeyed and was soon beside him. Before us, the slope at first steepened and then slackened, forming the south-eastern flank of a broad valley through which a small, shallow river meandered. Round about it was a whole town of tents, most of them basically dyed yellow, but all of them splashed with other bright colours in crude, barbaric patterns. One tent, set midmost, was especially large and was tinted as red as a robin's breast. Beside it was a high pole from which a tongue-shaped banner of the same hue stirred idly in the breeze.

'A red banner,' Avran muttered, 'and the device in black . . . Three chevrons . . . No . . . three spearheads rather, the middle one the largest. The emblem of Mestei! That means we have ridden far west, in fact, or they have moved further east. But the river . . .?' He furrowed his brows in thought. 'No, I can't give it a name, though it must be tributary to the Werenthin.'

There were many hasedain grazing in and around the camp and, though their yellow robes made them hard to see against the grass, many men and women too were moving among the tents. If guards were set, it was not obvious. Yet I knew the Montariotans were ready always for attack, for battle.

'Well, we cannot go that way.' Avran said quietly. 'We must divert to the northeast and be away from here quickly, before their warriors ride forth. Come now, Simon.'

Soon we were mounted and on the move again, as rapidly as Yerezinth's condition allowed. Even when we were an hour's ride away from the camp, we were reluctant to descend into the valley, where bushes grew thick about the river and ambush was a danger. Instead we kept to the high ground. However, the course of the river was swinging steadily toward the east. This meant we were riding, not northward, as we wished, but back eastward, to our increasing unease.

At length, Avran stopped Zembelen and, having waited for me to catch him up, said: 'This won't do. We cannot chance meeting the ukhuren again. We'll simply have to cross the valley.'

I concurred without enthusiasm.

'Very well then,' Avran responded decisively. 'I'll ride ahead down the slope. You follow, but make sure you stay at least twenty strides behind me.'

The slope was open and shallow enough, no peril being apparent. As they descended, Zembelen was kept to a steady walk. Avran had strung his bow and was holding it loosely in his left hand, his right fingering the arrows in the quiver, while he gazed watchfully about him.

As he neared the bushes, there burst forth a sudden flurry of movement, and he started back, setting arrow hastily to bow. However, it was only four deer-like creatures, two fully grown, two mere fawns, racing frantically away. I noticed the short, stout, three-branched horns of the adults, in shape like a caltrap set upside-down; their yellow pelts with brown dapple-patterns on their flanks; and even the tufts of coarse hair about their flying hooves as they fled away upslope. Avran had been greatly startled, but now he was laughing merrily. 'Come on down, Simon! There can be no Montariotans in these bushes.'

Relieved, I descended, and soon we were splashing across the river. As we were thrusting a way through the denser bushes on the farther slope, Avran stopped again.

'Fool that I am!' he exclaimed. 'Here we are, about to ride up from this admirable valley out into the grasslands. And yet this is the only cover we've found in two days. I realize that it's only mid-afternoon, but your beast has been injured and needs rest. Also, both sevdreyen deserve a feed on something better than grass. Simon, we must hide up here for the remainder of today. After all, it'll mean we can start earlier and ride farther tomorrow.'

And so we took our ease and refreshment by the quiet stream. For a second time, we trusted to the sevdreyen to stand guard. Wrapped in cloaks that had been again turned green side outermost and hidden deep within the bushes, we slept well and long, never dreaming what perils the next day might bring.

At its outset, indeed, everything about that day seemed auspicious. First of all, the long rest had conferred great benefit on Yerezinth. The stiffness was gone from his hind limbs, and a jagged, whitish scar had formed over the gash left by the ukhur's tusk. Secondly, though the morning was fine, a fresh wind was driving a procession of woolpack clouds before it from the southwest, producing a patchwork of brightness and shadow, which, we trusted, might make us less conspicuous even in so open a landscape. Thirdly, Avran had risen before me and had caught four trout-like fishes by the tickling method employed by English poachers and hungry Sandastrians. He lit a tiny fire and cooked the fishes on a spit, furnishing us with our first good meal since fleeing Doriolupata.

Dawn was three hours in the past before the ashes of the fire had been scattered and we were mounted. However, with Yerezinth better, we could hope to cover a much greater distance today. Avran was uncertain how far the grasslands extended – two more days' journey, at least, he estimated – but he hoped that by late evening, we might reach parklands, where there would be better shelter. With luck and swift travelling, we might even reach the deeper shade and greater safety of the forest itself. Thus, we were in good heart, as we left the undergrowth by the river and rode up out of its valley.

As we ascended its highest and steepest declivity, we did so cautiously. There were hasedain grazing in the grasslands beyond. We looked for herdsmen, but there were none to be seen. The feeding beasts, though certainly domesticated and probably part of the Mestei herds, took no particular notice of us. Clad as we were in our yellow cloaks, we must have seemed familiar enough to them to occasion no alarm, even though we were riding sevdreyen.

There were a number of fawns, some so newly born that they could not raise themselves onto twig-slender legs even to totter from our path. We saw also one dead male hasedu, the overnight kill of some predator and partially devoured. However, by the relaxed behaviour of the hasedain grazing nearby, we knew the killer must be gone far away. Soon we were beyond the herd and riding away northwards with a sense of relief into grasslands whose emptiness was, by comparison, welcome.

The wind had become intermittent, rippling the grasses into waves that faded quickly into stillness, only to be recreated by the next gust. Its cool freshness was exhilirating and raised our spirits further. A large flock of starling-sized birds with azure-blue plumage – *isitelnen,* Avran called them – flew over us around noon, eddying briefly about us like gnats in a rising air current, then flying on. A while later we saw grazing hasedain far to the east, but we were not tempted to view them more closely. Otherwise it was a steady ride, as fast as a horse's trot, for hour upon hour across golden grass flecked with bright flowers, with cloud shadows gathering above us, then passing to yield sunlight again.

We paused for a while early in the afternoon, to snatch a bite of bread and sip of wine, while Yerezinth and Zembelen munched grassheads without enthusiasm. Then on we rode again for two more hours over unchanging grasslands.

By that time, the pleasant monotony of riding was dulling our watchfulness. It was, I think, Yerezinth who first perceived the men behind us. I sensed his awareness of them and turned around. I could just glimpse a group of riders, so far to the south of us that only their motion enabled me to distinguish them. I tried to discern which way they were moving, then realized they were moving toward us, and approaching quite rapidly.

Through Zembelen, Avran had by then been brought to attentiveness. 'Better ride faster,' Avran said briefly. 'It may be they haven't noticed us, but we can't chance it.'

Our sevdreyen needed no other urging than the thought. Soon we were riding at a gallop, a gentler, more fluid motion than that of a horse and quite as speedy, yet below the fastest pace of a sevdru. The faster speed was one reserved for a more immediate emergency.

It was difficult to tell whether the riders were pursuing us or merely headed the same way. At our more rapid pace, they were not gaining on us, nor were they falling behind. We began to speculate that they had speeded up. Since we had not gauged their earlier pace, we could not be sure, but our tension mounted.

Looking ahead, I became aware that at last the landscape was changing. Not dramatically at first. It was just a gradual transition into undulating terrain, as a water surface begins to stir before one becomes aware of the breeze that is urging it into motion. The grasses became sparser, and I glimpsed sandy soil. It was clear that these had been sand-dunes before the vegetation stabilized them. Just as waves become ampler as a wind freshens, so did the height of these dunes increase as we galloped onward, their broad lateral spread growing less, even as their slopes were steepening. Our pursuers, if indeed we were being pursued, were soon lost to view. Our hope now was that we might evade them among these hillocks.

Yet westward there appeared another rider, high on a ridge-crest. He had seen us and was setting a horn to his lips. Its sound was like the bark of a red deer at rut. Now there were other riders mounting that crest, pouring over it and surging down in pursuit of us. Worse still, the horn call had alerted a third party of riders, to the east and much closer. There were more yellow cloaks, more bright spears coming after us.

As they descended into the hollows between dunes, the two groups of riders were lost to our view. We knew, however, that the Montariotans would soon be on our heels, since they were sure to have a better knowledge of this terrain than the two of us. Haste was now of the first importance.

Unfortunately, the dunes to the north were rising ever higher, and at the same time we dared not turn southwards. To make matters worse, the sun had slipped behind a cloud. Without its guiding position in the sky, it was hard for us to maintain a correct direction in such confusing terrain.

Avran glanced at me tight-lipped, then set Zembelen to ride straight up a high dune directly in our path. He was right. We needed to gain a view ahead and behind, at whatever cost in effort. It was not an easy ride, over tussocky grass in mats no bigger than a man's head, with sand between. Again and again hooves slipped, then gripped with an effort. Yerezinth was trembling. After such a long ride, the effects of yesterday's injury were starting to tell.

Finally, we reached the top. Here, we stopped for a moment and looked back. We could not see the pursuing riders, nor could we hear them, but that did not mean much, for sand absorbs sound. Still, they could not be far away. There was no time to waste. We plunged over the crest of the dune and down the other side, through a belt of dense brush growing in its lee and up onto the flank of another grass-grown sand mound. We descended into a second hollow and into closer-set, shoulder-high vegetation, where there seemed to be no paths, and the sevdreyen could scarce thrust their way through.

Behind us a horn sounded. We looked to see a rider, high on the crest of a dune to our left. Our pursuers were closing the gap. Frantic in our haste, we forced our way through the dense shrubs and, free of them, rode up onto and over the shoulder of a third, broader dune. Beyond it was a wider hollow, even more closely grown with shrubs and low trees, but beyond, again, there were gentler dunes and open grassland. If we could gain the grassland, then we stood a good chance of escape.

Yet penetration of the dense brush that lay immediately ahead posed a problem. At the same time, we could not linger, for there were horns braying behind us already. Down we went. We found a path. It was a broad game-path, leading through the brush towards an open pool where many creatures probably came to drink nightly. We rode along that path at full pace, splashing through mud on the pool's verge and then racing on toward the north and the lower dunes.

Yellow-cloaked riders were spilling down the slope behind us, but our lead was good. Into the second belt of trees we headed, almost abreast now. Yerezinth's chest was heaving, but I could sense there was yet enough stamina in him to keep us going for an hour or more. In open country, hasedain could not match sevdreyen for speed.

Avran was optimistic and turned to smile at me, as Yerezinth drew alongside Zembelen. But almost at that moment, the triumph we were sensing to be in our grasp turned into disaster. Both our mounts stumbled, and the ground crumbled away beneath us, as we plunged forward into a deep pit trap. Down we tumbled, into the meshes of a great rope net that closed around us. In a trice we were hanging in the darkness, as furious, frightened, and helpless as flies in the web of a hungry spider.

CHAPTER 9
The Purple Tent

Often the unfortunate fly caught in a spider's web is left long dangling in its meshes. In the Montariotan trap, we suffered no such fate. Within minutes we heard men's voices and laughter above us. The net began further to tighten around us, causing Yerezinth and Zembelen, Avran and me to fall against one another in a helpless jumble. Avran had the wit to lean forward and grasp Zembelen's brow-horn bases, to give himself some stability and protect himself from them. I did not react so intelligently and fell against Avran, my right leg caught and compressed between the sevdreyen's heaving flanks and my arms seizing my friend's shoulders in frantic alarm.

As we were drawn up to the surface, the back of the net was brought forward above us, so that we were pulled out of the pit with our heads foremost. My bowstave, carried so carefully for so many miles without discernible benefit, was again a nuisance. It had twisted around in the net and was pressing painfully into my back. My sword-hilt was driving up into my stomach, my right leg was numb, and altogether I was a bruised, miserable element in the writhing, kicking bundle that emerged.

We found ourselves in the midst of a crowd of yellow-cloaked men and the focus of a ring of spear-points. Had we been capable of resistance, it would have been wholly vain, but we were not. Though Avran was less bruised than me, he was much more thoroughly wrapped up in the meshes. Even after I had been extracted from the net, seized, and disarmed, he was still entangled.

After Avran in turn had been loosed and deprived of his weapons, the sevdreyen were lifted free of the net, quite tenderly, for these were valuable animals to the plains-dwellers. I was surprised and relieved to see that neither Zembelen nor Yerezinth had been much hurt by their fall. I understood this better when I learned later that such traps were designed to capture even the heavier hasedain without injuring them.

As we were drawn forth, there was much talk among the yellow-robed men. It turned out that not only their cloaks but also their tunics and cloth-topped boots were as yellow as spring primroses. However, though I imagined that their language was no doubt close to the Sandastrian tongue, I did not understand it at all. They spoke in spurts, their voices rising and then dying away as if wind-rippled, like the grass. It made quite an attractive sound, but was no more comprehensible to me than a jay's call. Nevertheless, I did perceive their surprise when they first noticed the jagged scar on Yerezinth's flank. Indeed, inexplicably, they seemed disconcerted by it.

Ropes were fastened around the horn-bases of our sevdreyen. Each of them was tied to the saddles of two riders whose heavier mounts would be able readily to control even big Yerezinth. As for Avran and me, our wrists were bound tightly together behind our backs, then we were lifted and set astride two other hasedain.

From this position we watched while the pit-trap was reset. After the net had been lowered back into place, a cross-weave of frail leafy branches was made. Then sand and clay were mixed and wetted with water fetched from the pool in leather buckets. This mixture was spread over the woven branches and smoothed, making a lid to be set over the trap. When this lid was in place, its edges were concealed by clay and leaves, after which dust was cast in handfuls over the whole. All was done with such quick skill that, within no more than thirty minutes, the game-trail looked as solid and inviting as ever. Bitterly, I wondered what unfortunate creature would be the next to blunder into the trap.

By that time, a third group of yellow-cloaked warriors, presumably those who had been following us from the south, had ridden up to join our captors. They eyed us with such evident surprise that I became convinced they had not been pursuing us after all. However, to my puzzlement, when their attention was drawn to Yerezinth's scar, they seemed quite as disturbed.

Among them was a tall man whose hood and yellow robe were embroidered in purple thread, evidently a leader. As he rode up to examine Avran and me, I saw that he had a grey beard trimmed like that of a Spaniard and bright brown eyes under brooding brows. He addressed me with what was evidently a series of questions, but I could not understand them, and he did not comprehend the Sandastrian phrases with which I tried to respond. Nor did he and Avran have any greater success in communicating.

The tall newcomer turned away in disgust. By a sweeping gesture of his arm, the other Montariotans were sped to their mounts and, within seconds, the whole party was riding northward along the game path.

I had Montariotans riding before, behind, and on either side of me. Avran was further to the rear, and the sevdreyen, trotting between the riders to whose mounts they were roped, were yet further back. All four of us, beasts and men, were under the close scrutiny of fierce eyes. My sword, bowstaff, arrows, and belt of knives had been taken from me and, though I still had the other knives concealed in my clothing, my arms were tied too tightly for me to reach them, even had this watchful guard been relaxed.

The hasedu on which I was riding, a slender doe, moved with a placid forward lurch like the gait of an ass, with none of the fluidity and grace of a sevdru. I could make no mental contact with her and suspected she was incapable of such communication. Probably, in fact, she had been given me as mount because of her slowness and stupidity. I saw not the least bit of hope of escape and, with my bruised body resenting every jolt, felt utterly disheartened and miserable.

Once clear of the hollow, choked as it was with undergrowth, the Montariotans bore left, westwards, following an irregular course that found the easiest route through the tussocky dunes to the grasslands beyond. Westwards they rode. The lands of the Mestei had been left behind. I fell to considering who these riders could be. Were they men of Eldernet or were they a marauding band of Ayanessei? I had no means of telling, but at least the question furnished something for my mind to ponder during the uncomfortable monotony of that journey.

Abruptly our course veered northward, across a shallow dip and around the skirts of a marsh, whose greenness gave brief relief from the tedious yellow of the grass. As we rode up out of the dip, the riders checked and there

were exclamations of surprise. Ahead of us, still a considerable distance away, but clearly to be seen in such a dull,
unvaried landscape, was a tent.

And a splendid tent it was. As we approached it, I saw
that it was huge, much bigger than any in the Montariotan
camp Avran and I had seen yesterday, bigger even than any
I had seen at a tournament. Beside it stood a high pole,
topped by a cross, each of whose four symmetrical limbs had
crutch-shaped ends. As I recalled, it was termed in heraldry a
'cross potent' and served as emblem for the crusader kings of
Jerusalem, being often depicted in the coloured scrolls sold at
fairs. I wondered what it signified. Around the pole and tent
were grazing some animals much like sevdreyen, but furred in
dappled brown, not grey, and with horns differently shaped.

The Montariotans rode toward the tent, not in any
disciplined order, but in a series of surges and eddies that
suggested excitement and unease. As we drew closer, I could
see that the fabric of the tent was elaborately embroidered
in gold, silver, green and red, with stick-like figures of
men and animals and with numerous cabalistic signs, some
familiar to me, but most unfamiliar. Three armed men
were sitting around the tent's closed entrance-flap, as if on
guard. As we approached, they rose to stand at attention.
Each was clad in purple and armed with a sword and a
mighty axe with a crescent blade.

At a word from their tall leader, the Montariotans stopped
and raised their long spears to the position of salute. One
of them rode forward a little before raising his weapon.
As he did so, I saw that it bore a fishtail-shaped green
pennant with the device of a jagged lightning-bolt and,
remembering Senraidar Estantesec's words, knew at last
what tribe had captured us – Ayanessei.

Whoever the inhabitant of the tent was, it was clear that the Montariotans respected – maybe even feared – him. Their leader rode forward, then dismounted and stood with arms apart in what was surely a gesture of welcome. A purple guard came forward to stand before him, making the same gesture and then offering the clasped hands of friendship. As the leader grasped them, both men inclined their heads respectfully and a few quick words were exchanged. Then the guard returned to the tent and went inside it, while the Montariotan leader waited.

The other Montariotans sat relaxed yet attentive on their mounts. Avran and I were equally attentive, but rather more uncomfortable, on ours. Somewhere behind us, the sevdreyen were moving uneasily, and I could sense Yerezinth's unhappiness.

How many minutes we waited, I don't know, but, in my discomfort, it seemed a long time. Eventually, however, the guard emerged and walked briskly over to speak to the tall leader. There was a mutual, gracious inclination of heads, and the encounter ended. The Montariotan directed a brief flurry of sentences at his men that caused a ripple of excitement – gratified excitement, if I judged correctly – and we were once again under way. We rode past the tent in a respectfully wide sweep and, watched incuriously by its guards, headed westward once more.

The rest of our ride was not long. Though the grassland ahead had seemed to me to continue unbroken into infinity, we were in fact quite close to another valley. This one was cut deep into the plain like a plough-slot into tilth and had flanks nearly as vertical as those of such a slot. However, hasedain, like sevdreyen, are unworried by steep descents. Together with the riders, we continued over and down with as little hesitation as water flowing over a fall. Below us stretched quite a wide space, with a shallow shrunken stream at its centre and, around the stream, many yellow tents, a whole town of them.

As we came closer, women emerged to watch our approach, and children – boys clad like riders in miniature, barefooted girls in dresses as long as those of English country children – ran noisily to meet us with excitement. While Avran and I evoked much interest, our sevdreyen did so even more. Yerezinth, indeed, seemed again to amaze and disconcert these people, though I could not comprehend why.

The majority of the riders dispersed among the tents, but a dozen escorted the sevdreyen, Avran, and me to the very heart of this tent city. Close by the edge of the stream stood the biggest of the tents and, before it, a tall pole from which a much larger green fishtail banner fluttered in the wind. The leader dismounted, inclined his head to the banner with the grave respect of a soldier to his warlord, and walked over to the tent. At its opening he was welcomed by an elderly woman, in a dress thickly broidered with silver thread. He followed her within.

Two of the riders of our guard also dismounted. A pile of stakes was lying at one edge of a space of open ground, before the tent and beside the stream. One of the Montariotans seized a stake and held it upright, to be driven deep into the earth by blows of a stone wielded by the other. A second stake was driven in close alongside the first and two others, at a greater distance apart, by the stream banks. Yerezinth was tethered to one of the latter, Zembelen to the second. Both animals were close enough to the stream to be able to drink at will from its waters.

Then Avran and I were lifted from our mounts and set down by the first two stakes, after which each one of us was tied to a stake by a rope attached to our already-bound wrists. The two dismounted Montariotans squatted down to guard us, each keeping his spear at hand. The others rode away.

A knot of women and children gathered to look at us. All had darkly tanned faces and black hair. Some were brown-eyed, but many had eyes as blue as the petals of a speedwell. They evinced no hostility to us and, indeed, seemed much more interested in the sevdreyen. After a while, the women went about their business, and even the children drifted away.

At that point, Avran spoke to me for the first time and, to my surprise, in English. 'I think we can talk, Simon, but we should use your tongue, for our guards may understand Sandastrian. Well, yet again we are in trouble, friend. It seems we have tumbled – how is it that you phrase it? – out of the cauldron into the flames.'

'These people are the Ayanessei, aren't they?' I said.

'They are.' Avran nodded.

'Well, they've not harmed us yet – not truly harmed us.'

'Not yet, Simon, not yet. However, think to yourself that no travellers – *no* travellers, Simon – have been captured by these people and survived to report it.'

'Perhaps we'll be the first, then,' I replied, feigning a cheerfulness I did not feel. 'I wonder why they're so interested in Yerezinth?'

'I do not know, Simon. He is a fine sevdru, of course, and very big – bigger, perhaps, than they have seen. Yet he is no bigger than a large hasedu . . . No, I do not understand it.'

'Can you comprehend their language? I can't.'

'It is difficult, certainly. I can pick out a few words, odd phrases, little more. The tall man is their leader, their eslef. They style him *akhled,* but it means the same. They did not call him by his own name, only by that word of respect. This place is the *akhledet,* the leader's town; but only part of the tribe lives here. They have several, perhaps many, other settlements.'

'And who lives in that splendid purple tent?'

'Ah, that is interesting. I am not sure, but some important personage – a great doctor, a prophet perhaps, or a wizard. Whoever it is that dwells there, they seem both respectful and afraid. Indeed, he must have power, to travel safely on these battle-torn plains with so small a guard.'

The evening was well advanced by then and the light fading fast, shadows reaching out ever farther from the valley sides. Cooking fires were being lit among the tents, their smoke spiralling upward in the relatively still air of the valley until caught and torn into grey shreds by the wind from the plains above. A group of women brought sticks and dry grass sods into the clearing, arranging them into piles before the big tent somewhat to the right and left of it. A tripod of iron rods was erected over one, a turnspit built over the other, and a burning taper brought to set each fire alight. Soon a cauldron of stew was cooking over the first and a joint of hasedu meat was being roasted over the other.

The stew, in particular, smelled delightful. I licked my lips hungrily. Even if these Montariotans intended to kill us, it would be an appreciated courtesy if they fed us beforehand, I thought wryly. In this, at least, we were to be fortunate. The akhled and his wife the akhledan emerged from their tent, to accept food proffered to them with solemn deference on trenchers and in dishes of polished metal. Rather to my surprise, they ate standing upright. I speculated whether this might be a Montariotan custom. When they had eaten, they astonished me – and, it has to be said, impressed me – by proceeding to serve food to those who had served them.

I was even more pleasantly surprised at what followed. After serving the two guards and receiving brief instructions from the akhled, two of the women brought food for Avran and me. Mouthfuls of deliciously flavourful stew were given to us in horn spoons and hunks of meat presented to us on skewers. We ate well.

Meantime, the akhled and akhledan were drinking wine poured from elegant glass flagons into metal cups. Of this also we were given our share, though in beakers of earthenware. Afterwards our lips and cheeks were wiped with coarse, moist cloths. When Avran endeavoured to express our gratitude, the women may not have understood his words, but certainly grasped his intent, for they gave us pleasant smiles before hastening away.

Night was coming on now. Tripod and spit were removed, and the two fires built up to a much larger size, so that the whole open space was lit by their brightness. The children were long since gone, and the women – the akhledan among them – were leaving. In contrast, men were assembling, singly or in groups, to squat down in rows around us. Soon there was a whole crowd of them, in a great arc extending from the stream bank to beyond the further fire.

'I feel better for that good meal,' Avran said quietly, 'but my arms are numb – as yours must be, I'm sure. And this gathering – what does it mean? Whatever it be, I doubt that it bodes well for us.'

CHAPTER 10

Riders Into The Firelight

By then, the whole valley lay in black shadow. This late in the month, there was only a rind of a moon, and it was not within sight. If any stars shone overhead, they were masked from view by the more local brightness of the fires.

Two wooden stools were set between those fires, one closer to us, one further away. When this had been done, a group of musicians assembled and began to play – a strange tune, with a sustained trembling beat on oddly-shaped double drums and a soughing wail-like overlay from horn-tipped pipes. It was an uneasy sound, disturbingly like the irregular heartbeat and gasping breath of someone very sick, and it increased my own feeling of tension. The crowd of men fell silent, as if charmed or drugged by the music. Belatedly I noticed that the akhled had emerged unheralded from his tent and was sitting on the further stool, waiting. Waiting. We were all waiting.

Suddenly there came a whooping of horns from beyond the camp. The music ceased, and everyone jerked to attention. There was a pause, then the horns sounded again, louder and brassier.

All of us looked in their direction, straining our ears. Yet we did not hear or see the riders until, suddenly, they were coming out from between the tents into the firelight glow. Two black shapes on black mounts, they seemed at first, each bearing aloft a flaming torch; then two more following, each with a long golden trumpet in hand.

As they entered the firelight, I saw them better. They were not clad in black after all, but in purple. Indeed, these were the three guards who had stood before the purple tent, as well as another similarly attired. Their mounts were the same dapple-brown animals that had grazed by that tent, but wrapped now in purple saddle-cloths. I perceived that their horns were quite different from those of hasedain or sevdreyen – a single, blunt nasal horn and two brow-horns that reached forward. Each brow-horn had five tines, clustered together like five fingers and making the horns seem like hands reaching out to seize.

The four riders stopped, forming a lesser arc between the fires and before the akhled, the torchbearers outermost. The two trumpeters raised horns to lips and blew a final, peremptory blast, then lowered their instruments and sat at ease. Again, we waited.

Then, from the shadows, there emerged a fifth and yet more splendid rider. In the firelight, he seemed a shining vision of silver, for he wore shirt, cloak, and hose of that colour, a strange tricorn cap that seemed made of scintillant metal and long boots of palest grey leather. His mount was caparisoned from head to rump in cloth of silver patterned with blue stars, while its hooves were sheathed with silver and its horns tipped with silver too. He rode forward till his mount stood midmost among the four purple-clad riders. Though I had seen King Henry among his noblemen at tournament and court, I had never seen any group so magnificent.

Yet, within moments, the scene had ceased to be simply splendid and had become almost eerie. The newcomer reached out a gloved hand for the torch of the outermost rider to his right, was handed it, and flung it immediately into the fire nearby. As it engulfed the torch, the fire changed in colour, its leaping flames turning from orange-yellow to a strange, unnatural green.

As I, and those about me, watched in awestruck wonder, the second torch was taken and flung into the other fire. Its flames also changed colour, not to green but to a bright magenta, causing the Montariotans to gasp in awe and fear. I heard the alarmed snorts of Zembelen and Yerezinth, as they strove vainly to pull free from the ropes that bound them, and I sensed their fright. Indeed, their emotions matched my own.

The two trumpets whooped again, in a strange double wail. The akhled was on his feet now, head bowed and arms outstretched in deferential welcome. In the interplay of colour from the two fires, his robe and those of his followers seemed to shift in hue from orange through brown and green to almost white. Their brown skins were turned sickly pale, and the purple robes of the four riders changed to brown. Only the silver garb of the fifth rider was unaltered in hue. Indeed, it seemed to shine brighter, so that he became gigantic, radiant, superhuman.

Then the colour in the flames began to fade. The fifth rider dismounted and accepted the clasped hands of the akhled. And I saw that he was only a man clothed in silver fur. Indeed, he was considerably shorter than the Montariotan leader, for the topmost tip of his tricorn hat barely reached to the level of the other's yellow coif.

After an exchange of courtesy, the akhled resumed his stool, and the newcomer sat down facing him. The watching Montariotans seemed to sigh and relax, and the

scene resumed normalcy. Nevertheless, that magical trans-
formation of the flames had left its shadow of awe upon
us, and our tension did not ease.

The akhled clapped his hands. Instantly two women
appeared from his tent, one bearing two splendid goblets of
ruby-red glass, the other a flagon of wine. One goblet was
filled and handed to the akhled. He drank from it, swallowed, and then, after a moment's pause, handed the goblet
to his guest. (This action, I presumed, was to demonstrate
that the wine was not poisoned or drugged). The second
goblet was filled and handed to the akhled. Then he and
his guest drank deeply, completing what was evidently a
ritual signifying honour and friendship.

There followed an exchange of sentences, the akhled
speaking in eddying gusts of words, his guest responding
with slow, sonorous cadences equally incomprehensible
to me. However, it was soon to be made clear that we,
their captives, were the subject of their talk. At a call of
command from the akhled, our two guards scrambled to
their feet and bent to free Avran and me from the chains
holding us to the posts. We were assisted up, steadied
(for our legs were cramped after sitting so long), and then
conducted over to stand between the two stools.

We stood there for fully three minutes, under the steady
scrutiny of the akhled and his guest. During that time, not
a word was addressed to us, nor did we speak. The face
of the fur-clad man was partly shadowed, but I saw dark
brows and bright, brooding eyes. Eventually he made a
dismissive gesture and said: '*Khadrashlesar iga khafeslar atim*'

This was the first phrase whose meaning I could guess.
If the Montariotan 'kha' prefix was equivalent to the
Sandastrian 'ksa,' it must mean: 'Unbind them and keep

them near to hand.' It was swiftly demonstrated that my guess had been right, for our guards freed our wrists from their ropes and then led us to stand beside the akhled's great tent.

In response to another brief order, Yerezinth and Zembelen were brought for inspection. Zembelen attracted only cursory attention, but at the sight of Yerezinth the fur-clad man rose to his feet. He walked forward and stopped to make a close, careful inspection of the jagged scar that disfigured my sevdru's flank.

As he did so, there came a sudden gust of wind that drove the smoke from the fires across into our eyes. I grimaced at this, blinking and throwing back my head. When the smoke cleared, it so chanced that I looked upward and saw the fishtail banner streaming against the sky. Then I looked again at Yerezinth and, for the first time, understood the surprise and awe of the Montariotans. My sevdru's healing wound had exactly the shape of the lightning-bolt emblem of Ayanessei!

The fur-clad man turned and spoke again to the akhled. This time I did not catch his words, but their import was made apparent when the two beasts were led away, to stand just beyond the fire almost at the centre of the arc of watching men.

The shadows were lengthening anew, for the fires were dying down. Yet no attempt was made to replenish them. The four mounted riders were becoming again creatures of darkness and the watching Montariotans reduced to a rim of smoky yellow from which gleamed many eyes. In contrast, the yellow robe of the akhled seemed golden-bright, and the silver furs of his guest shone in the fire-glow like an unsheathed sword.

Of a sudden, the latter turned about and, raising his hands in a gesture of invocation, cried *'Khasadin! Tsoned khasenast!'*

Again I understood him: 'Come to me!' he had called. 'Grant strength to me!' As if in response, the two fires crackled and flared up into great pillars of yellow light, causing Yerezinth and Zembelen to buck and ululate in terror and the watching men to gasp and tumble backwards. As for me, I was very sure in that moment that the silver-shining man was more than mortal and that he was a prophet or a wizard.

He stood with arms outstretched to the dark sky for a long moment, then turned away. As he did so, the fires dwindled.

With mutterings of awe and amazement, the tribesmen crawled back to their positions around us. Two of the riders – those at the centre – dismounted and came forward, to place before their leader a tall, narrow stand and set on it a bowl that seemed wrought of shimmering, scintillant silver. Each bowed, then both returned to their mounts.

The wizard, if such indeed he was, bowed in turn. Then, with a flick of his fingers, he set the bowl spinning, touching it again and again so that it rotated faster and faster. He passed his hands over it, and suddenly there was a column of smoke rising from the bowl, turning quickly into a little leaping point of red fire. He was nodding and crooning now, his fingers flickering about the flame as if caressing it.

As the bigger fires subsided into dullness, their fuel almost consumed, this little flame glowed ever brighter, a red eye looking out between the scintillant tricorn covering the bowed head of the wizard and the sharp coruscations from the spinning bowl. Then the wizard straightened his head and stepped back.

Now the wizard began speaking to the Montariotans in measured, doomful cadences, his voice like the roar of a gale in a gully and no more comprehensible to me. The silver of his robes was reflecting the last red fire-gleam, but with ever duller hues, like a horseshoe cooling on an anvil. The flame dissolved into smoke, dwindled, and expired. The spinning of the bowl slowed and stopped.

As the bowl stopped spinning, the wizard ceased speaking. The two trumpets blared, as he walked back to his mount. Within moments, the five riders, their leader midmost, were hastening away. There was a last bray of horns, then they were gone into the night.

After their going, the Montariotans stayed silent a while, then stirred into movement and noise. Yerezinth and Zembelen, still trembling, were led away. Though I could feel my sevdru's mental turmoil, I could transmit no calming thoughts to steady him, for my own mind was too uneasy and confused to be of aid. I sensed an increased respect on account of the very fashion in which the two beasts were being led away, but it gave me little comfort. I couldn't tell if they were destined for continued good treatment or for sacrifice.

The way they treated Avran and me allowed for a similarly ambiguous interpretation. We were conducted to a tent not far from that of the akhled. Our own clothes were taken from us – to my bitter regret as far as my remaining knives were concerned. While it seemed that they had not been discovered, they were removed beyond my reach. At the same time, we were provided with clean robes and new hide blankets in which to sleep. So far, it was all well and good, but we were kept under close guard and so firmly apart that we could not even converse.

I was unable, therefore, to learn how Avran interpreted this change of behaviour. For my own part, I had sufficient knowledge of the practices of the heathen cults still surviving in England to be set wondering with distinct uneasiness. We were indeed being treated well, but it was not uncommon for future sacrificial victims to be treated in exactly this way during their last hours on earth.

Despite my unease, I fell into sleep with the speed of a stone settling in a deep pool and slumbered without ill dreams.

CHAPTER 11

The Creatures Of The Night

It was a stray beam of sunshine, probing in through the open tent-flap onto my face, that awakened me. I stretched, blinked, and realized sluggishly that it must be mid-morning already. I had been allowed a long sleep.

When she saw that I was awake, an old woman who had been waiting patiently nearby came over to tend me. With dampened cloths and a coarse towel, she washed and dried my face and hands as tenderly as if I had been her infant. This done, she brought me a wooden platter laden with slices of cold cooked meat and different breads. These, with an earthenware beaker of hasedu milk, furnished an excellent and welcome breakfast. As I ate and drank, two squatting guards, each with spear in hand, watched impassively.

I must have been only half-awake until then, for I did not notice that Avran was missing until he returned to the tent. He was dressed in the yellow robes of a Montariotan and seemed remarkably cheerful.

'Awake at last, then, Simon?' He was speaking in English, as he had done last night. 'You were snoring as loudly as a timber-saw, and I thought you would sleep the day through. For my part, I am not such a sloth. I have been up and about for two hours or more. We're still prisoners, of course, but these Montariotans do not seem likely to kill us out of hand. In fact, they've allowed me to wander around quite freely. They barred my way, though, when I tried to walk beyond the camp, and they wouldn't let me approach our sevdreyen. Nevertheless, there's plenty to see. Come, get yourself dressed and let's go out and have a look.'

I found that, like Avran, I had been furnished with cream-white underwear and a yellow tunic and cloak in the Montariotan style, garments unfamiliar enough for me to welcome the old woman's help in dressing. Short boots of tawny-yellow leather completed the outfit. In warm weather, such a garb would be admirable, as it is light and cool. Presumably cloaks of fur would be substituted in chillier conditions. Out into the sunshine we went and, followed but not impeded by the guards, walked around the camp city for the rest of the morning.

There was much indeed to be seen. Some of the women were weaving cloth from long strands of vegetable fibre, using strange looms that rotated horizontally, not vertically like those I had seen in England. Lengths of the cloth thus produced were being dipped by other women into odoriferous vats, afterwards either to be bleached or dowsed in shallow troughs full of a yellow dye. We discovered by further watching that this dye was made from decoctions of the crushed bodies of a grassland grasshopper. We saw the white cloth being made into undergarments and the yellow into over-garments for men, women, or children. Meanwhile, by the stream banks, clothes were being washed or draped on stones to dry. Other women were preparing food, cutting up sun-dried meat, scraping or chopping root vegetables with little stone adzes, or crushing grain with rollers on shallow saddle-querns.

Some elderly men were moulding leather in troughs of steaming water or decorating it with sharp graving tools. Others were shaping pots with quick skill on treadle-turned wheels or fashioning vessels from thin silver by means of swift blows from tiny hammers or merely by use of their strong fingers. Two brawny individuals, stripped to the waist, were shaping arrow and spear heads in bright flames, then passing them to younger assistants who sharpened them on rough stones. Among their busy elders skipped and ran many children, while others either played with toy hasedain or competed in elaborate games, using patterns of lines graven by sticks into the streamside muds.

All in all, it was a busy and cheerful place. Though many of the women and children paused to watch with interest as we passed by, we suffered neither insult nor any abuse. Again and again, I heard the word *drahaklen* and knew it was being applied to us. I wished heartily that I knew its meaning. Avran did not understand the word either.

'I presume it must mean "stranger" or "foreigner",' he hazarded cheerfully. 'These people are so friendly that I can't believe they mean us harm.'

Twice we walked across the open space where, the previous night, those strange fires had burned. The scars from those fires were still to be seen in the turf, but the ashes had been cleared away and the stakes to which the sevdreyen and the two of us had been tied had been drawn out of the ground and restacked. The flaps of the akhled's tent were closed. We presumed he must have gone hunting or raiding, along with most of the younger men.

I was hoping Avran might have comprehended more of the wizard's pronouncements than I had. Unfortunately, he had not. All the same, he was inclined to be grateful to that gentleman, believing as he did that it was his words that had caused us to be freed and treated well. I was less confident, but, in that bright morning, my dark anxieties of last night seemed too ridiculous to mention.

At about one hour past noon, one of our four guards seized Avran by the sleeve, made a pantomime of eating, and gestured to us to follow him. Back we went to the tent in which we had slept, to find the old woman engaged in cooking scraps of meat on a spit over a little fire. Soon we and the guards were eating these from platters that also held hunks of bread and slices of a green vegetable tasting much like onion. One of the guards then served the old woman with grave courtesy, after which we all sat together, drinking wine poured from a tall earthenware flask into crimson glass beakers. These, Avran told me, were made in faraway Fachane and must have been acquired by trade or theft.

Scarcely was our meal ended when we saw a group of riders approaching the tent. Evidently our guards had been expecting this, for they leapt immediately to their feet and gestured to us to rise as well.

The riders – there were twelve of them – halted in a half-circle around us. One, evidently a leader from the elaborate green embroidery on his hood, uttered brief orders. Two hasedain, each saddled for riding, were brought forward, and we were urged quite courteously to mount.

Our former guards raised their spears in what was evidently a salute of farewell. Then, with green-hood in the lead, we turned around and threaded our way out through the woven paths of the tent city.

All whom we passed, men, women and children alike, stood still and watched us with a quiet intensity that I found disturbingly different from their casual attitude of the morning. I noticed too that two laden pack-hasedain were following. I wondered if we were going on a long journey. If that were the case, it boded well for us. Still, the silence of all the Montariotans seemed ominous.

The tents left behind, we splashed across the river downstream from the camp, at a ford used regularly and positioned so as to keep the tribe's waters clean. Steeply up the slope beyond we went and regained the general level of the plains, but now we were to the north of the valley. Two guards saluted with their spears as we passed.

After that, we headed steadily northward throughout the rest of that afternoon. Two riders had hastened ahead, two had dropped behind to serve as afterguard, and the other eight were bunched around Avran and me. The Ayanessei rode in a disciplined fashion and silence that contrasted sharply with their irregular order and gusty talk of yesterday. With our hands free, Avran and I could ride much more comfortably than we had done then. Since two of the Montariotans, one of them green-hood, separated us, we had no chance to converse. I could not gauge Avran's mood. For my part, I was in no better spirits than after our rescue from the trap.

It was a ride of few incidents. Once my hasedu bucked in fright when a long-tailed bird flew up with whirring wings from beneath his hooves. Twice we passed herds of hasedain grazing under the guard of armed Montariotans who responded gravely to our salutes, and, several times, fleet-footed wild creatures, perhaps wild hasedain, were glimpsed running from our path. The yellow grasslands seemed endless, yet we did not pause for rest or refreshment. Even when the sun began to set behind a phalanx of little clouds, the ride went on.

The light seemed to seep away southward, while, before us, there loomed a long, dark cloud on the northern horizon. I began to notice low green bushes studding the yellow grass, while ahead there loomed a darker shape that turned out to be a tree. Then we came on another tree, and another, and now a whole grove of them. And, in the fading light, the dark line ahead suggested not a cloud, but rather a forest, although it was hard to be sure.

Abruptly, green-hood raised his right hand, then gave a sweeping gesture to the left. If indeed that had been a forest, we no longer rode toward it, but we headed westward instead.

South of us, the sun was dipping below the horizon. The clouds were grey now and edged with red, while the sky above shaded from gold through turquoise to deep blue, a gradation of colour that would have astonished and defeated the most skilled heraldic artist. Steadily the light drained from the sky, until we were riding under an arch of deep blue, from which the first stars glimmered brighter than the pale rind of moon. Yet still that long ride did not end.

Ahead of us there loomed a dark shape, a hump against the western horizon. As we approached closer, I realized it was a hill, one that was flanked on all sides by a dense wood of trees.

It was not clear if it was a natural hill or some artificial creation, a motte built to elevate some fortification. We were no longer riding on grass, but on some sort of road. Even in the darkness, the changed sound of the hasedain's feet and their different manner of movement told me this was so. Yet, if this was in fact a man-made mound, it was surely very old. Soon we were passing among those trees. Though they were not tall, the thickness of their trunks showed them to be exceedingly ancient.

The road sloped ever more steeply till we were riding upward at an angle no horse could have managed. The riders had closed tighter around Avran and me, thinking perhaps that we might try to break away into the woods. Up and up we went. I seemed to glimpse stone courses to left and right about us and wondered if this might be the wreck of an ancient sun-temple, like the one Avran and I had seen in Menavedravard.

Then the slope eased, and we found ourselves atop the great mound in an open, flat area rimmed by trees on all sides. Underfoot were flagstones covered with mosses and lichens, with tall grasses and weeds thrusting up through cracks. At the exact centre of the clear area was one immense old tree, with great branches spreading widely. It was a tree that was nearly dead, for it retained few leaves, and its trunk had been repeatedly cloven by lightning-bolts.

Green-hood spread out his arms palm-backward, so that we ourselves and the other riders stopped. He rode forward, dismounted, and walked on a few paces before dropping to his knees. With arms spread again, but this time in the attitude of respectful greeting, he began to chant what sounded like a hymn to the ancient tree. The other Ayanessei dismounted and stood beside their hasedain with bowed heads. Puzzled and disturbed, but still uncomprehending, Avran and I watched and listened.

Suddenly green-hood turned around and clapped his hands. Instantly, four of the riders flung themselves upon each of us. Tumbling us from our mounts, they proceeded to strip us of our clothing. Naked, we were taken to stand beneath two great branches that reached outward in a broad V-shape, like two arms raised in invocation. Our arms were forced over our heads, spread widely apart, and bound by short lengths of rope to those branches. Avran cried out in angry protest, but he was ignored, if indeed he was even understood. Though very much afraid, I for my part remained silent.

Green-hood waved his men back to their mounts and then, standing between us, but looking toward the tree, uttered some wordy incantation that we did not comprehend at all. While he did so, the two pack-hasedain were brought forward into the clearing and unloaded. Though the light of the shrunken crescent moon was dim indeed, I could perceive what was being brought forth. Unbeknown to us, one hasedu had been bearing Avran's clothes and possessions and the other mine. These were set down in two heaps, but too far away from us to be reached even by our feet.

The garments that were stripped from us were rolled and put into the packs of the two hasedain, which were sent away. Green-hood began a new incantation, and the other Montariotans joined in it. Then, backing from the tree in the fashion of a courtier respectfully leaving the presence of his monarch, green-hood returned to his hasedu. He was still singing when, having mounted, he and the other Ayanessei retreated from the clearing. Their hasedain backed until their dark shapes blended into the trees. Then, at last, the chant ended. There was the sound of their descent down the steep road, then silence.

Allowing for the divergence of the branches to which we were bound, Avran and I were almost facing one another, though fully three poles apart. I saw him leap from the ground and hang from his bonds, pulling with all his might. All that resulted was that he chafed his wrists. The branch did not even bend, nor did the rope stretch. He repeated the action, with as little effect, then tried swinging from the branch, feet off the ground, in an attempt, I presumed, to cause the rope to fray. However, there was too great a distance between Avran and the branch for this to happen, and he did not keep up his attempt for long.

Half-heartedly, for I knew Avran to be much stronger and heavier than me, I attempted the same manoeuvres, but I gained only sore wrists. The rope was too strong for us, the knots unassailable.

Avran had relaxed and was looking across at me with a sort of wry amusement. He spoke in Sandastrian again, now that there were no listeners. 'Time for you to be thinking, Simon my friend! Nothing I can achieve will free us. Well, on this occasion I can be blamed only for being over-optimistic this morning. For the first time – and, I fear, for the last time – I can truly claim it was not I that led us into trouble!'

'A great consolation, no doubt,' I responded lightly, though, in truth, my spirits were very low. 'It would seem that we are some sort of sacrifice to this hunk of vegetation.' I pointed with my right toes at the tree-trunk. 'Well, men still make sacrifices to venerable oaks back in my own land. What a waste of effort it has been, crossing all those seas and mountains, merely to become an offering to an even more ancient and accursed plant!'

Avran laughed, then shivered. 'I wonder what is intended as our mode of demise? Starvation, or just sheer cold? I could wish they'd left us some clothes to wear.'

'I could wish they'd left me my knives. Yet I don't think our end will be so slow, nor will we be the first to meet it here. Look down at your feet, Avran. Can't you see the bones scattered around? Pieces of bone, rather. They seem all to have been split or bitten by strong teeth.'

Avran gazed around him as I had done, then shivered again. Yet his jaw had set grimly. 'Well, whatever our fate is to be, we must await it with due patience. *Not* the ukhuren, I hope. I have no desire to encounter those creatures again, however briefly!'

He paused, then said seriously: 'No, not the ukhuren. Look over yonder, Simon.'

My eyes followed his gaze. On the western side of the clearing, two animal shapes were moving among the long shadows of the trees. At first, I was reminded of the wolves so recently eliminated from England and still surviving, men said, in Ireland. However, wolves move much like dogs, whereas these moved in a curious, pouncing sort of lope. Moreover, wolves are brown, whereas the colour of these creatures was hard to determine, an uncertain wavering between light and shadow, as if they were formless. It was my turn to shiver now, and not from cold.

Clearly the creatures had perceived us, yet they were not approaching directly. Instead they were edging towards us in an oblique, weaving fashion, as if half eager, half afraid. Taller than any wolves they seemed, and gaunter, with long, flat-topped skulls that appeared earless and with forelimbs longer than hindlimbs, their bodies sloping backward to a sinuous, never-still tail.

There were two of them, at least. The moonlight was so pale that it was hard to see . . . No, three, and now there seemed to be a fourth, over where the road came up onto the mound.

One of the creatures emerged fully into the light and remained still for a moment. Now I could see why they seemed of such changeable colour. They were striped, but with stripes running not down their flanks as in the tyger of heraldry, but along their bodies in broad slashes in colours that were hard to make out – a dark grey and a dirty white, it seemed.

The creature looked towards me and snickered, revealing ugly, pointed teeth. Its bleak yellow eyes, like grave-lamps, met mine, but only for a moment. Then, as if in sudden alarm, all four animals – if indeed there were four of them – fled back into the trees.

I sighed in relief. 'They're gone, praise be to Our Lord. Excellent! For a while there, I thought we were about to provide dinner for a pack of spectral hounds.'

Avran was looking past me. 'No, Simon, they're not gone,' he said quietly. 'Two of them, or two others, are behind you now. I do not think much of our chances, friend.'

I tried to look back, but I could not twist my body around enough to see them, a fact that gave me no comfort. Moreover, within seconds I could see another sidling out from the trees near the clearing's rim, behind Avran. And, after that, there were two more.

'They're behind you too, I'm afraid. What are they, Avran? Can you give them a name?' Somehow it appeared to me important to be able at least to name them.

'Yes, I think so,' he said slowly. 'Our travellers' tales tell of a creature called the selth. It roams the plains at night, feeding on carrion, the injured, and the helpless. It is said to be hard to see, a ghost creature, yet with jaws strong enough to rend flesh and crush bone. None of our paintings depict one. Our savants have argued whether selths even exist. Well, we can reassure them on *that* point, if we are ever given opportunity. But, Simon, I fear we will not. It makes for a strange prospect, my friend – to be eaten by a creature of legend.'

Even now he was striving to be cheerful. For my own part, I was rigid with fear. The selths, if that's what they were, seemed reluctant to face our eyes, yet hungry for our blood. They were edging towards us with a deviousness that was more nerve-wracking than any direct attack. Moreover, it was also hard to keep them in view in the faint moonlight. They would fade into a patch of shadow, only to reappear in some lighter place, yet never quite where one anticipated. I shuddered.

'Avran, do you remember anything about them – anything that might help us?'

'So little is known of them, Simon . . . We know that they are cowardly, of course, but that much is quite evident, and I don't need to remember that. And yet . . . I believe I've hit on an idea that could help us. When they attack, if we were both to shout with all our might – not in fright, you understand, but by putting on an air of ferociousness – if we do that, it could be that they might flee. This is something we should try, but only when they attack.'

It seemed to me a faint hope, yet I could think of nothing better. Indeed, I was becoming so paralysed with fear, as those dreadful creatures wove their way ever closer, that I could scarcely think at all.

'Alright then. Let's – let's try your plan,' I said.

There were at least eight of the creatures in the clearing now. Some were still hugging its verges, but two were approaching ever closer to Avran. Moreover, two others, as fearful glimpses over my shoulders told me, were closing upon me. Abruptly, one of them opened its slab-like jaws and wailed. It was a shuddering, throaty sound that sounded like the mad laughter of ancient evil. Another echoed it, then a third. The sound stopped, and, in sudden decisiveness, they were running headlong towards us.

'Now, Simon! Shout will all your might!'

And we did so, bellowing like bulls at a baiting. The effect was immediate. All four of those attacking halted in their tracks, turned, and fled back to the bushes, the other selths preceding them. In a trice, the clearing was empty of them.

'It worked, Avran. It worked! Splendid – splendid!' Overjoyed and relaxing now, I found myself weak from the prolonged tension.

'For a while, Simon; for a while. Yet I'm fearful they will return soon enough. If only we could free ourselves!' He wrenched at his bonds, but with no effect. Those ropes were just too strong, those knots too well tied.

His words brought me up with a jolt. Avran was right, of course. The selths were sure to return. I pulled frantically at my own ropes, but they refused to yield.

As it turned out, the respite was in fact brief. All too soon, I glimpsed a sinister shape in a patch of light far over on my left; then saw another behind Avran. They were returning. For minute upon excruciating minute, they circled the clearing, approaching ever closer to us. When we shouted, again they fled, but they fled less far and resumed that circuitous approach more immediately.

Avran's chest was heaving, and he looked across at me gravely. 'That shouting – it worked for a while, friend, but it won't serve us much longer. Think, Simon, think – what else can we try?' But I could not think of anything. I was so terrified that I could scarcely think at all.

They attacked a third time. Again, we shouted as loudly as we could, and again they retreated. This time, however,

they went back only a few yards, breaking into an ulula-
tion of mocking wails as if to inform us that our stratagem
had been exposed.

All eight of the creatures were soon circling us. With a
sick, sinking feeling, I knew that their next charge would
mean our deaths.

Closer they came, ever closer. I could see now that they
were striped in dark brown and a pale, nauseous yellow. I
could see large, divided claws on their feet – strange claws;
and, as their jaws opened to howl, I could see great triangular teeth. Their evil earless heads, their yellow lamp-like
eyes that seemed windows into nothingness – the disfigured
horror of them was pressing ever harder upon me. They
were so close, so very close. I thought they would surely
attack soon, at any moment.

And so they did. I tensed, readying myself to give voice
to a last frantic shout. One was leaping at me, two others
at Avran. Our time had come.

However, as it leapt at me, the selth was suddenly transfixed by a spear – from nowhere, it seemed – so that the
creature fell sideways, howling in its death agony. Another
mysteriously flung spear had struck down one of those
attacking Avran. Then, in a moment, the remaining selths
were in panic flight.

With the very fangs of these dread beasts about to close
on us and rend us limb from limb, we had been preserved
from death, nor was it clear by whom.

CHAPTER 12

The Burning Of The Tree

Two men rushed to my side. Each was hooded and cloaked in dark brown, so that their faces and forms were hidden. Nor, at first, did they speak. While the Montariotans had been taller than me, both these men were shorter and found the knots out of their reach. One of them held me, therefore, while the other chopped awkwardly with his sword at one of the ropes binding my hands so high. To his consternation, the rope resisted such treatment, and, after a while, he tried sawing at it instead. Meanwhile, a third cloaked figure was standing watchful by Avran, a throwing spear in hand ready for use and two others held slackly by his side.

Several minutes passed before my right hand was free, and several more before the strands of the second rope were cut through. I collapsed forward, to be supported by one of the men – his bright brown eyes, glimpsed under the hood, seemed kind. He guided me over to the heap of my clothes. Shivering with cold and reaction, I was so helpless that I needed to be dressed. After that, my rescuer rubbed and pummelled my wrists and arms till they were warm and pulsing with returning blood. Meantime, his companion was trying to chop Avran free, with little effect, until the third man set down his spears and went to aid him by holding the ropes taut.

However, this meant that, for a while, none of the three was on watch. Suddenly, over the shoulder of the man who was tending me, I glimpsed anew the shadowy shape of a selth, edging toward him. Hastily, I thrust a hand into the pocket of my tunic and drew out my bowstring, then pushed my rescuer gently aside in order to pick up my bowstaff. In my weakened condition, to bend the bow was more than I could achieve, but he recognized what I was trying to do and helped me.

By then, the whole pack of selths was again ringing us. The deaths of two of them had not been the deterrent one might have expected, considering their evident cowardice. Possibly, the swiftness with which they had been slain was an occurrence that lay outside their comprehension. There were more of them than I had thought. At least ten of them were still living.

Avran had only one hand free and could not offer his help, as the swordsman was still trying to cut the other rope. The spearman was attempting without success to loosen a fourth throwing-spear from the body of the selth he had transfixed. Certainly, three spears – or even four – would not be enough to defend us long from so many potential attackers. I realized clearly that my long-bow would be needed. Yet, with my wrists as weak as they were, I was not sure I could use it effectively.

Normally, archery was a pleasure for me. On that night, it was an ordeal. As swiftly as I could, I set arrow to bow, but to draw the bow was almost beyond my powers. At my first attempt, I could not manage it and had to pull back on my draw in failure. The selths were closing in on us. I tried again, but could not do it.

The brown-eyed man had obtained a spear from his companion and held it ready for throwing, yet in a manner that suggested neither skill nor confidence. The spearman was standing at guard beyond Avran, while the third man sawed frantically at the single rope by which my friend was still bound. The selths were howling again, a dreadful, mocking sound that seemed calculated to fill their victims with despair. It was only a matter of time before they attacked once more.

For a third time I strove with all my strength to pull back on my bow, gasping at the sheer effort it took. At last the arrow was at its notch. And I barely managed it in time, for the selths were rushing forward and almost on us. My brown-eyed friend had thrown his spear, but missed. Already a selth was leaping at him, ugly jaws open and fangs bared. I let loose my arrow.

At such close range, I could hardly miss. My shaft drove deep into the creature's flank, throwing it backward against a second selth, which rolled over and promptly fled. Hastily I seized a second arrow and, by some freak reserve of strength, drew back the string at first attempt. A third selth leapt at us, but I was over-hasty in letting loose. All the same, the creature was sent tumbling over with an arrow through its forelimb and, after regaining its feet, it fled limping away.

Avran was free now and had fallen forward, with the sword-wielder standing over him. A thrown spear had slain a fourth selth, but the spearman had cast his remaining spear in vain and was reaching frantically for his sword. Four selths were closing in on him and Avran, while two others hesitated in the shadows.

I stepped forward to pick up another arrow, but, in my feeble condition, stumbled to my knees. The brown-eyed man leapt to my assistance, steadying me and helping me

to fit arrow to bow. With his aid, trembling, I managed
to draw back the string again and tried to align my aim on
one of the selths that were closing in on my fallen friend.
It was hard to keep the creatures in proper sight. They
seemed to fade from one spot and appear again in another.

One of them had paused to throw back its head and
howl. I hesitated, then for a third time I shot. It was a
fortunate shot, as it transfixed the creature's ugly head,
silencing that ghastly voice forever.

Almost at the same moment, the spearman hurled his
sword at another selth that was about to launch itself on
him. His weapon hit the beast on its shoulder and glanced
away, but the blow was enough to send that selth and the
two others into retreat. When he ran forward to retrieve
his spear, my brown-eyed rescuer turned that retreat into
panic flight. This time, I was sure, the selths would not
return. Which was a good thing, seeing as my strength
had been utterly drained, and I could not have drawn my
bowstring again.

Avran was helped into his clothes, and we were both
escorted – or, I should rather say, supported – away from
the tree. We were settled against a bank, with our weapons
by us, and allowed to rest while the spearman kept watch.

By then, he and his colleagues had thrown back their
hoods to reveal dark, curling hair and beards. They tried
to speak to us in Montariotan and in some other language
even more unfamiliar, but we could comprehend their
words no more than they could understand our replies in
Sandastrian.

While we rested, our two other rescuers were busy. The
thrown sword and spears were gathered up or withdrawn
with some effort from the corpses of slain selths, as was

my third arrow. My second arrow had gone with the selth it had injured, while the first was so deeply buried that it would have needed to be cut out, an effort not worthwhile.

The subsequent activities of brown-eyes and his companion were quite perplexing to me. With no small effort of labour, they began dragging the dead selths up to the trunk of the ancient tree, arranging them around it, and stacking branches over them. It struck me that this might be some sort of ceremony of tribute. Soon they were piling up twigs and leaves, until the dead creatures were covered completely. I wondered if this was to hide them from Montariotan view, as I was sure that these men were not themselves Montariotans.

I strained my eyes. It was hard to see in the difficult light, but brown-eyes seemed to be sprinkling something among the heaped twigs and leaves. By that stage I was entirely puzzled, then, in a moment, startled too, for they had set fire to the heap and were hurrying back towards us. The flames spread with amazing swiftness. Much to my astonishment, they were green flames, like those the wizard's spell had produced. I gasped in awe and leapt to my feet. Avran was on his feet as well.

'Avran, these men that rescued us – they must be the wizard's soldiers, the guards from the purple tent!'

Startled as I was, I had spoken in English. I was even more startled when our spearman guard replied in the same language. He was smiling.

'Excellent, so we can converse after all!' he said. 'You're quite correct, my friend. We are indeed the servants of him whom you call the wizard. But let's make haste to leave this place now. The fire is bright and growing more so, and other eyes may be watching.'

Indeed, the flames were leaping up around the old tree and engulfing it. One great dead branch was suddenly aflame, then another. The smoke was reaching a steadily thickening arm up toward the bright stars.

With friendly hands grasping and steadying us, we hastened over the rim of the great stone platform and down into the dark tunnel of trees. Suddenly I was aware that there were animals ahead of us, approaching us – not selths, thank goodness, but horned, deer-like creatures. By the way they moved, I could tell they were not hasedain or sevdreyen. I realized then that these must be animals of the sort we'd seen grazing by the wizard's tent and that had been ridden into the twilight by the purple guards. I was helped onto one, and Avran onto another. Brown-eyes climbed up behind me, the sword-wielder behind Avran, while the spearman mounted a third beast and led us away downslope into the darkness.

As we rode into the morning, I was aware of a billowing pillar of smoke and red flames, close at first and then further and further behind us, until I dropped into an abyss of sleep in which there was no awareness of anything.

When eventually I emerged from that sleep, it was with reluctance and pain. My eyelids felt as thick and sticky as if they were coated with resin. My arms – the right one, in particular – were throbbing and felt as heavy and weak as if they had been laden with weights. My mind too seemed reluctant to function, as if shuddering away from any recollection of that terrifying last night.

In spite of all that, I realized that all must be well now, since I was wrapped up warmly, and there was a sound of soft voices nearby. It was daytime again. Even with my eyes closed, I could tell. However, this was not the harsh sunlight of the grasslands, nor was there any wind. It was a pleasant place . . . we were in some pleasant place. Soothed, I relapsed into a drowse.

Many more minutes passed before, slowly, I climbed back to wakefulness and opened my eyes. I was indeed well wrapped in blankets and with a bed of cut boughs beneath me. A pillow, made from my rolled cloak, had been placed beneath my head. The light was filtering though branches clothed in the first green leaves of spring. The tree was of a kind I had never seen, with twigs arching upward and outward from its branches like ribs from a fish's backbone. Bright orange catkins hung down between the pale leaflets.

Two little green birds were nibbling at the catkins with long, curved beaks. They were swinging upside-down and performing the most extraordinary acrobatics, as if from sheer delight in living. I watched them with amusement for many minutes. Only when they flew away did I turn onto my side and look around me.

I realized that we were in the forest at last. These were not gigantic trees, like the ones around Lake Vanadha, but trees of a reasonable size, like the oaks and sycamores of Ecclesall Woods close to my Hallamshire home, and with many sunny patches between them. Yet all the trees were of unfamiliar sorts. Some had trunks as dark and smooth as the smoke-blackened beams of an old manor house; others had scaly trunks as russet-red as a squirrel's fur; yet others had brown trunks, corded like great, rigid ropes. In the patches of sunlight between their reaching roots, there grew many flowers. Some were of the same innocent blue as English bluebells in spring, others scarlet as pimpernels or yellow as campions, but all were of unfamiliar shape and leaf. Everything was beautiful, but at the same time all was very strange to me.

Avran was lying under the tree nearby me, still fast asleep among his blankets, and one of our rescuers of last night – it looked like the spearman – was just as deeply asleep close by him. At a little distance away, a fire burned in a hearth of rough stones. Over it was an iron tripod from which hung a pot, bubbling merrily. Squatting by the fire were our two other rescuers; it was their quiet voices that I had heard. Beyond, under other trees, the three horned beasts we had ridden were browsing quietly – and, no doubt, serving as guards. After so many days of strain, it was a delightfully tranquil scene.

I slipped out from my blankets, sat up, and, with an effort, got to my feet. My poor arms were sore and aching. One of the two men by the fire rose and came over to greet me. It turned out to be brown-eyes.

'Greetings, friend!' He spoke in English, although a strangeness in his intonation told me it was not his native tongue. 'I trust that you slumbered well?'

'Well indeed, thank you – and for quite a while, I imagine. What hour is it?' Under these trees as we were, I could not read the time from the sun.

He laughed. 'Long past noon! All of us slept late; and small wonder, after such a night. You are no mean bowman, friend. Even as weak as you were, your arrows saved us from those accursed selths. We owe you much.'

'Not as much as we owe you. Had you not come to our aid, by now we'd be merely a litter of chewed bone fragments under that terrible tree.'

He grimaced. 'It should not have been so close a call. We had been ordered to be there an hour earlier, but we

had presumed the Ayanessei would return immediately
to their town. They did not. And indeed it was a foolish
presumption, for we should have guessed they would stay
to learn what transpired. Instead, they camped out on the
grassland only a little way from Nekhalések – the temple of
the sun tree. We had to skirt them in order to reach you.
It was a tricky passage, for the ground was open, and they
are wary people. Consequently, it took us over-long. Even
so, we never guessed that the selths would gather so swiftly.'

I shuddered. 'Do not speak of them! Whether you were
late or not, we are deeply grateful to you. Yet why did
you burn their bodies, and the tree?'

'The tree deserved to be burned. It was ancient and
evil.' He was speaking solemnly now. 'Yet we did it, not
for that reason, but to serve as a sign.'

'A sign? I don't understand.'

'Ay, of course, you speak not the Montariotan tongue,
so you will not have comprehended what transpired in the
town of the Ayanessei. Well, your beast – or perhaps it was
your friend's beast – bears the lightning-bolt emblem of that
tribe. The Ayanessei believed that you must be harbingers
of good or of evil, but were hard pressed to decide which.
So they appealed to our master for his judgement. They
had come east to attack Eldernet, their ancient enemies.
They were not sure whether your coming meant that they
should continue east and ride triumphantly into battle or
whether they should avoid defeat by returning west to
their own territory.'

He paused and smiled at me. His eyes were as brown
as polished walnut wood, and his hair and beard almost of
that colour. I liked him very much. The other man was
watching from the fireside and listening.

'So the magician provided the sign?' I was eager to learn more.

He chuckled. 'Ay, you might say so! Our master, he has a kind heart. He knows that the Ayanessei slay all travellers from the south. At that, when it comes to it, they admit few enough from the north. Strange it is, for they're not evil folk, these plains peoples. Yet it's their custom. So our master contrived a way to save you and your friend. He urged them to expose you, in the old fashion, under the sacrifice tree. If the sacrifice was accepted and you were devoured by the selths, which they consider sacred, well and good. In that case, the Ayanessei might attack the Eldernet and be sure of victory. If anything went amiss, though, they would have to hop off back to their own lands. After last night, I reckon they'll be hopping away rather briskly!'

I laughed as well, and he went on more seriously. 'And so you can see that it is all due to our master's contrivance. Yes, the two of you have lived to see another day; but also quite a few other folk, who might otherwise have been slain, have been granted longer lives upon this earth. Our master's both wise and kind.'

'He must be so, indeed. But what about our beasts – our sevdreyen?'

'Is that how you name them? Well, they're not so unlike our own beasts in looks and not so unlike in name either, for ours are named *rafneyen* . . . Ay, but I'm straying away from your question. Well, I doubt that you'll ever see your beasts again, but they'll not fare badly. Was the marked beast yours, or your friend's?'

'Mine. His name is Yerezinth and he means much to me.'

He nodded. 'I comprehend your feeling well. Indeed, I have a like affection for my own rafenu. Well, Yerezinth is destined to be the mount of the akhled himself, so you may be certain he'll be well looked after. Since the other beast is to be ridden by the crown prince, the *indrakhled*, it will also fare well. You can be sure of that. The Montariotans depend much on their animals and so treat them well, even in the ordinary course of things. But royal beasts are treated royally.'

It was gratifying for me to know that my sevdru's future was assured. 'Thank you for that,' I said. 'Everything you say is good. But please, will you tell me your name?'

He chuckled again. 'Why, imagine me talking at such length, and us not being introduced! I'm Rahir Ravatseng, and yon hulk by the fire is my own brother Delhir. Both of us at your service.' He bowed in the English fashion, then beamed at me.

'Well, men name me Simon Vasianavar in this land, but in truth I'm Simon Branthwaite, from England and very much at *your* service. My sleeping friend is Avran Estantesec, prince of Sandastre.'

Rahir looked puzzled. 'I've heard of England, of course. There's plenty of folk from your land settled in these forests. Good men, some of them, and some bad. Yet, Sandastre? No, I've heard of no such realm. But then, few folk of these woodlands have ever heard of *our* native land of Reschora. It lies north of here, on the flank of the great mountains – no great distance after all, but not many folk travel so far. Yet enough of chatter. You'll be wanting your dinner. We can talk while we eat, or afterwards. Is your friend stirring yet?'

'I'm afraid he's a grand sleeper.' I chuckled to myself, remembering how only yesterday Avran had censured me for my sleeping habits. That seemed so long ago. Now, though, Avran was awakening. Gratifyingly soon, we were both dipping hunks of bread into stew hot from the pot. Before eating, I had introduced Avran to the two Reschorese and, between mouthfuls, I told him all that Rahir had told me.

Before we were done, the spearman had also awakened and had joined us, yawning. His name, we learned, was Felun Daretseng, and he appeared to be the leader of the three, if in fact they had a leader. He was much like the brothers in appearance, but quicker in thought and graver in mood.

'At the moment, you have a good opportunity to rest and relax,' he told us. 'Our master is travelling to join us, but he will not be here before the morrow's noon. In the meantime, there is nothing for us to do but wait.'

After we had eaten, Rahir took us to a place where a little stream wound its way through the trees. We drank, then bathed. The water was crisp and cold, but it served to take the aches from our limbs, and we returned to the fire considerably refreshed.

Delhir Ravatseng, who seemed a tranquil soul and less able in English than his brother, was playing sweetly on a little double pipe. After a while, Felun Daretseng began to sing softly. He sang in a language strange to us, yet with echoes of familiar words that made it seem not so very different from Sandastrian. Then Avran and I were persuaded to sing as well. Avran's song of his homeland meant much to me, but little to them. In contrast, my own two ballads, the old song of the cruel sister and the newer one of the combat in Chevy Chase, were understood well enough.

In this way, the afternoon passed pleasantly into evening. Since all five of us were still very weary, we retired early to our blankets, leaving the fire to dwindle to ashes. Under the placid guard of the rafneyen, we slept our weariness away and rose refreshed to a new day.

CHAPTER 13

In The Tent Of The Wizard

The next morning, I woke up earlier and more relaxed, as my weariness was gone and the ache in my arms had eased greatly. It also brought a breeze to rustle the new green leaves on the forest trees, with puffy white clouds that presaged showers rather than any considerable change in the weather.

Avran and I woke at almost the same time, to find that Felun Daretseng was gone hunting and the Ravatseng brothers were busy preparing breakfast. Thin pieces of dried meat were cooked to crispness over a little fire, then folded between slices of dark bread and served to us. We each drank draughts of sweet berry wine from a skin-covered flask. During this repast, we talked, or, rather, it's more accurate to say that Rahir questioned Avran about the peoples and realms of the southern hills. I interposed only an occasional comment, while Delhir sat smiling and silent.

'Well, that's a power of news, and no mistake,' Rahir said eventually. 'I'd heard tell of Denniffey and of the Fachnese. But, as for all these other kings and princes, it's information strange enough and wonderful to me. Mind you, I've little need to be surprised. How can tidings possibly travel north, when the Montariotans slay anyone who tries to traverse their lands?'

144

'They're a barrier indeed,' Avran responded. 'Yet we of Sandastre have heard a little about these forest realms. Word comes sometimes from the Montariotans, sometimes from Antomalata or Sapandella. Not that we trade often with those two kingdoms, for they seem forever to be at war.'

'Ay, well, maybe we'll venture into those lands someday. But we ourselves and the master, we don't often travel so far south. Mostly we stay among these forest earldoms or roam the northern plains.'

'Are there more plains, then, beyond the forests?'

'Yes, indeed, and some fine country, too. There's deserts that will match anything the Knights Templars tell of in their yarns of the Crusades, and there's grasslands richer than any that the Montariotans have for pasture. Beyond the plains, in the north, there are the mountains that are our home; and, in the east, other mountains. And beyond those mountains and ours, the great sea itself. Or so they say. My brother and I, we've never gone far to the north or to the east, nor yet has our master.'

'It seems that, even though Sandastre is so ancient a realm, we know little enough about our own island of Rockall,' Avran sighed. 'Why, even of the realms in the forest, our learned men can name only a few. Let me think.' He paused. 'There are Dellorain and Orelney – somewhere in the west, I think – and Atelone and, oh . . .'

'Dakalet and Seretta,' I prompted, for I had those names by heart.

Rahir laughed. 'Well, that's a few of them. Yet you're wrong in part. The realm of Seretta is not in these forests, but in grasslands by a great inlet of the sea. It lies north of Sapandella and northwest of that strange closed land, Dedesta. However, the others you mention are indeed forest realms. Dakalet lies far northeast of here. We travel there often, for its earl is a fine man and the friend of our master. Atelone is directly north of us, beyond the Bransworth River, and Orelney is over to the west, by the Mentonese sea. But, as for Dellorain, why you're in Dellorain at this very moment.'

It was strange to have a land cloaked in rumour transformed into a reality right there before our eyes. I gazed around at the trees with a new interest. Then, remembering my quest, I asked eagerly, 'And Lyonesse? It's Lyonesse that we're looking for. Surely it must be somewhere in these forests?'

To my deep disappointment, this name merely evoked a puzzled look from Rahir. 'Lyonesse? No, I can't say as ever I've heard of it. Would that be a realm or an earldom? Or is it just a town or fortress?'

'A realm, I think; and peopled by Englishmen.'

'Well, there's English folk a-plenty. Ay, and Welshmen and Gascons too, and even a few Frenchmen, all of them settling in these forests during the last three hundred years. Whenever there's a big war over in your countries, there are folk fleeing from it and settling here in Rockall. But Lyonesse? No, I've never heard tell of any such place. Have you, Delhir?'

His brother shook his head. 'Our master might know perhaps,' he ventured. Then, evidently tired of all this talk, Delhir produced his little double pipe and began to blow on it, a quiet, sweet, hypnotic tune.

The rest of the morning was passed in tranquillity. We went to wash in the little stream, then exercised with our swords and bows. The brothers watched us with keen interest. When, in our swordplay, Avran adroitly disarmed me, they applauded vigorously.

It chanced that Felun Daretseng returned just at that moment. He was bearing a small deerlike creature slain by a fortunate spear-cast. A *danatel* he called it. This he passed to Delhir, to be skinned and cooked. Then, with a smile, Felun invited Avran to a contest in swordsmanship.

I was made proud by the ease with which Avran disarmed him as well. To Felun's credit, he was more admiring than disconcerted.

'Well, friend,' he said a little ruefully, 'they rank me a good swordsman in my own land, but I am not of your quality. How do you fare with the throwing spear?'

This was a weapon with which Avran and I had been made to practise in Doriolupata. And, indeed, hunting with spears was a familiar Sandastrian art. Yet it was one at which my friend had little skill, and he was soon outmatched. I fared better, making casts that almost equalled, in accuracy and distance, those of Delhir, the Reschorese spearman. His praise was quite ungrudging.

'It is not only with the longbow that you have skill, Simon. Should it be that the two of you travel with us, your ability at arms may benefit us greatly. Though there are good men enough in these forests, there are evil men as well.'

It was long past noon before, with forewarning from the rafneyen, our friends became aware of the approach of those for whom we were waiting. First came two purple-clad riders, each with lances in hand, great axes slung over shoulders, and horns strapped to their saddles. I recognized them, for I had seen them as guards by the purple tent and riders into the firelight. Next came four rafneyen, harnessed in twos side-by-side. One pair carried a huge roll that had to be the tent itself, the other pair its

great supporting poles in a rope-secured bundle. Two more
riders followed, armed like the vanguard, but not bearing
horns. It was they who had carried the torches into the
Montariotan camp. Then came six more rafneyen, each
bearing packs. And lastly, came another rider in purple.
Remembering as I did a glorious figure in silver, it was
only when I took a second look that I realized this was
the wizard himself.

The other riders and the pack-rafneyen had already come
to a halt in the clearing. The Ravatseng brothers and Felun
greeted their comrades with cheery waves, then fell respectfully silent as the wizard approached. He had noticed Avran
and me, but it was Felun whom he addressed. He spoke
in swift sentences in a language I took to be Reschorese,
as it was incomprehensible to me and yet had none of the
gusty cadences of Montariotan.

While the two conversed, the other riders dismounted
and, setting down their weapons, began unloading the
pack-animals. Rahir and Delhir hastened to their assistance.
Heavy hammers and a narrow-bladed spade were produced
from one of the packs, and the great poles were extracted
from their bundle. There were six of these. One was slotted
into another and fastened to it with leather bindings, to
make a tall centre-post. This was planted in the exact middle
of the little clearing. The other four poles were set around
it at uniform distances from each other, then the fabric of
the great tent was wrapped about and over them all. This
was done with a swift skill that argued long practice. Avran
and I stood by, fidgeting uneasily, feeling we should help,
but fearing we might merely hinder.

I was surprised not to see the pole bearing the potent
cross emblem, which had stood so tall by the purple tent

out in the grasslands. Later I learned that this had signifi-
cance only to the Montariotans. As a result, it had been
left in concealment near the forest's edge, ready for use
next time the wizard visited the grasslands.

Having completed what I surmised was a detailed report
of the doings of his comrades, Felun assisted his master to
dismount. The wizard caressed his rafenu's head briefly and
dismissed it. Only then, for the first time since his arrival, did
he glance our way. At his word, Felun beckoned us over.

I had noticed before that the wizard was quite a small
man, but the tricorn hat had enhanced his apparent size. I
perceived now that, though burlier, he was shorter even
than me. Yet again, I found him impressive, for he had
a quality of forcefulness and authority that made a person
forget his height. His hair, his bushy eyebrows, and short
beard were all of a dark brown unflecked with grey, even
though he must be past middle age. His skin had been
tanned deeply by wind and weather. From that dark face,
there shone forth eyes of quite exceptional brightness,
so strikingly bright, in fact, that they seemed illuminated
from within by some errant shaft of sunlight. However, I
could never establish what colour they were. Sometimes
they seemed brown, sometimes honey-coloured, sometimes
– especially at night – as yellow as a cat's. Strange eyes,
indeed, but this was a strange man.

A vivid awareness that the wizard's orders had saved
our lives flooded my mind, and I fell to my knees before
him. Avran did likewise without hesitation. Immediately,
however, with a peremptory wave of his hand, he gestured
to us to rise and spoke to us in English.

'Stand, gentlemen! You are not servants, of myself or
any other. Nor do I hold such high rank as to merit your

reverence. I am a mere traveller, as you are – Vedlen Obiran, physician and alchemist of Reschora. I trust that my men have treated you well?'

'More than well,' Avran responded earnestly. 'We owe our lives to them, and to you. And for that, you do indeed merit our reverence. Avran Estantesec, at your service'.

'And Simon Branthwaite, at your service and deeply in your debt.'

A smile flickered across that dark face. 'Yet I think the debt is cancelled already, if matters be as my lieutenant tells. My men were tardy, and they owe their own lives, in turn, to you. The board is clear. We may converse this evening as equals. I shall look forward to that conversation.'

Without more ado he turned away, to vanish within the newly-erected tent.

After the unloading of the rafneyen was done, there was leisure for other introductions. Three of the men were also Reschorese. Drakht Belineg, a big, broad-faced man with the downwardly pursed lips of one forever striving to conceal an urge to laughter, was one of the trumpeters, and Narel Evateng, a lean man with a deeply lined face, the other. The third Reschorese had the same brown, curling hair and brown eyes as the Ravatseng brothers and was much like them, though bigger. When he proved to be their cousin, Hebehir Ravatseng, I was not a bit surprised. On the other hand, I was in fact quite surprised when I was introduced to the fourth of the wizard's soldiers, for he was an Englishman – or rather, a man of English descent. He was broad and short, round-faced, red-cheeked and beaming, his name Amos Sloly.

'Pleased am I to meet you, sor,' he said to me. 'And your friend likewise.' His voice had that deep, rich burr that I remembered from Bristol. 'Simon, is it? And from England. Well, 'tis from England that my grandfather travelled, seventy years back. From north Devon he came. Moses Sloly, his name was, and as foine and handsome a man as you could wish to meet. All of us Slolys be foine men!'

The gleam in his eye told me that this self-praise was intended in humour. Indeed, such phrases were often in his mouth, and he enjoyed them with huge relish. 'Whoy, let a real man carry it,' he would say, taking a pack from a burdened colleague; or 'That needs proper skill. I'll show you how 'tis done,' as he seized a hammer to drive in a pole. Rarely have I encountered a man who found more delight in life, or found it so continuously amusing. And yet, as I was to discover, there were depths in Amos Sloly that were not readily plumbed.

We were shortly to be grateful for the tent. Scarcely had we eaten our evening repast when there came a heavy shower. It did not last long, but the grass was left wet and the trees dripping. By then, however, we were sitting dry beneath a high, thin roof of hide that let in no moisture, yet permitted some light to penetrate. The tent interior was almost square. One-quarter of it was partitioned off by screens of purple cloth and served as private quarters for the wizard, who had indeed eaten within. The rest made a sort of messroom for his seven guards and us.

No watch was necessary, when fourteen rafneyen were grazing in the forest round about. It meant that all nine of us could relax and talk. Avran and I learned that the soldiers' master, Vedlen Obiran, was a man of renown in forests and plains alike, famed for his skills as physician and magician (for his men, as we did too, thought him more than a mere alchemist), his wisdom, and his ability to read men's thoughts. The purple robes worn by the men and by their master – whenever, that is, he did not choose more impressive attire – served, as it were, as a proclamation that they were not mere travellers, but wonder-workers and healers. And, in fact, as much as the seven were assistants to the wizard, they also functioned as his guards. In garb such as they wore, a man might travel freely across frontiers and through any of the realms of what they styled 'the middle lands' – the lands between the mountains of north and east and the highlands of the south. However, encounters with wild beasts and wilder men happened often enough to make the martial skills of the wizard's guards a necessity.

On the day of our departure from the camp of the Ayanessei, their akhled had sent the sick and the maimed of the tribe to the wizard to be cared for. Close by him were those four of his men whom we had seen in the firelight. I realized now belatedly that we had encountered no ill or injured people in our walk around the Montariotan camp. The wizard's other three men had been off hunting when the Montariotans chanced upon his tent. Once he had learned of our captivity and had been asked to judge us, their swift-thinking master had kept the three of them from the view of the suspicious nomads and had sent them to our rescue. Fortunately for Avran and me, the Ayanessei had never become aware of their existence.

Their work of healing done, the wizard and his four assistants had dismantled the tent and ridden away during the night. It was a departure that, by design, was mysterious enough to enhance their prestige in any future visit to the plains. They had slept in a sheltered place during much of the next day and after that had made an easy journey to join us.

'Can't say I'm sorry, usually, to leave those plains behind,' growled Drakht Belineg, 'but this time, I have my regrets. I'd have liked to be in that camp, to see the faces of those Ayanessei when they heard you two folk were gone, while that horrible old tree – we saw it once too – was burned to a cinder, as surely it was.'

Naral Evateng's trouble-creased face was lit by a smile. 'Ay, indeed!' he chortled. 'They'd be packing up and running like ants from a broken anthill. And more than that, they'll be considering our master a mighty magician!'

Felun Daretseng smiled at Avran and me. 'Better not cross the western plains again. If you do, they'll believe you're gods returning. No doubt they'd construct you a temple that would be all your own.'

Avran shivered. 'Do not speak of their temples!' he implored. 'I can't bring myself to think of such things without seeing those prowling selths again. I think it will be a long time before they fade from my nightmares.'

'True, all too true,' I said with an involuntary shiver, concurring with my friend most heartily.

In that very moment, the mellow sound of a bell interrupted our conversation. Instantly, Felun sprang to his feet and hastened into the wizard's sanctum. In a moment, he came out again to inform Avran and me that his master wished to speak with us. We rose and followed Felun inside.

The small space that formed the wizard's retreat was lighter than the rest of the tent, for a tall white candle, set in a silver holder, was burning with a bright flame of palest blue. I was reminded of the yarns spun by the Bristol quaymaster and I guessed the candle must have been traded from Mentone. By it sat Vedlen Obiran on a purple cushion tasselled with gold. His own garb echoed those colours, for he wore a purple tunic embroidered so elaborately with gold thread that it seemed to shimmer in the flickering light. His hands were tucked within the tunic's sleeves, and he seemed as still and motionless as a tree-stump. In the candle-glow, his eyes shone pale, like glow-worms in a hedge.

Felun gestured to us to sit on two other cushions that had been set before his master. We did so, while Felun stood at a deferential distance behind us. For what seemed many minutes, the wizard scrutinized us in silence. Under his gaze I found myself shifting in discomfort, like a child standing before a priest at first catechism. Avran bore the situation in rather better fettle. It was to Avran that the wizard's first words were addressed, although in a curiously oblique way.

'Red hair, I see. Yes, the Montariotans say it is common among you southerners. Even so, I've seen too few of you to form my own opinion. Some Englishmen are also redheaded, and many of the folk of Mionia over in the eastern mountains. Such hair is rare in the north. You would be noticed and remembered, if you were to venture there. But you, Simon Branthwaite' – he pronounced my name perfectly, his eyes bent upon me – 'would cause little remark. There are many among us that are much like you. You would not attract notice, and that, I think, is your special skill, not to attract notice.'

These remarks did not invite a response, nor did he seem to expect one. He went on, speaking pensively. 'Yet you have other skills also, Simon: a skill with the bow and, I think, with the thrown knife.' At this, I started in surprise. His men must have seen my weapons, of course, but their use would not be comprehended, even in England. 'Your other skill is with beasts. You watch, you understand, and they feel your sympathy. The animal you lost to the Ayanessei will be well treated, but he will remember you long and, as I foresee, to your great benefit someday. Yet there will be other beasts with whom you will forge an understanding, and always to your advantage.'

The evening was drawing on, and drops of rain were rattling again on the hide roof. Under the darkening sky, the light of the candle seemed even brighter, the shadows around us even darker. The wizard's attention was focused again on Avran.

'And you, prince of the realm beside the southern sea, have a skill with beasts as well, although learned and not innate. Yet you have only a small patience, and you cannot stay quiet in the shadows. You must be ever out in the sunshine and acting with vigour – often, indeed, with too much vigour and too little thought. Yet defeat will come to you only rarely, nor will you allow it to deter you overmuch. You are the stuff of travellers, for you are ever eager for fresh scenes and new contests. But you, Simon' – his eyes turned again to me – 'why do you travel so far, when your heart lies behind you?'

At this thrust of his, I blushed, started to speak, then hesitated, wondering how he had so readily perceived my love for Ilven and my reluctance in leaving Sandastre. I had not talked of Ilven in many days, even to Avran. And, though she was often in my thoughts, I had striven to put behind me all my doubts, concentrating my attention entirely on finding Lyonesse.

The wizard spoke again, with a kindness in his voice I had not heard up until then. 'Only your strong sense of duty, your commitment to your cause, can have torn you away from the woman whom you love. Tell me, Simon, why is that you seek that land of Lyonesse?'

Stumbling over my words, I tried to explain; and he nodded in understanding – an unexpectedly English gesture, for it's not one that the Rockalese make. 'So you reason that, since so many of your countrymen have settled in these forests, that realm must be in the forests as well. Yet most Englishmen that come here travel, not from Bristol, but from your city of London to the free port of Warringtown, far away in the east beyond the plains of Herador. True, some French or Gascon ships do sail to Saint Lorraine on the great bay. But your countrymen do not voyage on such vessels. I have not heard that any Englishmen have come to the forests from Bristol, nor that any others have voyaged to Rockall, as you did, with those heathen Mentonese.'

He paused and, when he resumed speaking, he seemed to be talking more to himself than to us. 'Yet Lyonesse . . . Lyonesse . . . no, not in the forests, but where in this great island? Is it a new realm in the dry plains or an old one in the eastern mountains? Of those mountains, I know little. Or is it somewhere in the far north; some valley in the Wainlands or the Delven Hills, or somewhere beyond the mountains? I do not know. Perhaps I shall never know. And these young men, will they discover it?'

It had become so dark now that no light penetrated the tent roof. The candle flame had flickered down. Its dimmer radiance picked out only the tracery of gold on the wizard's tunic and his eyes, making them shine brighter and yellower. Abruptly, and through no apparent cause, the flame flared up and burned brightly, seeming to awaken the wizard from his reverie.

'Simon and Avran, you must travel with me for a while. We have rafneyen that you can ride. Our beasts are laden lightly, and two can be spared. Felun, my good servant, not only must you find tunics of purple that will fit these new friends, but also you must teach them our Reschorese tongue. You will not find that difficult, for it is not much different from the language of the south that Avran has known from birth and Simon can now speak so freely.'

He paused, then went on: 'As we travel, we will ask questions. If the whereabouts of the land of Lyonesse can be learned, then, in some way, we will learn it. Be sure of that, Simon, and take heart.'

CHAPTER 14

Doubts In Dellorain

It was a night of tempest-driven winds and swift, brief showers. Each approaching gust rippled the trees into progressively more violent motion, beginning like a distant tide and culminating in a soughing sound, like waves breaking on a sandy shore. The first light drops of rain in each shower sounded like fingertips pattering on the taut tent fabric. As the raindrops fell harder and heavier, the noise would swell, like kettle-drums played during a joust in some tournament. Then, as the shower slackened, the rattle would die away into a muttering, like the hubbub of a distant, angry crowd, before ceasing altogether. After a pause, a breath-like sound of rising wind would signal the approach of the next squall.

Avran and the soldiers fell quickly asleep, the massive Drakht Belineg snoring like a blunt saw cutting beechwood. But I lay awake for a long time, and my thoughts were sombre. I considered the many leagues we had traversed, the many perils we had survived. I remembered our tense ascent of the tower and the snarls of the thassak, my fearful night ride with the grey warriors, our tumbling into the Montariotan pit-trap, and, worst of all, those dreadful prowling selths. Yet, having endured all this, still we had no idea where Lyonesse was.

It could not be in the forests, as we had guessed back in Sandastre, since these much-travelled men, even the wizard himself, had never even heard of its very name. After all, Lyonesse was not such a new settlement. More than sixteen years must have gone by since the ship of Sir Arthur Thurlstone and Sir John Warren had first set sail from Bristol.

If not in the forests, could Lyonesse be in the open lands beyond them to north or east? For the same reason, this seemed equally unlikely. It could not be hidden among desert sands, for it had been reached by ship. It must be close to a coast. In the mountains to the east, perhaps? Ships might find harbour there, unbeknown to the wizard. Or in the mountains of the north, maybe? But these Reschorese were men of the northern mountains, and yet they did not know of it.

I remained sure that Lyonesse was somewhere in Rockall. But I was becoming just as certain as well that it was still far away. I fell to wondering if Avran and I would ever discover it. And if we did in fact find Lyonesse, there arose the further question of whether we could hope safely to traverse again all those long leagues back to Sandarro, where lay my heart.

There had been an interval of silence, but now there was a new murmuring of wind among the trees. It was an uneasy sound, and it matched my uneasy thoughts. I asked myself whether we should go on. As I remembered my father and brother, I felt an upsurge of affection. Richard needed to learn about the fate of Anicia and their child, and both he and my father would be overjoyed to see me again. Moreover, my father would be proud that I had proved my mettle to him and that I was a worthy and dutiful son. But, realistically, the hopes of ever finding them were slim. Moreover, the attempt itself began to seem like a mission doomed to defeat, one in which Avran and I were merely casting away our lives to no purpose. At the same time, I longed to see Ilven again and embrace her, to reach a stage where all this strife-filled wandering was over, knowing that she and I could safely live and love together again.

The moan of the rising gale seemed to express the pain in my heart. Vedlen Obiran was right. I was not by nature a wanderer, but a person who longed for home and tranquillity, for a simple life and small pleasures. What was I doing, straying so far from the woman whom I adored? I began to think that now was the time for Avran and me to cut our losses and abandon this stupid search for a lost land. That way, we could return to Sandastre, and swiftly.

Yet this was impossible, I knew. It would mean admitting that we had summarily given up our quest. It would mean explaining with brazen shamelessness to Prince Vindicon and to Ilven that we had abandoned it. Not only that, but it would mean explaining my lack of fortitude and faintness of heart to Avran the brave – Avran, who had nothing to gain even from a successful outcome to the search, who was taking all these risks simply because it was my quest and I was his friend. I realized that I could not let them down by scurrying south to Sandarro. I had embarked on a path that allowed no turning back. I needed to follow it with singleness of purpose right to the end, even if that end brought death.

Though that dire thought was chilling, in a strange way it was calming as well. Outside, the sound of the gale reached a crescendo, then dropped in register and was lost in the steadier beat of a more continuous downpour. I had to go on. I had no other choice.

Like a drumbeat, the even new rhythm of the raindrops on the tent roof seemed to repeat to me, 'You must go on, you have no choice . . . You must go on, you have no choice . . . You must go on . . .' And at last I slid away into sleep.

We woke to bright sunshine and the sound of the steady drip of water from the trees. Breakfast was good, but the job of dismantling, folding, and rolling the wet tent, as well as drying and grooming the rafneyen and loading them up, were tiresome tasks. Clad in the purple tunics Felun had found for us, Avran and I felt ourselves now to be numbered among the wizard's men and, naturally, aided our new comrades in these chores. If we did not enjoy the work, we were gratified at least by the way they accepted us immediately and approved of our attempts to be helpful.

After that, Avran and I were introduced to our new mounts. Rafneyen are forest creatures and about as different from sevdreyen as roedeer are from red deer. Their whole build is slimmer, for one thing. Their nasal horns are not directed upward, but forward and outward, as short and sharp as the tusks of a wild boar. Their brow horns divide above a broad base into five unbranched tines, the three foremost longest, the two hindmost shortest. The central three tines curve, whereas the two outermost are straight. Because of this, the clustered tines are curiously like the spread fingers of a hand. Rafneyen are softer muzzled and larger-eyed than sevdreyen. Instead of being silver-grey, their pelage is as brown as polished walnut wood, but dappled or flecked with spots of cream-colour that make them hard to see among trees, whether in sunlight or in shade.

The mounts they found for us were both rather small animals, which suited me well enough, but made Avran look oversize, like a grown man on a child's pony. Yet he liked his new beast just as much as I liked mine. Both were bucks. Avran's was named Lanenot, 'small-spot' in Reschorese speech; mine was Gahelad, 'streaked-fur.' Amused by the similarity of their names to those of two of King Arthur's knights, I suggested we restyle them 'Lancelot' and 'Galahad.'

This renaming did not upset the rafneyen, since they recognized our thoughts rather than the sound of our words. Since my idea amused Avran, we adopted these new names definitively.

Galahad was an animal as noble as his name, or so it seemed to me. I was quick to forge a mental link with him, and, though he never supplanted Whitebrow and Yerezinth in my affections, I became very fond of him. Rafneyen are longerlegged than sevdreyen and move differently. The motion of riding him was strange at first, but soon came to seem just as familiar and pleasant. On flat ground a rafenu is quite as swift as a sevdru, and it is swifter in finding a path through woodland. However, as we were to discover later, rafneyen are much less agile than sevdreyen in rocky terrain and on steep slopes.

Our ride that morning was rendered less enjoyable by the steady, relentless dripping from the tree-branches over-head. I was reminded of that last wet ride to Doriolupata. Nevertheless, this ride was much happier. Many small birds serenaded us from the branches all around. Besides this, there was the occasional flash of bright butterfly wings, while the trees and flowers wove an ever-changing fabric of beauty that offered a feast of delight to our eyes.

We saw no people and no dwellings. Indeed, the first indication to us that Dellorain was inhabited came when we emerged onto a bridle track. Initially, this was little broader than a field path, a brown slash through the green grass. However, its beaten surface was pitted by the water-logged hoofmarks of rafneyen and the rain-filled furrows of cartwheels, showing that, while it may not have been used heavily, it was used by a varied traffic at least. Many of the marks were fresh. Men had been travelling that road today, and in the same direction as we were.

After a mile or so, a track joined ours from the left and two more from the right, so that the bridle path broadened into a road. Soon there were many tracks, and the road was becoming ever muddier. As we splashed along its slippery surface, I remembered wistfully the good roads of Sandastre. There were no stones or setts to make this road firm and no drains to make it dry. Nor, indeed, were we to encounter any well-constructed roads anywhere in the forestlands.

We rode that day in an order that was to change little on later days. The two trumpeters, leanly built Narel Evateng and huge Drakht Belineg, led the way – their habitual position, for they served as advance guards as well as heralds. Narel's watchfulness was reflected by a continual swing of his head from side to side. In contrast, Drakht's massive head remained still, but his eyes were forever roving. Felun Daretseng rode just behind them, seemingly relaxed, but ever ready to respond to an alarm. Avran and I followed at his rafenu's heels, and behind us came the pack-rafneyen that bore the tent and its poles. The Ravatseng brothers came next, then the four remaining pack-rafneyen, each now more heavily laden than yesterday. The burly Hebehir Ravatseng followed, with Amos Sloly alongside him.

Last of all rode the wizard (that was the way I was always to think of him). It was a vulnerable position perhaps, but one that allowed him to hasten or dawdle at whim. Sometimes, indeed, he would fall so far behind that Felun would stop our progress and go back in concern to seek his master. Either they would return together, or Felun would ride back to assure us all was well, after which we would await the wizard's tardy coming with patience or impatience, according to our feelings at the time. Sometimes, after delaying us for few or many minutes, Vedlen Obiran would arrive bearing a plant, berries, or a frond from a shrub, to be handed to Hebehir for storage into one of the packs. More often he bore nothing, and the delay remained forever unexplained.

The trees arched over our road, their branches forming, against the blue sky, a great green net through whose meshwork swam white clouds like a stately cavalcade of fish, soft as puffballs. When we set forth, there had been a ground-mist, but this had long since lifted, and, since the sun was behind us, our shadows rode before us down the path.

After so many days during which an exchange of conversation had been dangerous or difficult, it was a pleasure for Avran and me to be able to talk to each other in a relaxed way. Actually, with the strains and doubts of the night behind me, I was rather inclined to babble, with Avran contributing only an occasional word or smile. From time to time, Felun glanced back at us with amusement or threw out a comment to us that splashed like a pebble into the merry flow of my chatter and sank beneath it.

Suddenly we became aware of the sound of voices and movement ahead. Our two leaders checked their pace and went forward more slowly. The wizard, who had dropped behind, caught up and rode past us, his rafenu falling into step with Felun's.

As we rounded a shallow bend of the road, the trees opened out ahead of us to reveal a broad river. On its banks was a cluster of high pavilions, such as you see at a tournament. Around them were stalls, many beasts, and many people. Beyond, a broad wooden bridge without rails stretched across to a further bank similarly set with pavilions and swarming with people.

However, it was the figure in the middle of the bridge that caught my eye – a knight in the full splendour of plate armour. He wore a jousting helmet, its visor open, and his iron-gloved hand held a lance, upright and at rest. From its tip, a narrow green pennon floated in the breeze, and borne on his arm was a shield of similar hue, each of these displaying a device in gold which, later, I was to discover was a waterbird in flight.

The knight's mount was a massive animal, armoured in plate about the head and flanks. Curiously, I could see no horns. Only when we drew closer did I realize, to my surprise, that it was a horse – the first I had seen in Rockall. Horse and rider gleamed in the sunshine, throwing their reflection onto the bright water.

The crowd on our bank, though noisy enough, seemed far from happy. The men were chattering in that busy, but slightly furtive, fashion that the transmission of ill news seems to generate, while the children, instead of running around, listened open-mouthed or formed subdued groups at the tent skirts. As we came into view and it was noticed that we wore purple cloaks, they all stood back and fell silent.

One pavilion was larger than the others and tinted chevron-pattern in scarlet and silver. To it our heralds made their way, while their master and the rest of us followed. As we approached the pavilion, an elderly man, whose silver-broidered scarlet tunic showed him to be of high rank, emerged. He paused in surprise, then ran to us.

'Your coming is timely, Messer Obiran,' he cried. 'We have a knight here who is badly injured. On my lord's behalf, may I implore your assistance?' He spoke in English.

'My small skills are at your command,' the wizard responded gravely. He and Felun dismounted and went inside the pavilion, while the rest of us waited. The crowd had gathered all around us now. For a while, the awed silence continued, but soon the murmur of conversation began anew. At first I could make little sense of their talk. Fortunately, a late-arriving woman pushed through the crowd to join a man who was standing close to me. She demanded to be told what was happening. She spoke English, and I was just as interested as she was in his response. Indeed, I listened intently for many minutes, while Avran stood by me silent, trying to catch the gist of the conversation. Eventually his impatience became too much for him.

'Simon, what's going on here? I don't understand.' Avran addressed me in Sandastrian.

I answered in the same language. 'From what I can gather, there's been a long-standing dispute between the Lord of Dellorain and the Earl of Brantwood about fishing rights in this river. The Antoman the river seems to be called, and it marks the frontier between their two territories. Well, you'd imagine they'd be content to agree that half the river belonged to each; and so they do. However, there are islands just upstream, and in the shallows around these islands many fish spawn. Those islands are claimed by both realms. And so, they'd settled on a contest to decide the question, but now things have gone wrong.'

'What sort of contest? What has gone wrong?'

'A contest of champions, a joust on the bridge. The knight in armour is Sir Brian Beauchamp, son of the Earl of Brantwood. He was to be matched against the champion of the Lord of Dellorain, a French knight called Sir Guy de Guisdard — or something like that. I couldn't really make out the name. Well, the French knight appears to have stayed up too late last night, celebrating his victory in advance. He rode here fast this morning, too fast. His horse's hooves slid in the mud, and the horse fell sideways against a tree. The horse's leg is broken, and so, I gather, is the French knight's. The consequence is that they want Vedlen Obiran to set matters right for them — to perform a miracle, if possible.'

'Can't the Lord of Dellorain find another champion, or take up the challenge himself?'

'It seems not. The Lord is an experienced knight, but he is old, too old for jousting. He has many daughters, but only one son and that son's a cripple. Moreover, there are no other horses in Dellorain, believe it or not. The French knight was a traveller from some land called Rockaine. It was only his presence that caused the Lord of Dellorain to agree to a contest of this kind.'

'That really is a problem,' said Avran. 'Maybe the French knight might be mended well enough to be set in his saddle. However, I can't even begin to conceive how even our friend the wizard can have the horse back into good enough shape for any jousting today.'

'It's worse even than that. The champion of Dellorain must accept the challenge before noon. If he does not, the contest is lost and the islands are forfeit to Brantwood. Only two hours remain'.

We both fell silent, for there seemed nothing more to say. Behind us, Amos Sloly was explaining the position to the Reschorese. Soon after, Felun Daretseng emerged from the pavilion and spoke quickly to the Ravatseng brothers. They dismounted and, having extracted two bundles from the packs, followed him into the pavilion.

At a word from Drakht Belineg, the rest of us dismounted as well, and the rafneyen were sent away to browse among the trees by the river bank. Narel Evateng went with them to guard the packs. The rest of us stood and waited, the crowd eddying around us.

After a while, the Ravatseng brothers emerged from the pavilion. As always, it was Rahir who spoke, at first in Reschorese to his fellows and then in English to Avran and me. 'Our master's set yond Frenchman's leg for him, and done it well. He'll be hobbling for a while, but he'll ride again soon enough. However, there'll be no jousting for him today or for many days to come. As for the horse, 'tis in worse condition. Ay, the break will heal, but the beast will be too long pasture-bound to carry his master back to Rockaine, even by the year's end.'

Avran pulled a wry face. 'A sad disappointment for these folk of Dellorain.'

'Ay, 'tis so, but, that being how matters stand, there's no sense in repining.'

At that point, Felun emerged for a second time and beckoned to Avran and me. Surprised, we followed him into the pavilion.

It was very high and brightly lit by candles. On one of the several couches, a man lay wrapped in blankets; the injured knight, I thought. Beside him stood a group of richly dressed men and women, among them the wizard, the elderly man in red, and a taller, much older nobleman whose rich accoutrements marked him in no uncertain terms, I thought, as Lord of Dellorain. I bowed to him respectfully, and Avran followed suit. As we straightened, Vedlen Obiran spoke with a tone of urgency.

'My new friends, I know that you have many martial skills. Does it chance that either of you has any familiarity with the lance – any knowledge of jousting?'

We looked at one another. 'Not I,' Avran answered sadly. 'I have witnessed tournaments, but I have never ridden in one.' He would dearly have loved to respond otherwise, that I could see.

I hesitated, remembering my old life in England, my ventures at exercising with the old ashpole in that high field in Hallamshire. 'Well, I have a little knowledge of the art,' I stammered, 'but . . . but I cannot claim any great skill – any skill at all.'

The Lord of Dellorain's face looked worn and old, and his eyes were anxious, but he managed to smile at me. It was a gentle smile that made my heart warm to him.

'Are you willing to ride for me, then, as my champion?' he asked. 'I do not expect you to win, but it were better that my champion appear and be defeated than that Dellorain default on this contest.'

The red-robed man swelled indignantly. 'But this is ridiculous!' he spluttered. 'How can this unknown young man be our champion? He is too small to wear Sir Guy's armour. He would rattle about in it like a pea in a pot.

And what will he ride? The horse is lamed beyond mending – certainly beyond mending within two hours! The idea is absurd beyond comprehension.'

The Lord of Dellorain looked his way in stern reproof. 'This decision is mine and mine alone. Please remember that.'

At this reprimand, the man in the red cloak swallowed and fell silent, at which the Lord went on: 'As to the armour, why, there is the suit that was worn by the Prince, my son, when he was young. It will serve and can be fetched readily enough. And as to the mount . . .' He paused, uncertain.

'As to the mount, that is easily settled.' It was Vedlen Obiran who spoke now. 'The rules of the contest surely do not require that it be a horse?'

'I don't believe so,' said the Lord.

'My servant Drakht Belineg is a big man. His rafenu is amply strong enough to bear Simon in armour – if Simon proves willing to ride, that is. What is your decision, Simon? Will you serve as champion for the Lord of Dellorain?'

Again, I hesitated. For many years I had desired passionately to ride in a tourney, but I had not expected to be thrown so suddenly into a contest or to fight when so wholly out of practice. Nor had I even dreamed of riding in borrowed armour, on an unfamiliar mount, against a knight whose skill was undoubted. It was a daunting thing to attempt. However, I remembered the great debt that Avran and I owed to the wizard and his men. That sealed my decision. I would face the Lord of Dellorain.

'I am at your service, my lord.' The words rang out loud and resolute, infinitely more resolute than I felt.

The Lord nodded gravely. 'And I am in your debt,' he said solemnly. Then he turned to the others. 'The armour

ANTONY SWITHIN

must be fetched swiftly, and Simon's mount also. We have little time.' In a moment, the pavilion was all abustle.

The wizard's bright eyes turned on me. 'Good, Simon, good,' he said quietly. Then he chuckled. 'A joust of rafenu against horse! That will be something to remember. Consider your rafenu, Simon. Think of how you might best employ his special abilities to your advantage. For my part, I am by no means convinced that you need necessarily to experience defeat in this contest.'

171

CHAPTER 15

The Joust On The Bridge

With less than two hours remaining before noon, when the challenge from Brantwood would have to be either accepted or ignominiously declined, I had so much to do that there was little chance for pondering matters – or even for anxiety.

First of all, Drakht Belineg had to introduce me to his rafenu. This was a heavily striped male called Gahewen, 'broad-streak.' Remembering King Arthur's turbulent follower, I rechristened him 'Gawain.' He was doubtful of me at first, but we became friends quickly enough.

Watched by an uncomprehending crowd, one that was still unaware of my appointed role, I rode Gawain off into the forest and tried his paces. I was pleased to find that he was not merely obedient, but also quick and intelligent. Moreover, I knew that Drakht had ridden him in many fights. Gawain could be assumed to have an awareness of weapons that rafneyen without combat experience would lack.

When we returned, it was to find that the armour had been fetched not only for me but also for Gawain, since a rafenu could not wear a horse's accoutrements. The war armour of rafneyen is much like that worn by Sandastrian sevdreyen for battle. It comprises a cap of hammered steel, notched near the front to accommodate the nasal horns and closing about the bases of the brow horns. To protect the rafenu's chest and back, a coat of chain mail is provided, padded within and bearing a high metal saddle from which stirrups hang.

Gawain had never worn armour, and it took all of Drakht's cajoling before he would permit himself to be so accoutred. Even then he was most unhappy. He tossed his head, swayed his back, and heaved his flanks, so that the stirrups jangled against the chain mail, and he came close to bucking.

Wisely, Drakht decided to take Gawain off for a brief stint of exercise before the poor rafenu faced the added unfamiliarity of an armoured Simon as rider. Their emergence from the shadows of the pavilion provoked astonished comment from the people who watched.

While they were gone, it was my turn to be fitted. I put on a heavily padded gambeson which, when fastened, fitted my body snugly enough; then a padded hood was placed over my head. Next, they placed the hauberk of mail on me, and the heaume was set upon my head, to be fastened to the hauberk at front and back. Tournament gauntlets – the left bridle gauntlet heavy and stiff, the right one lighter and more flexible – were placed upon my hands, while greaves and sabatons, all of steel, were put on my legs and feet.

I felt almost overwhelmed by the weight of it all and wondered how I might manage ever to move, let alone ride. Moreover, although my vision was ample with the visor open, I was disconcerted by the narrowness of the slit through which I would have to look when the visor was closed. How could I watch and track an opponent properly, with such a restricted view?

I had been sitting while the greaves and sabatons were fitted. Urged to stand up, I did so with no small effort. Yet, having done so, I discovered that walking around was remarkably easy. The joints of the armour at elbows and knees were unexpectedly flexible, though I could not, of course, turn my head. Moreover, though the skirts of the hauberk were divided at front and back to permit sitting on a horse, I could not possibly mount unaided. I wondered what would happen if I were unseated.

However, when Avran showed me my reflection in a hand mirror, I was immediately comforted. I looked so splendid that I realized at that moment that a dream of my youth had come true. Though most of the armour was unadorned, the body of the hauberk had been lacquered scarlet, and the front of the heaume was adorned with a tiny shield, displaying the scarlet field with silver chevrons of Dellorain. The jousting shield I would soon be carrying was almost square in shape, but it curved inward at the base to be lodged on a horse's back and was notched at upper right to accommodate a lance. It bore the device of the French knight, a crowing scarlet cockerel that matched well with the colours of Dellorain. When Avran handed the shield to me, I beamed, gratified at my own martial image. Certainly, on the surface, I looked impressive enough to disconcert any opponent unaware of my lack of skill.

Unfortunately, when Drakht returned, his mount found my appearance even more alarming. Poor Gawain shied away, snorting with fear. And my soothing voice, issuing as it did from such a disconcerting source, failed entirely to comfort him. Only after much persuasion would he stand still, permitting me to be heaved up with a great effort by four sweating servants and set in the saddle.

After that, matters improved quickly. Gawain could sense my calming reassurances without being upset by the sight of me decked out in scarlet and silver, and I, for my own part, had to sustain the weight of the armour no longer. I took the shield and set it in place, then was handed the jousting lance. This I found hard to grasp in my metal-gauntleted hand, but it was less heavy than I had feared. By way of trial, I raised and lowered it, then flourished it – and promptly embedded it in the fabric of the pavilion, so that it was twitched from my hands and fell among the watching servants.

This accident amused them greatly, but they were courteous enough not to laugh aloud. One of them handed the lance back to me, and, holding it loosely before me, I emerged from the shadows of the pavilion into the sunlight.

By then, most people had wandered away to gaze over the river, examine stalls, or continue talking in low, dispirited voices. My unexpected appearance caused them to be startled at first. This was followed by cheers and a great deal of excitement.

Since it was not yet quite noon, there was time for another brief ride into the forest. The wizard had been right. Gawain was so strong that, even with the weight of the armour added to that of my small self, the burden was not overwhelming for him. As I rode along, I exercised with the lance, raising or lowering it, couching it or setting it upright, until the feel of it was more familiar. Then I tried a few mock charges at trees before turning and riding back reluctantly to the riverside.

By then the people were crowding about the skirts of the bridge, chattering like starlings on a cottage roof. At my reappearance, they raised a renewed cheer. They sounded so pleased and confident that I, knowing how inadequate a champion they had, felt quite embarrassed.

A platform had been raised by the bank. On it sat the Lord of Dellorain and his Lady, with Vedlen Obiran and the man in red, their chancellor. I rode over to this platform and raised my lance in salute, to receive smiles from three of them and a still-disapproving frown from the chancellor. Then I turned away and, with heart pounding, rode up onto the bridge.

The champion of Brantwood had, of course, seen an armoured figure riding on the riverside, but I did not know if he was aware that he had a new and different opponent. Though he must have seen the injured horse being brought back, he might well not know that the French knight himself was injured. He might well presume that his challenger had merely changed mounts. The fame of the French knight had been spread abroad, whereas I was a mere tyro, without renown, and that for good reason. Clearly it would help if Sir Brian were kept unaware that any substitution had taken place.

'Who are you that blocks zis bridge?' I asked, trying to imitate the accent proper to a Frenchman.

'I am Sir Brian Beauchamp,' he responded sturdily. 'I defend the right of my father, Earl of Brantwood and Lord of the Leafy Dales, to the proprietorship of all islands in this river between Brantwood and Dellorain. He who denies that proprietorship must contend with me.'

'Zat proprietorship I deny and zat right I challenge. Zose islands belong to ze Lord of Dellorain.' I wondered if I was overdoing the accent. I was beginning to sound pretty spurious, at least to my own ear.

'Zen . . . I mean, then' – his embarrassment evident, catching himself, he corrected his mimicry of my accent – 'you must joust with me. May he who wins claim those rights for his Lord henceforth and for ever.' Slipping off his right gauntlet, he flung it down on the bridge before me.

I knew I had to take up that gauntlet, but I dared not dismount. Fortunately, the problem had been anticipated. A soldier of Dellorain had followed me onto the bridge. He ran past me, picked up the gauntlet, and handed it to me. 'Ze challenge, it is accepted,' I said loudly. There was cheering on both banks, and I passed back the gauntlet to the soldier, who handed it to Sir Brian. Rather awkwardly, he slipped it back on – a feat I could not have managed unaided – and, turning his horse around, rode back to the Brantwood end of the bridge. Following his example, I turned back toward Dellorain, noting anew the lack of rails on the bridge and thinking gloomy thoughts, expecting I might soon be plunging into the waters beneath.

But I knew I needed to dispel such dark thoughts and be confident, so that Gawain in turn could gain confidence. Instead, with an attitude of determination, I made a mighty effort to think out manoeuvres for the joust and to instruct Gawain in his role. We were approaching the end of the bridge, and I knew we must turn. I braced myself for the sound of the bell that would be rung from Brantwood to signal the beginning of the joust. Sir Brian was couching his lance, and I knew I had to do the same.

The bell rang faint in the distance. A moment later, my opponent was riding swiftly towards me. At my mere thought, Gawain also was in full motion, moving even more swiftly, so that we had crossed the centre of the bridge before there was any coming-together.

Knight and horse seemed to be hurtling at us, as massive and implacable as a rock rolling down a hillside. Sir Brian was trying for the point stroke. Indeed, as I peered out from the slit in my helmet, his lance seemed to be coming right at my face with terrible swiftness.

As for me, I had no idea what I was trying for. I had never properly decided on this. By now I had time only to attempt a sweep of the lance. Whether I would have a chance to make any stroke at all was another question.

I crouched behind my shield and tried to sway away from that dreadful point – not that I needed to, for Gawain danced aside just at the right moment, swift as my thought. The lance-tip swung by me in an arc of brightness. My own lance, aimed so hastily, missed by a large margin. Then, we were past one another.

Sir Brian's impetus had carried him over the crown of the bridge. I could hear the sound of his horse's hooves scrabbling as he pulled on the reins and strove to turn around. For a moment, through my helmet-slit, I could see the bright tents and throngs of people on the Brantwood bank. No doubt they were shouting or cheering, but I did not hear them. Gawain had slowed and was already turning, as easily as if he were on a broad road. As it turned out, the small space posed no problem for him.

Again, I couched my lance, and again my mount and I were past the bridge centre before we met our opponent. Neither of us was moving so swiftly this time, and, with one encounter safely past, I was gaining confidence.

It was my turn to attempt the point stroke, but Sir Brian used his shield to divert my thrust. Despite Gawain's nimble sidestepping, the Brantwood knight's swinging lance came

178

so perilously close to my helmet that I felt the wind of its passing on my hot cheeks.

Down the bridge we went and turned around again, the Dellorain contingent cheering us wildly. Sir Brian had turned his mount more quickly this time, and we met right on the crown of the bridge. On this occasion I was wiser. I held my lance fairly loosely till the last moment, then clamped it tight and swung it at him. By then, his own lance-tip had skidded off my shield as Gawain danced aside with great agility. My swinging stroke cleared Sir Brian's shield, hit him in the middle of the chest, skidded up the plate armour, and then lodged under the gorget protecting his neck.

He was toppling backwards off his horse into the river, but I was in no better condition. Since my lance was still clamped to my body, I was thrown sideways and off balance. My feet were trapped firmly in the stirrups. I could not fall clear of Gawain, but was carrying him sideways with me.

My slit of a world view spun round. Frantically I leaned forward, somehow managing to clasp with my gauntlets his horn-bases and clinging to the high saddle with my knees as best as I could. The rafenu's hooves scrabbled for their grip on the wooden planks, then lost it. Then, with an enormous splash, Gawain and I fell helplessly down into the deepest channel of the bright-flowing Antoman.

It was, indeed, the very depth of the water that saved us. In a shallower river, by impact with the bottom, Gawain might well have broken a limb, and I might have been seriously injured. As it was, we plunged deep down, followed by a trail of bubbles, with Gawain's legs flailing and me gasping, as water flowed into my helmet. Somehow, in the plunge, Gawain righted himself. Up to the surface we bobbed, with him snorting and me spluttering. Then Gawain shook the water from his horns and, even as he transmitted calming confident thoughts to me, swam back to the Dellorain bank where the crowd was cheering in welcome.

''Tis a question to try the abilities of Solomon himself,' the Earl of Brantwood grumbled. He was a massive man, with fading blue eyes under knotted brows and a beard with the texture and colour of a Pennine sheep's fleece. 'Setting aside the question of the propriety of riding a rafenu in a tournament – a question that should have been argued ere the joust was begun and which, as you say, my Lord of Dellorain, was settled when our champions couched lances – I perceive no means for deciding who was victor. It may be true, as you claim, that your champion's lance upset my son from his mount, but then his mount, at least, remained on the bridge, while your champion and his rafenu, his mount, if you want to call it that, were both thrown into the river.'

'But then, Simon stayed in the saddle of his mount and rode it to the bank,' the Lord of Dellorain countered mildly. 'Your son had to be hauled out from the river mud and rescued by boat and then dried out ashore.'

'As to that, your champion's lance was broken, whereas my son's was not.'

'Broken or not, your son lost it, for he dropped it on the bridge. And he lost his shield as well, whereas Simon retained his.'

The Earl was purpling. 'But it was not your champion's skill that caused my son to drop his shield! He did so, sensibly, when he found himself in the water. And we recovered it without trouble.'

Sir Brian Beauchamp spoke up at this point. Having shed the concealment of his jousting helmet, he proved not nearly as formidable as I had imagined. He was a merry-eyed man of some twenty summers, with curling blond hair and a beard which, compared with that of his doughty father, seemed quite sparse.

'For my part, I consider myself defeated. My lance wrought no harm to Simon. It was his lance that sent us both into the river.'

His father would not yield to this argument. 'Yet was he an acceptable champion? He is not of Dellorain, but of the following of Messer Obiran here. Could he properly represent Dellorain anyway?'

The Lord of Dellorain was becoming annoyed. 'You put forward no objection when you thought a knight of Rockaine would represent me. And, if your son had emerged as winner of the joust, you would not now be crying "Unfair! Unfair!"'

We had crossed the river and were sitting around a table on the raised mound from which the Earl had watched the contest. A silent crowd of men and women from Dellorain and Brantwood stood about and below us, Avran and the wizard's men among them. The chancellor of Dellorain, more amicable now, together with Felun Daretseng, Sir Brian and myself, sat on one side – the north side-of the table. Facing us, their backs to the river, were the Earl of Brantwood and the Lord of Dellorain, with Vedlen Obiran seated between them. When flanked by the burliness of one and the tallness of the other, the wizard seemed smaller than ever. His ever-bright eyes flickered with amusement.

'Peace, peace!' he intoned. 'No one has won and no one has lost. The tourney showed your champions to be of equal ability and thus that your claims are of equal strength.'

'Then who owns the river islands henceforward?' the Earl demanded. 'Or must we bicker over them for years yet to come?'

'Not at all. Since your claims to them are of equivalent merit, it's quite evident that the islands belong both to Brantwood and to Dellorain. They must be conserved or fished at your joint will, by both your peoples. You must each nominate three men of wisdom to a council. That council must decide how the fishery should be administered and who should have rights in it. And those rights must be exactly equal. Do you both agree?'

The angry flush had faded from the cheeks of the Lord of Dellorain. 'That is acceptable to me. This quarrel has divided us for too many years.'

The Earl drummed his fingers on the table and glanced at his son. Then he rumbled, 'So be it. As you say, we have disputed long enough.'

At these words, there was frantic cheering from the listening crowd. The Earl waited till it had subsided, then went on. 'As for me' – a slow smile gave unexpected lightness to his heavy features – 'I never did care much for fish, anyway!'

There was laughter at this. The Earl slumped backward in his chair, his eyes roving, searching our faces. Again, he smiled. 'And this night ye shall all dine with my son and me at our castle of Brantley – the folk of Dellorain, Messer Obiran's men, and all.'

At this, the cheering was even more resounding, since, as we learned later, the Earl was renowned for the lavishness of his hospitality. So it was that, amidst a joyful crowd of men and women, after retrieving our rafneyen from the Dellorain bank, we made our way north through the forest to Brantley.

It was, to my eyes, a rather old-fashioned fortress, a simple motte-and-bailey encircled by a moat formed by diverting a tributary of the Antoman. Within the bailey were many small houses and, in the shadow of the keep, a spacious banqueting hall. There we dined, while musicians played their instruments – cittern, rebec, psaltery, and pommer – from a gallery above. Predictably, no fish was served.

Avran, Sir Brian, and I fast became friends, for the merry spirits of the Earl's son made him a most agreeable companion. At one point in our cheerful talk, Sir Brian eyed me curiously: 'Simon, why did you speak so strangely when you challenged me? Was the helmet distorting your voice?'

Reddening with embarrassment, I admitted: 'I was trying to sound like a Frenchman. I thought you might mistake me for the knight of Rockaine and perhaps fear me more.'

He laughed heartily. 'It was a vain device, Simon. I have seen that knight fighting in tournaments in the Deerlands. He is a much bigger man than you, and burlier. Not only that, but he does not speak in that way at all.'

Avran also broke out into a laugh. 'Well, it was a brave try, Simon my friend. And you rode bravely too. Indeed, when I remember that this was your first tournament, I marvel.'

Sir Brian had raised his ale to his lips, but at this he set it down so suddenly that the froth splashed out. 'Say not so! His first tourney? Why, from those skilled evasions of my lance, I had thought him a veteran of many contests!'

I was blushing again. 'It was my rafenu that was skilled, not I. Without him, I would have been unseated at the first joust.'

'Well, well!' Sir Brian said, marvelling. 'Though I do not accept your renunciation of all credit for your victory

– and you did in fact gain the victory, whatever my father and Messer Obiran might claim – I must believe also that your rafenu aided you. We ride rafneyen when hunting, of course, but never at tournaments. Yet horses are few here, and they're costly to buy and keep. It is time that we altered our ideas.'

He paused reflectively, then went on: 'Perhaps you have done more than fight in a tournament, Simon. Perhaps you have given a fresh twist to our games of war.'

CHAPTER 16

A Chart Is Rolled Up

Choleric though he had seemed at our first meeting, the Earl of Brantwood proved a large-hearted and generous host. So pressing and insistent was his hospitality that the wizard and his men, along with Avran and me, stayed at the castle of Brantley, not just for one night but for a whole sennight.

For Avran and me, it was a time of relaxation and recuperation, physical and emotional, from the strains of a journey that – hard as it was to believe – had only taken two months. It was strange to think that so much incident and so many perils had been packed into so short a time. I remembered my tranquil years in Hallamshire, not with real regret but rather with a vague nostalgia, as one recalls a peaceful dream upon awakening to a bright day of hard work.

The Lord of Dellorain and his Lady departed on the first morning, on the last day of Devbalet, the month we call February. They had wished to reward me handsomely for acting as Dellorain's champion. However, I would accept nothing from them, since I had fought in the tourney, not from any desire to serve Dellorain, but to pay off in part the debt that Avran and I owed to Vedlen Obiran. Though I tried hard to explain this, the Lord continued to protest his indebtedness to me with such vigour that I was relieved by his departure.

Indeed, even had I been willing to accept some gift, there was nothing they could have given me that I wanted. My only desire was to complete my quest swiftly and return to Sandarro and Ilven.

During those days in Brantwood, Avran and I learned much about the strange world of the forests and surrounding plains. It had been more than three hundred years at the very least, we gathered, since men fleeing from the wars or the laws of Europe had begun to arrive in Rockall. They had found the mountains of the north and east and the plains and hills of the south to be already quite densely inhabited and divided into many republics and princedoms. In contrast, the central lands of Rockall were almost empty. It was true that there had been a handful of people living in the grasslands east and north of the great forests, most of them fugitives from neighbouring realms, but these people had either welcomed, or else failed successfully to resist, the newcomers.

New realms had arisen amid those grasslands, often with Rockalese names but always with European rulers. Predominantly these were men of English birth or descent, like the self-styled Kings of Herador, Devoria, Tarnevost, and Merania and the Earls of Felessett, Bayansavar and Odunseth. England had been torn with fratricidal strife during those centuries, and many men had found it easier to leave their homeland than to disentangle the knots of conflicting loyalties.

However, numerous Frenchmen and Gascons had likewise come to Rockall, for their lands had been war-torn as well. Most of the Gascons had found new homes among the

English settlers. Yet they had also set up two independent realms, Rockaine and Haviland, in the foothills northwest of the plains. The Frenchmen had founded two realms. One of these, Delisle, lay in hills southwest of the forests. The other lay on the shores of the great bight north of Dedesta. It was centred upon the port of Saint Lorraine and named Bayard, after the great hero of chivalric legend.

In the winter of 1307-1308, a great party of Knights Templars had arrived, fleeing with their retinues and such wealth as they had saved from their greed-ridden, murderous betrayal by King Philip IV of France and his tame Pope at Avignon. Received sympathetically by the earlier settlers, the Templars had been permitted to settle in the last unoccupied area of grassland remaining between the forests and the northern mountains. The Gascon knights of Rockaine and Haviland were their neighbours to the south and the Reschorese to the north.

The lands allotted to the Templars were not very good, for by the early fourteenth century all the better areas, whether for grazing or the planting of crops, had been taken. Though new arrivals continued to be welcomed in some of the grassland realms, they were received less enthusiastically in others. Men came soon to regard a new land as theirs by right and become jealous of any whom they think might try to claim it. Moreover, among the descendants of earlier settlers there were many men of small fortune but high ambition, eager to set up fiefdoms of their own. Given that the grasslands were filling, hope arose that there might be room still to be found among the great forests.

About these, the native Rockalese seemed to know little but told uneasy stories – of haunted groves and poisoned rivers; of fell beasts and fearful ailments; of fairies and giants, goblins, and green men. The tales were so ominously recounted that the Frenchmen and Gascons had been wholly unwilling, and even the rasher Englishmen long reluctant, to venture into those endless-seeming forests.

However, when men did begin to make their explorations, they discovered that the stories had as little substance as those told around English firesides in winter. There were fell beasts, certainly, but none worse than might be encountered among the grasslands – no dragons, no cockatrices. It's true that some adventurers did disappear forever among the trees, but many more returned without having encountered excessive perils. And so, at first slowly, but then more swiftly, men began setting up homesteads and carving out new demesnes among the forest glades.

At the outset, they followed the practices of England, practices that had worked well enough in the plains, except where the land was too dry. They had cut down trees and cleared fields for their crops or had sought streamside meadows where their cattle might graze. However, such procedures were quickly abandoned. It was easier to harvest the forests than to plant and tend corn, oats, or barley, in a land where serfs were unknown and freemen reluctant to labour in the unremitting fashion that their ancestors had done. It was easier to keep hasedain, which would browse happily among the trees and underbrush, than to tend cows that seemed always to remain lean and sickly, however luxuriant the meadow grasses. Horses bred poorly and needed more attention here than in England, if they were to stay healthy. Moreover, they were hard to train. It was better to keep them for tournaments and, for the day-to-day activities of work or hunting, easier to ride instead the forest-loving, quicker-witted rafneyen.

Yet, however their mode of working their demesnes might be altered, the social practices of the settlers changed little. The tiny realms of the forestlands were mirrors in miniature of the greater realms of England and France. The little courts of the forest earls strove to emulate the greater courts of King Henry and King Charles. However, ships from France and England were not frequent, and their crews not likely to be well-informed concerning current court fashions and attitudes. Moreover, such tidings as they did in fact bring were altered or delayed, as they passed from mouth to mouth, from the ports of Saint Lorraine or Warringtown through the forest realms to these farthest and southernmost reaches of settlement.

In consequence, everything here was, in European terms, somewhat outdated. The houppelande, hennin, and pourpoint were unknown. Ladies wore the sleeveless surcoats and the crespines or pork-pie coifs fashionable in English courts of earlier times, while men still wore parti-coloured cote-hardies and hoods with long liripipes. The suits of mail worn by Sir Brian and me had seemed impressive enough to the watching crowds, for plate armour was rarely seen here in Rockall. But an English armourer would have scoffed at our mail, pointing out a number of faults in construction. That my lance, for example, had caught under the gorget protecting Sir Brian's neck was condemnation enough. In any decently constructed suit of armour, such a mishap would be impossible. Meanwhile, falconry was as popular here as in England, but the very hoods and jesses for the hawks were of an ancient style. All in all, to anyone from England, travelling in the great forests was like walking backward through the years.

However, I was not inclined either to criticize or to try to inculcate new ideas among the gentlemen and ladies of the court of the Earl of Brantwood. This was in part because it would not have been good manners, but largely because I found it curiously restful to be in such a tranquil backwater in the stream of Time. Sandastre had been an utterly different realm, a place where all things were new and there had been so much to learn every day. Here, everything was familiar, if a little antique. I enjoyed my stay at Brantley very much.

A factor in my enjoyment was the cheerful company of young Sir Brian. Both Avran and I found in him a companion very much to our liking. He was greatly taken by this new idea of riding rafneyen in tournaments. We were cajoled into exercising with him every day, riding mounts swathed in padded cloth and using light wooden lances. The greater intelligence of a rafenu in comprehending the wishes of his rider and evading the onslaught of an opponent was patent.

Sir Brian marvelled in retrospect that our encounter had been the first of its kind. He would beam with pleasure. 'Quite a historic joust!' he would exclaim, then go on. 'A privilege for me to take part in it. My word, how I'll run rings round my opponents in the Deerlands tournament this summer! Well, let's try it again. I think I'll have you this time, Simon.'

Neither buffets nor falls deterred him. And he suffered many during those early contests. If an unexpected flick of his lance set me swaying in my saddle, he would crow with delight. However, in contests with Avran, a skilled rider but quite without knowledge of jousting, Sir Brian would be always charmingly apologetic in victory. And always he remained merry in defeat.

With this game, as well as other martial pastimes, we passed our mornings and enhanced our skills. There were rides in the forest too, and races along narrow streamside meadows in which Galahad outmatched Lancelot and Sir Brian's mounts. Sometimes we went out with falcons at wrist, though the sport was poor so early in the year. Also, I was able, in a little chapel in the shadows of the castle walls, to express my thanks to God for bringing Avran and me safely through so many perils and to pray for a swift completion of my quest. All in all, that was a cheerful time.

The wizard we saw only rarely. Here in the castle, the duties of his men were few. Though Vedlen Obiran made himself daily available to treat the sick and injured of Brantwood and its forest glades, this did not occupy many of his hours, for the people of the Earldom were few and healthy. The Ravatseng brothers were his chosen assistants as he dispensed medical treatment, and Felun Daretseng was his preferred companion at other times. The remaining Reschorese found friends among the castle servants, as well as activities to occupy and divert them.

'Here, let a *real* man tackle that!' Amos Sloly could often be heard in the yards and kitchens, as he lent his aid to some task with the aim of displaying his own superior prowess.

On the fourth day, the wizard requested that Avran and I be brought to his room. This was a comfortable chamber above the banqueting hall to which little sound penetrated, with a large window through whose thin parchment panes the day-to-day activities of the castle could be watched unaware. We found him seated at a table and, at his gesture, sat down on the bench at its further side.

Rising from his seat, he unrolled a parchment and spread it before us.

'Come, look closer,' he said.

Avran and I rose from the bench to examine it. At first glance, it seemed only to depict a massive and elaborate letter U, such as one might see beginning a chapter in some monastery bible. However, when he turned the parchment onto its side so that the U opened toward the right, I perceived it was a chart. The hills were drawn in brown ink, the trees in green, and also in green was a vein-like pattern that I realized must represent rivers and coasts. Upon this chart many words had been written in black, the lettering in an angular alphabet unfamiliar to me. Avran did not comprehend it either. Nevertheless, both of us realized, even before Vedlen Obiran told us it was the case, that we were looking at a map of the forestlands and the realms around them.

'I have not attempted this before,' he went on, 'and I know that my attempt is both crude and inaccurate. However, if indeed we are to find Lyonesse for you, such a chart may aid us a little. Now, the lands of the Montariotans are here' – he indicated the lower side of the U – 'and Brantwood and Dellorain are here.' He pointed at a spot in the forests near the lowest curve of its base. 'Just east of us is Alberbrend' – he pointed again – 'and beyond again is a large area of dense forest which I believe to be still unsettled – here, between Alberbrend and Antomalata. If in fact Lyonesse is to be found in the forests, then it must be in this region, for it is certainly in no other.'

'You mean here?' I traced the area with my finger.

'Yes, just so.'

'How can we find out if Lyonesse is there?' I asked politely. I did not consider the prospect at all hopeful. The area he had indicated was much too far from the sea.

As happened so often, the wizard seemed to catch my thought. 'No, I do not believe it probable either, Simon.

That region has a strange reputation, and only exceptionally brave men would venture into it. Of course, your father and his predecessors in Rockall may have been valiant enough to do so, but I believe I would have heard tell of any such adventurings. The good thing is that we shall ride soon to the castle of Skarngrove in Alberbrend. That way, we can settle the question beyond doubt '

He paused and considered the map anew, before going on: 'If that particular search proves profitless, as we anticipate, then we must travel on northward. Even I do not choose to venture needlessly into those forest heartlands. Now, there are little-inhabited highlands just beyond the forests and above the Great Marshes that surround the mouth of the Aramassa.' He pointed this time to the upper left curve of the U. 'There, a new realm may have arisen; we can try that chance. Here to the north and east of the forests,' – he indicated the centre of the upper stroke of the U – 'realms rise and fade like storms in summer. However, those realms are products of quarrels over old boundaries, not new settlements. I doubt that prospect, although it should also be enquired into.'

He paused again, then said pensively: 'If those chances fail, then you must seek either in the eastern mountains, where the folk are fierce and strange' – he placed his finger on the furthest upper right of the U – 'or in the mountains of the north. Concerning those eastern mountains, I have learned a little during my travels, enough to think them an improbable, though not an impossible, location for Lyonesse. After all, they have long coasts.'

'Yet you believe those highlands above the Aramassa marshes to be more likely?' Avran was asking.

'It is a possibility to be explored. Yet it is not, I think, a strong one. However, that can be checked by only a small detour from our northward path.'

'But what of the northern mountains?'

'What indeed? Those mountains also have long coasts. My own land of Reschora lies here.' He set his finger at a position above the curve of the U. 'As you see, my chart depicts only a small part – the southernmost edge – of the northern mountains, for I have not travelled further. Yet, at least I can assure you that Lyonesse is not to be found among the southern ridges and valleys. Those realms and territories are all familiar to me, by name at least, and all are ancient. If Lyonesse be among those mountains, then it must lie much further to the north.'

He fell silent, and, for many minutes, Avran and I contemplated the chart with equal silence, striving to memorize its shape and to decipher its strange glyphs.

Abruptly the wizard sat back. In the thin light of the parchment window, his eyes seemed yellow. They were glinting with wry amusement. 'Hard to read, is it not? Well, both of you will have to make an effort to learn Reschorese speech and characters.'

With a quick twist, he rolled up the chart. 'We will ask in Alberbrend, but I expect little from that asking. Whatever your hopes, Simon, I fear your journeyings are far from their end.'

Then the wizard paused, eyeing us gravely. 'Yet I find other foreshadowings in my thoughts. I believe that our meeting happened not by mere hazard, but by design, and that our journeyings together were predestined, so as to achieve some end yet unknown to us. Moreover, these present journeyings will prove only a small part of that design, a small weaving-in of only a detail of the tapestry. In that tapestry, Simon and Avran, you are to prove important threads – perhaps even crucial in shaping its pattern. Well, we shall see, we shall see.' Then, with a peremptory impatience, turning his gaze from us, he waved us away and slipped again into his reverie.

As we left the chamber, its brightness was dimmed as clouds spread across the sun – clouds that seemed to me symbolic of troubles to come.

Though Avran remained the perennially cheerful traveller, I came away feeling quite daunted. The prospect of playing some large role in future events did not cheer me, for I was without large ambitions. So, there would be no quick end to my quests. It seemed that our travels were only just begun. For me, there was small comfort to be found in Vedlen Obiran's words.

CHAPTER 17

The Castle Of Chancelet

Of our visit to Alberbrend there is little to tell. Predictably, it was quite as brief as it was profitless. The Earl was away in his southern castle of Everbrend, and the castellan of Skarngrove was as reluctant to receive us as the Earl of Brantwood had been hospitable. The castellan was an elderly knight, thin and nervous, of the clerkly sort that executes decisions effectively enough, but is almost incapable of making them. After Vedlen Obrian, Avran, and I had consumed a meagre repast that had been grudgingly offered to us, he was persuaded to answer our question only because the magician was persistent.

'No, of course not; there have been no venturings into the deep forests. Why should men go there? Ridiculous idea. Much too dangerous. Trees too dense to pass. All sorts of evil beings – dragons, giants, witches, wizards – ' He paled and paused, then corrected himself, embarrassed. 'Evil wizards, I mean, present company excepted, of course. Absurd idea. Waste of time your seeking further . . . no need to stay and await my Lord's return. The Earl would only tell you the same thing as I'm telling you. There are no settlements, new or old, in those lands.'

And so, we turned north, passing from Alberbrend into The Deerlands. This was the largest of the forest earldoms and a very pleasant place. There were light sandy soils underfoot and many sunny spaces amid the trees, in which farms and little settlements seemed scattered as randomly as if they had grown from seeds blown from a dandelion-clock.

We were not heading directly northwards. Instead, we were following a meandering route that took in as many of these farms and hamlets as possible. Wherever we encountered people, we were welcomed and treated generously. However, there were several nights when we pitched tent in a glade far from any habitation.

As we travelled, Avran and I learned much. The Reschorese tongue proved little different from Sandastrian in essentials, though there were bewildering shifts of meaning – in Sandastrian, for example, *ushaz* means 'to condemn' and in Reschorese 'to praise' – and a whole range of unfamiliar words, for some of which we could not even find equivalences. The northern alphabet proved easy. Once we realized that the circles and curves of Sandastrian letters became squares and angles in the northern script, the letters were readily understood and mastered. Our progress was so rapid that, within a fortnight, both of us could read the place-names on the wizard's chart and take part, even though haltingly, in the conversations of our companions.

We found that, whereas the names of Sandastrian vardai are so ancient that they have no known meaning, the surnames of Reschorese families can be readily interpreted. The suffix 'eng' means simply 'man of.' Thus the Ravatsengs were men from Ravatar, and Felun Daretseng was from Dareten, both being valleys amid the southern hills of Reschora. Similarly, Narel Evateng was named from Evatel, a valley somewhere in its northern mountains, though it was long since his family had moved southward. 'Belineg' meant 'blacksmith,' while 'obiran' was the title given to the governor of a fortress. ('Seneschal' or 'castellan' are its nearest English equivalents, but they are not exact).

We learned also something of the arts of the physician and chirurgeon. Even in the smallest and remotest habitations, there seemed always to be someone requiring Vedlen Obiran's skills. As I have mentioned, the two Ravatseng brothers were his principal assistants, Delhir having a special delicacy of touch in bonesetting. Narel Evateng was responsible for the drying of herbs and the mixing of potions. The strange eyes and brusque manner of the wizard himself aroused awe and fear among those whom he treated, especially the women and children. Amos Sloly was of principal value because his cheerfulness and robust self-confidence were calming and reassuring. As for Avran and me, we looked on or else rendered aid only when required, even as we observed and we remembered.

Vedlen Obiran seemed never to expect recompense for the medicaments and treatments he provided, except in food, wine, or the small services of hospitality. Remembering the high charges extorted by quacksalvers at English fairgrounds, I was both surprised and impressed by this. In a spirit of genuine puzzlement, I asked Felun Daretseng how his master could contrive to live and maintain his men on such meagre profits. He hesitated before responding.

'Well, it's not easy to explain. In Reschora, there is a special caste of – what shall I call them? – alchemists, magicians, physicians – call them what you will. The Trident Mountains in the south of our land, and the valleys in their shadow, are a strange region, with strange earths from which one can prepare potions for healing or enchantment.

The people living there are strange as well, with abilities and skills quite out of the common. It is said that all the men are warlocks and all the women witches. Though I do not truly believe that, the saying is near enough right to be hard to dismiss. Many men from those mountains become travellers. It is their tradition that they must serve all people under God, whether barbarian nomads in tents or Christian kings in palaces. From the poor, no payment is exacted for services of healing. Indeed, even the rich are treated without any fees being demanded, though payment is accepted, gladly enough, if offered.'

'It sounds very noble and admirable,' I responded thoughtfully. 'Yet it must be an exhausting life, with no guarantee of adequate recompense. Such men must truly be saints.'

Felun smiled at this. 'Well, some of them are and some aren't. It is true that some of the Trident physicians travel far and undergo much hardship, in order to serve the needy. Our master is one of them. Much though he may enjoy his small luxuries, most certainly he earns them!'

'Yes, indeed,' I put in sincerely.

Felun smiled again at my earnestness, then went on reflectively: 'Unfortunately, there are others who journey only as far as the nearest mansion of a rich noble who fancies a personal physician or enchanter. For them, the risks are few and the comforts and rewards are many. When the rich require services in astromancy, necromancy, or any form of divination, in the breaking of seals or the setting of spells, a sizeable payment is always exacted. Even our master charges considerably for such tasks, but he performs them only rarely and reluctantly. Some of his fellow wizards are much less scrupulous, I fear.'

'I do not think I would like to encounter an unscrupulous magician,' I observed. Then, as my thoughts veered, I asked: 'Does our master return often to Reschora? Does he have a home there, and children perhaps?'

Felun's brow darkened. 'He had a wife whom he loved and a son who was precious to him, but they were murdered and his home was burned. Even though we Reschorese had no hand in that crime, the memory of it prevents him from returning to our land. Ask me no more. It is a story not for my telling.'

It was on the third day after leaving Alberbrend that we met with our next adventure. We were emerging from an area of thick forest into a clearing, with the wizard trailing behind as usual, when a cry of warning from Naral Evateng and a thrill of alarm from Galahad jolted me out of a daydream of Ilven. I glanced ahead and saw a huge brown creature, charging obliquely towards us with the ferocious pace of an angry bull.

At first, I perceived only its size and its speed, but then I noticed other details. It was much bigger than any bull and had only a single, huge Y-shaped horn on the front of its nose, lowered now to impale any unfortunate victim. I could see its ears, flattened against its short neck, and the red gleam of fury from little piggy eyes.

'A kalvak!' I heard Felun say in surprise. Then 'Ware kalvak!' he shouted, as his rafenu leapt from its path.

Fortunately, Galahad jumped aside equally nimbly. As the creature thundered by, I saw the massiveness of its shoulders and haunches, noticed its absurd little tail, held stiffly like an angry bull's, and heard the stertorous pants of its heavy breathing.

The pack-rafneyen were scattering, but one of the two bearing the tent-poles could not move fast enough. It screamed as a prong of that great horn slashed its haunches, then fell sideways, bringing its companion down as well.

Swift running by the rafneyen of the three Ravatsengs carried them well clear of the charging beast, but Amos Sloly was less fortunate. He had barely emerged into the glade and, taken unaware when his rafenu jumped aside, he was swept from its back by a low tree-branch. He yelped in fright and began burrowing into the foliage of a dense thorn bush with the scampering swiftness of a mole.

My heart pounded in alarm, for I thought the creature would surely turn on Amos, but it did not. Its attention was directed elsewhere. Just at that dangerous moment, the rafenu of Vedlen Obiran had emerged from the thicket.

It was evident that the wizard had not heard Felun's shout, nor had he seen the kalvak. More astonishingly, his rafenu did not seem conscious of danger either. The great beast was almost upon them before either rafenu or rider appeared to notice it. Even then, instead of leaping aside, the wizard's rafenu stood stock still.

My heart was thumping with a renewed and even greater apprehension. I had acquired a deep respect for Vedlen Obiran and now, it seemed, I was about to witness his obliteration. Yet no such thing happened. Quite casually, the wizard reached down to his saddle. There was a flick of his fingers, then of his wrists, and suddenly a ball of fiery green flame was hurtling at the kalvak.

The creature gave a mighty snort of astonishment and fear. It threw back its head and stopped, dropping its hindquarters and driving its great hooves so deeply into the turf that, afterward, one could see deep gouge-marks. As the ball of bright flame hit and burned its shoulders, the kalvak gave a convulsive leap and bray of pain. Then, with tail down, it thundered away into the forest.

Its path took the kalvak past the unfortunate Amos. Convinced that his last moment had come, he yelled in renewed fright and dived deeper among the thorns.

When the beast had gone and we gathered around him, Amos had to be pulled backward out of his uncomfortable refuge. The poor man's clothes, hair, and skin – his hands in particular – were so beset with prickles that we had all to lend a hand and pull them out.

Amos endured this passively, while Rahir rubbed his skin with soothing lotion, earning his gratitude. Yet, when Drakht Belineg rumbled, in tones very like Amos's, 'Why, let a *real* man tackle that thornbush!', the look that Amos shot him was not one of affection. Nonetheless, the imitation set the rest of us laughing.

The injured pack-rafenu had suffered less severely than we had feared, nothing worse than a gouge across its hindquarters and a strain of the muscles of its left hind leg in its fall. However, its load had to be removed, and those of the other pack-rafeneyen were adjusted in such a way as to free one of them to share the burden of the poles. The injured animal's leg and wound were then bound up by Hebehir under careful instruction from the wizard. Soon it was limping along cheerfully enough. All in all, more than two hours went by before our journey was resumed. As we rode, I reflected that the wizard, though he might trail behind us, was not quite so vulnerable as he might at first glance appear.

It was on the eighth afternoon that we reached Chancelet, a little town huddled around the banks of a narrow, swift-flowing river. The cottages, with their whitewashed walls and thatched roofs, looked very English, and the castle keep, on the great grass-covered motte behind and above them, was as tall, and with the same six buttresses, as that of Conisborough, a castle close to my Hallamshire home. Furthermore, like Conisborough Castle, it was built of white limestone. All the same, it was not of Conisborough that I thought as we rode into Chancelet, but of the great white castle of Sandarro, where I longed to be.

'Why, this river is flowing east, not west!' I commented with astonishment, as we rode over an arching bridge into town.

'You're right,' said Avran with no less surprise. 'And it's flowing fast, at that.'

Felun turned in his saddle and smiled at us. 'Indeed, that's the case. These are the headwaters of the Dainflete. If you were to follow its course, you would traverse the forest earldoms of Marcanlon and Dakalet and enter tidal waters where the river divides Seretta from Bayard. However, it would be a journey of many days.'

The little town proved quite as friendly a place as it had looked to me at first sight. The arrival of the wizard aroused pleasure and excitement, for he was a familiar and welcome visitor. It was only after many greetings and much merry chatter that we were allowed to pass up into the castle. The soldiers guarding its gate admitted us without hesitation.

Noting their surcoats – scarlet above, green below, and bearing the device of a running rafenu in brown – I winced a little and reflected that, in their passage across the water from England, the rules of heraldry must have suffered a sea-change. No English herald or king of arms would permit colour on colour. It would be considered an abomination.

Here there was no separate banqueting hall, only a high hall within the keep. However, bright with banners, it was a cheerful place, since the Earl of the March of the Deerlands – for that's how he styled himself – was as merry and benign as his people. He was a little, roly-poly man with short grey curls and a bristling fringe of beard, putting me in mind somehow of the tales of Old King Cole. I was quite gratified when I learned that his family name was in fact Colefax. His countess, in contrast, was quite tall and thin, graver than her husband, but with a twinkle of affection in her eye whenever she looked his way. There were six sons and three daughters, all of whom had happily avoided the physical extremes of their parents.

Though Avran and I made no friends as close as Sir Brian had been, our stay in Chancelet was to be almost as pleasant as that at Brantley, and quite as long. For us, at least, it was pleasant, but it was a demanding time for Vedlen Obiran. An elderly family retainer was in great pain after a fall from one of the keep's stone staircases. Even after Delhir Ravatseng had reset the woman's bones with care and skill, several days, many potions, and much attention were necessary before she was on the road to recovery.

Avran and I were not needed, nor was Felun Daretseng much in demand, which meant that we were able to receive many further lessons from him in the Reschorese language, letters, and customs. In between times, I would sit under a tree by the lowest slopes of the castle motte, strumming a cittern borrowed from a friendly court musician. Meanwhile, Avran did his best to master the fingering of a pommer bought in Chancelet market. Progressively, the early squeaks and breathy sounds gave place to more pleasing musical notes as the days passed.

I did not feel any impatience to be on the road, as I was beginning to lose confidence that we would ever find Lyonesse and had no eagerness for further perils and adventures. Even Avran was happy to relax for a while, taking pleasure in his growing mastery of Reschorese and also of his new instrument. Moreover, two of the Earl's daughters were casting amorous eyes his way and seemed always to find occasion for seeking his company. However, although he enjoyed their attentions and was always courteous in his responses, Avran showed no sign of succumbing to their blandishments.

The Countess of the Deerlands was, it seemed, a fervent believer in Vedlen Obiran's abilities when it came to divination. Repeatedly she implored him to predict for her what lay in the future for her family, her court, and herself. At first, concerned with their servant's condition, he was disinclined to oblige her. Only on the sixth evening did he yield to her continuing importunities, and, even then, he insisted that his services should also be made available to anyone else in Chancelet who sought them.

After an early dinner, eaten in haste, the courtiers and servants were sent out and the Earl's family was persuaded to retreat to their quarters. Within the great hall of the keep, a pavilion of purple cloth, open at one end, was set up, and other careful preparations made by his men, together with our help.

When the people were invited to return, everything had been arranged so as to impress them and, indeed, awe them. The lights in the hall had been dimmed, save only those above the gallery where the court musicians sat, and the fire had been put out. All attention was thus focussed upon Vedlen Obiran.

Around the pavilion there had been ranged four of the tall Mentonese candles, each contained in a slim lantern of crimson grass that altered their blue flames to bright purple. Within the pavilion sat the wizard, clad in his gold-embroidered tunic. He seemed still, and yet there was a shimmering aspect to him, like that of some strange ornament from the Saracen lands. Before him, on a little platform, was a broad, shallow copper dish, arched over by a sort of cupola of glass that was patterned and supported by a tracery of silver wires. The dish was filled to the very brim with water. In the water, there floated seven candles, each of a different hue and each burning with a flame of its particular hue. All the colours of the rainbow were there – red, saffron, yellow, green, blue, indigo and violet – and the flickering of the flames spilled many-coloured shadows on the stone flags.

Though Vedlen Obiran would never foretell the futures of any of his men – a policy loudly bemoaned by Amos Sloly – we were all permitted to join the throng in the great hall and witness the proceedings. In the gallery above, the musicians played. They played music that was solemn and slow, and that added to our tension. Not only that, but it kept us from hearing the requests of those who had come to seek the magician's prognostications, not to mention his responses. Nonetheless, we found it quite entertaining to watch the approach of each petitioner and to guess, from his or her expression, whether the forecast had been for good or ill.

It was mostly the ladies of Chancelet who were anxious to know their future. Three of the male courtiers and a handful of tradesmen also ventured up to the purple pavilion. But the other men, knowing all too well the hazards of a life filled with contests and combat, had no desire to learn how brief or how long their span of time on earth might be.

Usually, therefore, it would be a woman who approached. She would hand to Hebehir Ravatseng, who served as treasurer, the coins of gold or silver charged for the augury. Then she would walk with faltering step toward the wizard's seat, excitement and trepidation in her eyes.

There was a low bench placed just beyond the great copper dish. The woman would sit on that bench, her back to the hall and her eyes looking into the wizard's across the flames. He would ask her name and invite specific questions, then gaze silently at her for a while. Under the purple shade of the pavilion and in the flicker of the flames, his own eyes seemed sometimes black, sometimes golden, always as inhuman as a lizard's.

Abruptly he would reach into a coffer beside him and pick out a little coloured ball of some light material. It had the appearance of a bubble of wax, but I could not be sure. With a strangely casual gesture, he would toss the ball into the midst of the bright flames of the floating candles. Sometimes it would fall into the water between them, shining in their glow. This, it seemed, was a good omen, a promise of long life at least, though the woman's fortune would depend upon the colour of the candles to which it floated closest. Long life does not always bring other blessings.

More often, the ball would be caught in the up-draught over the flames and would bob up and down under the glass cupola for a longer or a shorter time until, eventually, in a puff of flame, it would vanish. The length of time in which it bobbed up and down reflected, we surmised, the likely span of life foretold for the petitioner, while its position among the flames foretold her fortune during that life. More than that, none of us could determine.

Before approaching the wizard, one of the earl's daughters threw such a bold glance at Avran that I guessed what her petition would be. The ball that Vedlen cast for her settled safely in the water close to the blue candle. However, by the clear look of annoyance she had on her face after returning, I knew that her hope of wedlock to my friend had been pronounced a vain one.

When the Countess herself stepped forward, the little ball did not have a long life above the flames. Yet she returned with such a composed bearing that the predictions must have been gratifying in other ways. Judging from their expressions, the fortunes of other petitioners were variable. However, once a ball went right into the green flame and vanished instantly. At this, the wizard covered his eyes, and his suppliant, the town carpenter, staggered away stricken. Just before we left Chancelet, we learned he had been killed by the collapse of the roof-arch of a house he was helping to build.

As the evening wore on and the line of petitioners dwindled, the number of people who were watching also dwindled. Husbands departed with wives who needed words of congratulation or consolation, while children were put to sleep, and the elderly sought their beds.

It was as the divinations were nearing their end that I noticed a stranger entering the hall. He remained so deeply in the shadows that I could not see him clearly. Only when the last trembling petitioner had departed and the musicians had ceased playing did the stranger emerge into view. He was a lean man of middle height, clad in brown leather and with a curl of grey beard, but with eyes as blue as Avran's. He tossed a gold coin to Hebehir, walked briskly up to the bench, and sat himself down on it.

'Prophesy for me, wizard,' he demanded, in ringing tones that carried clearly across the quiet hall. 'Is it to be in sack or in malmsey that we drink to celebrate our reunion?'

Vedlen Obiran leapt to his feet, put out the candle-flames with a sweep of his arm, and seized the stranger in a delighted embrace.

'Robin Randwulf, my old companion!' he cried. 'Met again, after so many years! This is truly a cause for celebration. My Lord of the Deerlands, may I crave the boon of your hospitality for my friend?'

CHAPTER 18

Out Of The Forests

Amid the bustle that followed the granting of Vedlen Obiran's request, I wondered with amusement how reliable the wizard's predictions were, when he could himself be so deeply surprised by a friend's coming. While the wine was being fetched, I voiced this thought to Rahir Ravatseng. I did it in a joking spirit, but there was no like humour in Rahir's voice when he answered.

'Do not doubt our master. It is true that he will not prefigure his own future, any more than he will ours, but for different reasons. For us, I think it is because he feels foreknowledge of our fate might either destroy our confidence or might so increase it that we became arrogant. For himself, it is because he believes that a foreknowledge of his fate might reduce his concern for the particular problems that each day brings. I know that to be his reasoning, for he has told us so. Be sure that whatever our master *does* predict always comes to pass!'

At the time his words did not convince me. It may be that I did not wish to be convinced, in view of the wizard's predictions for Avran and me. However, when I heard of the carpenter's death, I began to believe Rahir's words. Yet, even while I questioned Vedlen Obiran's necromantic powers, my liking and respect increased for a man who could welcome a friend with such clear and unaffected pleasure.

The health was drunk in malmsey. This is a wine rare in Rockall, since it has to be imported, at great cost, from Castile by way of London and Warringtown. I learned next day that the Earl had only one bottle in his cellars. Yet, with typical generosity, he fetched it out without hesitation for Vedlen Obiran's guest. At the Earl's invitation, it was Vedlen who proposed the toast.

'My Lord and Lady of the Deerlands, gentlemen and companions, I present to you a friend lost for many years but now found again – Sir Robert Randwulf of Jarmswayle, great traveller and soldier, the rightful Earl of Odunseth!'

As we drank to him, the newcomer smiled at the wizard and spoke in amiable reproach. 'Now, now, Vedlen my friend, that's an old story and better forgotten. Let us drink instead to our coming adventures!'

And so we did, in a wine of lesser but still palatable vintage. Shortly afterward, the courtiers were discreetly dismissed, and the Earl and his lady departed. Those of us in the wizard's retinue dismantled the canopy and took away the accoutrements, then were conducted away to our beds by Felun Daretseng. Sir Robert and Vedlen retired to the latter's chamber, to reminisce no doubt into the early hours.

Felun had told us that departure from Chancelet was planned for the seventh morning after our arrival. However, it was my guess, when I awoke, that the arrival of the knight of Odunseth would cause our stay to be prolonged. So it was, but only by a day. Nor did our departure mean an end to a reunion of the friends, for Sir Robert travelled with us.

I had expected him to be accompanied by a retinue
of servants or at least by a squire. But that was not the
case, for he had arrived in Chancelet quite alone, with
only a pack-rafenu to carry his armour and other possessions. Consequently, Amos Sloly decided to appoint himself
factotum to the knight, which was a turn of events tolerated
by the wizard and received with good-humoured resignation, it seemed, by Sir Robert.

During the onward journey, the pattern of our progress
changed. Instead of lagging, the wizard rode with his friend
in the van, just behind the two heralds and ahead of Felun,
Avran, and me. Though we did not deliberately eavesdrop
on their conversations, the snatches of their talk that we
heard convinced us that Sir Robert was indeed a great
traveller. Not only had he roamed the whole middle lands
of Rockall, but also he had carried his sword in campaigns
in many other countries. He had been to England and to
the various realms of Lower and Higher Germanie. He had
visited the heart of the church of God on earth in Rome.
He had even voyaged to the Holy Land itself, venturing
dangerously among the Saracens to visit its holiest places.
Then he had voyaged back westward to Navarre, Aragon,
and Castile, wearing the Cross again in battle against the
Moors. In part he had fought for conscience, in part for
gold, but largely, we became sure, because of a sheer love
of adventure.

Most recently Sir Robert had been in Merania, engaged
to fight in its monarch's service against the neighbouring
Kingdom of Marrafecca. He had left in disgust.

'That young king will never go to war. To be sure,
he loves to design uniforms for his soldiers – I've never
seen an army so elegant. Why, every least soldier has a

ANTONY SWITHIN

surcoat of fine green cloth to wear, with the crown and
the crossed sword and sceptre of Merania broidered on it
in gold, silver, and purple – and woe betide any soldier
whose surcoat is dirty or ragged or whose weapons do not
shine. The King's own guards bear swords and halberds
chased with gold and silver. For a while I was content
enough in his service, for I was encouraged to drill my
men to a perfection of discipline that would have made
them a formidable fighting force.

'But did they have the chance to fight? No, not they!'
There was deep disgust in his voice. 'Our beloved King
loves to watch their marches and countermarches and to
see the mock charges and formation rides of his cavalry
– oh yes, we officers all rode horses, and a pretty penny
they cost to keep – but he has no stomach for a real war.
When the King of Marrafecca, on a trumped-up excuse,
invades Merania and trims off its whole southeastern part
to make a puppet realm for one of his favourites, what
does our brave young monarch do? Nothing; nothing at
all. Just makes a few querulous noises and sends off to Saint
Lorraine for some new material for the court ladies' dresses!'

At this I broke in: 'Your pardon, sir, but could you
tell me what that new land was called? Not Lyonesse, by
any chance?'

He turned in his saddle and looked back at me in surprise:
'No, it is named Feyensinn, and its chief town is Wratney.
Lyonesse? That name is familiar, somehow . . . Oh yes,
now I recollect. Surely that was the name of the sunken
land from which came Tristan, to find adventure with King
Mark of Cornwall and suffer an ill-fated love with his queen,
Yseult? My mother taught me that tale. But I had thought
Lyonesse to be a realm of faery, not of the real world.'

'Yet Simon here, and Avran, seek that realm,' said Vedlen Obiran quietly. 'Simon's father and brother travelled to it. Simon is sure it is to be found somewhere on this island of Rockall.'

'To discover a lost land, that is a quest indeed!' Sir Robert was evidently impressed. 'Well, I've roved widely enough and I've heard the tales of many other travellers, yet never till now have I heard of any voyages to Lyonesse. Come, Simon my lad, tell me more. Expound to me the reasons why you're so sure Lyonesse is to be found in Rockall.'

To be truthful, I was wondering by then whether Lyonesse was to be found anywhere. However, as we rode along, I told the story of the settling of Lyonesse by Sir Arthur Thurlstone and Sir John Warren, recounted some stories of their doings that had drifted back to Hallamshire, and explained when and why my father and brother had fled to Lyonesse. When I was done, Sir Robert spoke again thoughtfully.

'Well, I have never visited Rockall's southern realms and would have surmised Lyonesse must be among them; but you know those lands, Avran, and you say that it is not. Certes, 'tis not among these great woodlands, for I have travelled them all. Nor is it in the east. I know the grassland realms well – too well! – and, though I know the eastern mountains only by report, I am sure Lyonesse cannot be found among their ridges or valleys. The Mionians occupy the northern heights, and the Sifatela peoples occupy the rest of those mountains. They are fierce fighters. If any Englishmen had settled there, they would have had to battle hard for their lands. And whilst in Merania, I would surely have heard of such adventurings. You need spend no time in eastward questing, for it would be wholly wasted.'

'There are new realms in the hills north of these Deerlands, or so men say,' Felun put in tentatively.

'Ay, so there be, but they are small and too far from the sea. Your English knights would have had to evade the Mentonese and cross the Great Marshes to reach them. Yet the stories you heard echo no such adventures as would have befallen in that crossing. No, Simon, if Lyonesse is to be found in Rockall, then it must be far in the north, beyond the barren uplands and the great peaks. I have heard rumours of lands beyond − tales of black, burning mountains, of men with winged helmets and of trees that are alive, of evil gods and strange sacrifices. Such stories would accord well enough with those you heard in Hallamshire, Simon. Yet, for my own part, I place little credence in them.'

Sir Robert fell silent, and we rode along quietly for a while. Then he spoke more pensively: 'Yours will be a mighty journey and a dangerous one.'

He was sounding a note of warning to us. Yet, strangely enough, it seemed to me that he was almost envious.

In this northern reach of the Deerlands forests, the trees were less varied and even stranger, but they were very beautiful. The dominant trees were of a sort we had seen first around Skarngrove, and, in fact, that place was named after them, for they are rare and remarkable in the southern forests. Here they were common enough. Skarns are massive trees, with a pitted, honey-brown bark whose layers overlap in a series of chevron patterns. In shape, their leaves are much like those of an oak, though even more deeply scalloped. In colour, however, they are very different − a much paler green and flecked with yellow. This was a useful tree to the settlers in the forests. The bark, soaked in baths of hot water, yielded a solution for the tanning of leather. The wood, when polished, made fine furniture, for it had a grain of broken spiral patterns that was very beautiful. And the branches, though too inflexible to be used for bows, furnished excellent arrow-wood.

These northern woods were even more open, with many flowers crowding between the tree roots and grasses springing luxuriantly in the glades. The birds were singing less now, for they were busy building nests and feeding nestlings. Every tree seemed a-flutter, except when the swift passing of a hawk froze everything into a brief scene of stillness.

That night we reach Dunfield, the northernmost of the settlements acknowledging the sway of the Earl of the March of the Deerlands. It straddled the Dun River, a little tributary of the Dainflete, and was girded about by stone walls and deep ditches. The ditches were dry then, but separated from the river waters only by narrow dikes. They could be readily filled by the diversion of its waters and would serve as moats in times of peril.

One of the Earl's sons had just been appointed governor of Dunfield. He had ridden with us to take up his duties and to ensure we were made welcome – a needless precaution, for the townspeople were as cheerful and friendly as those of Chancelet. Indeed, the Deerlands seemed to me altogether a happy place. I regret that the chances of my life have never taken me back there.

Three nights and two days were spent in Dunfield castle while Vedlen Obiran did his best to treat the sick and mend the maimed of the little town. There were not a great many, but enough to keep our master busy. During our hours of leisure, Sir Robert, who had heard from Felun Daretseng of Avran's skill with the sword, tried him out in contests with blunted weapons. These were exhilarating to watch, inasmuch as Sir Robert and Avran were very well matched. Each knew tricks that the other did not. However, since Sir Robert was more experienced in battle, Avran was repeatedly deceived into a misstep and either caught by a sword thrust or disarmed.

I was concerned at first as to how Avran would respond to his defeats, for my friend was quick-tempered and not accustomed to being bested, even in such mock-battles. Fortunately, Sir Robert was so cheery, and so willing to teach Avran how to emulate or to counter his own tricks of swordsmanship, that my friend found it impossible to be angry with him.

Felun ventured his sword in a few contests and acquitted himself honourably. The rest of us – even Amos Sloly – knew that we were amply outmatched and were content to watch and learn. Indeed, Sir Robert was prepared to provide lessons in swordsmanship to anybody who requested them. Most of us benefitted from these to some degree, but feats of this kind were beyond Amos.

'You use your sword like a spade, man!' Sir Robert told him. 'Better stick to your axe. You're strong and can wield that well enough. You'll never make a swordsman.'

Yet Amos, red-faced with frustration, remained sure that, by dint of persistence, this was a skill he could master, even though, again and again, his weapon would be deftly flicked from his hands. Nor did Sir Robert's patience with Amos, or Amos's respect for his teacher, ever seem to diminish.

It was on the third afternoon following our departure from Dunfield that we came to the end of the forests. There had been a morning rain, and a heavy haze was still hanging over the trees, so that I did not see the hills until we were almost at their foot. Then, suddenly I was conscious of what seemed a great wall rising before us, grey in the haze.

'Ah! the Ferekar Naur – the Stoney Mountains,' said Felun with satisfaction. 'Though we are yet many weeks' ride from Reschora, the sight of them always cheers me, for it means we are heading north toward home. However, these are lands where troubles can come unlooked for. I am always happier when I know they are behind us.'

Just as a sheepskin rug gets ruckled up when people's feet push it against a wooden chest, so did the forest seem to swell up against the wall of the hills and end abruptly. Where the trees ended, two bridle paths diverged, one climbing steeply upslope, the other following the forest edge eastward. We took the latter, ascending slowly and easily until the tree-tops were below us, a narrow shore of green with a sea of grey haze beyond. To our right was a steep rise of grass through which great crags protruded. They were formed of a rock I supposed to be granite – a mass of square pink shapes in a greyish ground, from which tiny glass-like crystals sparkled in the sunlight. As the path wound its gentle way ever higher up the hillside, the slope to our left became ever more precipitous and the grass sparser, while the trees below us became hidden altogether from view.

During that upward ride, we saw no other travellers, though we had seen many on the forest roads. Nor did we see any wild creatures, except for a single hovering falcon. The slow ascent was not arduous, but it seemed endless. I felt somehow that we were diminished, that we had become mere beetles obliquely climbing a stone field wall. We had all fallen silent, and it was as if to assert my humanity that I spoke to Felun.

'Surely we've left the Marches of the Deerlands behind us? What realm are we in now?'

'Yes, we've left Earl Hubert's lands. As to whose realm we are in, we must now be in the feofdom of the Lord of Owlsgard, who, we hope, will be our host this night.'

'Owlsgard? I didn't think there were any owls in Rockall, though we have plenty back in England.'

He laughed. 'Oh, indeed? I have seen that bird depicted on the arms of Sir Samuel Saville, but I thought it to be a fabulous creature, like the wyverns and cockatrices on the arms of other knights from England and Gascony.'

I laughed in my turn. However, I remembered the device of the Savilles, as they hold lands around Leeds, not so very far north from Hallamshire. I looked forward to a meeting with a nobleman who, if not a north-country Englishman himself, at least must have had ancestors who came from the lands near my home.

However, I was to be disappointed. It was late evening when we reached Owlsgard, but there were no lights. When we rode up onto the ridge upon which Owlsgard stood, we knew why. The keep stood out against the sky, hollow-windowed and smoke-blackened. Of the cottages that had relied so vainly upon it for protection, only charred ruins remained.

CHAPTER 19

The Trail Of The Marauders

In the shock of this discovery, we all stopped. The night wind brought to us the acrid reek of wet burnt wood. Somewhere nearby, we could hear a dog howling. It was long since I had heard that sound, and it did not cheer me. Then, without orders, our rafneyen bunched together around that of the wizard, for all of us felt the need of his wisdom.

Sir Robert sniffed the wind. 'That fire was recent. There is an odour of fresh charring. Yet it must have been before this morning's rain – last night, I would suppose.'

Vedlen Obiran sighed. 'Many unhappy chances have befallen those who settled in these hills, but I had not anticipated this. Sir Samuel was a worthy man and an honest one, but too trusting perhaps. I sense it was his very trustfulness that brought disaster upon him. Rahir and Delhir, the torches, please! It could be that someone is still alive amid these sad ruins. We must search carefully, but we must also be swift.'

The torches were brought forth and kindled. We divided into pairs, each pair taking one torch. Felun was my partner, while Avran went with Naral Evateng. It was I that found the dog, a poor pathetic creature, its hindquarters so smashed by a fallen beam that I wondered it were still alive. At least I was able to provide a swifter end to its misery. The discoveries of Naral and Avran were even more depressing: an elderly woman impaled by a thrown spear and a child dead amid the charred rafters of its home.

Other searchers found more dead men and women, yet not nearly enough to account for the settlement's whole population, and there were no other dead children. There was little sign of any armed resistance to the attackers, and everything suggested treachery. The stone keep would have been hard to assault, yet the dead men within it were few. They wore neither armour nor even jupons and seemed not to have borne weapons. The body of Sir Samuel was not found, though members of his household were recognized among the dead.

At least Avran and I had the good fortune not to have known these people that were slain. Our comrades, in contrast, gave vent to cries of grief, as they recognized murdered friends.

When the search was completed, we gathered again around Vedlen Obiran. By then it was quite dark, for the rind of the moon hung suspended above us, and the stars were masked by high, thin cloud. Our flaring torches formed a bright ring. In its light, his eyes shone as yellow as an owl's, and his voice was curiously calm.

'You are angry, my friends, and you are right to be angry. I know that you wish, as do I, to pursue those who have committed this vile crime. I also know that you hope, as I do, to release those who have been taken captive and to avenge friends who have been slain.'

He paused and surveyed us with a sombre eye, well aware that, like hounds in leash, we were straining to be away. Nevertheless, he went on: 'Yet we must not permit our anger to betray us into foolishness. In so dark a night as this, it would only be feasible to find and read tracks if we sought them by torchlight. We cannot do that, for the torchlight would proclaim our pursuit, leading us perhaps into ambush unawares. Also,, we must remember that the marauders greatly outnumber us. We must rest till the sun rises and, when we pursue, we must be as careful and thoughtful as we are swift.'

That night, though the rafneyen were freed from their loads, the tent was not erected. We ate and drank hastily and lightly, for our sombre mood and the reek of burning had stifled our appetites. Afterwards we rolled ourselves in our blankets and, guarded by our beasts, did our best to find sleep.

I was shaken into wakefulness in the soft grey of a misty morning. The haze from the forests seemed to have risen like a tide and washed over the hill ridges.

It was Rahir Ravatseng who had roused me. 'Our master says we must dress today, not for show as we have until now, but for combat. I have put out for you the surcoat and hose you wore when first in the forests. I have also found a padded jupon that you must wear beneath your surcoat, and a strong leather hood. They'll make you hot later on, no doubt, but you'll maybe need their protection. Look lively, now!'

He went on to awaken Avran and give him a similar message. I rolled over, shivered in the cool air and rose. Quickly I took off my purple tunic and put on this other clothing, while Avran did likewise. Neither of us guessed then that we would never again wear the wizard's livery.

The jupon fitted well enough beneath my surcoat, though it made me feel fat. The hood, however, was so uncomfortably large that, after fastening it around my neck, I allowed it to hang loose behind my shoulders. I put on my belt of knives over the surcoat and attached my scabbard and sword to it. Then I went to lend assistance in the loading of the rafneyen. They were all quite unhappy, the poor beasts, since they had not been able to feed on the smoke-spoiled vegetation and had found nothing to drink.

By then, Felun and Sir Robert had gone off to discover the trail of the marauders. Though they were back within minutes, they found us already loaded up, mounted, and eager to depart. 'They are striking away northwards,' Sir Robert said rather breathlessly. 'After two dewfalls and the rain of yesterday, their tracks are not easy to read. However, if we have understood them properly, the situation is a strange one. The robbers must have brought only their own horses and rafneyen and must have captured few or none in their assault. I cannot think why. Instead, they appear to be using their captives as beasts of burden for carrying away their loot. Well, that will slow them all down and gives us better hope of catching them, but it is puzzling.'

'How many are they?' asked Vedlen Obiran.

'Reivers or captives?'

'Whatever you know.'

'Well, it hardly matters, since my answer must be the same. I do not know. A good number, certainly.'

'Well, Robin, for a task such as confronts us, it is best that you should take command. You are a warrior; I am not, although it may be that my advice may prove of aid at times. What do you propose?'

The knight's answer was prompt. 'As you stated last night, my friend, we must be swift yet careful. We cannot afford to be encumbered by the pack-rafneyen.'

'It is true that the heavily laden beasts would slow us down,' said the wizard, nodding sagely. 'Yet,' he continued, 'I think at least two should accompany us. In particular we should take with us our supply of herbs and other medicaments, which surely will be needed to treat wounds and other injuries before this pursuit is over. Moreover, I can foresee other needs. If you concur, Robin, we shall take two with us and adjust their loads for lightness.'

'Very well,' responded Sir Robert. 'As for the remaining pack-rafneyen, I suggest that they be placed in the charge of Amos Sloly, as he understands them best. There is no cause for making such heavily laden beasts hasten. Amos can bring them along behind us at a more leisurely pace than the pace we must adopt.'

Knowing Amos's perpetual desire to be at the heart of things, I was sure he would protest. In fact, he did begin to frame a complaint, but, under the wizard's cold eye, he fell quickly silent.

I looked away while I listened to Sir Robert's other orders. Then, happening to glance back at Amos, I was surprised to see him smiling to himself. That made me wonder what compensation he had been given for being left behind. In any case, other matters held my attention, and I thought no more about Amos.

The rest of us separated into two groups. In the van were Sir Robert, Felun Daretseng, Avran and me – Sir Robert and Felun because of their knowledge of the terrain, Avran and I because of our skill in archery. The plan was for the others, including the wizard himself, the three Ravatsengs, lean Naral Evateng and massive Drakht Belineg, with the two lightly laden pack-animals, to follow far enough behind to serve as reserve if we were ambushed, yet close enough to keep in contact. Avran and Naral would serve as go-betweens whenever necessary. Amos, with the remaining pack-rafneyen, including Sir Robert's, would wait an hour or so before following and would not make haste.

We four rode off abreast, down into the dip between the Owlsgard ridge and the main southern shoulder of the mountains. The morning mist veiled the burned ruins from view, but the sour, smouldering smell of the devastation assailed our nostrils anew. Soon, however, the ruins were behind us, and their unpleasant reek subsided.

The long slope beyond was gentle but monotonous, its curve as smooth and as convex as the front of a bulging grain sack. The soil cover was meagre. The hooves and boots of those we were pursuing had scuffed and scarred the thin turf, but it was hard nonetheless to make sense of these insubstantial records of their passage. Even so, I became sure that the captives were being led by men mounted on shod horses, while other men on rafneyen herded them from behind and rode on either flank. I remarked on this to Sir Robert, and he seemed pleased.

'You have good eyes for a trail, Simon, better eyes than mine. Keep watchful. If you should notice any new details – any parting of ways, in particular – you must tell me immediately.'

For almost two hours we rode steadily northward, up onto and along the crest of land. The mist was lifting only slowly, the slopes around us seeming to fall gradually away into nothingness. When the ridge and the trail we were following began to swing eastward, I did not notice the change until Sir Robert remarked upon it.

'Heading east, then? Where can they be going, Felun? Not to Blackhill, for sure. I would not trust Sir Gabriel

Jacklyn very far, but it seems he will not prove to be the villain in this particular play.'

'Well, there's a ford across the Marolane River about three leagues upstream from Blackhill Castle,' said Felun. 'They may strike down to that crossing. That would take them to Becketsward or, by the high paths, to Rewlenscrag.'

'True enough,' replied Sir Robert. 'Yet I cannot conceive that the Lord of Ralphsland would resort to such treacherous raiding, nor even Sir Cuthbert Reddlestone for that matter, stiff-necked and vile-tempered though he can be. No, some other hand than theirs has wrought this infamous crime.'

Felun uttered no response, and we rode in silence for a while. Then Avran asked: 'I have seen no map of these mountains. Is it possible for you to chart them for me in words?'

Felun thought carefully, then answered slowly: 'Have you seen from above a duck flying swiftly, with its wings held close to its body? Well, if one ignores their most easterly ridges beyond the River Edflow, the Stoney Mountains are much of that shape. Conceive that your duck is flying from the west to a little north of east. Its tail would be defined by the valleys of the Pochard River on the north side and the Marolane on the south side. Its beak would be pointed to Takrallen, the easternmost stronghold of the Templars. Owlsgard would be on the outer pinions of its right wing, Becketsward on its back just above the base of the tail, and Rewlenscrag on the innermost pinions of its left wing.'

'Yes, I can visualize that readily enough,' responded Avran. 'Are those the only holds in these mountains?'

'By no means. Those are merely the western holds. Close to the tip of our duck's left wing is the castle of Wildfell and, at the very tip of its right wing, that of Falconward.

And then there is the hold of that Welsh knight. Some strange name he has, harder even to remember than your difficult English names.'

'Sir Hugh ap Llewellyn, do you mean?' Sir Robert was amused. 'His hold is called Merlinsward. It is in the valley separating the left wing from the neck of your flying duck. Yet there is some other castle, I believe, closer to hand than Merlinsward. Its name is on the tip of my tongue. I remember hearing dark rumours about it.'

Felun stopped his rafenu, so suddenly that we were all startled. 'Cat Crags!' he said excitedly. 'That filthy nest of carrion birds! Yes, of course; Casimir of Chattaine, whom they call the Wild Cat. It has always been well-known that he has gathered evil men around him. I would wager it is from that quarter that this dastardly blow was struck.'

'You may be right,' responded Sir Robert, 'but we cannot yet be sure. There may be quarrels of which we have not learned, or other knaves of whom we have no knowledge. I propose that we make no assumptions, but that we continue following the trail and find out where it leads.' Yet Felun's suspicions were to be confirmed within the hour, and in a most unexpected fashion.

Before that happened, however, we made some other discoveries. We were riding along quite swiftly, for, though those whom we were pursuing must have been travelling slowly, they had a lead of a whole day of marching time. The ground underfoot was covered with grass, little thicker than a coarse linen sheet laid out to dry in the sunshine and of almost the same hue, for it had died off and been bleached to a creamy yellow colour in which there were yet a few touches of spring green. On this monotonous surface, the footprints were even harder to see. Yet, suddenly I perceived, as Sir Robert and Felun had not, that the tracks were swinging away to our left.

'Hold hard!' I cried. 'We're over-riding the trail!'

The others stopped and examined the ground more intently. 'So we are!' said Sir Robert. 'I am obliged to you, Simon. Your eyes are indeed sharper than mine.'

Over to our left was a tor made up of huge granite blocks that seemed stacked atop one another, like cheeses outside a cheesewright's door. The trail led towards these. When we approached closer, we saw on the ground a litter of food fragments not yet found by birds and some broken earthenware flasks, plus many indentations and scrapings. Evidently the reivers and their captives had rested here during the day after the burning of Owlsgard. Discarded wine-flasks and a forgotten dagger indicated that the marauders themselves had sat up on the tor, doubtless so that they might oversee their captives. Felun examined the dagger carefully, but it told him nothing.

The onward trail was soon found. It led, not back to the hill-crest, but along the northern flank of the ridge, as if the marauders had not wished to risk being seen on the skyline. Below us, the valley of the Marolane was still hidden from view in haze. Hollows in its nearer slope contained stands of shrubs that had found enough soil to root in, and enough shelter from winds, to permit a ragged growth.

Where one patch of shrubs reached upward to the ridge we found the body of an elderly man. He had pitched forward on his face and seemed to have died from simple weariness, for he showed no wounds. This discovery caused us each a lurch at the heart and a tightening of lips, but our haste did not permit any last attentions. Instead, we knew we had to ride on and try to save the living.

As we prepared to do so, however, we heard a frantic call from the trees below. Looking down in surprise, we saw a boy scrambling up the slope towards us.

'Help, Messer Daretseng – help me!' he cried out breathlessly.

Felun dismounted and ran down to gather him up in his arms. As Felun walked back towards us, we saw that the boy was holding on to him frantically, sobbing into his shoulder. The boy could only have been about seven years old. He was slim and dark-haired, his clothes torn by the branches but of good quality.

By that time, the second party had caught us up and ranged themselves around us. However, Felun waved us away and sat down on the slope, speaking soothing words to the boy until his sobs ceased. We dismounted and waited.

Quite soon, Felun beckoned the wizard over, and the two of them talked a while with the boy. After a longer while, Vedlen Obiran returned to us.

'The child is the son of a servant who was slain in the castle. His mother, I am afraid, must also have been slain. When the marauders had plundered the castle, all who were still living were rounded up and made to shoulder burdens – yes, even he, small though he is. He attached himself to the old man – his grandfather, I think. When the old fellow collapsed from exhaustion, the boy threw down his burden and ran off into the bushes. Though his flight was noticed, he was not pursued.'

'Whatever happened at Owlsgard, then?' Sir Robert asked eagerly. 'Was it treachery?'

'Yes, treachery brought about by greed, but' – and a wintry smile passed over the wizard's usually impassive features – 'treachery that failed of its main object. The boy's father was a trusted servant of Sir Samuel Saville, and the boy himself is quite sharp. He has the story clear in mind. Gold is at the root of it, as it is so often at the root of quarrels between you Europeans. It seems there is a dry stream-bed just above Owlsgard keep. This was dug into by chance when a ditch was being extended. In a pocket in that old stream-bed, they found many little pebbles of gold. By careful washing, they also obtained much gold dust – enough, in all, to fill a small coffer, or so the boy claims.'

Seeing how we all stirred at this news, Vedlen Obiran gave a somewhat more wry smile, then he continued: 'Well, Sir Samuel had no thought of hoarding the gold – he is no miser – but he was interested rather in what it might buy for his people – weapons, tools, small comforts. He decided to take the gold to Thraincross in Herador, whence merchants travel regularly to Warringtown, and he was to have departed today.'

The wizard paused, and, when he resumed speaking, there was anger in his voice. 'As I guessed, though, Sir Samuel had been too trusting. A while back, his seneschal died in an accident, and there was no obvious successor. So, when a wandering Gascon man-at-arms turned up at the castle and proved intelligent and amusing, that man was appointed to be the new seneschal.'

'What was his name?' Sir Robert demanded abruptly, his moustache bristling like the whiskers of a cat that has smelled a mouse.

'Pierre Paradis, he called himself,' responded the wizard. 'A lean fellow, the boy tells me, with greying hair that formed a widow's peak over his brow.'

'Pierre Paradis, you say? That's interesting,' said Sir Robert.

'Ah, do you know him, Robin?'

'I have not encountered him, but I've heard tell of him – a wily fox of a man, they say, but, like a fox, he leaves a trail of ill odour behind. He does not always use that name, though.' Sir Robert seemed disinclined to say more.

'Well, it seems this unworthy seneschal was overcome with lust for the gold. And so he plotted to gain it – or some share of it. He arranged the raid on Owlsgard and, when the raiders came by night, he opened the gates to them. But they came too late. Sir Samuel had learned by chance that a party of Mentonese merchants was at Trayad-in-Riotte, where, as you might know, the Mentonese have a trading station. So, seeking to save himself a longer journey, Sir Samuel loaded his rafneyen with the gold and other goods for sale and hastened off to Trayad, two days before his announced date of departure. The seneschal sought desperately to delay Sir Samuel's leaving, I gather – the boy's father seems to have remarked on this and wondered why – but he could not persuade his master to linger. So off went Sir Samuel, with his lady and their two sons, many of his men, and most of the rafneyen. When the raiders came, the gold was gone already.'

We laughed at this, but the wizard said: 'Yes, it is pleasing to think of evil men discomfited, but it was certainly not good for the people of Owlsgard that remained behind – Sir Samuel's daughter among them. In their frustration and wrath, the raiders sacked and burned both castle and village, slaying any that stood in their path. And now they are driving away the people of Owlsgard like laden hase-dain, but with less mercy than such beasts receive. They have said they will free their captives – or most of them, though not the younger women – when they reach Cat Crags. For my part, I would place no trust in that promise.'

'Cat Crags!' Sir Robert, Avran and I exclaimed almost with one voice. Vedlen Obiran nodded gently. 'Yes, indeed. Felun guessed right. Along with the evil Gascon, the other principal culprit in this crime is he whom men call the Wild Cat – Casimir of Chattaine. Well, maybe we shall bell that cat.'

He paused, then went on thoughtfully: 'Cats and owls are both night creatures, I understand. Yet men tell me that, if a cat should ever attack an owl, it rues bitterly having done so. I believe that Casimir and his kindle of vile kittens will come soon to wish they had never marched on Owlsgard.'

CHAPTER 20
The Pen On The Hillside

Already we had been a small party to be pursuing so large a band of reivers. In the next few minutes, our numbers were further reduced. After only the briefest of discussions with the wizard, Sir Robert gave us new orders. Though they might not have much love for one another, the Lord of Ralphsland and Sir Cuthbert Reddlestone were known to have even less liking for the Wild Cat of the Crags. As a result, Felun Daretseng and Hebehir Ravatseng were sent off to seek their aid against him. Felun, carrying the little boy before him on his saddle, was to ride to Becketsward and rally Ralphsland. Hebehir would take the longer road to Rewlenscrag and seek to rouse the people of Pochardsvale.

Narel Evateng, who had great endurance and whose rafenu was reckoned the swiftest, was sent off on the still longer trail after Sir Samuel Saville and his company. They had been gone two days and more, but they would not be travelling with speed. It was hoped that, as of yet, they might only have crossed the Edflow to Amsetch, an isolated stronghold of Dakalet whose castellan was known to be friendly to the men of Owlsgard. If that were the case, then Narel might catch up with Sir Samuel within a long day's hard riding. However, since Narel could not hope to bring Sir Samuel's company back in less than three days, they were likely to be of little service in freeing the Owlsgard captives.

When we rode onward, therefore, there were only three in the advance party – Sir Robert, Avran and me – and only four in the second group – Drakht Belineg, the Ravatseng brothers, and Vedlen Obiran himself. We were a small number, but I comforted myself that, with the wizard among us, we were much more formidable than we seemed.

Narel had ridden away swiftly. Soon Felun, with the little boy sitting before him and chattering away happily and with Hebehir riding beside him, rode away back along the slopes to seek a path down to the Marolane crossing.

As they departed, a light wind rose, rippling the grass heads and shredding the haze into cobwebs that faded swiftly in the emergent sunshine. Below us, I could now perceive a broad valley down which a river threaded its way through patches of trees, green beads on a sparklingly blue string. Beyond was a line of greater hills that looked much more rugged than the cow's-back ridge on whose flanks we were standing. Gazing down river, I could see a cluster of turrets that must be the castle of Blackhill, that stronghold whose castellan was so much distrusted that his help was not even being sought. Looking upriver, I could see only more trees and a confusion of rocky hilltops. The lair of the Wild Cat, I presumed, must be hidden among those crags.

Before we moved onwards, Sir Robert and the wizard had a brief conference. Sir Robert was sure that the marauders would continue to herd their captives along the ridge top. At the head of the Marolane, it seemed, there were many streams, bogs, and patches of woodland.

Among these, so large a party could not be kept together, especially when it included captives eager to escape. Thus, though a crossing of the valley might have shortened their journey to Cat Crags, it would be considered too hazardous to be attempted.

The question was whether we needed to continue following the trail along the exposed hill ridge and thus risk being seen by those we were pursuing before we could come close to them, when we knew their destination already. Alternatively, we considered it might be wiser to take another route that would allow for more concealment, along the southern shoulder of the hill or among the trees of the Marolane valley. Two of Vedlen Obiran's arguments seemed to decide the question. First of all, he pointed out that the Marolane valley was more populated than the southern hill slopes. The marauders would be apprehensive of chance encounters on that flank and especially watchful in that direction. In contrast, the raid on Owlsgard had destroyed the principal settlement on the southern side of the hills, which meant that that flank would not be watched so closely. Moreover, with the sun so bright, the raiders would be reluctant to gaze long into its glare.

So it was that the three of us of the advance party crossed the ridge at speed and headed down its southern side, till the out-arch of the slope concealed us from view from above. Then we found our way, as best we could, along that steep flank of the Stoney Mountains. Stony indeed they were. We had to thread our way across or around curving outbulges of granite – their angle was too shallow for them to deserve the name 'cliff' – and across downward incurvations of turf so thin that it tore away under the hooves of our mounts, causing them to slip again and again.

How I longed to be riding a sevdru, those masters of rock and steep slope! Our poor, forest-bred rafneyen had no skill in pathfinding on such hillsides. Indeed, they were so unhappy and insecure, and dropped to so slow a pace, that we found it easier to dismount and lead them along.

Chancing on a spring from which a little waterfall cascaded in a deep slot down the hillside, we took the opportunity to allow our thirsty beasts to drink their fill, then drank ourselves. While we were doing so, the wizard's party caught up with us. Vedlen Obiran looked hot and annoyed.

'We cannot go on with this absurd scrabbling across rocks and steep hillsides,' he announced firmly. 'The idea was mine, but it has proved a stupid one. What do you suggest, Robin?'

Sir Robert grinned at him. 'Now, now, Vedlen, it wasn't so very bad a concept, just a mite too difficult in execution, maybe. You were right, in that we couldn't all go traipsing along that ridge, as obvious as coals on a snowbank, and I reckon this flank of the hills is indeed the safer. Yet it's a tiresome traverse, that I'll agree. I suggest, Vedlen, that the three of you and the pack-rafneyen should go down to the foot of the slope and ride along just inside the trees. We'll send Simon up onto the ridgetop. He can read sign and he's watchful. Avran and I, we'll follow along far enough behind him that he's only in distant sight for us, and we should be quite out of sight of any other watchers. If Simon is in fact spotted, why then, he's only a single rider. He won't alarm them, for they'll consider him just a wandering hunter. That suit you, Simon?'

'Well enough,' I answered promptly, although, to be truthful, I was a little dismayed at being given primary responsibility in the pursuit.

'Good. Then we'd best have a quick bite before you take those pack-beasts and the food away, Vedlen. We'll all be the better for it.'

The meal was welcome indeed. While we ate, our beasts took the opportunity to browse on the plants that fringed the streamlet.

Twenty minutes later – a *vekruan* or 'hour-third,' as the Sandastrians would say – I was leading Galahad awkwardly and apprehensively back up the steep hill shoulder. Below me, Avran and Sir Robert waited on their beasts; and farther below, welcoming the relief, our four other companions were descending with their rafneyen to seek that simpler path along the forest edge.

When I reached the hill crest again, I looked around me very carefully before daring to mount. The ridgetop stretched empty away to the eastward, but I was able to find again the tracks of those we were pursuing. They were still following the ridge, which was good.

Though I could not relax my vigilance even for a moment, after the ordeal of the slopes, I found it pleasant to be riding at speed along a flat surface again. Galahad was very much happier and more confident, tossing his horns blithely and making that strange sniffing sound which, in a rafenu, signifies contentment.

As I rode along, I tried to reason out in my mind how far the marauders and their captives might have travelled by now. They must have set forth, I presumed, sometime in the morning after the burning of Owlsgard. Though the plundering of castle and village would have preceded their burning of the place, the binding and loading of reluctant captives would have occupied some hours. I did not think they could have set forth until well after first light. From Owlsgard to the tor where they had rested was, say, five leagues. We could not tell how long they had paused. An hour at least, I guessed. Could those poor prisoners have been made to march another six leagues before darkness fell and another halt was enforced? Well, perhaps as many as seven, but not more, certainly. I surmised that the overnight resting-place would have to be close now. Then I saw it: a churning of tracks, scrapes and hollows in the grass where people had lain, more empty flasks, the rubble of a meal, and the rag of a torn garment.

So, all in all, they had travelled about eleven leagues in that first day – a long, hard day's march for those poor captives when some were children, some old, and all of them heavily laden. Assuming they had set forth at first light on this second day, the question was how much farther they might have gone before stopping again. Six leagues at most, I thought, probably less, since the captives would be all the more exhausted. After that third stop, the reivers would certainly make their captives march as far as they could. Nevertheless, another six leagues seemed the absolute limit. So, they must be no more than nine leagues ahead of Galahad and me, perhaps less.

While we were eating, Sir Robert had told me a little about the terrain. This hill ridge would end soon. Then there was a broad, lower saddle of land to cross before the central mass of the Stoney Mountains was reached and, after that, a difficult path through rocky country to the castle of Cat Crags. Laden down as they were, those prisoners could not go all that way before nightfall.

They would be too weary and the path too arduous. I thought it likely they would cross the saddle and then rest for the night.

If so, it raised the question of whether we should seek to attack the marauders before they stopped and put themselves on guard. That might be effective, but I doubted it, as it seemed highly improbable that so few of us could successfully attack so many. By now I knew, from the tracks, that there were at least fifty of the reivers, with nigh on a hundred captives – some of them men, certainly, but most of them women and children.

Another problem was that the weather was changing. Long fingers of cloud were reaching up across the forests from the southwest. The sun seemed to be skipping across them like a child across stepping-stones, sometimes shining brightly, sometimes hidden. I was riding across moving lines of shadow, my view ahead at times brightly lit, at other times shaded.

A line of deer-like animals traversed the ridge ahead in an irregular straggle until, sighting me, they plunged downslope to disappear amid the dense shades of the narrowing Marolane valley – narrowing, and also ending, for the land below me was rising to meet my ridge, and the inner heights were looming closer now.

Turning in the saddle, I could just discern Avran, far behind me and hugging the hill slope. Of Sir Robert I could see no sign.

While I rode onward, the cloud fingers reached ever farther north, till they were above me, with more massive clouds darkening the southern horizon. My ridge was tilting northward, and slots had been cut into its flanks by several small streams, among which the Marolane could no longer to be distinguished. The path of those we were pursuing still followed the ridge crest, but the ridge would have to end soon. Why weren't they heading downslope?

I saw the reason, in a last gleam of the sun's light before the great hand of cloud closed over and hid its rays. Much of the saddle was occupied by marshes, its hummocky surface, with tufts of rushes and coarse grasses, being unmistakeable. The marauders would follow the ridge until they could no longer do so, then take a northward path across the higher, drier land beyond those marshes. Since I was riding much more rapidly than the captives could walk, the distance between us had to be closing.

Slowly the trail I was following began to swing away from the ridge crest and downhill. I had a brief view of the great granite bulwarks that ended the ridge on its southern side, then they and the forests passed from my sight.

I followed the trail obliquely downward across the much gentler slope linking the ridge with the bridge of land to the central mass of the Stoney Mountains. The higher marshes were dotted with bushes. These became ever more numerous as the ground became drier, until they formed an irregular pattern of thickets. In this grey light, it would be hard for me to see the marchers amid those thickets, but, of course, it would also be hard for them to see me.

Now I found the spot where they had taken another rest. There was more debris of a meal, the shards of some broken flasks, and the trodden husk of a loaf of bread. Also, off to the side, I discovered the body of an old woman, dead from exhaustion apparently, for she showed no obvious injury. Someone had regarded her with affection even in death, for her poor limbs had been straightened and her face covered with a silken cloth. As I gazed upon her, the tide of anger against the marauders rose so high within me that I felt like shouting my fury to the skies.

A movement beside me caused me to start, but it was only Avran. 'Another victim,' he remarked grimly. 'Indeed, these reivers have a debt to discharge for their brutality.'

'Do you think you should have caught up with me?' I asked with some concern. 'Wasn't the idea that you should stay well behind me?'

'Sir Robert instructed me to join you. He crossed the ridge to speak to me, and now he has gone to summon our comrades. He thinks the marauders cannot be far ahead now and believes they may have left a rearguard hidden amongst these thickets. He suggests we ride together, keeping our bows strung and our arrows ready. He told me to take heed and that a watchful eye remains more important than haste.'

I made a mental reckoning again to myself. 'Nearly seven more leagues since their overnight camp. They must have driven these poor souls without resting for six full hours.'

'They would have been here around noon, then, and stayed for an hour, at least.'

'Aye, and since then, how far can they have marched? Two leagues . . . three . . . maybe four. That would be their limit, I think. It would take them across this bridge of land to the hills beyond. There, surely, they would have to camp. Indeed, they won't be able to reach Cat Crags this night, if the distance is as far as Sir Robert estimates.'

'So, they will be keeping guard and looking back. When they start to climb again, they will be well situated to spot us. We must be especially watchful now, so that we see them before they see us.'

Our crossing of that saddle was made with all the care we could contrive. We would ride only when we knew that a thicket shielded us from view from ahead, and then never together. Usually I led while Avran watched, and I watched while he followed. Where the screen of bushes was minimal, I would dismount and run or walk forward at a crouch, while Galahad came after me in so wide a circle that we would not be viewed together. Then Avran would come on ahead more swiftly, while Lancelot came circling after him.

At the centre of the saddle there was no cover at all, just an open expanse of tussocky grass. I had to drop onto all fours and crawl, like a hunter stalking a stag, with Avran behind me and the rafneyen waiting. Only when we had safely found shelter in a little thicket beyond this open space did we summon our beasts to us.

If the Wild Cat's men had thought to leave a rearguard at that point, we would surely have been seen and slain, but they were too confident and did not. Maybe it was the darkening skies that urged them to haste and carelessness, for in fact the clouds seemed to be ever more lowering, and the air had that throat-catching dryness that precedes a storm. It was already late afternoon. On such a day, night would fall early.

On the northern slope of the saddle, the bushes were low and scattered, affording no concealment for a rider.

'Avran,' I asked, 'can you wait here with Galahad and Lancelot? Sir Robert and the others cannot be far behind us, and, as you can tell, there's no good cover ahead. I'll go forward on foot and try to spy out their camp.'

'Yes, I'll wait here,' he said, visibly anxious.

'Look after my bow, would you? It'll be too awkward to carry.'

'Must you take this risk, Simon? Remember, there are many evil men that you may have to face, and they will be at their most watchful. Let me go instead, or at least allow me to come with you. We can leave our rafneyen here with a message.'

As he spoke, I was slipping off my unwelcome leather hood and heavy jupon. Now they would be more a hindrance than help.

'No, Avran,' I replied, as I buckled the belt around my waist again. 'If we were both to go, it would more than double our chance of being detected. Moreover, my friend, you're a less able tracker than am I, just as I am a less able swordsman. I won't be weaponless, remember. I have my knives. Please wait here. Honestly, Avran, I'll be both swifter and safer alone.'

My friend threw up his hands in exasperation. 'So be it! I will pray for your return.'

'Do so,' I said cheerfully in reply, before setting off up the slope.

Were it not for my anxiety about those whom we were hoping to rescue, I would have been enjoying myself thoroughly. This shallow hillside, with its tufty bushes, was much like a Pennine slope dotted with broom and gorse. Indeed, some of the bushes were quite as prickly. On just such slopes in my native England I had been able to approach a watchful fox at the mouth of its lair, provided the wind were with me. Which meant that I was confident that I could approach any average human guard undetected. However, it was an effortful climb. I was glad I was not encumbered by the jupon and my bow.

There was now no need to follow the tracks closely, for they were easy to see, even from a distance. The captives would have to be very weary. They must have almost crawled up the hill, for they had displaced grass-sods and beaten down small bushes as they heaved and sweated their way upwards. Criss-crossing tracks of horses and rafneyen showed how the marauders had been driving those poor men and women onward. I pictured the cursing and the cracking of whips, the stumbles, the whimperings of tired children, and the agonized cries of the elderly. I felt a renewed surge of anger.

Where the slope slackened, a guard was sitting astride a big brown horse. He was a heavy-set man, in brown leather jupon and armed with sword and longbow. On his head was a mail cap adorned with the device of a leaping, clawing cat. After following the marauders for so long, it was almost a shock to have the imaginings of my mind transformed into reality. The guard seemed more bored than watchful, and I managed to pass by him unnoticed.

Beyond, the hill widened out into a broad, shallow hollow, like the lap of an alewife dressed in an apron and sitting in her chair. At sometime past, a great pen for beasts had been built there, hemmed closely on all sides by high bushes. It had a containing wall solidly made from blocks of slate, wide enough for a man to walk along. Indeed, half a dozen armed men were on watch upon it – not walking, though, but sitting at ease.

Carefully, I made my way forward till I was in the welcome screen of the bushes and, finding a strong stump, clambered onto it, so that I could peer over the wall. The pen was clear of vegetation and had a single entrance on its further, upslope side, closed by a heavy gate. Within the pen, additional guards stood on watch, while other armed men walked about distributing food to a concourse of captives sitting or lying on the short grass. I could hear the wail of a hungry baby and saw children lying asleep, too tired even to eat. On the far side of the enclosure were stacked bundles, packages, and kegs, the plunder of Owlsgard.

I wondered where the rest of the Wild Cat's men were. I imagined they must be higher up the hill. It steepened again sharply beyond the pen, and, high against the grey sky, I could perceive another taller wall of slates. Beyond that second wall was some sort of a tower and a thread of smoke that showed a fire to be burning within.

It was not hard to evade the attention of the guards on the wall, for they were looking, not outward, but inward. Passing silently through the bushes round about was much harder, for they were densely intergrown and there were many brittle fallen branches to be avoided.

Fortunately I chanced on an animal trackway, made by some creature the size of a roebuck. Crouching low, I was able to make my way along this track quietly and with speed. I found that it did not join, but ran closely parallel to, the broader path up from the pen entrance to the old tower above. The path had been overgrown until some recent time, when men with swords – the cuts were too clumsy for scythes or axes – had opened it up by trimming back the bushes. The trimmed-off twigs and branchlets, though trampled underfoot, still showed the fresh green of newly-opened buds.

As the slope steepened, the animal track swung away from the main path and headed westward. Fortunately, the foliage was becoming less dense, so that, without joining the path, I was able to find my way upwards, slowly, carefully, and above all quietly. When the slope became steeper still, I was forced to haul myself up from one root or strong stem to the next, blessing my good fortune that the bushes were not spiny here. Then the slope slackened again, and the brush grew thicker. I could hear movements and voices. With infinite care I edged toward them.

I realized this had been a castle of sorts, a wall of stone surrounding a small bailey, in the midst of which was a tall, square tower. It was a typical hall-keep of the sort once built by the Normans in England, but now long out of favour. Whether it had become ruined, or had simply never been finished, was not clear. The uppermost part of the keep had so jagged an outline that I presumed hall and chamber must now be open to the sky. However, there was a spire of chimney protruding up beyond one corner, from which smoke was spiralling skyward. There were men within, for I could hear the intermittent sound of voices. Yet it was the men nearer at hand that commanded my attention.

There were eight of them, five on horseback and three standing by on foot. Four of the five horsemen and two of the men on foot wore chain-mail tunics, with yellow surcoats bearing a rather clumsily drawn device that I read as a cat salient sable – a leaping black cat. However, these men had chain-mail hoods, presently thrown back, instead of steel caps. Each was armed with sword and axe, and each bore a round shield of coppered iron, with a boss at centre. They were solid, rather squat men, with low foreheads, black curling hair, and black beards – surely Gascons, I thought to myself.

It was the foremost horseman who took my attention. His surcoat was of yellow silk, and the leaping cat had been embroidered upon it with much more care, its claws done in silver and its tongue in red. He was armed like the others, but his sword-hilt and scabbard were chased with gold. His face was strangely shaped, broad and yet flat at front and back. When he turned toward me, I saw that he had a little, hooked nose between two unusually large eyes – strange eyes, with yellowish-brown irises and black pinpoint pupils. He had a way of suddenly smiling, twitching his cheeks so that the ends of his moustache stuck out like feelers and drawing back his upper lip to reveal irregular, discoloured teeth. He was, in fact, very much like a cat, a fighting cat of town alleys.

That this was Casimir of Chattaine, I did not doubt for a moment. It was important to know what he was saying. Screened by a low bush, I crawled as close as I dared.

He was addressing the third of the men on foot, a thinnish man with greying hair and clad in a plain brown surcoat over mail. His back was to me. He and Casimir were speaking in French, and I blessed Lord Furnival's chaplain, who had taught me that language so well. I understood them easily. Casimir's voice was unpleasant, harsh and throbbing like the growl of an angry tom-cat before battle.

'No, Pierre, I shall not wait any longer. I am bored by this endless slow driving of these stupid villagers. After a night of storm such as comes upon us now, they will be drenched and dismal, and even slower. Edmond,' – he turned to one of the other men standing by – 'make sure all our loot is covered and kept dry. Little enough have we gained by this expedition; we must not lose that little.'

'It was not my fault that Sir Samuel was gone with the gold,' the man called Pierre protested. I realized in that moment that he must be the traitorous seneschal, Pierre Paradis. 'How could I anticipate that he would depart so early? I did my best to delay him and the pack animals. You know that.'

247

'Not a very good best, though, was it, Pierre?' Casimir's smile was not attractive. 'And your reward will not be very great either, will it, dear friend? Indeed, I am not sure whether you deserve to be given the woman you desire so much. We shall see . . . tomorrow.'

The man Paradis had stepped backwards as if struck, but now he spoke up bravely enough. 'At what hour must we expect you, cousin Casimir? And what shall we do with all those villagers – drive them away, or just keep them here?'

'Why, keep them here, of course!' Casimir's voice was almost caressing. 'For tonight, that is. Tomorrow – why, we'll take along the few girls and wenches that we fancy, and perhaps some of the young boys. As for the rest, we don't need them. So, what shall we do with them, eh, Edmond?'

'Slay them, of course, just like we always do!' The other man had contemptuous amusement in his coarse voice. 'No cause for leaving tale-bearers behind, is there, eh?'

The lean Pierre appeared as horrified as was I by the brutality of this proposal, but the other soldiers were expressionless and Casimir positively purring.

'Always you're so very sensible, Edmond, I leave matters in your charge with complete confidence. Not in yours, dear cousin Pierre' – he twitched another smile at the lean man, his teeth gleaming unpleasantly – 'for, after all, you're not always quite trustworthy, are you? I should not wish you to be tempted again. Adieu, then, till morning.'

Without more ado, Casimir drove his spurs into his horse's flanks with such vicious force that the poor beast neighed in pain and leapt into motion. Off westward he went, the other riders following without a word and swiftly passing from my view.

CHAPTER 21

The End Of Pierre Paradis

As Pierre Paradis turned to watch them go, I saw for the first time his narrow face, close-trimmed beard, and greying hair, with its widow's peak almost reaching down to the base of his nose. There was concern, even a sort of guilt, in his expression. The burly Edmond perceived this, for he nudged the lean man and laughed.

'Shaken you a bit, has he? Aye, he's a tough one, our Casimir. No room for weaklings in *his* following. Better have your wench tonight, if you want her. No sense waiting for tomorrow, for then you might never get her.'

Laughing heartily, he walked away through an arch and into the castle bailey. The third man, though, seemed reluctant to follow. He was almost as broad as the others, but was younger and seemed of a more imaginative, nervous type. His next words underlined my impression.

'I like it not, Messer Paradis.' He spoke so quietly that I almost missed his words. 'I like it not. This expedition has been misfortunate from the very outset. No gold, no rafneyen, and that woman screaming her curses at us, till Edmond slew her in the doorway of her home. And now, this talk of a greater slaying tomorrow. The thought of it makes me sick at heart. Evil fortune will follow such a deed, surely. I would that I had never left Takrallen. I fear I shall never see it again.'

Paradis looked at him sharply and seemed briefly to mirror his fear. Then, with an effort, he drew himself together and assumed a very different guise. He cocked his head, and his face wrinkled into a smile. As for his voice, why, it was positively caressing.

'Do not let our lack of luck dishearten you, Gilles! It may be we'll gain that gold yet, who knows? And we have food and wine a-plenty among our plunder. And women, too! No cause for being so downcast, man. Why, 'tis merely the imminence of the storm that is affecting your spirits.'

At this point, I noted that Pierre Paradis could exude an astonishing warmth and charm. Spurious though I knew this to be, I could comprehend now how he had bemused poor Sir Samuel Saville. It was impossible to imagine for a moment that such a man, with such a smile, could be anything other than trustworthy. The very thought seemed absurd.

The simple Gascon soldier responded immediately to this encouragement. 'Ay, you're right of course, Messer Paradis. Just as you say, it must be the storm as has upset me. Well, doubtless I'll be cheerful enough when it's past. I'd best go down and make sure our loot is well covered against the rain, else we'll all rue the day.'

He hastened away down the hill, but Pierre Paradis did not follow. I saw his lips twitch in what, I am sure, was wry amusement at the simplicity of the other man, but then he became grave, stroking his cheek pensively. He was speaking to himself now, so quietly that I was barely able to hear him.

'Well enough, but I think Gilles is right. This adventure *is* ill-fated . . . and Edmond Arsenac spoke sense as well. If I delay till tomorrow, I may indeed never enjoy her, and it's for her that I have risked so much. It grieves me to have to take her tonight, in such rough surroundings, but I must. I cannot risk waiting . . .' His voice trailed off altogether, and he stood silent.

Perhaps I made some slight sound, for he glanced suddenly toward me. Fortunately, I was lying quite still, and he did not notice me. Instead, in a sudden impulse, he strode away – not into the castle bailey, but down the path. The woman whom he had been speaking about had to be one of the prisoners, and I pitied her.

It was time also for me to move, for I had to acquaint Sir Robert and the others of the situation and of the dreadful fate that menaced the other captives. Yet I dared not move too quickly and in haste. There were many men close by. There would be other reivers on the path. And there were the guards around the beast-pen that I had to pass. If I fell into Edmond Arsenac's bloody hands, I would be putting at risk much more than my own life.

It had been hard enough to ascend that steep slope silently, but it was very much harder to descend quietly, and I was much slower. Careful though I was, at one point both my feet slipped in the leaf-litter. To save myself from falling, I seized the stout stem of a bush. Unfortunately, its root tore free from the shallow soil, and I found myself hanging by one hand over a steep slope.

Just as I was about to lose my hold and drop, I heard voices on the path close by. For an uncomfortable minute, clinging desperately to the bush, I froze, while eight of the Wild Cat's men walked by, strolling leisurely, but without noticing me. Then, my wrist aching, I let myself drop.

It should have been easy enough. Unfortunately, an old log was concealed beneath the leaf-mold. My feet slipped on it, and I sprawled sideways, my left leg twisting under me. As I fell, some dry branches broke under my weight and the log, displaced, rolled away downslope.

The volume of noise I caused seemed to me immense. Again, I froze. My heart was pounding madly. I was quite sure that I would either receive an arrow in my back or be hauled away by investigating soldiers.

However, everything remained quiet. Carefully I sat up and probed my knee anxiously. I winced at the touch, but nothing seemed to be broken. Again, there came the sound of voices on the path. I froze a third time, but the men were passing by uphill, not coming my way.

'All that good bread wasted, eh?' I heard one of them grumble. 'Senseless to feed 'em first, ere we've had chance to eat. Senseless to feed 'em at all, come to that!' They must have been some of the men who had been serving the prisoners.

Another voice growled in the affirmative, and then they passed from my hearing.

I stretched my leg carefully, massaging the knee with hands and palm. I had eased it a little, and it felt better. I flexed my leg again, stretching the ankle to test it, then rose carefully to my feet, standing as upright as the slope allowed. I was pleased. The pain was easing. Slowly, ever so carefully, I descended to the level where the slope slackened and found the animal path again.

My knee had behaved well enough for the brief time that I had to walk upright. However, now that I had to crouch, it began again to throb uncomfortably. Painfully I moved forward, yard by yard, as quietly as I could manage, since I was still dangerously close to the path from the beast-pen.

I crawled perhaps seventy yards, then sat for a while, stretching and relaxing my knee, trying to ease it. I felt safe enough, for I was well concealed, but, as it happened, a gap in the branches enabled me to see some way along the path toward the pen.

So it was that I saw Pierre Paradis for a second time. As I might have expected, he was not alone. Before him walked a girl, slim, with a tangle of dark hair and wearing a dark red surcoat that was obviously of good quality, though its hem was torn and streaked with mud. Her feet and arms were bare and scratched. She stumbled as she walked, with a sort of forward stoop, her arms thrust out behind her. As the two came closer, I saw that her arms were roped together and that Paradis had so twisted the rope as to force her wrists upward. She was not accompanying him of her own free will. He was speaking to her, and in English, not in French. 'Well, my dear Lauretta, the decision is yours. You may become mine willingly or unwillingly, yet you *shall* be mine, and on this night. You are entirely at my mercy, you know. Whatever happens, there will be no-one to help you.' His voice was so triumphant, so gloating, that it sickened me.

Though she was so obviously helpless, there was yet a fire of anger in her. 'I shall never be yours willingly, be sure of that! You, the devil who betrayed us, robbed us, caused our people to be killed – why, I'd rather be had by the meanest scullion than by you!'

There was such disgust and contempt in her voice that Pierre Paradis responded furiously. He hauled viciously on the rope, so that she was pulled backwards and fell sideways. As she fell, he struck her twice around the face, causing her to cry out in pain.

I was angry already, and that was altogether too much for me. I do not remember rising and stepping forward. I do not even remember drawing the knife from my belt, but there it was in my hand. As Paradis stepped back – I think he was intending to kick the girl, as he had slackened the rope – I threw. The knife caught him full in the throat. He gasped and, spouting blood, collapsed backward onto the path as he left this life.

My painful knee altogether forgotten, in a moment I had thrust my way through the bushes and was kneeling by the fallen girl. She was breathing in gasps, her breasts heaving. She looked at me searchingly with large, dark eyes, then wordlessly allowed me to turn her around and undo the rope from her arms. I raised her to her feet, and she stood before me trembling. Only then did she speak.

'I was praying to God for vengeance on that monster, and vengeance came. Are you some sort of angel?' The incongruity of the question made me laugh aloud. 'Not really,' I said, 'though I may have usurped the role of an avenging angel on this occasion. However, we must be swift and careful. We can talk later. Into the bushes, quickly. There's a path just a few yards in. I'll follow you, but first I have to retrieve my knife and try to hide the traces of our going. Quickly now!'

Obediently, although still shaky, she scurried away out of view. I withdrew my knife and cleaned it by driving it deep into the earth. Then I dragged Paradis's body a few yards up the path, so that it would be less evident from where his assailant had come.

The effort reminded me again of my twisted knee. I was limping as I returned. As I followed Lauretta into the bushes, I did my best to smooth away our tracks and to interlace the branches in such a way that our passage would be concealed.

Lauretta had not gone far along the path. She was kneeling and waiting for me. As I came up to her, I saw that she was smiling.

'No, not an angel, maybe. Angels are supposed to be tall and blond and handsome, aren't they? And you're so slight and so dark. Yet you do very well for me. Tell me, please, what's your name? I can't go on without knowing that, at least.'

'I'm Simon Branthwaite and you, I suppose, must be Lauretta Saville. I'm sorry to be so direct, but we're in a lot of danger. Listen! Already somebody's coming. Quiet now!'

We were out of sight of the path now, but still perilously close to it. Two men at least were coming down the path from the direction of the pen. I heard one call out in French: 'What's that? Someone's fallen?'

There was a sound of heavy feet running a few paces, then the same voice cried out: 'Why, it's Messer Paradis – and dead. Yes, he's dead. What's happened?'

The next voice I recognized. It was that of Gilles. He sounded frightened.

'His throat has been torn out, by some beast or some devil. I was saying to him, not even an hour ago, that this expedition had a curse overshadowing it. Yet he would have none of it. And now, as everyone can see, the curse has fallen on him.'

The first speaker seemed equally alarmed now. 'Ay, happen you're right. Well, we'd best tell Messer Edmond. Quickly now!' And they fled away uphill.

As they went, I beckoned to Lauretta and led the way through the bushes. However, it was becoming increasingly difficult for me to move fast. After a while she whispered. 'You're limping. What's the matter?'

'Oh, I had a fall, that's all. I was stupidly careless. Come on, we can't waste time.'

All too soon, though, the pain became too much for me, and I had to rest. Lauretta stopped beside me.

'You must go on!' I whispered. 'I'm too slow. You remember the wizard, Vedlen Obiran, don't you?

'Yes, I do,' she replied.

'Well, he's below, with some of his men. Go to him and tell him about the old castle where the Wild Cat's men are, and about the pen. Tell him as well that the Wild Cat intends, tomorrow, to kill all your people – except, maybe, the young women and boys. You can't wait for me. You have to hurry. Be careful and quiet, though. And beware of the mounted guard at the place where the slope steepens.'

She was evidently shocked by my words, but she said: 'Let me examine your knee, please. I have some skill at healing but little skill, I'm afraid, at moving swiftly and unobserved in the woods. I'll need your help, Simon.'

'Oh, very well,' I groaned.

Soon I felt her fingers probing about the bones of my knee, then winced as she found and manipulated some tendon or muscle. There was a flare of pain, which made me groan a second time and for a different reason. 'You have to try to move it,' she said to me. 'Now, isn't that better?'

'It does feel better,' I said.

'That's good. Carry on, then, and please lead the way again. It's so dark in here.'

And so, I set off again along the animal track. It was indeed much darker now in the deep shade of the bushes and with the storm-clouds massing overhead. We passed the beast-pen without seeing it, for the path led down-hill by a different route than the one that I had followed when ascending. Nor, this time, did I glimpse the guard on the horse.

My knee was in fact easier now that Lauretta had manipulated it, but I found the descent painful and difficult, enduring many jolting stumbles. At long last, the slope began to slacken and the bushes to thin out. We were some way to the west of where I had left Avran, but not too far.

We paused in the shadow of a last high bush at the foot of the slope. For the first time, I was able to straighten. Suddenly, I realised that Lauretta had come very close to me. She put her arms around me.

'Thank you, Simon,' she said. 'Even though you're an injured angel, I think you're a very effective one.'

She kissed me full on the lips, then loosened her hold, after which, moving carefully in a crouch from bush to bush, we made our way to where Avran and the others were waiting.

CHAPTER 22

The Taking Of Alunsward

'So Casimir of Chattaine is gone to his hold, and Pierre Paradis is dead,' Vedlen Obiran mused.

We were all sitting in the deep shade of a thicket, a ring of browsing but watchful rafneyen around us serving as guards. Lauretta and I had just finished recounting our adventures. We had also related all the other bits of information that we knew. I told about the old castle, the beast-pen and its guards, while she described the condition and present spirits of the captives.

'Aye, it's good to know that villain is finished with,' growled Drakht Belineg. 'Though I could wish I had been privileged to set my hands on him. He'd have died, but much more slowly. He did not merit a swift end.'

'He died fittingly.' To my surprise, it was the normally silent Delhir Ravatseng who was speaking now. 'He wrought much evil and he died while striving to commit further evil. Be sure he has gone straight to Hell.'

As if exhausted by this rush of words, he began playing quietly on his little double pipe.

'The important point is that he is dead,' Sir Robert was speaking now. 'This land is cleaner for his going. Soon, I trust, we will be despatching that dastardly Casimir after him to Hell. Simon has done well, better even than I anticipated.'

At those words, Lauretta, who was keeping very close to me, seized and pressed my hand. Even in the greyness, I could see that her eyes were shining.

The wizard gave one of his rare chuckles. 'Simon has done very well, better even than any of you yet conceive. Consider now. Their most intelligent leader, Casimir, is gone to Cat Crags. Pierre Paradis, the only other man among them capable of any perceptiveness, is dead – and dead in a way that seems to them, as we know, strange and inexplicable. We can be sure that the man Gilles is busy spreading alarming rumour among them. As for Edmond Arsenac, he may not be at all afraid himself and will surely try to pacify them. However, he can do it only by force, not by persuasion, as he is no sort of reasoner. If they are left in tranquillity, their fears will die down. But they are not going to be left in tranquillity. We shall see to that.'

There pealed a low mutter of thunder in the far distance, and Vedlen Obiran laughed again. 'Why, even the weather is coming to our aid. An approaching storm always induces disquiet and unease in men's minds, especially when they have nothing to occupy them immediately when it comes to tasks at hand. That castle will be a brew of tension, you can be sure. We'll cause this tension to spill over. Look now – already their fear is becoming evident. See there, up on the hillside?'

All of us looked from our place of concealment up towards the reivers' camp. There were gleams of brightness among the trees.

'I can tell you what they have done,' said the wizard quietly. 'They have ringed the beast-pen with torches. The guards are fearful, not of men, but of the fierce creature which, they believe, ripped out the throat of Pierre Paradis.

So, by lighting torches, they believe they are protecting themselves. Wise fools! For they will be looking from light into darkness, and we can be so much surer of approaching them unseen. Again, Simon, remind me. How many men were on watch?'

'I counted six,' I answered.

'Well, it may be the number has been increased, but it cannot be by many. Edmond Arsenac will be finding it hard even to maintain that guard, let alone to augment it. His men will be most reluctant to go down to the beast-pen when, as they believe, some monster is on the prowl. Robin, my friend, I'm going to take back command from you just for this evening. You are the better warrior, but this will be a time when we employ the devices of wizardry.'

Sir Robert laughed. 'Well, Vedlen, you're the one for devious doings in darkness, not I. I relinquish my command to you gladly.'

'My thanks to you, Robin. Well, we cannot commence operations until complete darkness has fallen, and we must trust that the storm does not arrive too swiftly. Even so, we can make our preparations. Delhir, will you serve out food and drink to us? While he is doing so, would you unload the pack-sevdreyen, Avran and Drakht? Rahir, I shall need your assistance. We must set Simon's knee altogether to rights if we can, for we shall need his skills again this night.'

Within the hour, we ventured forth up the hill. My knee had undergone further examination and manipulation. It had then been bound in flexible fibre made from some sort of tree-bark, the bindings being stitched into place by the neat-fingered Rahir. This extra support enabled me to walk freely and even to crawl, though I could not have run far.

We had all received careful instructions from Vedlen Obiran, and some of us had been furnished with special supplies from the rafenu-packs. All of us were travelling on foot, the rafneyen awaiting our summons below.

We were moving, not in a single group, but in three smaller parties. Rahir and Delhir had left early and gone off eastward, to discover some new route up the hill. Though Rahir was no woodsman, Delhir was skilled enough to find them a way. Sir Robert and Drakht Belineg were cautiously climbing the main path, to deal silently with the horseman-guard if he happened still to be on watch. This was only a precaution, as the wizard believed the guard had probably been withdrawn, which proved to be the case. My partner was Lauretta, our task being to find and follow the animal trackway again. Just a little way behind us were the wizard and Avran, neither of them good woodsmen, though Vedlen Obiran could see as well as a badger in the darkness.

It had indeed been the wizard's intention for Avran, not Lauretta, to be my immediate companion on this venture, but she would not leave my side. As for her reason, she proposed that she might be able to help me, should my leg prove bothersome again. Vedlen Obiran had appeared to accept this. As far as I was concerned, however, I suspected strongly that Lauretta had some other motivation. A residual distrust of my companions, possibly? Or else . . . I did not feel inclined to speculate further.

We found the trackway without difficulty, and up it we ventured. I had my bow over my shoulder this time and my quiver at my hip, which made this second crouching ascent more awkward than the first had been. However, my knee, though throbbing a little, behaved well enough.

I speculated what might happen if we encountered the animal that had made the track. And maybe we did, for we heard a grunt and a scrambling sound, as something up ahead fled before us. The noise caused Lauretta to seize my arm in alarm. She pressed herself against me for a long moment before we resumed our slow climb.

When we were over the first rise and at the level of the beast-pen, we began to glimpse, through the dense mass of leaves, the firefly-light of the torches. As the animal track converged with the main path, the lights shone brighter and larger.

Eventually, knowing we had to be beyond the further end of the pen, I found a place where the branches seemed less dense, gave my bow to Lauretta, and wormed my way cautiously through the underbrush to the path. Having made the passage, I enlarged it by breaking off or bending back branches and twigs, then I fetched my bow. As I crawled again to the path, Avran was following close behind. For a while Lauretta stayed within the screen of bushes, then she in turn came out onto the path. As for the wizard, he had gone on up the hill.

Cautiously, with bows at the ready and arrows at string, Avran and I made our way along that path. For some distance, it continued as a narrow slot through the thicket, but then it swung to the left and widened, approaching the pen gate.

Hugging the shade as best we could, we looked past the bend. There, ahead of us, were the high slate wall and the entrance to the beast-pen, flanked by crudely shaped sandstone pillars and closed by a heavy wooden gate. A torch flared and smoked on each pillar, forming a patch of brightness and causing the shadows to dance around it.

On the nearer side of the wall, a guard was standing. He was clad in mail and quite still. I could see the bow slung over his shoulder, the scabbard hanging from his belt at left, and the quiver at right. Since he was facing towards us, we could see as well that on his breast there hung a horn. Beyond the gate was a second guard, similarly equipped, but seeming much more nervous, for he was pacing up and down on the wall and glancing uneasily to left and right.

'You need to deal with that nearer guard when the time comes, Avran, my friend,' I whispered. 'Then you have to go forward to the gate and see if any of our friends need help. As for me, I'll try to edge closer to that other guard.'

Avran gave a rueful smile. 'Today it seems my part to remain still while you adventure, Simon. Well, so be it, but again I ask you, take care. That last bit of waiting aged me by a good many years.'

I smiled at him. It was good to know I had such a friend. We clasped hands, and then, dropping to my knees, I crawled round the bend in the deep shade of the bushes. Though the first guard was still looking toward me, I knew he could not see me. The question was whether, with the bow burdening me, I could pass him without being heard. It was impossible, I thought. The torch-flames lit the area around the gate too brightly. Moreover, the bushes by my side were so dense that I was not sure I could force my way into them. Certainly, I could not do so without causing noise.

I approached the gateway as closely as I dared, then waited in the last patch of deep shade before the lit area. I could see now that there were seven guards on the wall, the two around the gate and five at further stations, some of them pacing up and down, some still. Between each two guards a torch burned. Cautiously I sat back on my heels and then straightened, wincing, as the effort caused a brief flare of pain in my knee. Slipping the bow from my shoulder, I raised it and, taking from my quiver an arrow, set it to string. By now, our other comrades must be in position. I waited for the signal with bated breath.

Then it came – a curiously eerie, wailing whistle from somewhere up on the hill, close to the tower. Even though I was expecting it, the sound startled me. It must have unnerved the guards even more. All of them became still, gazing upward toward the source of the whistle. I could hear uneasy sounds from the captives within the beast-pen, some of whom seemed not to be asleep.

This was the moment. Quickly I drew back the string and loosed, aiming at the further guard. The nearer one was Avran's concern. Had my target been moving, I do not think I would have hit him. The flickering light was too uncertain. As it was, he dropped without a sound, falling backwards beyond the wall. Almost at that moment, the guard close by me grunted and crumpled. Before he fell from view, I glimpsed the feathered end of Avran's arrow protruding from his chest.

As Avran ran out from the shadow, I straightened with an effort and walked toward the gate, scanning the wall as I did so in my anxiety. I was relieved. All the guards were gone from it, and this had been achieved without a horn being sounded. I wondered how it had been managed. Each of our comrades must have been ready to act, of course, but one of them must have dealt with two guards. Later I was to learn that had been Delhir, whose sling had proved quite as deadly as any longbow. Rahir and Sir Richard had employed flung nooses, after which they bound their victims and left them under the wall's shade, while mighty Drakht Belineg had simply leapt at a guard and dragged him from the wall.

As Avran and I slipped back the catch of the heavy gate and swung it outward, we realized that Lauretta had joined us.

'Bravely done! Oh, bravely done!' There was a sobbing catch in her voice and tears in her eyes. Yet, in the torch-light, I could see that her face was almost radiant with joy.

'Now it's your task!' Avran said urgently. 'Speak quickly to your people, before they become alarmed.' I could see that many more of the captives were awake and some leaping to their feet.

She ran quickly into the pen and then stopped. 'It's me, Lauretta,' she called out. 'All is well. You'll soon be free, but' – as a hubbub of sound began to rise – 'please, please be quiet. We're still in a lot of danger! Now, is anyone too unwell to be able to walk? If so, let me know quickly. And the children, you must awaken them, if they're still sleeping. Get them ready to leave – but you cannot let them be noisy. John Stanton, Bevis, Alban, Bernard, come to me quickly, please. I'll need your help. You have to uncover the pile of the reivers' loot and distribute the bundles – all that can be carried. This time, remember, you'll be taking your own possessions homeward, and you'll no longer be serving as beasts of burden for brigands.' There was a ragged cheer at this, as Lauretta's words and vigour had lit a flame of hope in their breasts quite as bright as the torches. She silenced them, then spoke again with a more bitter anger in her tone.

'You will wish to know as well, I think, that our betrayer is dead. Pierre Paradis was slain earlier today by our main saviour, Simon Branthwaite.'

She set her arm on mine, beaming at me. This time, the shout of joy was so loud that it alarmed me.

'Keep them quiet, Lauretta,' I said urgently. 'There are still nearly forty of the reivers in the castle above. There are too few of us to deal with them.'

'I'm sorry, Simon,' she said in a contrite tone. 'Quietly, good people, please – and quickly. We have to go away from here, before they discover us or the storm breaks.'

There was a growing turbulence in the air, a gusty wind ruffling the women's dresses and causing the wrappings of the bundles to flap. The two Ravatsengs and Drakht Belineg had clambered over the wall by then. Soon they were treating the injured as speedily as they could or speaking words of comfort to those who were bereaved.

Before long, Sir Robert was riding into the pen on the foremost of a line of nine rafneyen. Two of the women and one elderly man were so ill that they required to be carried. Each of them was placed on the back of a rafenu, the soothing thoughts of each owner reconciling it to an unfamiliar rider. The other beasts were laden with the bundles carried up to that time by the children and by all the men that were determined to participate in our own harassment of the marauders. Then, in a surprisingly orderly procession, the freed captives made their way out from their place of confinement. Led by one of the Owlsgard men, who knew the Marolane valley well enough to find his way even by night, they set off to seek the road to Becketsward.

Lauretta was to go with them as well. Briefly she returned to my side, watching while the last of them were going out of the gate. Then she embarrassed me deeply by flinging her arms around me and, in the full view of my colleagues, kissing me again upon the lips. After that, without a word, she hastened off to follow her people down the path and out of view.

Avran grinned at me. 'Careful now, Simon my friend. Remember, you're betrothed to my sister. None of these wayside romances, please!'

I blushed with embarrassment. Fortunately, I was spared from having to respond by another gust of wind, which set the torches guttering and sent smoke across the beast-pen.

'Come, we must be moving,' Sir Robert urged. 'Drakht, would you swing back the gate?' Drakht moved to do Sir Robert's bidding. 'But do not quite close it until Rahir has joined you,' Sir Robert added. 'He has a last task to perform. You men of Owlsgard, follow me, please. The rest of you know your next tasks. Do not waste any time. The storm is sure to come upon us soon.'

As Avran and I hurried off along the path, we became aware of a strange change in the light behind us and looked back. The torches were still flaring, but they were no longer burning white. Instead they had become a pale, eerie green, like the strange corpse-lights that can be seen sometimes over marshes at night. I presumed that this must have been contrived by Rahir during his last hasty circuit of the beast-pen, but I could not guess what he had done.

As we rounded the bend of the path and the torches vanished from view, we heard another wailing whistle. This time, though, the sound was more sustained and throbbing. The Owlsgard men, who were ahead of us and following Sir Robert, hesitated and seemed inclined to turn tail. However, when he beckoned them, they hastened on uphill. The Ravatseng brothers and Drakht Belineg had vanished from view. As for Avran and me, we found the tunnel I had made through the brush and, following it, returned to the beast-track.

We followed that track to the point where it swung westward. Then, for the second time that day, I faced the prospect of clambering up the steep slope toward the castle. In the darkness, carrying a bow and with my unreliable knee, this was an even more difficult task. Fortunately, this time I had less need to move silently and could rely at need on Avran's sturdy support.

However, the gustiness of the wind was a hindrance. At one moment, it would be blowing so hard that I had to lean against it, with branches whipping across my face. The next moment, it would drop off, and I would find oneself caught off balance. There was a strange throbbing, ululating note in that wind, like derisive spectral laughter. I had never heard such a sound in any storm before. I wondered if it was merely the wind that was wailing around the stones of the castle or whether it was a contrivance of the wizard's, a device to rattle the nerves of Casimir's men even further.

At last the arduous ascent was done, and we were again on the ridge top, close to the castle. The wizard had told us that it was called Alunsward and that it had never been completed, its people being slain or driven away in some raid. He thought that crime might also have been committed by the Wild Cat's men, but he was not sure. As, with extreme care, we crawled closer to its gate, we could see the bright fire in the keep and the torches burning around the bailey.

There was a considerable commotion within. Soon six horsemen were riding out from the gate, the guards swinging it open to allow them to pass. The riders stopped at the top of the hill beside us, at that last level point before the path plunged steeply. They were talking urgently together in French and were clearly uneasy.

'Strange green lights,' one of them said. 'Go and find out what's wrong,' says Messer Arsenac. But does he come with us? No, not he. Stays snug in the castle, he does. And the rafneyen all gone, too. Whatever became of *them*, I wonder?'

'Stop snivelling,' said another, evidently the leader. 'Come on, now! The guards'll still be on duty, you may be sure. Those lights, they're just some queer effect of the storm – nothing to worry about. Hurry now. Soonest gone, soonest back.' And, spurring their beasts, they all set off down the hill.

'What were they saying?' asked Avran eagerly.

'Well, they're in for a surprise,' he said with a chuckle, when I told him.

Indeed, they were. Amid the wail of the wind, we heard a sudden outburst of shouts from below us and the brief sound of a horn, so quickly silenced that its note could not have carried to the guards at the castle gate. We knew well what had happened. The riders had been ambushed by Sir Robert and the Owlsgard men. Hastily we set arrows to our bows and waited by the path, in case any rider should escape back up the hill. None came. Six more men accounted for. Thirty or so still to go.

According to instructions, I left Avran in hiding by the gate and, after making a cautious way westward far enough to be quite out of view of the guards on the castle gate, traversed the rough road. Somewhere near, I knew, Vedlen Obiran must be awaiting me.

From the air beyond the castle, there came a wailing, chuckling voice – amused, questioning, suggestive of the demonic. Then another and louder voice, quite as sinister-sounding, seemed to answer from close by. This was so startling to me that I stopped short, but then I heard a much more human chuckle. It was the wizard. As good as I believed my night sight to be, he had seen me long before I was aware of him. The wailing ebbed away on our side, though the spectral voice to the east still continued with its chuckling.

'Welcome, Simon,' the wizard said cheerily. 'Delhir tells me that the captives are safely away – excellent news!'

'Why, has Delhir met up with you already?' I asked, astonished.

'Oh, yes. He moves swiftly in the darkness, that one. I believe we are stirring up those rats in the castle to no small extent. They appear not to be enjoying the singing of my thunderstick very much.'

'Oh, is *that* what the sound is?' I said, suddenly enlightened, for I had made them for myself often enough when young.

'Would you like to try it?' he answered, then handed it to me. Soon I was happily whirling over my head the wooden slat on the end of its string. The sound would have been startling on a bright day, in a light wind. On a night like this, in such a gusty gale, it was truly devastating.

A third 'spectral voice' had joined in now, on another side of the castle. It left me wondering which two of our comrades were whirling the other thundersticks. To add to the effect, real thunder was rumbling away in the distance, with brief flashes of lightning.

'Hand me the thunderstick now, Simon, and take this device instead. Whenever the sound of my thunderstick subsides, set it to your lips and speak into it loudly with a throbbing intonation of your voice. This is what you must say – but in French. Since I cannot speak French, you must translate for yourself.'

He gave me brief instructions, then said, 'Let's try it now.'

This second device was a sort of long conical tube, with thin leaves of wood slotted into its sides within. Even when I spoke into the open tip of the cone, my voice was amplified and strangely distorted. When I shouted – or rather, wailed – into it, my voice sounded so utterly inhuman as to be truly eerie.

'The curse is falling upon the evil followers of the Wild Cat!' I shouted as the ululating note of the thunderstick subsided. Then it throbbed louder for a while. I waited till the sound dwindled. 'Flee!' I wailed. 'Flee, before it is too late! Flee, for God's wrath is upon you!'

After that first trial, we moved closer to the castle, repeating the performance several times as we did so. There would be silence for a while, then the thunderstick would wail, and, as its sound diminished, I would shout: 'Flee, before it is too late! Flee! Flee!'

The massive gate had been left open, presumably to permit the re-entry of the six riders when they returned. Its two guards had huddled together and were gazing outward in silence. Nor was there any sound within the castle, except for the crackling of the torches.

Suddenly a green flame was to be seen among the bushes close to the castle wall; and another, burning in a second position; and another; and another, till the whole castle wall seemed ringed in a virescent glow. Immediately and with frantic haste, the guards slammed the gate shut. Again, the thundersticks screamed their mocking laughter, while the real thunder rolled closer and lightning flashed in the

southern sky. Again, I wailed into the cone. 'The curse
. . . The wrath . . . Flee, flee!'

'Now for the next act,' said the wizard in a tone of amusement. He ceased whirling the thunderstick and, instead,
raised a little wooden pipe to his lips. This was the third
time I heard that strange high whistle.

At that moment, from all sides, it seemed, balls of bright
magenta fire were hurled over the stone wall into the castle
bailey, so that its whole interior was bathed in a weird
purplish light.

Once more I shouted into the cone: 'Flee, before doom
falls on you! The curse is come!'

Then, strangest sight of all on that eventful evening,
a wavering white shape rose high into the air above the
wall of the castle over to our left. It appeared to have two
great eyes of green fire and a curving, red-lipped mouth.
There rose a wail of fear, and someone shot an arrow at
the strange thing, but the arrow passed through it without
doing it harm.

One last time I wailed through the cone: 'Doom is
coming upon you. Flee! Flee!'

At that, the nerves of the reivers finally cracked. There
was a surging rush for the castle gateway. The two guards
were bowled over, and out came a terrified crowd of men,
fifteen of them at least.

As they scurried past us, another magenta fire-ball – this
one flung by the wizard himself – fell among them. Never
till then had I heard men whinny like horses in terror, but
I heard the sound now, and away they fled into the night.

Only a few had stayed behind in the castle. They tried
to close its gates, but it was too late. Before they could do
so, Sir Robert, Avran, and the men of Owlsgard, armed

with weapons taken from the slain horsemen, had stormed the gates and found their way within.

There was a brief, frantic fight. Edmond Arsenac was one of those who had kept his nerve, and it was Avran who slew him, after a short but fierce duel. When the wizard and I entered its gate, all of Casimir's men remaining in the castle either had surrendered or were dead.

Gilles must have been one of those who had fled into the night, as he was not to be found among those slain or taken prisoner. I was glad about this, since inadvertently he had served us well. Also, I believed that, after such a fright, there was every chance he would turn away forever from evil-doing.

CHAPTER 23

The Return Of Casimir

I was roused from deep sleep. Somebody was shaking me gently. In the moment that I awakened, I gazed around me in bewilderment. I was in a strange place below a broken stone arch that cast its shade over me, as I lay on a silken-sheeted couch. I stretched, groaning at the pain of a knee that had stiffened overnight. Only then did I become aware that Rahir Ravatseng was bending over me.

'Is all well with you, Simon?' he inquired anxiously. 'Last night – or this morning, rather, for 'twas amply past midnight – either you fainted or else you fell asleep on your feet. Friend Avran caught you, and 'twas our master himself that put you to bed here, on Edmond Arsenac's own couch. Not that *he'll* be needing it any more . . . 'Tis a shame to be rousing you so early, before your slumber be properly done, but we must be moving soon. Will you be able to manage it, think you?'

I blinked at him and then contrived a smile. 'Oh, I'm well enough, I'm sure. I needed that sleep, though. Are we still in Alunsward, then?'

'Aye, but we must be shifting out shortly. Now then, how's that leg of yours?'

I tried to flex it and winced anew. 'A bit stiff, I'm afraid.'

'Well then, I'll just take that wrapping off and give you a massage.'

He drew back the sheets. Then, using a little knife, he cut the stitches in the bandage and peeled it off. I winced as his firm fingers probed the muscles of my knee, but soon he had it feeling easier and was stitching a new tree-bark wrapping about it. While he was doing this, he talked steadily with an amicable cheerfulness. 'While you were dreaming, Simon me lad, we had a real old storm. The thunder was something to hear. I'd have thought it would have awakened anyone, but no, you slept sweetly right through. And the rain, it came down positively in pailfuls. Funny thing, though. It was just around here. Those folk from Owlsgard – the old folk, the women and children, and your friend Lauretta – they would be far enough down the track not to have felt it at all, I reckon – a few drops at worst. It's like as if the very heavens arranged to lave this place clean of all the foulness of the Wild Cat's doings – the dirt, the blood, the very tracks, all washed away.'

'How strange! And yet it's clear that Alunsward needed to be cleansed.'

'That it did. And, you know, those fellows that ran out from here, none of 'em headed for Cat Crags. Sir Robert followed them some way, before the storm really set in. They were all fleeing off east, headed towards Falconward and Lukeyne. We put a proper scare into 'em. I doubt not that they're running yet.'

I laughed. 'It was a good performance, right enough. I understand how the wailing was managed and, as for the talking, I did it myself, though I don't really comprehend how that hailer device works. But those fire-balls, and especially that shape in the sky. How in the world were those contrived?'

'The fireballs I don't rightly understand, either. They're made up in the Trident Mountains. We brought them along with us from Reschora. As you throw, you pull out a sort of roughened rod and that sets 'em burning.'

Rahir paused reflectively, then went on: 'Come to think of it, those wands our master carries inside his cloak must work the same way. He has a piece of coarse stone fixed to his belt. When he's in danger, he pulls out one of the wands and strokes it briskly across that stone before throwing it. By then, the wand's blazing. You saw how he scared off that kalvak, back in the forests? Many's the time I've seen him use those wands to frighten off men who tried to rob or kill him. But as to what causes the burning, I've no idea. Some sort of magical element, I suppose.'

'And the shape in the sky?'

He chuckled. 'Why, I fashioned *that* myself, and brother Delhir touched it up! 'Tis composed of gossamer-thin cloth, woven from plant fibres. Delhir drew the eyes and mouth, using tinctures that our master prepared. They're made of some stuff that shines in moonlight. The cloth rolls up small, so you can carry it easily, and there are four thin bladders of skin fixed to the top edge, which you blow up and tie so that the breath won't leak out. Then you let 'em go, and up she floats. En-Dor I call her, after that witch in the Bible. She's frightened plenty of other folk before this.'

I laughed in response. 'She's quite a sight! Not beautiful, maybe, but striking. And the arrow didn't damage her?'

'No, it went straight through. I'll just have to stitch up the hole sometime. Now if that archer had shot higher and punctured one of the bladders, we might have been in trouble . . . There, that's done. You'll find your knee a sight easier today, and, given a couple more days, it'll be as right as ever it was. Time to rise, lad. The sun's shining, and there's an ample breakfast, courtesy of Casimir the Cat.'

Indeed, when I emerged from the shade of the arch, I found that the sun was already quite high in the sky. The morning had to be half over already. The darker colour of the soil of the paths and the brighter greenness of the turf within the bailey gave evidence of the overnight rain, but the puddles were already shrinking.

A cloth had been spread on a fallen stone. On it were placed platters of bread and meats, with slices of dried apple and a flask of wine set about by horn goblets. Sir Robert, Drakht Belineg, and Avran were sitting on other stones nearby. They had just finished eating, and Avran greeted me in a cheerful spirit.

'Ah, the sleeper awakes, now that the worst of the work is done. I'm blithe to see you looking so well, though, Simon. Your knee must be much better. I can tell by the easy way in which you're walking.' Indeed, after the first hesitant paces, I was finding that I could step out freely. 'Here, have something to eat and drink.'

As I provided myself with food, I asked, 'What have you been doing this morning?'

'Tidying up this place, mostly,' he replied. 'Taking away the bodies of the slain, first of all. Eight of Casimir's men died here in our little fracas last night, and three more surrendered. Then there were the six riders who were ambushed on the path. None of them survived.'

'They were given no opportunity to surrender, I fear,' Sir Robert commented grimly. 'The men of Owlsgard

277

were not in a forgiving mood. Had you not slain Edmond Arsenac, Avran, he would surely have been torn to pieces, for he had earned much hatred. I was hard put to it to protect the other three, even though they were lesser villains. Those who fled were wise in their terror.'

Avran gave a wry smile. 'Curious, isn't it, how often it is the brave who die and the cowards who survive? Yet if they'd not fled, we wouldn't have taken the castle.'

Nay, Avran, you're wrong there,' Drakht Belineg rumbled. 'Our master would have seized this keep somehow. He does not fail.' With an air of finality, he seized the flagon of wine, refilled his goblet, and took a long swig.

'And those seven guards down by the beast-pen, were all of them slain?'

Rahir chuckled. 'No, three live yet, but they had a sorry night of it. We tied 'em up, you see, but then had so much else to do that we forgot all about 'em. When we went down there this morning, we found them sodden with rain and stiff with cold and fright. Serve 'em right, of course. The trouble was, it meant that Delhir and I had not only to massage their limbs to life but also to calm them down. Not that we carried *that* too far. Truly I believe that they've had such a scare, one way and another, as to make honest men of 'em.'

'Where are they now?'

'On their way to Becketsward, all seven of 'em, in the charge of three of the Owlsgard men. This time the Owlsgard men are doing the riding, upon rafneyen captured last night, while it's the reivers who are walking. And what's more, they're chained together and carrying the rest of the food and loot that we recovered from this place. The Owlsgard men are enjoying *that* turnabout, you may be sure.'

'So, what do we have to do next and how much time have we?'

It was Sir Robert who answered. 'Difficult questions, Simon. We're assuming that Casimir and his villains will not have started out early from Cat Crags, yet we cannot be certain. The storm did not extend even that far, so they will not have been delayed by it. Nor can we know how many men will accompany Casimir when he *does* return. More than the four he took with him, assuredly, and with many more beasts, for he plans to be carrying away both loot and women.'

I started up in alarm. 'But that means they may be arriving any time, and in force.'

He smiled at me. 'Now, Simon, think you that I'd be sitting here so calmly if that were the case? No, no. There's a guard on the gate and watchers on the ridge. We've arranged our signals and we'll be given ample warning of Casimir's approach.'

I relaxed again and took a sip of wine. 'What are we to do, then? Ambush them on the road or here in the castle? That should be easy enough.'

'Oh, Simon, come now! You're capable of being more astute than that. I don't think you're properly awake yet. If they were riding horses, of course we might ambush them – if not on the ridge, then certainly here in this castle or in the coppice below. But they'll be bringing rafneyen, many rafneyen. Would rafneyen advance into such danger, or allow their riders to do so? Of course not. They'd sense the ambush half a league away. No, what we must do is to puzzle Casimir so thoroughly that he wastes time and rides too far away from his hold. By then, I hope, we'll have the men of Becketsward and Rewlenscrag to aid us.

Delhir and my good friend Vedlen rode away early to arrange the setting of the trap which, we trust, may today catch the Cat.'

He rose to his feet. 'Are you done then, gentlemen?' All nodded their agreement.

'Good, then. We must complete our preparations. The first step for us will be the final abandonment of this castle.'

As it was, the ruin of Alunsward already looked as if it had long stood desolate. Rising early and working energetically while I was still sleeping, the wizard's men and those of Owlsgard had removed not only the bodies of the slain, but also all traces of occupancy, except only the food and vessels from which we had breakfasted and the bedding in which I had slept. The latter were now packed up into a satchel that Rahir slung over his shoulder, while Drakht used a thorny branch broken from a bush to obscure our footmarks.

Having seen this done, Rahir and Sir Robert left us and walked out of the castle bailey, each towing a thorny branch behind him to conceal his own footsteps. The big wooden gates were not only standing widely open, but were held so by huge blocks of stone. As they approached the gates, Sir Robert whistled, and a lean, sandy-haired man carrying a bow – the Owlsgard man who had been guarding the gate – scrambled down from the wall to join them. Before the three were gone from view, Avran turned to me. 'So, friend, we are to be among the custodians of this place. It's good that we both have our bows. We may be needing them. I'm afraid you face a bit of a climb, though, Simon. I trust your leg won't prove troublesome.'

However, it was not my knee, but my nerve that came close to failing me. We went inside the square shell of the keep and ascended a broad stone stairway that led up to an uncompleted first floor high above the hall. Stepping cautiously across its widely spaced beams, we reached a much narrower second stairway. This zigzagged upward without any kind of parapet past the levels of two higher floors, both marked by lines of protruding stones, but neither yet constructed. The stairs ended about thirty cloth-yards above the framework of beams and about twenty more below the irregular upper rim of the keep. The wall inside was poorly built and crumbling. Nevertheless, someone had climbed it, for a strong rope was dangling down to us.

'The last stretch is a little more difficult,' announced Avran cheerfully. 'Just do what I do, though, and you won't have any problems.'

Taking the rope in both hands, he placed a foot against the wall, leaned backward and just walked up that vertical face of stone. After reaching the top, he slung a leg over and pulled himself up out of my view.

'Easy enough, Simon, isn't it?' he called down. 'Your turn now!'

The very thought of emulating Avran, of climbing the wall so calmly and easily, appalled me. Already my heart was pounding, and not because of my ascent of the stairs. Unwisely I gazed down from this highest stone step to the gridwork of beams far below. A long way to fall already, and if I slipped . . . Then I looked up at the dangling rope and felt sick. Apprehensive, I took a deep breath. Then my nerves failed me entirely. I could not make the climb. I would have to turn back.

'What's the matter, Simon?' Avran called down to me impatiently. 'Recovering your breath? Don't waste time now!'

Courage works in strange ways. In that moment, it seemed to me preferable to attempt the climb, even though I might fall and break my neck, than to be shamed in Avran's eyes by showing fright. I took two deep, shuddering breaths, closed my eyes, and grasped the rope with shaking hands. Then, setting my right foot against the wall and leaning outward so that my body was at the proper angle, I took my first step.

Well, that was all right, even though my legs were shaking . . . another step, and another. I wasn't finding it so difficult, after all. I dared to open my eyes, then wished I hadn't, for I was at a dizzying angle to the stones. My sweat-moist palms slipped a little on the rope; I tightened my grip frantically and half-closed my eyes again. Another step, another, then another . . . Finally, Avran's strong hands were seizing me by the shoulders and hauling me up onto the top.

As I lay there panting and with eyes closed again for fear of looking down, my friend spoke, his voice remorseful.

'Oh, Simon, I do apologize for hurrying you. I'd quite forgotten your injured knee. Take your ease and relax for a while. You'll recover soon enough, I'm sure.'

Lying there with heart beating away frantically, I was too dishonest or maybe too craven to admit that I was suffering, not from physical pain, but from sheer fright.

Then, far away, I heard a sweet, high trill, much like the call of a whimbrel. The sound was repeated closer by, and I raised my head. The keep of the castle stood high above its walls, and we were perched atop its westernmost corner. In front and over to our left, the land fell away shallow into the marshy upper reaches of the Marolane valley. Exactly to our left was the saddle we had crossed yesterday. I found I could see down into the more distant half-circle of the beast-pen, though its nearer end was hidden from view. Almost in front of us was the open bailey gate, and beyond it lay the rough track leading away northwestwards into the hills, fringed by a bristle of bushes like the hairs on the chin of a man who had remained for a week unshaven. (At that thought, I felt my own upper lip and chin, still so hairless and unmasculine – rather appropriate, I thought with self-disapproval, for a coward like me.)

Hearing a sound of scrambling below us, I looked back for the first time into the hollow shell of the keep. There, dangling, was that dreadful rope. And there, further below, was Drakht Belineg, satchel on back and bow over shoulder. He was running – actually running – up that stone staircase with its dizzying lack of parapets. He reached the top and then, in the most easy, confident way imaginable, grasped the rope and walked up the wall. Soon he hauled himself up and turned around to pull up the rope, coiling it neatly beside us.

'Casimir's lot are on their way here,' he announced briefly. He seemed only slightly out of breath, big and heavy though he was, and I felt ashamed. 'Can't say how many of 'em yet, though. We should see 'em soon. Keep down. They mustn't spot us.'

'Won't their rafneyen detect us, though?'

'Nay, they won't sense us – or not as a danger, for they'll know we're intending them no immediate harm. Aye, we might make 'em uneasy, but I don't mind that. Nor will Casimir's men look up so high. Why should they? Look! There they are.'

As a drifting cloud took away its shadow from the grey, irregular hills ahead and to our right, I perceived the approaching reivers. At first, I could distinguish only their movement. Then I began to descry the riders themselves and, as they came closer, the character of their mounts. I counted only five men who were on horseback, then a sixth. One of them had surely to be Casimir himself. Eighteen other men were riding rafneyen, and there were around fifteen other rafneyen bearing empty pack-saddles.

As they came closer, one of the leading riders hollered a formless cry, presumably a prearranged signal of greeting. Of course, there was no response. The reivers rode a little closer and then halted in evident puzzlement. After they had conferred briefly, five riders on rafneyen were sent out in front, the rest following them at a slower pace.

When it was realized that the gates of Alunsward Castle were standing open, there were startled exclamations, another halt, and a second hasty conference. On this occasion, only the advance guard of five riders proceeded closer, so very slowly and with such caution that it was evident they were expecting an ambush, even though it was not likely the rafneyen were giving any warning of one. Within the range of a long arrow shot, the five halted and conferred once more before approaching the castle gateway, timorous and watchful as they advanced.

At last, one, bolder than the rest, urged his mount in through the open gates. His cry of astonishment caused the four others hastily to follow him. Soon the main party of reivers came up. I could distinguish Casimir of Chattaine now. He and the other horsemen rode just inside the gates and halted there, the remainder of the rafenu-men staying outside with the pack-rafneyen. I whispered Casimir's name to Avran and Drakht, pointing him out to them.

'So that's him,' murmured Avran. 'One well-placed arrow, Simon, and Rockall would be a sweeter place.'

'Ay, and those other brigands would be pulling this keep down stone by stone to get at us.' Drakht rebuked him in a rumbling undertone. 'Don't thee be so daft, Avran.'

It was evident that the reivers were not just surprised, but very much disconcerted. On an order from Casimir, the five rafenu-men and two of the horsemen dismounted and, while the other horsemen remained on watch, began a careful exploration of the bailey. Eventually some of them ventured into the keep. Voices below us told us of their entry, then we heard feet on the stone steps.

However, the reivers did not climb much higher than that skeletal first floor. There was no reason for them to ascend, when the stairs beyond were so evidently empty and the rope no longer within view.

We heard the dwindling sound of their footsteps and, a minute later, saw that they were remounting and gathering with the other horsemen around Casimir. I could hear their voices, but they were talking too rapidly and in tones too low for me to distinguish any words, hard though I tried. However, their gestures showed that they were dismayed and uncertain.

Casimir's anger was evident from the peremptory manner in which he waved his men out of the castle, even though he must have been just as puzzled as they were. All the same, he did not hesitate any longer. Soon the whole party of the reivers was cascading down the path and out from our view.

Drakht Belineg straightened and gave a sigh of satisfaction. 'They're gone to discover whether their captives are still safely penned, I'd suppose. Well, that'll give 'em no joy. Indeed, I doubt now if they expect anything joyful. I reckon we've got yon Casimir properly rattled. Well, he doesn't know it yet, but his troubles are just beginning.'

CHAPTER 24

The Trap Is Sprung

Avran sat up, stretched and then stood upright, a move of daunting hardihood that did nothing to soothe my still-fragile nerves, for the stonework crowning the keep was not broad. 'Well, Drakht, do we go down now?'

'Best wait a while longer,' the big man rumbled. 'I'd like to be sure what those reivers will do when they've reached the beast-pen. If all goes as our master guesses, they'll be off along the track of the Owlsgard folk.' He also rose to his feet. 'Aye, we can see down well enough. They'll be back in view shortly. And, meanwhile, 'tis good to have a stretch. Don't you want one too, Simon, after all that crouching?'

'No . . . I'm quite all right lying here, thanks.' The thought of standing on that narrow edge of stone quite horrified me.

'Simon's injured knee made the climb difficult for him,' Avran said with sympathy, even though somewhat inaccurately.

'Aye, of course it would,' responded the big man in a spirit of concern. 'If I'd borne that in mind, Simon could have gone off with Sir Robert instead.'

All this undeserved sympathy was embarrassing me, so I spoke hastily to change the subject. 'Actually, I'm not quite clear why we came up here at all. Of course, I know we were able to watch the coming of Casimir and his brigands, but surely we could all have done that from outside, from a distance, along with Sir Robert? Besides, we haven't learned anything, since we were much too high to hear what they were saying.'

Drakht Belineg rubbed his cheek. 'Ay, but suppose yon Casimir had split his party and left some of his men as garrison here? He'd have been able to use this place as a refuge at need. And last night's tricks wouldn't serve to scare *him* out. But three stout fellows like us, right in their midst, unbeknown to 'em and armed with these good bows – why, we'd have accounted pretty speedily for any guards he'd left. As it chances, though, Casimir didn't leave any, and we weren't needed.'

And my having to endure that dreadful climb was all in vain, I thought bitterly to myself. However, an exclamation from Avran diverted my thoughts: 'Ah, there they are!'

The greater height gained by standing brought Casimir's men more quickly into the sightlines of my comrades than mine, but soon I could see them as well – or some of them, at least. Men on rafneyen were circling within the beast-pen, no doubt questing for pieces of evidence that might explain how their prisoners had escaped and what had happened to their vanished comrades. Soon, however, the riders withdrew from our view.

'Time to go down,' Drakht said. 'They'll not miss the tracks toward Becketsward, we may be sure. However, there's a chance – a small chance – that yon Casimir might decide not to follow 'em. Just in case, we'd best close the gates against him.'

He picked up the rope, checked its point of anchorage, then uncoiled it and threw it down again within the keep.

'I'll go down first. Then, Simon, you'd better follow – I can catch you if that wobbly leg of yours causes you to slip.'

In a moment, he had swung himself over and was clambering down, as fast as a dormouse running down a plant-stem.

'All right, then, Simon,' he called up. 'I'll hold the rope away from the wall, to make it easier for you. I gulped in apprehension and then, grasping the rope, swung myself off the wall, with about as much enthusiasm and willingness as a condemned man mounting a scaffold.

In my fear and haste, my feet failed to find proper purchase on the wall. As they slipped, I rotated dizzily, clasping my knees frantically around the rope and hugging it with thumping heart. Then, taking a deep breath, I began to lower myself hand over hand inch by inch down the rope, keeping my eyes firmly shut. The descent seemed to take hours. Eventually, feeling Drakht's big hands steadying me, I opened my eyes again and saw that I had just about reached the stairhead.

'Well, that was a funny way of doing it,' Drakht commented, his face puzzled. Then, as my legs gave way under me and I collapsed backward against the welcome solidity of the wall, he went on in a more sympathetic vein. 'Your leg's hurting again, I can see. Rest easy for a bit, lad. Me and Avran, we can see to the gate.'

Avran was already on his way, walking backward down the wall, with the rope gripped confidently in his hands. Within moments, he was beside me again. Evidently, he had heard Drakht's words, for he echoed them: 'Yes, do rest awhile, Simon. You can follow us whenever you're ready.'

The thought of being left to descend that stairway, bereft as it was of parapets, made me shudder. Hastily I rose to my feet. 'No, I'll come down with you,' I said decisively.

'Good for you. But take my arm. It'll steady you.'

When I had first climbed the stairs, they had not worried me too much. Now, however, after my experiences on the rope, the least bit of height held terrors. Clutching Avran's arm really was a comfort. I was grateful as well to be able to keep close to the wall, with his solid body between me and the drop. Thus, we descended, past the gridwork of beams and down to the very welcome firmness of the floor within the keep. There I released Avran's arm. 'Thanks, Avran,' I said. 'I'll be all right now.'

He looked at me steadily and gave a half-smile. 'Your knee wasn't truly the problem, though, was it, Simon? Oh, don't look so shamefaced. There are many otherwise courageous people who find heights frightening. Yet, when you were climbing the narrow stair on that tower in the Trantevrin Hills, you showed no fear.'

It was a relief to know that my friend had been astute enough to perceive my weakness and forgive it. 'Well, that ascent was made in darkness. I had no view of what was below,' I answered. 'Yet I might have managed here well enough, but for that – that *awful* rope . . . I'd never climbed a rope, anyway, and to watch it swinging . . .'

Avran's smile had broadened, but it remained an understanding smile, untouched by mockery. 'Yet, after all, you did very well, Simon. However afraid you felt, you *did* manage the climb and, when you were told to go down, you didn't hesitate. I was quite anxious for a moment, though, when your feet slipped.'

'Not nearly so anxious as I was, I'm sure. I thought my last hour had come. I can only be grateful to God that we're down safely. And I'm grateful to you for being so understanding – and for concealing my weakness from Drakht.'

Avran laughed and, putting his arm around my shoulders, gave me the briefest of hugs. 'Come on, then. We mustn't leave all the hard labour to Drakht!'

However, by the time we emerged from the keep, our powerful friend had rolled the great stones away from the gates already and was swinging one of them shut. We helped him with the other and dropped the massive bar that secured both gates into its socket.

'Avran, will you go up on the wall and keep watch?' Drakht asked. 'If Casimir and his pack of cutthroats do come back this way, we'd best be ready. If not, no doubt Sir Robert'll be sending his orders to us shortly. Sit down for a while, Simon lad, and rest that leg. We'll be needing your assistance soon enough, I don't doubt.'

I caught Avran's wink as he turned away and I blushed. Fortunately, Drakht did not notice. Yet I was glad enough to sit down on one of the stones. The ascent had in fact put some strain on my knee, and I was suffering as well from the reaction that often follows a thorough fright. Drakht sat down beside me and, producing some hunks of bread and cheese from his satchel, shared them with me.

We munched in silence until Avran called down. 'Here comes that Owlsgard archer. He needs the gates to be opened for him.'

It was the lean, sandy-haired man who had been on watch earlier. Seeing him again more closely at hand, I recalled that Lauretta had addressed him as Bernard last night. As he stepped inside the gateway, his freckled face was beaming.

'All proceeds well, masters,' he said. 'Sir Robert said to tell you that the robbers have ridden off westward and that the trap will soon begin to close about them. You can be easy for an hour at least, and maybe more. Some of my friends are on watch outside. They'll give us warning if there's trouble.'

So Avran came down from the wall, and, while we shared the bread and cheese and drank from a flask from Drakht's pack, we talked. Bernard knew this area of the Stoney Mountains intimately. Not only was he able to explain Sir Robert's plans, but also to tell us how they depended on the character of the landscape.

'Cat Crags is easy enough to approach from the north, but it's difficult to reach from south or east. It's wild country indeed. There's two roads – this bad one up the hill from Alunsward and another, better road from Blackhill, up through the Marolane meadows and the valley of the Swiftling Brook. Once the robbers have followed my people down from Alunsward into the upper Marolane valley, there's no way they can turn, either southward or back into the hills, between here and the Swiftling. There's marshes in the valley bottom and there's dense, spiny scrub on the slopes, with cliffs above. Since they can't gain the Swiftling road, they'll have to come back toward Alunsward.'

'And why can't they use the Swiftling road?' Avran asked.

'Because they won't be allowed to, that's why. Our Owlsgard folk mostly crossed the Swiftling last night. There's a stone bridge just above where it joins the Marolane. Even our three friends that went off with the prisoners this morning should be safely across by now.

Well, according to the messages we've had from Felun Daretseng, the men of Ralphsland were really angry when they learned that Casimir had pillaged Owlsgard and burned our homes – they're good neighbours, the Ralphsland folk. They were already on the march last night, hoping to rescue us – although I fear that, but for you and your friends, they'd have been too late.'

He leaned forward to take another hunk of the bread and cheese, then continued: 'Anyhow, they met our people this morning. Half of 'em turned back to render aid. The others, under the Lord of Ralphsland, came on. But not too far, for they'd had word from Sir Robert what to do. There's a coppice, just where the Swiftling flows into the Marolane. When Casimir gets to it, he's going to find the men of Ralphsland waiting for him in ambush. He won't pass through that way, you may be sure.'

Bernard paused to take a large bite of his bread and cheese, then resumed speaking, his mouth full and voice a little muffled. 'But, if he did manage to get past, he'd find no joy. Pochardsvale has been roused as well, thanks to your friend Hebehir. Sir Cuthbert Reddlestone and his men are marching upon Cat Crags.'

'Excellent!' said Avran. 'Will they attack it, then?'

Bernard swallowed, then continued more clearly. 'No, they can't hope to take the castle, for it's well-nigh impregnable. However, they'll prevent Casimir from bolting back to his lair, or his other men from riding out to his aid – supposing Casimir could get word to them, which I doubt. So, since the robbers won't be allowed to reach the Swiftling road and can't find a path either westward or southward, they'll need to come back this way if they're to regain their roost – or so they'll think. And, since the

Ralphsland men will be on their tails, they'll be riding fast and frantic.'

'That'll be pleasant,' rumbled Drakht. 'I was fearing we might not be seeing 'em again.' He took a swig from the flask and beamed at us benignly.

'So what then?' Avran asked eagerly.

'Sir Robert believes they'll pass this castle and try to take the ridge road back towards Cat Crags. Well, we're not going to let 'em. There'll not be another ambush on that road, but there'll be a real scare for 'em. Your master the wizard has plenty of tricks up his sleeve. He'll be there, with Rahir and Delhir. He says he won't need anyone else.'

Bernard paused again, took another huge bite and masticated it between bulging cheeks.

'But what then?' asked Avran impatiently.

'Why, Casmir'll turn back into Alunsward,' Bernard responded, with a sort of muffled glee. 'The gates will be standing open. It'll be looking as deserted as ever it was. But this time, the rest of us'll all be waiting inside to welcome him.'

Drakht laughed uproariously and gave Bernard so hearty a thump on his back that it caused the poor man to choke. 'That'll be a welcome indeed. How long must we wait for that pleasure?'

Bernard was coughing and spluttering. It was a few seconds before he could speak. 'An hour,' he gasped at last. 'About an hour, Sir Robert estimates. It depends how fast the robbers ride. Yet our men are on watch, and you may be sure they'll warn us beforehand. My, but you've got a heavy hand,' he said half-resentfully, half in admiration to Drakht. 'I'd sooner be your friend than your enemy

– but it's painful enough to be your friend.' And Drakht's rumbling chuckle was heard again.

So, for a second time, the gates to Alunsward bailey were propped open, Drakht taking care to place the great stones back as exactly as possible into their original positions. Then there was nothing for us to do but wait. Drakht leaned back against one of the door-stones and drowsed. Avran, Bernard, and I were too excited to follow his example and, instead, continued to talk.

On prompting from Avran, Bernard gave us a brief and reluctant account of the robbers' taking of Owlsgard – an assault that came, of course, entirely without warning, since the gates were opened to them while most folk were sleeping. He would say even less about the hardships of that forced march – the whips, the blows, the jeers – but enough for us to glimpse the bleak fire of anger that burned beneath his placid exterior.

'Aye, and you killed that accursed traitor Paradis, Simon, while you finished off that hard-handed rogue Arsenac, Avran. We folk of Owlsgard, we'll be forever indebted to you both. Yet I could envy you the pleasure, for all that. I'm looking forward to this next encounter, you may be sure.'

The bright weather of the morning had proved insubstantial. When we had been up the tower, the sun, though still it shone bravely, was already hemmed in by phalanxes of clouds marching from the southwest. By now, they had overwhelmed it. The sky had become uniformly grey, and the light was fading, while intermittent wind gusts set the grasses rippling.

As one gust found its chill way in through the open gateway, Drakht shivered and woke up. Stretching and yawning, he rose to his feet and inspected the sky.

'This'll suit our master fine,' he observed cheerfully. 'Just so long as the rain doesn't come before the reivers do, that is.'

His comment puzzled me, though I was to understand it later.

Almost at that moment we heard sounds from outside. In through the gate, in undisciplined array, but with cheerful faces, came the twenty other Owlsgard men, each now armed with a sword or an axe, a bow, or a spear, obtained during or after last night's fighting. Though we were given smiles, they spoke no word but scattered about the bailey to find concealment. That was not a difficult task, for there were numerous crumbling walls and stone-heaps, the roofless ruins of houses and store places that had once hugged the inner side of the bailey wall. Sir Robert, who had followed the men in, stopped to speak to us.

'Everything is going well enough, though not quite so well as I would have wished. Casimir and his brigands are in flight back up the valley, but they – or, more likely, their rafneyen – detected the ambush too soon. None were slain or taken. The Ralphsland men are not as close on Casimir's heels as I had hoped, although they are in pursuit.'

He paused to consider the matter, then ordered: 'Bernard, you'd best conceal yourself inside the keep. I won't have it used as a refuge by our enemies. Avran and Drakht, I want you to make sure that no one is readily visible and no tracks are obvious. When you've done that, you must both hide as well. Simon, you're the best archer. You need to come with me.'

Just to the right of the gates on the inner side, a flight of steps wound up to the top of the wall. Since anyone up there would be seen easily from outside, that would not have been a good position for keeping watch. Fortunately for us, however, there was a place three-quarters of the way up, where some stones had fallen out, leaving a gap in the masonry through which one might peer without much likelihood of being spotted.

When we had taken up position, I strung my bow and placed a line of arrows ready to hand on the step beside me. Then I crouched beside Sir Robert to look out. I found that, though we could not see any distance down the hill, we could see quite some way along the road toward Cat Crags. The light was indeed poor by now, and, though I thought I could see the figures of men concealed among the roadside bushes, I was not sure.

'Hark! Here they come,' Sir Robert whispered. 'Be very still, now.'

Up the road from the cattle-pen, in an irregular straggle, came the reivers. In front were an advance guard of five rafenu-riders. Then seven or eight of the pack-rafneyen. Then the six horsemen in a tight group, a grim-faced Casimir midmost. And, after that, the remaining thirteen rafenu-riders, with the other pack-rafneyen among them. The flanks of the horses and rafneyen were heaving, after so steep an ascent at speed.

The advance guard checked outside Alunsward, as if to consider taking immediate refuge, but Casimir bellowed in French. 'Back to Cat Crags, idiots!' At that, they hastened onward.

But not far. Suddenly there were creeping lines of greenish fire crossing the rough track before them, beyond which could be glimpsed what seemed to be the shapes of many men. Strange, stiff figures they were, in the eerie green glow. After brief spell of bafflement, I realized that these must be the bodies of the reivers that had fallen last night, propped up in gruesome rows.

Whether Casimir's men recognized dead comrades and were appalled, or whether they merely thought they faced another ambush, I cannot say. Anyway, the leading rafneyen reared up in fright, one rider being thrown, and the others halted. At that moment, two fireballs were hurled among them. A second rider fell from his mount, slain, as I learned later, by a stone from Delhir's sling. By then, the other reivers and rafneyen were milling about in confusion.

As two more fireballs dropped in their midst, the confusion turned to panic. Back they all streamed towards Alunsward. The pack-rafneyen fled away downhill, but the riders poured in through the gateway.

'Quick! Quick! Shut the gates!' someone called in French. Immediately four of the rafenu-riders leapt down from their saddles to obey.

At that moment, prematurely, the trap was sprung. Whether some Owlsgard man was seen too soon by one of Casimir's men or whether one reacted too quickly in excitement, I am not sure. But suddenly there were shouts, and the reivers were being attacked from all sides.

In terms of numbers, the fight was more or less even. However, the reivers were already demoralized, and our people had the advantage of surprise. I saw Drakht Belineg leap at a rafenu-rider and pluck him from his saddle. I saw Avran hurling himself, sword in hand, upon another rider. And I saw the reivers who had dismounted, striving, too late, to remount their beasts before the men of Owlsgard caught up with them. Then, remembering my duty, I seized my bow and set arrow to string.

Amid the confusion, the six horsemen – Casimir and his particular guard – had kept together. Moreover, they had not ventured far within the gates before the attack was launched. Now they were turning in flight, and the gates were still open.

Hastily, I loosed an arrow and had the satisfaction of seeing one chainmail-clad figure tumble from his horse. Sir Robert had run some way down the steps. As the others rode by, he leapt down upon one of them, he and the rider struggling briefly before the horse threw them both off and fled. I loosed a second time, but missed. It was an arrow of Bernard's, though, that emptied a third saddle. However, Casimir and his two remaining cohorts rode down two Owlsgard men that tried to oppose them and passed out of the gate, four rafenu-riders following.

I seized my arrows, stuffed them back into the quiver, and, forgetful of my injured knee, scurried down the stone steps. As I reached their foot, Sir Robert, who had finished his opponent, came up to me.

'Quickly! Out of the gate!' he cried. 'I hope and believe we'll find Rahir outside with our rafneyen. Hasten, now!'

Swiftly he ran before me, while I hobbled after him as best I might. We found that the wizard, Rahir, and Delhir were already approaching on rafenu-back, followed by six other beasts, Galahad and Lancelot among them.

Our three friends did not pause, but set off immediately down the hill in pursuit of the fleeing brigands. However, Sir Robert and I were soon mounted and following. Down the hill we cascaded, Galahad making me very aware how he hated such a rapid descent – and into another turmoil of action, for the reivers had ridden straight into their pursuers of Ralphsland.

In that brief affray, the brigands did not seek quarter. Soon all were slain – all save one. Casimir cut down two of the men of Ralphsland and, spurring his horse viciously, rode through the press of men, out past the beast-pen and away.

Immediately Sir Robert, who had already slain another of the horsemen, rallied the rest of us in pursuit. We were joined by six of the Ralphsland men, the rest of them continuing up the hill toward Alunsward.

It proved a long chase. We could see Casimir far in front of us, well out of arrow-shot, but we could not catch up with him. His horse was a splendid beast and, even after so long a ride and so much mishandling, possessed such remarkable endurance that it had not tired.

Back across the saddle below Alunsward we rode, at a speed vastly greater than during our careful crossing of yesterday, and up onto the ridge along which the Owlsgard folk had been driven.

Quite why Casimir took that route I do not know, though I puzzled over the question as we rode along. He cannot have been hoping to find refuge with Sir Gabriel Jacklyn. If that were the case, he would surely have sought the Marolane valley. I considered the possibility that he might be aiming to ride down from the ridge as fast as possible, in order to seek refuge in the forests. Yet neither the Earl of the Deerlands nor the Earl of Marcanlon would knowingly have given him sanctuary.

Whatever his reasons, Casimir chose to follow the ridge crest, under ever-darkening skies and amid the mutter of distant thunder. I caught glimpses of him whenever lightning flashed to the south, as a dark shape fleeing along the skyline.

At first, his lead was quite a long one. However, when we too had gained the ridge crest, minute by minute we approached closer to him. I believe, indeed, that we would have caught him eventually. In a straight race on level ground, rafneyen are faster than horses, and our mounts were much less tired than his. Yet a different fate awaited Casimir.

Suddenly, both Casimir and we ourselves too became aware that other riders were coming eastward along the ridge toward us. Caught between his pursuers and the approaching party, Casimir reined up and gazed around him, his eyes wild. Then, in desperation, he urged his horse directly down that steep southern flank of the granite ridge.

We raced onward to the point where he had halted. Indeed, some of us might well have ridden down after him, despite the dangers of the descent. Wisely, however, Sir Robert held up his gloved hand to arrest us from this course of action. Casimir was riding downward at great speed and, for a while, was going well, keeping to the turf and avoiding those dangerously smooth outswells of granite. Yet, as we had learned yesterday, that turf was extremely thin.

Abruptly a whole sheet of it peeled away from the granite, crumpling and shredding under his horse's hooves. With a neigh of terror, the horse lost its footing and fell sideways, tumbling down the hill.

His foot caught in the stirrup, screaming now, he was dragged after the horse and then under it. A flash of lightning gave us a brief glimpse of man and beast rolling down in a mass together. Then they were hidden by the slope of the hill, gone into darkness and silence.

Since there seemed no point in risking the lives of others in an effort to aid a man so evil, Casimir was not sought until next morning. The unfortunate horse was broken-backed and dead. The body of Casimir, bruised and battered almost into shapelessness, lay beneath it. Curiously enough, though, his head was little damaged. On his dead face was an expression, not of pain, but of such stark fear that men said he must have seen the gates of Hell opening to receive him. Delhir Ravatseng was quite sure this in fact was what he had seen.

CHAPTER 25

The Cleansing Of Cat Crags

As we gazed down the hill slope, the other party had joined us. However, it was only when the rolling horse and rider had vanished from view that I became truly aware of them. Their leader spoke first.

'Well now, who was that, Messer Obiran? One of those accursed robbers, I presume, since you were pursuing him?' He was a slight but forceful-seeming person, with thinning hair and a forward-thrusting beard that had been dark but was now flecked with white.

'Their leader himself,' answered the wizard. 'You knew him, I think, Sir Samuel — Casimir of Chattaine. He has done you grave injury, but he can never do so again.'

'Grave injury indeed! When your man Narel Evateng came up with us, I could scarce believe his terrible tidings. Yet, when I saw the burnt-out ruins of our castle and village, I was forced to do so. Tell me quickly! What has become of the rest of my people? And my daughter?'

'Some few of your people have died, I regret to say, but most live yet and are well enough. The women and children, and the older men, are safe in Becketsward, with all the property that Casimir had made them bear away for him. As for your daughter, she is with them and safe as well.'

Sir Samuel Saville drew in his breath and released it in a long sigh. 'I thank God to hear it. After seeing the ruin of our little settlement, I came close to losing hope. But, tell me, what has been the fate of the rest of those robbers? And what about that vile creature Pierre Paradis, whom I trusted so foolishly? Most bitterly do I rue the day that ever I allowed him within my gates.'

'Some of Casimir's men are fled and some taken. Some remain to be smoked out from their retreat in Cat Crags. But the greater part of those who raided Owlsgard are slain, Paradis among them. Here is the rain at last. We need to be moving. I will recount the story to you as we go.'

So, the two parties became one, and, as we rode back along the granite ridge, the events of the last two days were told and told again. Not only was Sir Samuel eager to hear the tale, but also Narel Evateng and the other men of Owlsgard who had ridden with Sir Samuel. Among them was his elder son Dominic, a darker-haired replica of his father. His lady and younger son had remained for safety in Amsetch, where Narel had found them all.

After two rides of such length and at so great a pace, Narel Evateng himself was soon nodding in his saddle. I felt almost as tired and left it to Sir Robert and Rahir to repeat the story of our doings to those who were out of earshot of Vedlen Obiran's recounting. It seemed to me an even longer ride back. Nor was it an enjoyable one, for the rain fell steadily. Yet our spirits remained high, for we had achieved all that we had set out to do.

It was late in the evening when, looking up towards Alunsward, I saw again the bright spark of flames, though this time the beast-pen was unlit. When, at long last, we rode up to the gates of Alunsward, we found them still standing widely open. Now, however, there were torches burning all around the bailey and a bright fire before the keep. The men of Owlsgard and Ralphsland were singing and making merry in the fire-glow. Though the rain was still falling steadily, such was their mood that no-one seemed to mind.

They were on watch for us, however, and surrounded us with greetings and eager questions. Sir Samuel's return was welcomed with joy by his people. Among the crowd were Bernard and Avran, but Avran's eyes were only for me.

'You're back, friend – excellent!' he said, then added in quick concern. 'Yet you seem very weary. Is all well with you, Simon?'

'Oh yes, I'm tired. It was a long ride. But otherwise I'm well and glad to see that you're safe. Were there many killed in the fight?'

'Four of Owlsgard died, and three were injured. Felun has been tending them. Alas, three men of Ralphsland were also slain. But, of the reivers, none remains alive. The Owlsgard men were not inclined to be merciful. As for me, I'm fine and flourishing – and most thankful to know you're uninjured. What happened to that foul creature Casimir?'

'He must be dead also, I'm sure,' I said and went on to tell Avran what had happened. Then, at long last, I dismounted and, after giving Galahad the caresses he merited, sent him off to browse. Many other rafneyen were feeding around and within the bailey, and I noted several horses tethered in sheltered places among the long grasses.

Avran conducted me over to the fire and found me bread and meat, as well as wine of a strange, aromatic sort. Before I had eaten, however, I was beckoned over to be introduced to Sir Henry Harbayne, Lord of Ralphsland – grey-haired, grey-bearded and as lean and keen as a gaze-hound – and a second time, more formally, to Sir Samuel Saville, who seized me by the hand.

'Vedlen has told me how you rescued my daughter, how you slew that dastardly seneschal of mine, and of your part in the saving of my people. I cannot hope to repay you for your services and courtesies, but I shall not forget them.'

For my part, I shall never forget the warm tenor of his voice and his smile, as he spoke to me in this way. It gave me an ampler reward than ever I deserved.

Soon I was seeking my blankets and a sheltered place in the lee of a ruined wall. As I fell away into sleep, the men were still singing and carousing round the fire, their joy at the day's victories undampened by the rain.

Maybe some men woke with the dawn next morning, but I was not one of them. Indeed, I suspect that the only ones who were about early were those few hardy souls who had continued celebrating right through the night. When I was awakened, it was to find the sun shining and the sky blue and clear. The sun's height told me that the time was almost noon.

Again, it was Rahir who had awakened me. His brown face was beaming. 'There was no cause to rouse you so soon today, Simon. Indeed, I was not about early myself. Yet I thought that, having slept past breakfast, you'd not wish to sleep past luncheon also. Moreover, I'm needing to look again at that knee of yours.'

So he did, expressing satisfaction at its condition before re-bandaging it. We talked of small matters while he gave it attention. When he was finishing, I asked idly: 'What are the plans for today, then, Rahir?'

'Why, we'll be finishing our task by riding on Cat Crags. While that evil roost remains undestroyed, there's too much chance of other carrion birds settling in these hills. So, we go to lop it away. The task should not prove a great one, with Casimir the Cat and most of his kittens accounted for already.'

We were cheerful, as we rode forth. A small garrison, under the charge of Alban Daintree of Owlsgard, was left in Alunsward. The wounded were sent away to Becketsward, in charge of two of the Ralphsland men who had themselves suffered slight injuries. The rest of us, wizard's men, men of Owlsgard and Ralphsland, all set off together up the track northwestward.

We made no great haste, since we knew that Cat Crags was already invested by the men of Pochardsvale. Nor, indeed, was it a track on which haste was desirable, for it was of the very roughest and led through the most difficult country I had yet experienced. The rocks appeared to be shales or slates, sometimes hard and sticking upward in irregular masses, sometimes crumbly and decayed to form pools or sudden, deep bogs that had to be skirted with care. Within the pools and bogs, a myriad frogs, toads, and other slimy things seemed to have their habitation. their cachinnating choruses sounding loud in our ears. In sheltered places, thorny bushes grew in profusion, and a few misshapen trees reminded us of the strength of winter winds in these parts.

We made many descents and many climbs as we followed the winding track, but, in general, we were mounting ever higher into the hills. After nearly three hours of riding, we saw before us, upon the highest crest of all, the fortress of Cat Crags.

It was a simple enough structure, a circular tower-keep set upon a high, narrow ridge, but its situation made it almost impregnable. On its southern and western sides and, as I was to learn, on its northern side as well, the ridge fell away into steep cliffs, crowned by tall, machicolated walls that were overseen by a single western tower. On the eastern side, where the ridge narrowed, it had been excavated away into a deep slot, crossed by a drawbridge beyond which loomed twin defensive towers. The whole fortification was constructed of slabs of purplish-grey slate. Rising as it did from cliffs of similar character, it seemed more a natural phenomenon, a rugged growth from the rock itself, than a product of man's labour.

On a flat place some way to the east of the gatehouse, and safely out of arrowshot, the men of Pochardsvale had made their camp. There the main group of Sir Cuthbert Reddlestone's force were waiting at leisure. However, they bore arms and were ready to leap into action at any call from the guards watching the castle. As we approached, the Lord of Ralphsland, the wizard, Sir Robert, and Sir Samuel moved into the lead. It was Sir Cuthbert himself who came forward to meet them. He was a large man, clad in chain armour from head to foot, with a surcoat of white bearing the device of a black tower atop a scarlet rock (the latter being punning reference, I presumed, to his surname, 'red rock,' Reddlestone). Swinging from his waist, in a silver-chased scabbard, was a massive sword of the two-handed type which was now becoming rare but which his mighty thews permitted him to wield with ease. His hair and moustache were silver grey, his cheeks rather jowly, and he had a look of arrogance to which I took an immediate dislike. However, his greeting was courteous enough.

'My Lord of Ralphsland, Sir Samuel, and Messer Obiran, welcome to you! We have prepared some small refreshment for your men and yourselves. May I ask you to join us? My soldiers will ensure that the vermin that remain in this bleak rat hole do not venture forth while we eat. But indeed, they show little evidence of courage.'

A considerable feast was awaiting us, laid out on great wooden platters on trestle tables. There were roasted ducks; great fishes of a sort unknown to me, each cooked, boned, and skinned; haunches of some sort of venison; and a variety of fruits and vegetables, some familiar to me but most unfamiliar. Though Sir Cuthbert had made his way in haste to Cat Crags, he had managed to arrange an ample provisioning. We ate better than we had done in many days, the men of Pochardsvale serving us and cross-questioning us eagerly about the downfall of Casimir. They were jubilant at this, for he had been a menace to all who desired to live peacefully in or about the Stoney Mountains.

They were contemptuous about the garrison remaining in Cat Crags Castle. 'Only a handful of soldiers, most of 'em old or feeble; and maybe a few women and children. Your master the wizard will frighten them out briskly enough. There's no courage in 'em.'

That latter estimate was soon to be tested. As the afternoon was ending, Drakht Belineg was sent as emissary, to speak to the men in the fortress. He was conducted up to the castle by two men of Pochardsvale, one bearing the triangular white flag which, throughout Rockall, signifies a desire for peaceful parley and the other carrying a slim trumpet. As they neared the moat before the castle gate, the trumpeter blew five shrill blasts, then lowered his instrument and waited.

There seemed some hesitation within the castle. It was only after a relatively long delay that the drawbridge was lowered and two men ventured forth. Each wore, over chain mail, the yellow surcoat with the leaping cat that Casimir had chosen as his device. Otherwise, they were very different. The first was as broad and swarthy as the general run of Casimir's men, but the second, who seemed the more senior, was thin and clerkly. It was he whom Drakht addressed.

'I speak for my lords of Pochardsvale, Ralphsland, and Owlsgard and for the mighty wizard Vedlen Obiran. Know that your Lord Casimir is dead and his men have also been slain, in just retribution for their treacherous ravaging of Owlsgard. As you can no doubt see, your castle is closely invested by forces overwhelmingly greater than those remaining to you. You may choose between surrendering peacefully, in which case your lives will be spared, or being forced out from this last refuge, in which case you are in gravest peril. Which do you choose: to yield or to be destroyed?'

I did not hear the response, but I gathered it must have been a request for time for consideration. The two men withdrew onto the drawbridge. The thin man seemed, from his gestures, to be urging surrender, while the other seemed to be urging resistance.

At length they returned over the bridge. Unexpectedly, it was the burly man who spoke, in a growling tone that carried almost as well as Drakht's mighty voice. I cannot attempt to reproduce his accent, but his words were clear.

'We defy you! You cannot seize Cat Crags, and we are amply provisioned. You may lay siege, of course. However, you will become weary as the days pass and you spend your time without profit. Be wise and leave now. Cat Crags has never been taken, nor will it be taken.'

Drakht laughed. 'You are quite wrong. Not only will it be taken, but it will be taken swiftly. Very soon, we will put an end to your wish to stay in that wretched bolthole. When you desire to capitulate, you must come forth bearing a brown flag – and perhaps, even then, your lives may be spared. Adieu for now!' With that, he turned away.

The thin man seemed disconcerted and again hesitant, but his burly companion seized him by the arm and hurried him back into the castle. They vanished from view and the drawbridge was lifted swiftly.

As Drakht and his companions walked back toward us, I chanced to be standing close enough to Sir Cuthbert Reddlestone to hear his words to Vedlen Obiran. 'Are you quite confident that you can do this thing, wizard?'

'Oh, yes.' There was a glimmer of amusement in Vedlen's brown eyes – they had a honey-brown gleam in the setting sun's light. 'With a wind blowing steadily from the south-west, as now it is, and with the help of your men, I can guarantee that those brigands will soon be eager to forsake their refuge.'

The task we were set was one that surprised most of us, though Drahkt and the three Ravatsengs – Hebehir, who had ridden to Rewlenscrag, had rejoined us now – knew well enough what the wizard had in mind. We were instructed to collect all the dead branches that we could obtain from thornbush or tree and bring them to be heaped on the southwestern side of the castle.

Since there seemed only the slightest of chances that any flames would reach high enough to trouble those within the castle with their heat, and none at all that so solid a stone structure could be caused to burn, I failed to understand this plan. I comprehended it even less when I saw that the burnable materials were being piled not immediately beneath the castle walls, but on the further side of the narrow Swiftling valley. Certainly, the smoke from the burning would carry into the castle, but that would be of little avail, except to cause some small annoyance to its inmates.

However, like the others, I worked with a will at collecting the branches. We hacked through plant-stems and tree-roots with our swords, cursed as thorns pricked our fingers, and carried back as much as we might manage, on journey after journey, while the sun went down behind the southern hill-ridges and the light dwindled.

The combustible materials we had assembled were arranged into two piles. A long, hayrick-high mound was made on the upper slope of the southern flank of the Swiftling valley and a much larger mound of reserve fuel piled on the ridge-top behind, from which the fire would be fed as it burned down. After heaping up all the branches we could bring, we rested awhile, and flasks of beer were circulated. Our throats were so dry by then as to make this refreshment particularly welcome.

I had wondered if the wind might drop with the coming of night, but it did not. Instead, it waxed stronger and gustier. This was the time of the dark of the moon, but the stars were bright and the clouds few. I glimpsed a night-hawk overhead and, remembering Sandastre, thought it a good omen.

Then, suddenly, I saw a series of pinpoints of light. Sparks were being struck from flints to set the fire alight. Soon the heaped-up branches were beginning to burn. However, they were damp and green. They would produce much smoke, but little flame.

In the slight addition of brightness caused by their burning, I noticed that four men were walking along the lee side of the smoking pile and casting onto it handfuls of some sort of powder. I thought that the lean one must surely be Narel Evateng and the burly one Hebehir. Which meant that the other two must be Hebehir's two cousins.

As they passed by, the smoke from the burning seemed to increase and to take on a yellowish tinge. It was blowing across the valley in ample billows and reaching the castle, that was sure. Yet the change in the smoke's colour was not spectacular, and I did not believe it would frighten those within.

After a while, the flames burned brighter as they used up their fuel. I was one of those who carried more branches over to feed the fire. I passed Rahir, who, with the other three, was ambling along at his leisure and throwing more powder onto the burning twigs. He gave me a smile and a wink.

As I cast my load into the flames, one branch fell short. I bent to pick it up and toss it after the others. Just at that moment the wind shifted, and the smoke eddied a little. I caught a whiff of it and instantly began gasping and coughing. The smell was revolting. Hastily I ran back upslope, coughing and coughing till my eyes were streaming.

As I ran, the wizard's words of last night came back to my mind. He had said he would smoke out the remaining robbers and I had presumed he was speaking figuratively, but now I realized that he was merely speaking the literal truth.

After blinking several times, I managed to clear my running eyes, though I was still shaken by coughs. As I looked back, I saw that Drakht Belineg and the wizard himself were both walking along the line of smoking branches, each casting some different, lighter-coloured powder onto them.

This time, the result was much more spectacular. Each grain was transformed into a brightly burning spark, almost agonizing in its whiteness and intensity, only to be carried along with the smoke, which then rained down into the castle. Soon it seemed as if a torrent of light was flowing across the Swiftling valley, to bathe the castle walls and towers in a radiance brighter than the full moon.

This strange, magical method of attack was having its effect. Even here, across the valley, I could hear desperate cries and the noise of frantic movement from within the castle. I thought I heard the sound of fighting as well, but I was not sure. Then, as I returned downslope bearing more of the dead branches, I heard a trumpet sound once, twice, three times from the hilltop behind me. Instantly, the wizard raised and let fall his right arm by way of signal, after which he and his five men stepped back from the fire.

A man-at-arms of Pochardsvale was running down toward us. 'They've yielded!' he shouted, hoarse but exultant. 'The drawbridge has been lowered, and they're showing the brown flag. They'll be coming forth in a moment – if they can manage it. I've never heard such coughings and gaspings.'

After that whiff, I could sympathize with them. Yet I found myself laughing at the ease with which the impregnable Cat Crags Castle had been taken. I waited till Rahir caught up with me and found he was chuckling too.

'Simple enough, wasn't it, Simon?'

'Yes, it was simple. But how was the trick worked, and why couldn't we have used it in the taking of Alunsward?'

'Ask me not how 'tis done! Aye, we performed a similar trick once before, long ago, to rout out a murderous band of thieves from their forest hiding place in Dakalet. Yet I've no idea what potions we were using. Some strange, alchemical preparations, I don't doubt, and from the Trident Mountains. The first needs a strong, steady wind to carry its odours, while the fuel must be green and moist. Maybe that's why we couldn't employ the same trick at Alunsward, for there'd been no recent rain. As you'll recall, the rain came afterward. The second preparation you have to be much more careful with. It's strange stuff indeed. If your fingers are wet, it'll burn them. We keep it very well wrapped and very dry, you may be sure.'

'But what do these preparations contain?' I asked.

'I don't know at all what either of those powders contains. I'm not even certain our master does, wise though he be.'

As the Pochardsvale men had surmised, the garrison of Cat Crags Castle was not large – some twenty-five men, fifteen or so unhappy and worn-looking women, and a few ragged children. All of them were coughing as if their hearts would burst, and, once again, I felt sorry for them. I trusted that neither the Owlsgard people, nor any others, would desire to wreak vengeance on such pitiful figures, and I was glad to find that they did not.

The burly man was not among those who had surrendered. I was to learn later that, while attempting to prevent the capitulation, he had been struck down and slain by his frantic comrades. That was no cause for regret, for, though courageous, he had been one of the Cat's closest henchmen and very evil.

The others were treated well enough. After the lean man, Casimir's seneschal – and chosen for that office, I think, because he was too weak-spirited to be disobedient to his master – had surrendered the keys and he and the other men had set down their weapons, each was allowed to seat himself on the ground and was given a cooling drink. Afterward, however, the men were fettered and marched away.

In contrast, the women and children were given moistened cloths with which to lave themselves and invited to eat and drink at will from the ample remains of our feast. Though three or four of the women seemed as wild and wicked as the reivers themselves, all were treated with like courtesy. Some, who had been captured from settlements in the hills or villages in the forests and plains, were weeping with joy at their release. The tales they told of what had been done to them made us furious again at Casimir's crimes. It was just as well that the last of his cohorts had been removed already from our reach.

About their ultimate fate, I should perhaps add a brief note. Needless to say, the women and children were all freed, allowed to go wherever they wished, although most chose to go at first to Becketsward. As for the surviving reivers, it was decreed that all of them – including the six captured earlier – would be taken in chains back to Owlsgard and made to labour in its rebuilding. When that work was done, they would be compelled to assist for two further years in tilling and planting the fields of Owlswatch, harvesting its crops. Then, if they had worked well, they would be allowed to go their way in freedom. It seemed to me, remembering the sentences of execution meted out in our realm of England for crimes much lesser than theirs, a very merciful treatment. But that is the way of Rockall.

As for the rest of us, we built a large bonfire on the hilltop with the other branches we had collected. We sat around it, drinking and eating, singing and talking, men of Pochardsvale and Ralphsland, Owlsgard folk, and wizard's men all mixing together in a shared camaraderie, till the first hues of dawn were tinting the southern horizon. Then we slept well and long.

CHAPTER 26

The Days In Ralphsland

'Whatever can have become of Amos Sloly?'

We were riding down the Swiftling track, on our way to Becketsward at last, when I voiced that question. 'At last,' I write here, for three full days had elapsed since the remainder of Casimir's robbers had been smoked out from their roost. The first day had been an idle one, for the castle had remained too odoriferous to be entered. Our only solemn occupation had been a thanksgiving for victory, with Sir Samuel Saville leading our prayers. Afterwards, there had been more feasting and singing. When brisk overnight winds had done their cleansing work, we entered Cat Crags on the second morning and searched it very thoroughly. Though Casimir's brigandage had gained for his men and him many unmerited luxuries, it seemed to me a dismal place. It was very dirty and communicated none of the sense of communal pride that characterises any ordinary English castle. Of its dungeons and the sad relics they contained, I will not speak, though it is in vain that I have tried to put them from my memory.

The castle could not readily be burned or levelled and was too important a strongpoint to be left unguarded. Moreover, there was reasonably good pastureland for rafneyen in the

Swiftling valley, as well as good prospects for hunting and the planting of crops in the terrain to the north. It was decided that families from Becketsward and Pochardsvale and even from Owlswatch be invited to settle there and form a new community. For the moment, the plan was that it be garrisoned by men from all those three places, under the charge of John Stanton of Owlsgard, who was unmarried and willing to become its seneschal. The loot that Casimir had accumulated was divided up. Much of it was allocated as compensation to the Owlsgard folk, the rest being apportioned between Sir Henry Harbayne of Ralphsland and Sir Cuthbert Reddlestone of Pochardsvale for the use of their communities. Here in Rockall, nobles did not seize such plunder for themselves, as would have been usual in France or Britain.

Sir Cuthbert and the majority of his men were on their way back to Pochardsvale, while most of the men of Owlsgard had set off directly homeward on rafneyen that had once been Casimir's, taking with them the twenty-five prisoners. Moreover, the Lord of Ralphsland had sent some of his men, with the women and children from Cat Crags, off to Becketsward two days earlier. Hebehir Ravatseng travelled with them, to provide medical attention if necessary.

So it was that only a comparatively small party rode down the Swiftling valley that day. There were some thirty soldiers of Ralphsland and six men of Owlsgard, Bernard the archer and Sir Samuel's son among them. All of them, plus two dozen laden pack-rafneyen, were following behind Avran and me. Beside us were the Ravatseng brothers and, in the van, the Lord of Ralphsland, with the wizard, Sir Samuel, and Sir Robert.

The three knights were engaged in a lighthearted discussion, but the wizard was silent and seemed asleep in his saddle. Since his mount was entirely trustworthy and since he had a capacity for complete relaxation whenever the opportunity arose, it is probable that Vedlen Obiran *was* indeed asleep.

'Amos Sloly?' Avran echoed my query, his surprise evident. 'Why of course, he and the pack-rafneyen should have caught up with us long ago. Maybe he stayed at Alunsward. We left a small garrison there, didn't we?'

'Aye, we did.' Rahir Ravatseng was speaking now and sounding unexpectedly grim. 'But Amos is not there, for our master sent Narel back yesterday to ask. And so, this morning, our master ordered a proper search to be made. Narel and Drakht are riding back towards Owlsgard, to see if they can find our absent friend.'

Those last words had so ironic a ring that I asked: 'Why, Rahir, what could be wrong? Likely enough Amos has stayed close to Owlsgard. Possibly he felt it the safest option. What else could have happened?' As I spoke, however, I recalled my last glimpse of Amos and his strange secret smile.

'Well, 'tis possible that he and all our belongings might have finished up in Blackhill Castle. Sir Gabriel Jacklyn wouldn't mind putting his hands on other folks' property. Yet I hardly think so. For myself, I believe Amos has taken the most valuable of our goods and skipped away with his loot.'

Avran was as shocked at that idea as I was. 'Oh, surely not, Rahir! Amos is such a cheerful soul, always smiling, always so eager to help.'

'And always so careful not to miss anything that might give him a bit of profit for himself,' Rahir added dryly. 'For my part, I've never been so sure of that one.'

'He was wholly self-seeking.' Delhir's observations were

so few that they always came as a surprise. 'He did not merit our master's trust.'

I found myself resenting these unexpected criticisms of someone who was, after all, an Englishman like myself. 'Why, then, was he employed? Surely our master would not have taken into his service someone who was false-hearted? And surely he would not have left his tents, his gold, and his other possessions in the charge of a man he could not rely on?'

'Amos Sloly was useful to our master, of course.' It was Rahir who proffered an answer. 'He spoke the English of your people who have settled here in Rockall. He could gain their trust easily and he gave them confidence when we were treating their ailments or injuries. Yet, as to Amos being left in charge of the packs, you must remember that our master sets little value upon such material things. Consider instead that, when he was seeking to rescue the Owlsgard folk and needed comrades whom he could trust, our master preferred to leave Amos Sloly behind.'

Such an inversion of my argument was disconcerting. On the other hand, it appeared perfectly plausible. I had come to understand and respect Vedlen Obiran's dedication and selflessness. Alhough he enjoyed his luxuries, they were not important to him.

Avran was impressed as well, yet he remained unconvinced. 'Yet Amos is so jovial, so willing, so good-natured . . . I cannot believe him to be a thief, Rahir. He must have encountered some mischance – some accident or raid – surely?'

'I pray that you're right and I'm wrong, Avran friend. Our master can ill afford to lose so much. Nor do I think that Sir Robert would be pleased, either, to find his armour and his store of gold gone. Well, no doubt Narel and Drakht will discover all that's to be learned.'

We rode on for a while in silence. Soon, on our left, we were passing the stone bridge that spanned, in a double arch, the waters of the Swiftling and the Marolane just above their confluence. To the right of the bridle-path was the thicket where the men of Ralphsland had waited to ambush Casimir's men, yet had succeeded only in turning them back. It was formed of bushes of a type I had not seen, with dark green, shining leaves of oval shape, dense enough to afford excellent concealment. The tip of each twig had opened into a seven-petalled flower, each petal having a blush-pink base and white tip.

The sight of these blossoms caused a stir of excitement among the Ralphsland men. Apparently, these bushes, which were called saints-wreathes, flowered only rarely. The men were sure that the flowers had opened in celebration of Casimir's downfall. Eagerly they broke off branches to carry to Becketsward.

Beyond the bridge, the bridle-path climbed slowly up the hillside between irregular crags of slate. Our rafneyen's hooves skittered perilously on the broken shards that had fallen from these crags onto the path, though none of the beasts lost balance. After an hour of difficult riding, the slate-filled terrain ended, the bushes faded out, and we passed onto a swelling, grassy hillside, much like the ridge on which we had ridden from Owlsgard. There were rafneyen feeding among the few, low bushes, under the watchful eyes of herd-boys who shouted cheerful greetings to us.

With arrival home imminent, the Ralphsland men began chanting a carol of joy and victory. The chorus was simple. I joined in, while Avran produced his pommer and managed to tootle the tune as well. In this way, cheerfully, we passed the last few leagues, as we rode over the round hill and down to Becketsward.

Like the two others we had seen in the Stoney Mountains, its castle was relatively recent in date and simple in structure. It had a square tower-keep that was set centrally in a bailey of no great size designed on a quadrate plan and with mural towers at the four corners. On the northern side, moreover, the castle was protected by granite cliffs and by the swift waters of the Belden Brook below; on the southern and eastern sides, by a deep, dry moat whose further flank had been set hedgehog-like with pointed stakes. A drawbridge led over this to the southeastern tower, which served also as gatehouse.

As we approached, still singing, from the bailey there issued sounds of music and cheering in response. A crowd of men and women, with excited children cavorting and prancing among them, surged out over the bridge to welcome us. Happiest of all were the wives, sons, and daughters of Owlsgard, many of whom were weeping with joy.

Soon the knights and the wizard – wide awake now and beaming – were garlanded with flowers, while posies were thrust beneath our front saddle-straps. By that point, we were riding slowly, as the press of people around us increased. Suddenly a garland was tossed over my own head, and I saw Lauretta in the crowd.

'That is for you, my angel!' she cried. 'Halt your mount for a moment, and let me come up beside you.'

As Galahad stopped, directed by my thoughts, and I made place for her, she scrambled up onto his back. She sat side-saddle before me, clinging on to me in a way that half-delighted and half-embarrassed me, while chattering away to me in a babble of pleasure, as we rode through the arching gateway into the bailey of Becketsward.

Sir Samuel turned in his saddle to look back at us, but gave us only his smile. Avran, however, raised his eyebrows and winked at me, after which he stared steadfastly ahead.

That evening we feasted in the great hall of Becketsward keep. We were not a very large group. Many of the Ralphsland men had returned to their farms and families in the valleys west of Becketsward, while most of the Owlsgard folk and their new-found friends were celebrating around bonfires burning outside in the bailey. Apart from a few servants, therefore, there were only seventeen of us at that feast – the Lord of Ralphsland and his Lady, tall, grey, and grave; their two handsome daughters (they had no son); the seneschal of Becketsward and his lady; Sir Samuel, Dominic, and Lauretta; Vedlen Obiran and the three Ravatseng cousins; Sir Robert Randwulf, Avran and me; and, to our great pleasure, Felun Daretseng, whom we had not seen for six hectic days.

With him, during the earlier part of the evening, was the small boy whom he had adopted or who had adopted him – it was hard to tell which, for they showed great mutual affection. Later Felun took the boy off to bed and returned, a little sheepishly, I thought, to rejoin us.

While we ate, the talk was merry enough. But, when the dishes had been removed and the wine was circulating, Sir Henry Harbayne spoke more gravely.

'For the destruction of your village and castle, Sir Samuel, I am in part to blame, as you are yourself in part to blame. Yes, yes, I know we have just obliterated an evil, but that evil was allowed to fester too long. Each of us has ruled his own small feoff in the Ferekar Naur and has been content with that. Oftentimes we have disputed our boundaries with neighbouring feofdoms, often we have traded with each other, and sometimes we have enjoyed each other's hospitality, but that has been all. When Casimir made his first small raids on farms or barns, we chased the reivers away and watched our own bounds more carefully. We did no more. When he seized and devastated Alunsward, we expressed shock, but we took no action. We learned of his other fell deeds in the lands to eastward and northward, but still we did nothing.'

'All true enough,' said Sir Samuel, 'but what could we have done?'

The fist of the Lord of Ralphsland smote the trestle table with such a mighty blow that goblets and flasks danced. 'Why, we ought to have co-operated then, as we are doing now! Alone, none of us was strong enough to extirpate the evil of Cat Crags, but if we had acted together as men of goodwill, we could have accomplished this long ago. Yes, I recognise that Messer Obiran and his men have given us great assistance' – he inclined his head politely to the wizard – 'but if you, Sir Samuel, and I had combined our forces with those of Sir Cuthbert and our neighbours to west and north, we would have been easily able to destroy Casimir and his knaves. The Lord of Wildfell and Sir Hugh ap Llewellyn of Merlinward – they have suffered much from Casimir and would certainly have joined us. Sir Gabriel Jacklyn I dislike and mistrust – I know he traded with Cat Crags and I suspect that, on occasion, he lent his aid to Casimir's misdeeds. Yet he would not have dared rally to the support of the Cat, had we others decided to act in concert. But instead, we thought only of our own concerns. This was the reason that Owlsgard burned. If that deed had gone unavenged, Becketsward might have been next to be put to the flame, situated as it is between Cat Crags and Blackhill.'

As Sir Henry paused and sipped from his goblet, Sir Samuel nodded his head. 'Aye, you are right. And now we *are* acting together, a fact for which we the folk of Owlsgard are profoundly grateful. Yet how should we proceed?'

'Why, we must form a league, an alliance of those willing to take action against future evils. We must establish a system of rapid alert against danger. We must agree to rally, not merely when all are threatened but when any one of us is threatened. Yes, I know we have our disagreements about land and water, grazing and hunting rights, but those can be settled readily enough, given goodwill. Casimir the Cat is dead and, I trust and believe, in Hell. But there are other Casimirs that will prey on us, if we afford them opportunity. We must ensure that they are given no opportunity. Such men must learn that evil deeds are followed by swift vengeance.'

Sir Samuel was nodding again. 'Your words are most wise, my friend. What, then, do you propose?'

'That we must gather to confer – and soon. A fortnight from this day, let us say? I shall propose to Sir Cuthbert that we meet at Rewlenscrag, not here in Becketsward. You must understand, I do not wish to seem to be setting myself up as leader – and Sir Cuthbert can be – how shall I put this? – rather sensitive. If he concurs, then messages shall be sent out to the rulers of all the feofdoms in these hills, not just our western feofdoms, but to Falconward, Starkward, and even to Amsetch, though I suspect the Lord of Amsetch may feel his feofdom too remote either to be aided by us or to aid us.'

'Even to Blackhill?' enquired Sir Samuel.

'Even to Blackhill, though I question whether Sir Gabriel will come or, if he does come, will want to co-operate.'

The wizard had been listening intently, a smile on his face. His eyes looked honey-brown and benign in the firelight. Now he spoke.

'My lord of Ralphsland, your idea is excellent. I congratulate you most sincerely. If what you propose is carried through, then out of the evil of Casimir's deed there may spring a lasting good.'

In the days that followed, Avran and I enjoyed a pleasant and relaxing time in the lordship of Ralphsland. We continued to give aid to the wizard and his men in their medical tasks as physicians and surgeons wherever it was required. However, that was seldom, as the people of this realm were mostly healthy. Moreover, the folk of Owlswatch were recovering well from their ordeal. Indeed, the rest of them set off back to Owlsgard on the third day, under the charge of young Dominic Saville and with some skilled masons and carpenters that accompanied them to aid in the rebuilding of the village and castle. Lauretta, Avran, and I rode with the group to the Marolane ford three leagues upstream from Blackhill. There we were bidden an affectionate farewell. If Sir Gabriel Jacklyn's men witnessed the crossing – we were within his lands – they gave no sign, and we returned unmolested to Becketsward.

That evening, we learned that Sir Cuthbert Reddlestone had agreed to stage the gathering of the lords of the Ferekar Naur and proposed to celebrate it with a tournament. He had asked especially that Vedlen Obiran be present, a request to which the wizard immediately acceded.

That was good news, but the other news that we received that evening was much less auspicious. It was brought by Bevis, Sir Samuel's rafenu-master at Owlsgard, who had arrived with five pack-rafneyen. These bore the wizard's tents and tent-furniture, found abandoned in a gully of the Stoney Mountains not far north of Owlsgard. Drakht Belineg and Narel Evateng had made the discovery. Unfortunately, since the storm that had followed our taking of Alunsward had washed away most traces, neither they nor a skilled hunter from Amsetch whom they had recruited to their service could make clear sense of what had happened.

They could not decide whether Amos Sloly had been captured, along with the pack-rafneyen and the other possessions of the wizard and Sir Richard, or whether Amos had jettisoned the more unwieldy items and fled with all he could conveniently steal. However, they were sure the rafneyen had gone away eastward, down into the valley of the Brunflow and away towards Riotte. Drakht and Narel had taken the recovered items to Owlsgard, then had ridden away to continue the search for Amos Sloly.

Avran was still inclined to give Amos the benefit of what small doubt remained. 'Perhaps he was ambushed,' he argued. 'The scouring of Cat Crags does not mean we have driven all evildoers from these hills.'

However, the discovery served to shake even further my own diminished faith in my fellow countryman. I remembered again that strange smile of Amos's and recalled also that Trayad-in-Riotte was a trading post of the Mentonese, where a thief might dispose of whatever goods he had for sale. As for the Ravatseng brothers, they just nodded their heads sadly, not showing any surprise.

A much more pressing problem for me was Lauretta. She regarded me as a romantic figure, a sort of knight-errant who had saved her from a cruel fate. Well, I didn't mind that. The trouble was that it was quite evident that she assumed a marriage between us to be the only proper ending to such a romance. In consequence, she regarded me in an almost proprietary fashion, a fact I found increasingly disturbing.

Now that we were ensconced in the castle, she was unwilling to allow Rahir Ravatseng to tend my still-troublesome knee, nor would she permit any servant do so. Instead, each morning, she came to my chamber high in the keep and insisted on re-dressing it herself. I was grateful that Avran, who shared that chamber, was present on those occasions. I was not sure, however, that Lauretta was equally grateful.

An additional problem was that I found her both attractive and amusing. She was slim and graceful in her movements, with brown eyes set in an oval face that was rarely lacking in animation. Much more often it reflected vividly her mood of the moment – interest, enquiry, attention or, most commonly, a bubbling enjoyment of life. I liked Lauretta very much. However, though Sandarro might be far away and though I knew well that I might never see Ilven again, it was she who possessed my heart. All the same, I found it hard to repulse Lauretta's attentions and, in my weakness, I made little attempt to do so.

Avran might by all rights have been angry, had he not known that my feelings for his sister remained unchanged. As it was, he merely felt sorry for Lauretta and rather annoyed with me for not having the courage to break off our developing relationship – a relationship, to make matters even worse, that her father and mother quite evidently approved of.

So it was that I spent much of each day with Lauretta, while taking care never to be left alone in her company. On some days we went out riding, though always with Avran, Sir Robert, or some others coming along, up onto the hill behind Becketsward, northward along the steep valley of the Belden Brook or westward into the broader vale of the Marolane, with its little riverside farms. At other times we would join groups of musicians under the castle walls. Lauretta and I would sing the old ballads and carols of England, and she would teach me some of the new ones of Rockall, while Avran persuaded his pommer into following the melody and musicians of Ralphsland, who strummed citole and cittern or played their plaintive notes on psaltery. On Saturday, we wandered round the town's weekly market, inspecting the stalls of food and wine, admiring the cloths and tapestries brought from England and Gascony and the hawks and falcons sitting hooded and stiff in the sunshine. Once, I was persuaded into a game of chess with Lauretta and had her laughing at my ineptitude. On another occasion, we sat in a crowd about a travelling storyteller, enthralled by his tales of ancient valour and entertained by his stories of scandal from the courts of Herador and Kelcestre.

It was on the day before our departure to Rewlenscrag that I found myself at last alone with Lauretta. Somewhere outside the castle walls, Avran was again trying his skills of swordmanship with Sir Robert and, no doubt, was again finding himself outmatched by that wily warrior. The wizard was engaged with a difficult delivery, one that the Becketsward midwife had despaired of, and was aided in this by the Ravatseng brothers. I was not sure of the whereabouts of our other friends, but they were not in evidence.

So it was that I found myself sitting with Lauretta up on a stone seat atop the northwestern tower of Becketsward castle, looking out over the green valley of the Marolane, with the deeper green of the Great Marshes in the distance. Though the castle was humming with preparations for tomorrow's expedition to Rewlenscrag, we were not involved, and the prospect before us was tranquil. I remember that Lauretta was looking most attractive, in a dress of green velvet, tight-bodiced and high-belted, her long dark hair combed to sleekness and capped by a crisp white coif. She had been unusually quiet as we climbed the stair, but now she spoke with a sort of earnest desperation. 'Simon, it is time for a decision. You know that I am yours if you want me. My father likes you and knows he is in your debt. If you should choose to come to Owlsgard, you are certain to receive high honours from him. If, though, you prefer to go on with a wandering life, well, I would go with you, with or without my father's consent. But I believe he would agree even to that. Whatever you want, I want, so long as I can be with you.'

I looked at her sadly. 'I have been afraid of this. My dear Lauretta, I like you very much and I enjoy your company. You know that. However, things between us can go no farther. You need to know that I am promised solemnly in marriage to the sister of my friend Avran, to Princess Ilven of Sandastre.'

It was as if I had given her a buffet across the face. 'Please don't say it's so!' she said, her voice faltering. 'Tell me it's not true, Simon. I cannot – I shall not believe it!'

'Yet it *is* so, Lauretta. If you don't believe me, then you must ask Avran.'

'If you assure me that it's so, then I have to believe you,' Lauretta said with sadness. Then, desperately, she added: 'But you can't truly love her, when you have left her so far behind. Oh Simon, I love you so much. Can't you forget her and . . . and be kind to me, even if you don't love me?'

Poor Lauretta. Her voice had a further catch in it now, and her eyes were brimming with tears. She had dropped to her knees before me and was clutching my hands. My heart went out to her, but there was nothing I could do.

'Oh Lauretta, I am so sorry,' I said. 'You need to understand that I have no desire to hurt you. However, I'm afraid I do love Ilven and I'm entirely certain that I don't want to leave her. If it weren't for a vow I made before I met her, I would never have left Sandastre.'

I tried to explain the quest I had undertaken for my father and brother. However, I don't think Lauretta understood or even tried to understand. Suddenly her hands slipped from mine, and she rose to her feet. When she spoke, her voice held a note of profound desperation that was heartrending.

'Well, you do not want me or need me, that's clear. Farewell, my angel!' Lauretta turned and ran sobbing down the stair, out of my view.

As it was, I was not to see her again. She did not appear at dinner that evening. Next morning, we learned that, along with two servants, she had fled away, back to Owlsgard.

CHAPTER 27

The Quarrel At The Butts

The castle of Rewlenscrag was the most impressive I had seen in the Stoney Mountains, not so much because of its design – the keep was simply a square tower – as because of its position and colour. That keep was set on a crag isolated by a deep, narrow ravine from the hill behind. The crag was so small in extent that the keep occupied its whole summit. The only approach was by a steep stair, without balustrades and cut straight into the rock. A broad terrace below the crag was enclosed by high, machicolated walls to form the bailey. Beyond that, the ground fell steeply again to the meadows of the Pochard River.

This was a splendid defensive site, sure enough, but, as I have remarked, the colour was also striking. The keep and fortifications were built of blocks of white marble veined with green, but the cliffs under the keep and beneath the curtain wall of the bailey were of a black rock in which tiny green crystals sparkled in the sunshine. Add to this the verdant green of the grass of the meadowlands and the sward and shrubs within the bailey, plus the brown of the wooden houses set against the bailey walls, and you have a scene of strikingly varied colour. Nor was that an end to it. In and about the castle there were many tents, most dyed in bright hues and many with the banners of their owners displayed upon poles alongside. Nine tents, for the eight lords and the wizard visiting Rewlenscrag, were set in the bailey, while the many smaller tents that housed the followers of these lords were distributed throughout the meadows below. All in all, I have rarely viewed such a brilliant scene.

I refer here to eight lords, for indeed the Lords of Amsetch and Blackhill had both elected to attend this rally of the rulers of the Ferekar Naur. Soon, I learned the heraldry of the eight realms and could pick out, by his surcoat, where it was that any man came from.

The arms of Amsetch were simple enough: *argent, a fess doubly cotised azure* – which is to say a silver field traversed by a broad horizontal line of blue, with two narrower blue lines parallel to it on either side. The others were all more elaborate. The men of Merlinward bore the old Welsh symbol, which I read as *gules, a dragon sejant erect or* – which is to say a golden dragon on a field of red, and a fierce enough beast it looked, with barbed tail and protruding, forked tongue. The green surcoats of Wildfell depicted a wild man, naked except for a wreath of green leaves round his loins and very fierce-looking, brandishing a massive black club. The blue surcoats of Falconward depicted, fittingly enough, a falcon in jesses and bells, hoodless and with a writhing lizard clutched in its claws. That was more difficult to blazon, but I thought it must be *azure, a falcon argent belled and jessed gules, preying on a lizard or*. In similar canting fashion, the black surcoats of Starkward showed a silver castle set on a green hilltop, its stones neatly indicated. (*Sable, a castle argent masoned sable, upon a hill vert*).

The friendly arms of Ralphsward, green again and bearing a running rafenu in gold, were familiar enough (*vert, a rafenu courant or).* The silver surcoats of Blackhill I regarded with proper mistrust, being moreover rather puzzled by their charge. Of course, the black mount meant Blackhill, but I wondered why it was surmounted by that unusual emblem of a scarlet lion stretched out horizontally, as if in sleep. Even when I had blazoned it carefully as *argent, a lion jacent surmounting a mount sable,* I missed the laborious canting reference to the name of its owner till Sir Robert pointed it out – 'jacent lion,' that is to say, Jacklyn. The lion, though stretched out, seemed to be watching through narrowed eyes. If its nobility did not make it a suitable emblem for Sir Gabriel, that shifty glance suggested him well enough.

The arms that caused me most pain, however, were the three owls on a blue field that symbolized the Savilles. Since his daughter's abrupt departure, Sir Samuel had continued to be perfectly courteous to me, but without the warmth of cordiality he had shown up to that time. And I could scarcely blame him. For my own part, I was missing Lauretta acutely. At one moment, I was condemning myself as all sorts of a fool for allowing her to go out of my life. After all, I thought it unlikely I'd ever find my way back to Sandarro and Ilven. At the next, I was chiding myself for my lack of consideration in permitting her hopes to rise as they had done. I should have told her earlier of Ilven. What an insensitive brute I had been to her!

All the time, I was thoroughly unhappy, sometimes wanting to pour out confidences to my friend, at other times too surly to speak any word. For poor Avran, it must have been a difficult period, but he bore my ill-nature very well, as only the truest of friends will.

Together with the wizard's men, we had another cause for unhappiness. It was that we looked so tawdry amid all this splendour. For sure, the wizard's tent stood proudly amid the others in the bailey, its multitude of cabalistic signs evoking awe in its beholders. However, the splendid purple livery we should have worn had been stolen, along with so much else. For Avran and me, the situation was not too bad. Our Doriolupatan cloaks, worn yellow side outermost, looked sufficently colourful, even if they bore no charge to indicate our allegiance. The wizard's men, however, had only their field gear to wear and for this reason were decidedly dispirited.

Their situation was especially poignant, because most folk at Rewlenscrag seemed to assume that a real wizard might, if he so cared, magick his followers into a more impressive garb. A wizard who did not, their glances implied, must be a mere charlatan or a second-class operator at best.

To add to our problems, Avran and I had too little to do. Vedlen Obiran and the eight lords of the Ferekar Naur were closeted together all day in a chamber high in the keep, while they argued out plans for a league of mutual defence. Before this could be done, they had to agree on the fate of Cat Crags and Alunsward, now become a no-man's-land, and also on the exact boundaries of their lands, on hunting rights and fishing rights, and on many other things. Felun Daretseng, who attended these deliberations with the wizard, was of the opinion that Sir Cuthbert's invitation to Vedlen Obiran had proved a crucial factor in the negotiations. Again and again, they appealed to the wizard as an adjudicator, and he seemed always to find an acceptable route around an apparent impasse.

Our evenings were pleasant enough, for then we would all join together. We met sometimes at banquets in the castle, sometimes to prepare and eat our own meals before the wizard's tent, and sometimes, when the wizard was not present, to dine and drink in the cook-shops and ale-houses that had been set up in the meadow. During the daytime, the Ravatseng brothers had enough injured or sick people applying for treatment to keep them occupied, while Sir Robert was heavily involved in the planning of the tournament. Avran and I, on the other hand, were left without any tasks.

What we should have done, of course, was to set forth again on our quest. The difficulty was that we were still without any clear idea where we should be heading. It was evident that we needed to go beyond the northern mountains, but we were not certain by what road and in what direction. Those mountains, we had been told, were greater both in extent and altitude than those of the south, and passes through them were few and difficult. It seemed advisable to wait till the Rewlenscrag council had ended and then, if all went well, to travel north to Reschora with our good friends, the wizard and his men. At the same time, it was not clear whether in fact Vedlen Obiran would be travelling north, in the event that Amos Sloly was not found.

So, we occupied our hours as best we could. Although Avran can't have found me an agreeable companion, depressed and irritable as I was, he stayed by my side loyally throughout most of those long days. In view of an atmosphere of intense preoccupation with the martial arts that prevails anywhere before a tournament, it was natural enough that we should exercise with our arms. Avran sought patiently to improve my swordsmanship, trying to impart to me the tricks Sir Robert had taught him. In point of fact, my skill with that weapon did increase, though it would never match his own. As well, I practised with my throwing-knives, an exercise that had become all the more necessary insofar as I had not done anything of this kind for many weeks. And both of us went daily to the butts, to refurbish our skills with the longbow. It was there that we ran into trouble.

The great hall of Rewlenscrag castle was large enough for most normal occasions, but much too small to contain the host that had assembled this time. After a first evening, in which Sir Cuthbert had entertained only his fellow lords and the wizard, on each subsequent night he bade to his table two or three of the lords, along with their principal followers. Since the combination of the folk he invited had been varied nightly, we quickly came to meet men and women from each of the little realms of the Stoney Mountains. Most of them were quite pleasant.

There were, however, exceptions. One of them, most unfortunately, was Fulk Reddlestone, Sir Cuthbert's eldest son. He was quite as big a man as his father, with huge shoulders that hunched forward, a mane-like mass of yellow hair, light blue eyes as bright and unfeeling as sapphires, and full lips set into a perpetual curl of contempt.

When he was introduced to me, Fulk appeared merely uninterested and faintly condescending. However, when Avran was presented under his proper title of Prince of Sandastre, Fulk registered a sort of angry surprise. The handclasp he offered had been very brief and quite token in nature. Afterward, I heard him whisper to his neighbour a petty comment about the ease with which a person could claim high rank in a realm that nobody had heard of. Unhappily, Avran was also listening, and I saw his flush of anger.

On subsequent nights, when we dined in the castle, Fulk addressed not a word to Avran and me, but his whispered comments about us to his neighbours at table, followed by their amused glances and their titters, had several times irritated me and brought my volatile friend dangerously close to losing his temper.

Fulk had his own particular associates among the sons of the lords of the Ferekar Naur and their followers. His younger brother Berenger seemed always to be attending on him in an annoyingly fawning way, while Humphry Stethren, scion of the Lord of Starkward, and Aldwyn Ennerling, the son of its seneschal, were almost as constant in their cloying admiration.

A more surprising associate of Fulk's, and certainly a new one, was Hubert Jacklyn of Blackhill. A youth as dark, lean, and ever-smirking as his father, he was, in my judgement, quite as untrustworthy. He seemed at once to irritate and to amuse Fulk, stirring the bigger youth into brief anger at one moment and, in the next, pacifying him with honeyed words and provoking him to laughter by some barbed witticism. I felt that I disliked Hubert even more than Fulk. Young Reddlestone was merely a boor, but young Jacklyn was quite evidently a self-seeking mischiefmaker.

Given this combustive mix of personalities, it was not without reason that I felt disquiet when, on the eighth day at Rewlenscrag and the seventh day of our archery exercises, I noticed that Fulk and his four cronies had joined the watching crowd. Most of the archers, whatever the lordship to which they belonged, were friendly enough, and, on that day, we chanced to be matching our skills with those of two archers of Starkward. We had shot at

the target already from a relatively short distance – about
eighty yards – and had all shot well, our four arrows clus-
tering around the gold. Now we were trying again from
double that distance. Just before the first man of Starkward,
a grizzled veteran with a face as lined as an onion-slice,
set his arrow at the nock, I heard Humphry Stethren cry
out: 'I'll wager five gold marks that my man will outshoot
the wizard's man!'

'Nay, I'll not place my money on such a long chance,'
Fulk Reddlestone responded contemptuously.

Yet Hubert Jacklyn said with a laugh: 'Taken! I believe
always in betting on a dark horse – and that one is dark
enough!'

Thus it was that, when I stepped up to the mark, I knew
that five gold pieces of Blackhill money were depending
on my skill. For me, this was an annoying and troublesome
situation. While I cared not a jot whether young Jacklyn
won or lost his wager, all the same I felt impelled to strive
to my utmost in making the shot – for the honour of our
master, if for no other reason.

The old archer had shot well. His arrow had struck only
just outside the gold. It would be a hard shot to match
and harder still to excel.

Take it easy, I told myself. Back straight, chest open,
arrow at nock. Good, now draw slowly. Watch the wind.
There are gusts from the right, but the grass is not rippling,
so the air should be still. Aim a little higher, so the arrow
will drop right, and . . .

I was about to loose when there was a cry of 'Fast!' I
relaxed as a small boy chased his wooden ball onto the
grass just in front of the butt, seized it, and, with the
remonstrances of the bystanders ringing in his ears, ran

back among them. Again, I set arrow to nock, but now the rippling of the grass warned me of a wind-gust, and I waited a moment to gauge its intensity. I realized that I had to aim more to the right to compensate . . . Pushing into my bow, I anchored for a second, then loosed just before the gust died away.

It was a good shot, yet not quite good enough. When men went to measure whether my arrow had hit the target closer to the centre than that of the Starkward archer, they judged it a tie.

Sure that his man had won, Humphry Stethren flung his hands skyward in irritation, but Hubert Jacklyn merely chuckled and said, 'Let your wager ride on your other archer, Humphry, and mine on the prince from the south. Indeed, I'll double it, if you care to cover me.'

'Nay, I have not the gold,' young Humphry muttered in embarrassment.

'But I have,' Fulk Reddlestone announced. 'I'll take you, Hubert, and I shall have your money. The youth with the dark complexion may know something of archery, but I question whether that self-styled princeling' – he jerked his chin contemptuously toward Avran – 'can even tell the fletching of an arrow from its point.'

This set his followers laughing sycophantically – all but Hubert, who merely smiled and said, 'We'll see, friend Fulk.'

As for Avran, he had so tensed and reddened in fury at Fulk's derisive words that I whispered urgently to him, 'Be calm, Avran! If you allow yourself to become annoyed, you'll never shoot well.'

He nodded and tried to relax, moving away so as to be out of earshot of Fulk's jibes.

The wind was blowing across the butts more steadily now, and clouds were massing above the spur of hills behind the castle, causing shadows to advance across the sward. I shivered, not with cold, but in anticipation of trouble to come. Yet, for the moment, all seemed well.

The Starkward archer, a younger man with a mop of brown hair and only a wisp of beard, took up his position, drew, and loosed. He had not allowed enough for the wind. His arrow struck only in the outer ring of the target.

Fulk and his associates groaned, and I heard Humphry mutter to them, 'I'll settle with that bungling young fool, be sure!'

The question remained whether Avran could do better. He stepped up to the mark, looking less angry, but still more tense than I would have wanted. I saw him breathe deeply. Then he set arrow to nock and drew back his string.

At the very moment when he was about to loose, young Berenger Reddlestone, who had been by his brother's side in his usual attitude of fawning admiration, coughed loudly and then gave a braying, embarrassed laugh. Distracted, Avran shot too much to the left and, in anticipation of a miss, a ripple of chuckles spread among Fulk's cronies.

They laughed too soon. By some freak of chance, the wind was changing in strength and direction even as Avran shot. His arrow, which ought to have missed the target amply, veered in its flight and, instead, embedded itself close to the centre. Not quite in the gold, but near enough.

There was an awestruck mutter among the crowd, then hesitant applause. I noticed that Vedlen Obiran was standing a little way further up the hill, smiling and silent. It left me wondering . . .

Humphry Stethren stamped his foot in anger. 'That arrow should have gone wide. That was witches' work!'

'Nonsense, Humphry,' responded Hubert Jacklyn coolly. 'Just good shooting. You owe me five gold marks, friend. And so do you, Fulk.'

'So I do, Hubert, so I do,' said Fulk calmly. 'I deserve to lose. I know now I was foolish. I was assuming that the redhead was really a prince. Of course, no prince would trouble to teach himself skill with a bow, so I had expected him to lose handsomely. I should have known better. No true prince would be content to travel in the rag-tag of a wizard's train.'

He turned as if to go back up the hill, but Avran, scarlet with fury now, seized him by the arm and spun him around.

'You will apologise for those words,' he demanded, his voice hoarse with anger. 'You have not the slightest idea what you're talking about. My father is ruler of a land that is greater than all these hills combined and of such antiquity that you cannot even begin to conceive. I will not allow my land and my lineage to be insulted in this way.'

In comparison with my friend's anger, Fulk seemed dangerously cool. He was much bigger than Avran, looking like a wolfhound beside a terrier.

'Odd, then,' he answered contemptuously, 'that it should be a realm of which no-one has heard – your dark-haired friend, of course, excepted. If we were all endowed with such rich imaginations, we might all be scions of such realms.'

This renewed insult set his friends chuckling, but it caused Avran's fury to rise to fever pitch. 'Do you dare again to call me a liar? Then you need to back your claim by the strength of your arms!' He drew off the glove with which he had held his bow and flung it into Fulk's face.

The big man recoiled in shock, his face flushing with colour – partly as a result of the buffet it had received but largely in a response of unfettered anger. 'By God, this insolent mountebank dares to challenge me!' His voice evinced as much surprise as fury. 'Humphry, will you serve as my second?'

'Of course,' answered young Stethren with gratified alacrity.

Fulk stroked his bruised cheek. 'Well, then, it is for me to choose weapons, is it not? Normally, I would suggest that we meet during the tourney with lances, as gentlemen should. However, since I hear you strangers ride rafneyen on such occasions and not horses, I am not sure whether that would be an equal match. It might allow too much opportunity for tricks of wizardry, perhaps. And of course' – he inclined his head in mock-courtesy – 'I cannot match you with the bow, as I freely admit.' This oblique renewal of insult set his friends chuckling again. Fulk paused till their amusement had died down, then went on very deliberately. 'So, I choose that our weapon be the sword and that we meet on foot. May I request also that your second *not* be your friend here' – he jerked his head at me – 'who is perhaps a little too knowledgeable by now in the arts of necromancy, but rather Sir Robert Randwulf, whom I know to be a gentleman?'

Avran had flushed anew at this insult directed to me, but he merely said, 'Very well. We shall leave it to our seconds to arrange time and place.' Without further word, he picked up his glove and turned away to retrieve bow and quiver.

Fulk and his followers went away up the hill, chattering with as much animation and excitement as starlings. The two Starkward archers, who seemed to feel some responsibility for the scene, muttered words of embarrassed apology and hastened away, while the crowd broke up into eddies of gossip. As for Vedlen Obiran, he came up to me, shaking his head from side to side in a sort of grim amusement. His eyes were black and inscrutable.

'Your friend can be fiery, can he not? Well, he has had provocation. Both Sir Cuthbert and his son are becoming uncomfortably arrogant. It can do no harm for them to suffer a rebuff. Yet I could wish that this incident had been postponed a little. Our negotiations are near to completion – so near, indeed, that I have been able to leave the lords at their task for a while without fear of acrimony. It would be unfortunate if the prospect of peace in these hills were to be destroyed by such a trivial incident.'

Avran had rejoined us, dragging his feet and with a hangdog look. Evidently the flare of his fury had burned out already.

'I am sorry,' he said, with a sincerity that nobody could doubt. 'I've been an utter fool, but that Fulk, he is so – so absolutely infuriating . . . Nevertheless, I cannot allow my stupidity to wreck your plans. I will apologize to him and withdraw my challenge if you wish, though I confess it will go hard . . .' He relapsed into an embarrassed silence.

Vedlen Obiran looked at Avran steadily for a moment. The wizard's eyes had an unexpected light of amusement in them. 'No, you must not do that. Not only would it further inflate that young man's already overblown opinion of himself and confirm his ideas about you, but also it would reflect adversely upon all who are my followers and my friends. Be sure, instead, that, when you meet him in battle, you emerge as the victor. On the other hand, try not quite to kill him!'

Avran's back, which had been bowed, straightened. He breathed deeply in relief. 'Thank you,' he said simply.

The wizard eyed him again, speculatively this time. 'However, it will be politic if I appear not to approve your actions and if I set myself a little apart from them. Sir Robert, Felun, and I are to dine this night in the great hall, but it would be preferable that you and the Ravatsengs found some excuse for absenting yourselves.'

Noting my puzzled brow at his mention of the brothers, he smiled and explained. 'Rahir and Delhir are your good friends, you know, and they do not like Fulk Reddlestone very much.' The wizard paused, then added: 'Nor, for that matter, do I.' After this, he walked away uphill without any further word.

CHAPTER 28

Tidings And Trepidations

Drakht Belineg and Narel Evateng arrived at Rewlenscrag that evening. They reported to the wizard first, then came down to join us for dinner. The Ravatseng brothers had elected to prepare that repast, for they were weary of the limited fare of the cook-tents. We ate in the castle bailey, beside the great pavilion of the wizard – a good meal of stew made from the meat of some rabbit-sized creature, flavoured with herbs and slivers of shallot and accompanied by hunks of good wheaten bread and flagons of strong ale.

Our two newly-returned comrades were both very weary and were content, while we ate, to listen passively to the gossip of the castle. Our conversation was in Reschorese, good practice for Avran and me, for at Rewlenscrag most talk was in English. Only when Drakht, having three times emptied his great beaker, had visibly relaxed, did Rahir address to him the question we were all desiring to ask.

'Well, Drakht, you didn't bring Amos back with you, that's evident enough. So what happened to him? Was he victim or was he rogue?'

'Ay, that's the question,' Drakht sighed heavily. 'If only we could answer it, but we cannot. Ours was a vain search.' He fell silent, staring unhappily into his beaker.

'Could you not trace him, then?'

'Did you find no trail?'

These two startled questions, one from Rahir and the other from me, were uttered simultaneously. It was Narel who replied.

'In honesty, friends, I am not sure. I wish you'd been with us, Simon, or you, Delhir. Drakht and me, we're not trackers, and the man from Amsetch had left us. Indeed, we'd not expected to have to rely on tracks. We thought to pick up information from people we met, hear of sightings maybe, for Amos is not a man to mistake.'

'That he is not,' growled Rahir.

Narel smiled at this, then continued: 'To cover the ground better, we elected not to travel together. Drakht went to Amsetch and from there into the skirts of the forest, but he gained no news of any strange travellers, either on rafenu-back or on foot. I searched the hill ridges south of Falconward. It is dry ground and stony, affording little chance of discovering tracks. Sometimes I did find a few fresh hoofmarks, but I could make little sense of them. So, I headed eastward, out onto the dusty plains of Lukeyne – a harsh land, that, and with few settlers. I heard tales of men fleeing on foot from the phantom terrors of Alunsward' – he smiled briefly – 'and also of rafenu-riders. Yet always they'd been glimpsed from afar, in the mists of morning or the gloom of evening. Nothing definite.'

He drank deeply from his beaker, then went on: 'Well, in the end I traversed Lukeyne and swam my beast across the All Saints River into Riotte. At Trayad-inRiotte I encountered Lady Saville, her son, and their escort, trading their gold for supplies to aid in the rebuilding of Owlsgard. However, no other strangers had come there. The Mentonese will not discuss their deals, of course. Yet I am sure that my questions evoked no responsive echoes in their minds. Our master's and Sir Robert's possessions have not passed into Mentonese hands. Of that I am convinced. Indeed, that was the only fact I gleaned in my long ride.' He sighed and shook his head sadly.

'So, we cannot tell whether Amos is alive or dead.' Avran sounded almost relieved.

'Aye, that's so.' Drakht was speaking again now. 'Alive or dead, you ask. And Rahir asks whether he is victim or rogue. I cannot answer either of you properly. Yet my belief is that Amos is alive and is a thief. Together, Narel and I scoured the hills east of Alunsward and then I searched Amsetch, from the Hillebren pass in the north to the banks of the Brunflow in the south. Yet we discovered only the jettisoned tent, nothing more. If Amos were dead, then surely we should have found his body.'

'But what if he is alive and a prisoner of thieves?' Avran was still battling to retain his good impression of our former friend.

'That does remain possible,' Drakht responded heavily, but his disbelief was patent. Though Narel said nothing, a downward curve of his lips told me that he also could not accept Avran's idea.

'And what next? Will we search further for Amos?' Rahir was eager and indignant.

Narel sighed again and answered: 'Drakht and I, we would like to do so. Our master, though, says we've wasted enough time chasing after lost trifles. He says that other and more important tasks lie before us. He will not permit us to spend any more time questing for Amos.'

Quite evidently, Narel was disgusted by this decision. As for Drakht, he was nodding sombrely.

Delhir Ravatseng had been sitting under the shadow of the tent, as usual so quiet that almost one forgot his presence. At Narel's words, however, he leaned forward and struck his left palm with his right fist. His eyes were bright.

'Why, that *proves* Amos to be alive and a villain! Don't you see? If Amos were an innocent captive or if he were lying dead in some rocky place, wouldn't our master strive to rescue or to avenge him? Of course, he would!' Nodding to himself, Delhir sat back and fell silent again.

Delhir's deduction was so evidently correct that all of us tensed at his words. Drakht's nostrils were flaring and his eyes smouldering in wrath.

'Ay, Delhir, ay! You don't say much, my friend, but there's times when you're quicker in thought than any of us. So, we must not seek our departed friend. Yet it may be that, someday, our paths will cross again. If so – why then, Amos will rue that day!'

From the vigorous way in which Drakht was twisting his great hands together, I believed him.

After that, the current of our talk shifted into other channels. To my surprise, the duel was not mentioned, though everybody knew of it – or everybody, it seemed, except for Sir Cuthbert Reddlestone. It was certain that he would have been angry at such news, and it was probable that he would have stopped the encounter. For this reason, word of the duel was being kept carefully from his ears.

The time had been set already – for the morrow, at one hour after the prime. The place had been decided as well: a dingle on the north flank of the Stoney Mountains about three hours' ride from Rewlenscrag.

After eight days of waiting while their masters negotiated, the followers of the lords of the Ferekar Naur were becoming as bored as Avran and I had been. If a nearer staging place had been set for the encounter, a large crowd would certainly have assembled to watch. Wisely, the seconds – possibly Humphry Stethren, but more probably, I thought, Sir Robert – had chosen that more distant setting in hopes of preventing any such gathering. Moreover, they had been careful not to let either time or location be known widely.

For my part, I viewed the prospect of the duel with such deep disquiet that I was tempted to tell Sir Cuthbert about it myself. Only the knowledge that Avran would never forgive such a betrayal prevented me.

It was true that my friend was an excellent swordsman, his skills enhanced by his practicing with Sir Robert. But, by reputation at least, Fulk Reddlestone was quite as good. Moreover, Fulk was much bigger – and, I assumed, much stronger – than Avran, with a reach that was considerably longer. I doubted if my friend could survive such an encounter without injury. I asked myself in fact if he would survive at all. My mind flinched away from that question. Though I sought my blankets early, I slept little that night and rose hollow-eyed to a day that seemed unfairly bright and sunny.

Avran had risen before me and was as full of energy as I was listless. Already, I learned, he had been exercising with his sword for an hour or more. He devoured a large breakfast with enthusiasm, chaffing me because I was inclined to eat so little. If he guessed at my fears for him, he made no remark. And if he suffered from any disquiet himself, it was not evident.

Normally the wizard breakfasted in his tent. On that day, however, he surprised us by joining us. Yet he was in a rather pensive mood and not talkative. His strange eyes were as deeply brown as a peaty pool in shadow, while his face was as lacking in expression as the inscrutable face of a saint carved on a Celtic cross. Only when his meal was done did he bestir himself, rising to his feet and addressing Avran.

'I cannot be with you today, my friend,' he said. 'The lords of these hills are meeting as usual, and I must be with them in their discussions. They have decided their new boundaries and divided up the disputed lands. While all their realms except for Amsetch and Starkward have gained some new territory, the greater part of those lands have been placed into two new lordships. Alunsland, in the area around Alunsward, will have Alban Daintree of Owlsgard for its lord. It seems he is to marry the daughter of the Earl of Amsetch, a union that should make for peace and strengthen his authority. A new realm, to be named Peakland, will be centred on Cat Crags. John Stanton will serve as its governor for five years, under the joint overlordship of Sir Cuthbert and Sir Henry. After that, its settlers will choose their own lord. That is good, but better still, the idea of a league for mutual protection has been accepted by all – even by Sir Gabriel Jacklyn, though he has been wriggling somewhat under the pressure of his peers' opinions.'

He paused and surveyed us with searching eyes before continuing. 'So, it seems we have redrawn the chart of these hills into a new and, I trust, happier shape. We can take much contentment in that. In such a balance, the loss of our gold and possessions weighs lightly.'

Vedlen Obiran was smiling now, his brown eyes gleaming like a pool on whose surface the sunlight plays and dances. His pleasure was reflected in our faces, even my own, dispirited though I had been. Then the wizard addressed Avran again.

'Sir Robert will be waiting for you down by the river, beyond the tents. Drakht, Delhir, and Rahir will ride with you – and also Simon, of course – but I am afraid Felun, Narel, and Hebehir have tasks to perform that will detain them here in Rewlenscrag. Be on the watch for treachery, each of you. One cannot trust all those young men who follow Fulk to observe the ordinances of chivalry.'

He paused again, then gazed at my friend and me. 'My thanks and my blessings go with you, Avran and Simon, on this day and on all days. The road ahead of you is long, and you will each encounter many problems and many dangers. Sometimes you will be afraid, sometimes almost overwhelmed by doubt, but you must never allow despair to take you in its black embrace. If you employ your mind, Simon, and if you keep your skills, Avran, you will surmount every obstacle and achieve all your desires.'

Solemnly he clasped hands with Avran and then with me. His words and this subsequent action pleased me, but they disconcerted me as well, for they seemed very much like a ceremonious adieu to friends setting forth on a long journey. His manner struck me as odd and incongruous, since I felt sure that, if all went well in the duel, we would be back in Rewlenscrag that very evening.

If Avran was similarly disconcerted, it was not evident. No doubt he was too preoccupied with thoughts of the duel to read any particular meaning into the wizard's words.

In contrast, Vedlen bade only the most casual of farewells to our other comrades before striding away up the hill. Hebehir followed him hastily. Narel had already gone, and Felun was nowhere to be seen that morning. After seeing to the needs of his young lad, Felun would no doubt be attending the meeting in the castle. It left me wondering, though, what tasks had been found for Narel and Hebehir.

Speedily Delhir and Rahir cleared up after our repast, refusing any aid from Avran or me. For my part I checked over my throwing-knives, making sure that those concealed in the sheaths in the shoulders of my jacket and the spines of my boots could still be readily extracted if the need arose. Then I fetched my bowstave and arrows from the bundle by my bed and advised Avran to do likewise.

To his surprised protest I responded: 'Quite evidently, Master Obiran anticipates trouble. I know you'll be wielding your sword in the duel, but we can't tell how events may shape themselves afterwards. We had better be prepared, don't you think?'

'I suppose so,' Avran replied diffidently.

Within minutes, we were walking down the steep path from the castle bailey toward the meadows. Never had Rewlenscrag seemed more beautiful than it did in that hour of departure. The grasses were freshly bedecked with flowers, some as coolly blue as cornflowers, others as flaringly scarlet as poppies. The tents seemed to glow with colour, and the clothes of the people we passed seemed new-dyed into brighter hues. The very sky was the limpid blue of a songthrush's egg and speckled, not with black, but with white woolly puffs of cloud, too few and too innocent to hint at changing weather. A splendid scene it was. In my altered mood, I wondered if I might be seeing it for the last time and I gazed around me almost wistfully as we descended the slope.

We had been warned not to seem to be leaving in a group. Drakht had gone ahead, while the Ravatseng brothers sauntered along behind us. Even so, we were the object of many curious glances and traversed the meadows on a rising tide of whispered comments.

In a glade half a league or so beyond the tent town, Sir Robert and Drakht were waiting with the six rafneyen. We knew that Fulk and his followers, on the other hand, would be riding to our common destination by a different path. As soon as the Ravatsengs had caught up with us, we set forth, following the Pochard's banks downstream for two more leagues and splashing across a place where its waters shallowed at a rock bar. Through a thicket and up a long hill we rode. The ascent was not continuous in its steepness, but intermittent rather, as if we were climbing a series of poorly made steps with small clifflets of shale as risers. There were marshy patches in the flatter places, the treads of these steps. Even after several days of sunshine, our rafneyen's hooves sometimes sank deeply into the mud.

It was hot. I slipped off my cloak and folded it across the saddle in front of me. Galahad, who was just as hot as I was, shared my uneasy mood and tossed his horns irritably in his usual fashion.

Once we reached it, the ridge crest proved broad and fairly flat. Also, there was a welcome stir of air to cool us. Soon we could see beyond the ridge. The viridian hue of the Great Marshes extended into the distance over to our left. Below us, in a broad valley, there flowed a great river, bordered by lush green meadows and intermittently concealed by clumps of trees. Beyond it, a range of lesser hills made for humps on the horizon.

All of us paused at this sight. 'Those are the Ferekar Rokanair, the Rockaine Hills,' said Sir Robert quietly. 'Gascon territory. They're a tempestuous folk, but most of them are good and chivalrous. Evil men like Casimir are as few among them as among the English or the Reschorese. The valley you see is that of the Aramassa, perhaps the greatest of all the rivers of Rockall – unless you have greater streams in the south, Avran?'

My friend shook his head, and Sir Robert continued. 'We've left Sir Cuthbert's lands behind now, by the way. We're in the Wilderward, the feoff of Sir Amyas Aydenburgh of Wildfell. We thought it better that the duel be held on neutral territory.'

Then he gazed around him. 'Many years have passed since I was last here. I am a little uncertain of our way. Do you recall it, Drakht?'

'Not I,' responded the big man. 'Never been here before.'

Fortunately, Rahir said: 'I remember it well enough. Over to the left a furlong or so, and then down. Am I right, Delhir?' At his brother's nod, Rahir led the way confidently, and our rafneyen followed his.

The dingle was certainly well concealed from above. It was a notch cut into the slope of the hill as sharply as if by some giant axe. Only when one rode up to its very edge did it become suddenly visible. Perhaps some stream had flowed through it once, but now there was just a space of green sward between two dense banks of bushes.

Fulk and his party were waiting for us already – not just the five we had encountered at the butts, but also a score of other nobles' sons and their hangers-on. Someone raised a derisory cheer when we were sighted on the skyline. He was quickly hushed, however, and, when we

355

had ridden down among them, we were greeted with proper courtesy.

However, I noted with some disquiet that all the young men were armed with swords, axes, or spears. Berenger Reddlestone even bore a shield on his arm, its highly polished surface shining in the sunlight. If the duel happened to expand into a general mellay, we would be outnumbered five to one – not a pleasant prospect.

An ample space near the centre of the dingle had already been roped off as an arena for the combat. The polygonal pattern of its surface showed it to be a dried-out marsh, the crust of the mud so very desiccated that it had crumbled to dust wherever feet had stepped. Even as we dismounted, Fulk's followers were already gathered in thick ranks around the ropes. I hesitated whether to extract my bowstaff from its sling beside the saddle, but decided reluctantly that my carrying a strung bow might merely stir up animosity. Instead I picked up my cloak and, after instructing Galahad to stay reasonably close by, walked over with my friends to join the watchers.

Humphry Stethren had brought with him the two swords that were to be used, and he and Sir Robert compared them with close attention. In this respect, at least, the contest would be even. Each blade was exactly a clothyard in length, and the two were so alike in shape that they would have fit into the same scabbard. It was Sir Robert who chose which should be handed to Avran and which to Fulk.

Before he took his weapon, Avran said: 'I do not wish to proceed with this fight, if it can be avoided without dishonour. Master Reddlestone, if you will withdraw your imputations concerning my status and my family, I am prepared to lay down this weapon and to take your hand in friendship. Will you do so?'

At that, there were hoots and catcalls from Fulk's supporters, but Fulk himself merely responded coldly: 'What I have said, I have said.' At that, Avran sighed and accepted the sword. Weighing up the two adversaries, I thought again that my friend was outmatched and felt anew the cold clutch of fear at my heart. Even if you ignored Avran's smaller size and lesser strength, he was at a disadvantage in armour as well. Fulk Reddlestone was wearing a tunic of chain mail over a padded hauqueton. On his head was a steel helmet, and his stockings and boots were studded with iron plates. In contrast, Avran wore only the padded jupon and the leather hood that Rahir had issued to him at Owlsgard. His stockings, though thick enough, had no plating, and his boots were merely of leather. Add to this advantage of armour Fulk's other advantages in strength, height, and reach, and the contest seemed so manifestly unfair that I wondered how Sir Robert could allow it to proceed.

However, Sir Robert seemed to feel no disquiet, and arrangements were soon made for its commencement. The contestants were stationed eight paces apart, their swords pointing at the ground. Then Sir Robert turned to the crowd.

'This duel shall begin when Master Stethren throws down the kerchief he is carrying. It shall end when 'Pax' is called, either by Master Reddlestone or the Prince of Sandastre or, if one of them be unable so to cry, by Master Stethren or me. All of you who are spectators, I charge you to obey the laws of chivalry, not only in letter but also in spirit. You must neither intervene in this fight nor protest its outcome, whatever that may be.'

This stern command was received in a silence in which I seemed to detect some unease. Then, as the contestants raised their swords, I was startled to hear Hubert Jacklyn mutter to Aldwyn Ennerling: 'I have still my five gold marks and, once again, I'll wager them on the Prince.'

Aldwyn Ennerling responded in a tone of surprise: 'Why, you've lost your senses, man! Still, if you're such a fool, you deserve to lose your money. Taken!' So, for a second time, as I watched my friend begin a contest, I knew that Blackhill gold was riding on him. Somehow, this time, I took comfort in this knowledge.

CHAPTER 29
The Duel In The Dingle

Sir Robert stepped away now and went to stand on the north side of the arena. His hand rested on his sword-hilt, but that was his right, for, by the rules that govern such contests in Rockall, the second can intercede on his principal's behalf whenever a foul blow is struck or any other base deed is attempted. Once Humphry had dropped the kerchief, he would take up a similar position on the arena's south side and be likewise ready to intercede if necessary.

At present, Humphry was standing in the centre of the rope-bounded space, his eyes bright and his lips parted. His excitement was evident. In his right hand, he clasped the kerchief, gaily coloured in green and no doubt borrowed from some girl in Rewlenscrag. Slowly he raised that hand and, with all eyes upon him, released the kerchief before backing away in haste to the ropes.

As the kerchief fluttered to the ground, the two contestants advanced toward one another, not directly, but in a crab-wise motion, each with sword at the ready and eyes watchful. Fulk made a half-stroke, then checked himself. Then, for what seemed a considerable while, but was probably no more than the space of a minute, the two circled each other warily.

Predictably, it was Fulk who made the first onslaught, leaping at Avran with a suddenness that startled me and striking downward in a series of powerful hacking slashes which, it seemed to me, my friend parried only with difficulty. Avran was backing away, and Fulk's friends were cheering lustily.

However, as Fulk's blade flashed back and forth in strokes from left and right, Avran's continued to meet and block it. Moreover, although Avran kept giving ground, he did not do so in a straight line and so risk being trapped in an angle of the ropes, but rather in a broad circle that kept him never far from the centre of the space. His strategy was perceived by the onlookers, and the cheering died away.

Fulk halted, his sword drooping as if his wrist was weary. Nevertheless, when Avran thrust at him swiftly, Fulk was ready. His sword swept upwards with such force that Avran's blade was turned back. Indeed, such was the strength of that counterstroke and the speed with which Avran's blade was carried upward that I feared my friend had lost his hold on his weapon.

There was a collective gasp from the watchers. Somehow, though, Avran kept his grip on his sword hilt. Even as he was backing again, his blade caught and deflected Fulk's mighty downward sweep.

After that, for several minutes, there ensued such a quicksilver sequence of thrust and parry that their two blades seemed to weave a meshwork of light. Always it was Fulk who was on the attack, employing his greater strength to try to break through Avran's guard. Always it was Avran who was on the retreat, but it was a retreat closely calculated, never rash or headstrong. The footmarks they left in the mud crust made a circle, the centre of which was very close to the centre of the arena. The dust thrown up by their rapid footwork powdered their legs and hazed the sunlight.

The sun was at its height now, and the dingle was quite without cooling draughts of air. Even for us onlookers, to be enclosed in that sun-baked space became a cause for perspiration. It was hardly to be doubted that the contestants themselves were becoming very hot too.

Since Fulk was both the bigger and the more heavily armoured, it was predictable that he began to tire quickest. By almost imperceptible degrees, the fury of his onslaught was losing its force. Instead of trying by sheer strength to break through Avran's guard, he sought instead to benefit from the asset of his longer reach. The massive sweeping strokes at short range were being succeeded now by probing thrusts and wrist-flick counters.

Yet, as Avran's blade blocked each thrust and avoided the flicks and twists of Fulk's sinuously weaving sword, the bigger man seemed to be advancing more and more slowly, his step in measure with the retreat of the smaller man.

For a moment, the two were at a standstill, their blades criss-crossing. Fulk was facing toward me. I could see that he was breathing fast and that the sweat was coursing down his brow. Then he took a deeper breath and, calling on a fresh reserve of strength, launched a new onslaught that forced Avran again into retreat. However, as the dust eddied around them, the circle of their movements closed tighter around the arena's centre, and Fulk's massive hacks seemed to become more and more laboured.

Then, suddenly, as we looked on, we realized Fulk was in retreat. There was a great inhalation of breath and a lot of excited comment. Hubert Jacklyn, standing behind

Humphry on the far side, nodded in satisfaction, his dark eyes agleam, while Aldwyn Ennerling registered resentful astonishment.

As it chanced, Berenger Reddlestone was standing just to my right. Where he had positioned himself had surprised me, not only because his other close friends were all standing behind Humphry, but also because it meant that he was looking south into the sun. The shield was still on his arm. It puzzled me why he had not set it down. Berenger had been shouting with mad delight during the first few minutes of the combat, but his cockcrows had faded into silence as it unfolded. Now he gave vent to a long moan of dismay.

Fulk was managing to block all of Avran's thrusts, but that he was finding this difficult was becoming more and more evident. As their paths changed again, I realized that Fulk was backing into us, even as Avran was advancing towards us.

At this, Berenger tensed. A slight movement of his caught my eye. Glancing toward him, I noticed that his attention was turned to his shield-arm and that he was raising his shield with care, at a curious angle.

Suddenly, I realized Berenger's purpose. He planned to use the highly polished metal of the shield to reflect the sun into Avran's eyes and so to dazzle him and expose him to big brother Fulk's thrust. As it happened, I was carrying my cloak on my arm. Quickly I stepped behind Berenger and, as the sun's rays shone bright on the rising shield, I slung my cloak over it, green side outermost.

Berenger started in astonishment, then turned on me with a snarl. I responded, speaking loudly enough for everyone around me to hear. 'Sorry to do that, friend, but

I was afraid you might dazzle the swordsmen. It was quite inadvertent, I'm sure!'

Berenger looked at me with fury, but other eyes were upon him now. Seeing his ruse exposed, he muttered: 'Oh, yes, of course. Foolish of me. I should have put my shield down.'

'Then why not do so now?' I asked in a tone of marked politeness. As I drew back and folded my cloak, he set the shield on the ground with very obvious ill grace.

Sir Robert had heard my words and looked toward us. He gave me a brief smile of approval and turned back toward the ring. My gaze followed his.

It was then that I witnessed Avran's feinting thrust, checked at the last moment. This drew an unnecessary counterstroke from Fulk and left him open to Avran's blade. I watched that blade slide inward and upward in a strange, spiral twist that sent Fulk's sword spinning from his hand. And I witnessed the mighty thrust that, had it not been checked, would surely have pierced Fulk's coat of mail and slain him. As it was, it caused the big man to collapse backwards onto his knees. Then, with Avran standing over him, eyes ablaze, his sword hovering over his throat, Fulk grunted hoarsely the reluctant word 'Pax!'

Since Humphry Stethren seemed too stupefied for speech, it was Sir Robert who stepped forward and shouted to the crowd: 'Victory and honour belong to the Prince of Sandastre!'

There were delighted shouts from Rahir and Drakht, while even Delhir, typically quiet, was clapping his hands in joy. As for me, I was jumping with delight. And alhough Aldwyn Ennerling, Berenger Reddlestone, and a few others were glumly silent, the greater number of those watching were sporting enough to applaud my friend's victory. With this, I realized that we were in no danger of any mass assault and felt a second surge of relief.

Already Avran had sheathed his weapon and had fetched Fulk's sword. Now, with characteristic courtesy, he handed it to Fulk, hilt foremost. The big man, who was still sitting back on his haunches, took it and rose laboriously to his feet. He looked white and was breathing heavily, the perspiration coursing down his cheeks. For a moment he stood still and unsteady. Then he thrust his sword into its scabbard and held out his arms to Avran. As they clasped hands, Fulk spoke for the first time.

'Prince of Sandastre – wherever that is – you may be. A prince of swordsmen most certainly you are. I withdraw my words, but, since they have brought about this bonny fight, I am not so sure that I regret them.'

In that moment, I knew that Fulk could not have been aware of his younger brother's treacherous devices. Such an honourable an antagonist would never stoop to such base practices.

Avran laughed joyously and responded: 'A bonny fight indeed! I am fortunate to have encountered so fine a swordsman and doubly fortunate to be victorious.'

With these fair words did an unhappy affair end in the best of fashions. This exchange between Avran and Fulk brought more applause from the onlookers and much favourable comment, but there were still some who were unhappy. Reluctantly, Aldwyn Ennerling payed his forfeit of gold to Hubert Jacklyn and grumbled: 'More wizardry! Just as Humphry was, I was a fool to wager against any of Vedlen Obiran's men.'

But Hubert Jacklyn responded lightly: 'Did you notice any evidences of wizardry, then? Did you see any strange green fogs, hear any weird chants, or witness any dragons emerging from the earth to eat up the combatants? Nay, my friend, I fear you're just a fool!'

As he turned away, Hubert noticed my amusement and winked at me before going to join Humphry and Fulk.

Sobbing in his fury and humiliation, Berenger had seized his shield and, summoning his rafenu, had fled away already toward Rewlenscrag. Others of the onlookers were soon riding away as well, but, even though they had also summoned their mounts, Sir Robert and our other friends seemed inclined to linger. As it turned out, after bidding a properly courteous farewell to Fulk, Humphry, and the others, we were the last to remain in the dingle. I fell to wondering why.

I was to discover the answer quickly enough. Sir Robert mounted his rafenu, then turned it around, so that he faced Avran and me. 'Well, friends, that was a worthy victory. I am glad, Simon, that you anticipated that young villain's stratagem in time.'

When Avran expressed surprise, Sir Robert responded with a brief explanation that gained me a grateful smile from my friend. Then, before Avran could speak, he went on: 'Yet you cannot return to Rewlenscrag, you know. Very soon, sweet little brother Berenger will be pouring out the story of this afternoon – or his own special version of it – into his father's ear. Even though Fulk has accepted defeat well, his father will neither forgive nor forget what he will view as being a smirching of his precious family honour. Sir Cuthbert has his good points, but he has a stiff neck and an ill temper too. I am afraid, Simon and Avran, that you're going to have to be sent on your way toward Lyonesse.'

Seeing our expressions of dismay, he smiled and went on: 'Yet you must not worry. Vedlen foresaw this, of course, and all is prepared for you. Your possessions are waiting for you, down the hill in the Aramassa valley. Vedlen had hoped to escort you to Reschora himself, but, following the loss of his gold and goods, he cannot afford to do that. He must return instead to his work in the forestlands. However, he has charged me to set you on your way. As far as Reschora, at least, I shall travel with you, and maybe further if you'll welcome my company. I've long thought of traversing the Northern Mountains, to discover what lies beyond.'

For both of us, this news softened the blow of knowing that we would be leaving behind our friends. To our protestations of relief and pleasure, Sir Robert answered quite simply: 'Splendid! Then let us be riding down to the river.'

So, instead of retracing our tracks towards Rewlenscrag, we rode together across the dingle, over its abrupt lowest rim, and down a moderately steep slope into the Aramassa valley. As we jogged along, it was with undue cause that my friends made much of my scotching of Berenger's little scheme. In some detail, Drakht outlined what he would have done to that young villain, had it succeeded. Then the flow of our talk dried up, as each of us, filled with regret, became conscious of the imminence of a parting of ways.

We rode through the belt of trees that hugged the lee of the slope and out into a broad meadow of green grasses, as colourfully flower-flecked as that at Rewlenscrag had been. On the very bank of the river was a hurst covered by well-grown trees whose dusty, arrow-shaped leaves showed them to be evergreens. The trees grew so densely that I was surprised when Sir Robert led us straight toward this grove. But as it turned out, there was a bridle-path winding among the trees, along which we were able to pass in single file to the riverside.

There, waiting patiently for us beside the broad flood of the Aramassa, were seven persons. Four were short, dark men in faded blue tunics and light cloth shoes, whom I did not recognize. The others, however, were delightfully familiar – Felun Daretseng, his small boy from Owlsgard, and big Hebehir Ravatseng. They were sitting in the shade of a tree, but they leapt to their feet at our approach and hastened forward to greet us.

Hebehir actually lifted Avran from his rafenu and hugged him with delight. 'Why, man, you're in fine fettle! Surely you must have vanquished that arrogant young cub Fulk?'

'Careful, Hebehir! You're squeezing the breath out of me. Yes, I defeated him, but he's not so bad, you know. He's a fine swordsman.'

'Magnificent! Why, we're proud of you.' Hebehir hugged Avran again, beaming with such unalloyed delight that I realized again how fortunate we had been to make such friends. It saddened me to think that we would be saying farewell to them so soon.

While Felun's pleasure was less vigorously demonstrated, it was no less great. And, as for the little boy, he was hopping with joy. They added their round of congratulations to Hebehir's and received from Rahir a highly-coloured account of the combat. In it, my own small service gained fuller mention than it merited. Meanwhile, the four strangers watched and listened inscrutably.

When that account was ended, Felun introduced them, speaking in Reschorese. 'Sir Robert, Simon, and Avran,

I would like you to meet Etvan and Dazlan Garavet and Ulim and Terim Lazadel, boatmen of the Aramassa.'

We exchanged the clasped-hands grip of friendship, and he went on: 'To ride in so small a party to Reschora would be difficult and dangerous, for perilous lands lie between. Our master the wizard has arranged that these men should take you there more speedily, by boat. It will mean that you need to leave behind your rafneyen, I fear. But then, rafneyen would be of small service in the mountains.'

'Thank you indeed!' Avran's response was surprising. 'That will be splendid!'

I managed to echo his gratitude. However, when I recalled my past ineptitude in boats, I felt scant enthusiasm for any prolonged voyaging.

Then Felun solemnly conveyed to us Vedlen Obiran's farewell and repeated his blessing, adding: 'Our master regrets the loss, not only of your company, but also of your services. He asked me to tell you, however, that he is recruiting a new assistant – young Henry Ellis here, who prefers to stay with us than to return to Owlsgard.' The small boy blushed with pleasure, then turned a couple of somersaults in glee. 'Narel Evateng, who took my place today in the council chamber, sends his blessings as well, regretting that he cannot express them personally. He will be as overjoyed as we are at the news of your victory, Avran. But now we must, I fear, be setting you on your way and returning to Rewlenscrag. You'll find the rest of your gear stowed in the boats. Our master has already made payment to the boatmen, so you need have no anxieties in that regard.'

That parting ended up being as painful as I had expected. Not only was our gratitude to the wizard profound, but also our affection for his men had become very strong. I found it especially hard to say goodbye to Rahir and Delhir, those two brothers who had saved our lives at Nekhalések. Almost as difficult was my farewell to my rafenu, the noble Galahad.

All too soon we were ensconced in the two boats that had been moored in the trees' shade, Sir Robert with the Garavet brothers in the first, Avran and I with the Lazadel cousins in the second. The boatmen pushed off from the sandy shore and paddled out onto the broad, slow-flowing river, using strange long-shafted, long-bladed oars. All too soon, they were rowing upstream in a steady, effortless-seeming rhythm. All too soon, our friends and the beasts who had served us so faithfully were lost to sight in the shadow of the trees.

Once again, it seemed to me, a part of my life was fading from reality into dream. In the shadow of that parting, I felt daunted and depressed and fell to wondering what lay ahead. No doubt there were more perils awaiting us among those greater mountains that we had yet to traverse. I asked myself if I was destined ever to find Lyonesse, ever to meet again my father and brother, the objects of my arduous search. Would I manage ever to return to Ilven, the love I had left behind in Sandastre?

I glimpsed Sir Robert in the boat ahead of us, gazing eagerly at the scene around him, and I became conscious that Avran, sitting behind me, was dozing, relaxed in the aftermath of his exertions. Suddenly, I was ashamed of my fears. Blessed as I was with these two strong companions, both of them willing, in a spirit of adventure and friendship, to share all the risks with me, I felt I should be feeling humble and grateful. Moreover, the words of comfort offered by the wizard came back to my mind. There was every chance that there were indeed perils ahead, yet somehow Avran and I would survive them and, some day, we would find Lyonesse.

Glossary Of Rockalese Words

All Rockalese words are defined when first used in this account. However, for the convenience of any reader who finds them hard to remember, they are brought together here for ready reference. Four Rockalese languages are represented, of which the three principal ones are Sandastrian, herein {Sand.}, Montrion {Mont.} and Reschorese {Resch.}. Where words are common to two or more languages, this is indicated.

A

aftal, n. one hundred {Sand.: Resch.}

agiru (pl. **agireyen**), n. nobleman {Sand.: but <u>not</u> used in Sandastre itself}

akhled (pl. **akhledai**), n. chief of a Montariotan tribe {Mont.}

akhledan (pl. **akhedanai**), n. consort of the chief of a Montariotan tribe {Mont.}

akhledet (pl. **akhledetei**), n. chief town of a Montariotan tribe {Mont.}

aldreslef (pl. **aldreslevei**), n. princess of secondary status {Sand.}

asalbek (pl. **aselbekai**), n. short-trunked deciduous tree with branches forming an upwardly-directed cup: leaves lanceolate; berries black and sour; used as a laxative. {Sand.}

aseklin (pl. **asekleyin**), n. arrowslit window of a fortification or castle {Sand.}

ashlesar, v. to chain {Mont.}

askatal, n. one thousand {Sand.: Resch.}

aspadarn (pl. **aspadin**), n. component unit of a **padarn**, q.v. {Sand.}

astre (pl. **astrei**), n. land, nation {Sand.}

atim, adv. near, nearby {Mont.}

atra, n. or adj. southwest {Sand.}

ava, n. or adj. one (numeral); first {Sand.}

Avbalet, n. January {Sand.}

azesse (pl. **azessen**), n. marsh, swamp {Resch.}

B

bavalin, (pl. **bavalneyen**), n. rhinoceros--herbivore of southern Rockall; hide brown; two immense, cone-shaped brown horns, bases almost confludent, tips sharp {Sand.}

belineg (pl. **belnegen**), n. blacksmith {Resch.}

bevnu (pl. **bevneyen**), n. beast [used of domesticated qudrupeds only] {Sand.}

biek, conj. placed between personal name and surname of a convicted criminal {Sand.}

D

dakheslef (pl. **dakheslevei**), n. king {Sand.}

dakheslevat (pl. **dakheslevatai**), n. kingdom {Sand.}

dakhvardavat, n. Ruling Council of Sandastre {Sand.}

danatel (pl. **danatelen**), n. antelope-like herbivore of hare/jackrabbit size, with simple, short horns, forwardly directed (cf. muntjac) {Resch.}

deva, n. two {Sand.}

Devbalet, n. February {Sand.}

dort (pl. **dortan**), n. ward of a fortified city {Sand.}

dr, **dri**, pref. to verbs indicating a reversal of action [equiv. to English 'un-'] {Mont.}

drahakhal (pl. **drahaklen**), n. sacrificial victim {Mont.}

drashlesar, v. to unchain, unbind {Mont.}

E

ebelmek (pl. **ebelmekai**), n. deciduous tree with flowers of bright orange hue {Sand.}

embelin (pl. **embeleyin**), n. musical instrument of half-melon shape with four strings (cf. citole) {Sand.}

eng, suff. 'man of . . .' {Resch.}

enor (pl. **enten**), n. spot, blotch {Sand.: Resch.}

eslef (pl. **eslevei**), n. ruling prince {Sand.}

eslevar (pl. **eslevaren**), n. consort of ruling prince {Sand.}

estelen (pl. **estelnai**), n. yellow-flowering deciduous tree of northern Sandastre: the symbol of Estantegard {Sand.}

F

faraslef (pl. **faraslevei**), n. earl {Sand.}

faraslevat (pl. **faraslevatai**), n. earldom {Sand.}

felbra, n. or adj. southeast {Sand.}

ferek (pl. **ferekar**), n. hill, mountain {Resch.}

feslar, v. to keep, maintain, hold {Sand.: Mont.}

festikier (pl. **festikieren**), n. water bird of southern Rockall {Sand.}

fil, pref. inner {Sand.}

G

gahe (**gaheà**), adj. streaked {Sand.: Resch.}

galikhu (pl. **galikheyen**), n. water-hog: amphibious riverine herbivore with short tusks and a grey hide; related to the pigs but only of piglet size and proportions; gregarious; resembles a pygmy hippopotamus in habits, but smaller {Sand.}

gard (pl. **gardai**), n. ruling family (of Sandastre) {Sand.}

H

haleàsek (pl. **haleàsekar**), n. temple, holy place {Mont.}

hasedu (pl. **hasedain**), n. heavy antelope-like herbivore; pelage dark brown; having two spiralling, lyre-shaped horns. Used as a beast of burden and source of meat and milk throughout Rockall; by the Montariotans, used also for riding. {Sand.}

I

iga, conj. and {Sand.: Mont.}

ikhoras (pl. **ikhoranai**), n. tree whose branches are used for arrow-making {Sand.}

indrakhled (pl. **indrakhledai**), n. heir to a Montariotan chiefdom {Mont.}

indreslef (pl. **indreslevei**), n. prince of secondary rank {Sand.}

isitelen (pl. **isitelnen**), n. starling-sized bird with azure blue plumage {Sand.}

K

kal, (pl. **kalai**), n. etched sphere of quartz, used as a low-value monetary token [equiv. to a penny or cent] {Sand.}

kalvak, (pl. **kalvaken**), n. rhinoceros-like forest herbivore of central Rockall; brown, small eared and with a single, Y-shpaed nasal horn {Resch.}

kha, pref. imperative prefix {Mont.: equiv. to Sand. **ksa**}

koiru (pl. **koirneyen**), n. merchant, tradesman {Sand.}

ksa, pref. imperative prefix {Sand.}

'**Ksakeren!**', imp. v. 'Move!' [to a person or animal] {Grey Riders}

'**Ksashassat!**', imp. v. 'Be still!' [to a person or animal] {Grey Riders}

L

lad (pl. **ladar**), n. fur {Resch.}

lan, pref. lacking, without {Resch.}

M

marnis, n. or adj. south {Sand.}

mekret (pl. **mekreyet**), n. rascal {Sand.}

N

naradat (pl. **naradaten**) n. republic {Sand.}

narat (pl. **naratai**), n. ruler (or president) of a republic {Sand.}

naur, adj. stoney

nekh (pl. **nekhai**), n. sun-tree; large deciduous tree, with spreading branches. Survives in isolated hill situations in central and southern Rockall, but flourishes only in Vragansarat {Sand.: Mont.}

nendra, n. or adj. northeast {Sand.}

nos (pl. **nosan**), n. heart {Sand.}

not, suff. diminutive {Sand.: Resch.}

O

obiran (pl. **obiranar**), n. seneschal, castellan {Resch.}

osumlet (pl. **osumleten**), n. aquatic wildfowl [general term] {Sand.}

P

padarn (pl. **padin**), n. circular house {Sand.}

pevenek (pl. **pevenekar**), n. huge coniferous trees; bark creamy brown, punctate, resistant to impact and fire; cones very small, with tiny seeds (cf. sequoia) {Sand.}

R

rafenu (pl. **rafneyen**), n. antelope-like forest herbivore having two nasal and two brow horns; nasal horns directed outward, brow horns five-tined with three foremost tines curving and moderately long, two rear tines shorter and straight; pelage walnut-brown, flecked with creamy spots; used as a mount and capable of simple telepathic exchanges with its rider {Resch.}

ramora (pl. **ramoren**), n. large forest herbivore having a long, straight nasal horn, a pair of long, straight brow horns and a pair of coiled, ram's-horn like horns behind the ears; a line of erectile spines along the back and a spiked tail; pelage of almost Prussian blue hue; telepathic abilities exceptional {Sand.: Resch.}

rewlen (pl. **rewlnen**), n. grey, raven-like bird of central Rockall {Resch.: English}

rokh (pl. **rokhei**), n. warrior {Sand.}

ruan (pl. **ruanan**), n. hour {Sand.: Resch.}

S

sadnar, v. to approach {Mont.}

salis, n. or adj. north {Sand.}

sasayin (pl. **sasayinar**), n. catapult-like weapon set between the brow horns of a **sevdru** {Sand.}

sasialin (pl. **sasialinar**), n. the dart propelled from a **sasayin** {Sand.}

selth (pl. **selthen**), n. nocturnal scavenging carnivores, gaunt, with long, flat-topped skulls; forelimbs longer than hind; canines pointed, first premolars converted into carnassials for shearing, other cheek-teeth strong, for bone-cracking; fur off-white, with irregular, longitudinal grey streaks {Sand.: Resch.}

senetar, v. to give or bestow {Mont.}

sevdru (pl. **sevdreyen**), n. antelope-like herbivore having two forwardly-directed nasal horns and two brow horns, branching twice symmetrically in Y-fashion so that each horn has four tines; pelage grey, with white underparts and central white line down neck and back; used as a mount and capable of simple telepathic exchanges with its rider {Sand.}

skarn (pl. **skarnar**), n. deciduous tree of central Rockall; bark honey-brown, pitted, overlapping in chevron-like layers; leaves pale green with yellow flecks and scalloped edges (cf. oak); bark used for tanning, branches for fletching {Resch.: English}

soven (pl. **sovenei**), n. stranger, foreigner {Sand.}

T

tal, n. ten {Sand.}

tala (pl. **talnan**), n. village or hamlet, usu. a cluster of **padin** {Sand.}

Taltegis, n. Sunday {Sand.}

tavelnek (pl. **tavelnekar**), n. deciduous tree with dark green foliage opening in fan-like fashion above a short trunk: bitter yellow berries, used as purgatives {Sand.}

thassak (pl. **thasskeyen**), n. sabretooth carnivore of central and south Rockall; lion-sized; fur silver-grey, with darker patches {Sand.: Mont.: Resch.}

tsoned, n. strength, fitness {Mont.}

U

uen (**wen**), adj. or suff. broad {Sand.: Resch.}

ukhur (pl. **ukhuren**), n. large, long-legged hog-like omnivore of the grasslands; cheeks warty; ears with swollen tips; tushes short and sharp; nocturnal and gregarious, capable of rapid running {Sand.}

uld, pref. outer {Sand.}

urut (pl. **uruten**), n. small, shaggy-furred, rotund insec-
tivore of southern Rockall, with strong claws for
opening up anthills {Sand.}
ushazar, v. to condemn {Sand.}; to praise {Resch.}
ustres, n. or adj. west {Sand.}

V

vakhast, n. ejaculation of surprise ('My goodness!')
{Sand.}
vard (pl. **vardai**), n. family-clan {Sand.}
vardaf (pl. **vardavai**), n. chief of a family-clan {Sand.}
vasian (pl. **vasianar**), n. small, tarsier-like arboreal
primate of southern Rockall, large-eyed and with grey
pelage; capable of moderately extensive telepathic
interchanges with its owner; very faithful {Sand.}
vekra, n. one-third {Sand.}
vekruan, n. twenty-minutes [one-third of an hour] {Sand.}

X

xalihu (pl. **xaliheyen**), n. horse-like herbivore with single
long, spiralling brow-horn; cloven-hoofed, otherwise cf.
unicorn; pelage black (northeast Rockall) or silver-grey
to white (eastern mountains) {Sand.: Resch.}

Z

zembel, adj. dark in hue {Sand.}
zikadath (pl. **zikadathen**), n. venomous, arboreal snake
of southern Rockall; skin patterned in yellow and
green {Sand.}

Antony Swithin (1935-2002)

William Antony Swithin ('Bill') Sarjeant was born in Sheffield, England. An only child, with a vivid imaginative life nourished not only by science but by the fiction of writers like Rider Haggard, Edgar Rice Burroughs, and T.H. White, he survived the German blitz during World War II and went on to complete a PhD and DSc in geology. In 1972 he was appointed as a professor at the University of Saskatchewan in Canada, where he was to remain until his death. Besides being a renowned paleontologist and historian of geology, he was also a naturalist, novelist, bibliophile, local historian, folksinger, and Sherlockian scholar— in other words, a brilliant Renaissance man, a polymath of rare and astonishing versatility.

One of his grand projects was *The Perilous Quest for Lyonesse*, an ambitious 12-novel cycle set in the alternative world of Rockall, an island continent that he construed as the legendary Atlantis, albeit as a place existing in another dimension. Situated northwest of the British Isles in the Atlantic Ocean and named after a tiny islet only 20 metres in size, it had sparked his fertile imagination as a child and held an enduring fascination for him. 'Rockall,' he once remarked, 'is for me a lifetime quest and a continuing, very beguiling dream which I delight in sharing with my readers.' The first four books of Sarjeant's series were published under his pen-name, Antony Swithin, in the 1990s, but then further progress on the series was forestalled by his untimely death. Sarjeant's richly conceived project has been resurrected under the editorship of Canadian novelist and independent scholar, Mark Sebanc.

Mark Sebanc (1953-)

A novelist and independent scholar, Mark Sebanc lives deep in the rural hinterland of Ontario some 200 kilometres west of Ottawa near Algonquin Park, Canada's famed wilderness area, with his Costa Rican wife. Trained as a classicist, with a B.A. and M.A. in Latin and Greek from the University of Toronto, he has worked as an editor and translator of numerous scholarly works. His editorial credits include, for example, *The Flame Imperishable*, Jonathan McIntosh's landmark work on the metaphysical underpinnings of Tolkien's legendarium. He is also the originating co-author of *The Stoneholding and Darkling Fields of Arvon*, the first two books of the *Legacy of the Stone Harp* epic fantasy series. Both are published by Baen as part of a project expected to run to five titles. Most recently, he was given the commission by the Estate of the late William A.S. Sarjeant to edit and overhaul extensively Sarjeant's monumental 12 novel *Perilous Quest for Lyonesse* epic historical fantasy series.

If you've enjoyed this book and would like to read more great SF, you'll find literally thousands of classic Science Fiction & Fantasy titles through the SF Gateway.

For the new home of Science Fiction & Fantasy . . .

For the most comprehensive collection of classic SF on the internet . . .

Visit the SF Gateway.

www.sfgateway.com